MW01231076

A WALK THROUGH HEAVEN & HELL

WADE J. CAREY

CROSSBOOKS
PUBLISHING

CrossBooks™
A Division of LifeWay
1663 Liberty Drive
Bloomington, IN 47403
www.crossbooks.com
Phone: 1-866-879-0502

Cover artwork by Robert "Hobo" Chadwick

Certain stock imagery for the following chapter headings are used by permission from www.bigstockphoto.com: 1, 3–5, 7–16, 18, 20, 22–29, 31, Epilogue, Mythology, Prayer of Salvation, Biblical Verses Used.

All characters appearing in this work are fictitious. Any resemblance to real persons, living or dead, is purely coincidental.

First published by CrossBooks   1/7/2014

ISBN: 978-1-4627-3369-9 (sc)
ISBN: 978-1-4627-3371-2 (hc)
ISBN: 978-1-4627-3370-5 (e)

Library of Congress Control Number: 2013922507

Printed in the United States of America.

This book is printed on acid-free paper.

FACT VS. FICTION

Just a quick note, before you begin reading . . . .

As a novel, this book is fictional by its very nature. However, its real purpose is to demonstrate essential biblical concepts within the context of a story. Admittedly, this can be a very slippery slope, indeed. So allow me to make this abundantly clear, right up front—*the Bible is the holy, inerrant Word of God.* There is absolutely no question in my mind about that. I also believe it to be the unquestioned authority in all matters.

Since the writing of novels can be a challenging way to draw someone towards biblical truth—which is the unambiguous goal of this book—I cannot recommend strongly enough that you also read the "Mythology" section at the end of the story. It briefly explains the major concepts being utilized throughout the book. It also separates biblical fact, from biblical speculation (fiction).

Personally, for those who love Jesus Christ, I feel very strongly that the exploration of some of God's wonderful mysteries to be a natural and spiritually healthy endeavor. To me, it only shows that one wishes to know more about Him. However, we must be cautious as we do so. Therefore, as you read this story, I ask you to please consider my reverence towards the Bible, and the critically important role I believe it plays in our walk with the LORD.

All glory goes to Jesus Christ, who died for our sins. I hope you enjoy your *walk through Heaven & Hell!*

Wade

CAST OF CHARACTERS
PREVIOUSLY INTRODUCED IN

"A Walk Through The Market"
&
"A Walk Through The Mall"

On Earth

Wyatt Hunter—Christian author and lead human character. He is in his mid-forties, slightly stocky build, with a shaved head and short graying goatee. He lost his wife, Vanessa, to a demonic attack a couple of years previous.

Caleb Hunter—Wyatt's identical twin; leader of an earthly group of Satan's army; takes his orders from demons.

Danny Hunter—Wyatt's son with Vanessa. Danny is in his mid-twenties.

Mi-Cha Hunter—Danny's wife. She recently gave birth to their son, DJ.

Cam Hunter—Danny's half-brother and Wyatt's son; ex-Marine with outstanding battle skills; his mother is Cammie Spears, Wyatt's ex-girlfriend.

Candace Johnson-Richardson—retired attorney and leader of Flaming Sword Communications; in her mid-fifties; intelligent, strong, lively and beautiful.

Charlene Harris ("Miss Charlene")—older sister of Candace; back-lines support for the group. She is in her late sixties.

Bobby James—recovering alcoholic; was present when Wyatt's wife was killed; in his late fifties, medium build, southern accent, has a blonde, comb-over hair style.

Chul Moo ("Moo") Kim—former Taekwondo instructor and brother of Mi-Cha; brother-in-law to Danny Hunter.

Jacques O. Baugh Sr.—demon warfare expert; in the process of turning his duties over to his son, JJ.

Jacques Baugh Jr. ("JJ")—has a somewhat separate, but related ministry with Flaming Sword Communications; a front-lines soldier who battles demons. Is in constant search for Donovan, his demonic nemesis.

Juan Montoya—over the road truck driver with mysterious background and connection to the group; experienced in confrontations with demons and those with addictions.

Sampson—leader and of the vigilante group, I.F.I. ("eye for an eye"), which believes in the Old Testament ways of justice; tall, with long, dark hair; speaks in a European accent; very articulate mannerisms.

Ezekiel—Sampson's second-in-command at I.F.I.; short, very thin and muscular, with an exceedingly bushy mustache; shaved head; an angry man.

Saul—assistant to Sampson and Ezekiel; tall, husky physique, shaved head with indistinct eyebrows. Physically imposing, but gentle-mannered.

In Heaven

Abbie Hunter—Wyatt's mother and Earl Hunter's earthly ex-wife.

Earl Hunter—Wyatt's father; lived virtually all of his life for himself, but surrendered to Jesus before he died.

Cammie Spears—Cam's mother who was murdered by Caleb Hunter; Wyatt's ex-girlfriend.

Willie Richardson—Candace's earthly husband; was also murdered by Caleb Hunter.

Menelik Richardson—son of Candace and Willie Richardson; died of leukemia when he was ten years old.

George & Edrie James—parents of Bobby James.

Robert Harris—Charlene's earthly husband; was also murdered by Caleb Hunter.

Angels

Mick—the primary angel character; appears on Earth as a man in his fifties; famous for his grayish blond ponytail and propensity to use the word "dude"; leader of "The Dozen" angel group.

Jimmy & Ruth—Mick's lead assistants; Jimmy is short, bald and slightly pudgy; Ruth is taller, with red hair. Both appear on Earth as if they were in their forties.

Esther & Rebecca—guardian angels who work within the Hunter, Johnson, James, and Harris families.

Demons

Damon—a "lead demon"; arch-enemy of Mick and the characters in the Hunter and Johnson families; nowadays, he always is seen wearing a well-tailored suit; he is in charge of Chas & Blake.

Chas & Blake—Damon's direct-report demons. Chas enjoys fighting; Blake specializes in reconnaissance.

Donovan—lead demon who attacks the Baugh family.

PROLOGUE

Jefferson, GA
July, 1967

**"But the Lord is faithful, and he will strengthen you
and protect you from the evil one"
2 Thessalonians 3:3**

Appearing sullen and feeling emotionally withdrawn, Abbie Hunter sensed outright defeat looming at her doorstep as the north Georgia scorching sun slowly baked her quaint southern hamlet. Unfortunately, the oppressive heat had only thus far added an insulting layer to the raging war on her psyche. This was largely due to the furious emotional tempest which had been plowing through her feelings for a full week now, leaving in its wake a swath of total despair right down the Main Street of her heart.

In an effort to regain her composure, Abbie slumped in a creaky wooden rocking chair on the front porch of her small home. She finally sighed in frustration at her fruitless attempt to cool off in front of an old, rusty metal fan—which had certainly seen its better days. Thus far, the onerous heat was completely overpowering the rickety fan.

Finally resigning herself to the fact that overcoming the heat that day was outright senseless, she groggily gazed over at the temperature gauge on the wall to her right.

Her suspicion was confirmed.

Hanging lazily on an old rusty nail, the Coca Cola thermometer appeared to be slowly melting as the rising red mercury hit triple-digits under the oppressive temperature's assault.

She sighed once again, shaking her head.

Because of her depleted emotional condition, Abbie had been unable to muster the energy to shower that morning. Her skin felt sticky and uncomfortable. The occasional droplet of sweat slipped onto her lips, bringing with it an obnoxious, salty kiss. She quickly used a cloth handkerchief to blot the fresh tears and sweat from her face.

Abbie was now facing the daunting task of attempting to move on from a week-long marathon of trepidation, confusion, and anger. This monumental undertaking now loomed over her like an inexperienced climber trembling at the foot of Mount Everest.

Abbie's emotional crucible had been hatched exactly one week earlier—a day she would never forget. On that fateful afternoon, she was surprised to discover her husband, Earl Hunter, secretly packing his clothes and a few things for their son Caleb. When she asked him what he was doing, Earl dropped an emotional nuclear bomb on her like no other: he announced that he was leaving her, and was also taking the elder of their identical twin sons with him to his home state of Massachusetts. Without mincing his words, Earl informed Abbie that their marriage was over—not because he no longer loved her, but because he no longer had any time for her. He said that big things were in store for him.

For weeks previous to that dreadful moment, Abbie had sensed that something was definitely amiss with Earl. His strangely withdrawn behavior had caused her to wonder if he was actually having an affair. In retrospect, that would have been a relatively easy thing to deal with. However, she was totally unprepared when Earl informed her that:

"God has big plans for one of our sons, and I intend on making sure that Caleb gets his chance to achieve great things."

After arguing non-stop for a day or so, Abbie was shocked to realize that Earl was determined to carry out his ambitious, evil plan. At that point, her survival instincts kicked-in, and she emotionally withdrew. Although it might have seemed odd to some people, from an emotional perspective, Abbie felt that she needed to concentrate on keeping her other son, Wyatt, with her in Georgia. Somehow, this gave her a great measure of solace with which to cling to.

Earl Hunter was a very successful and strong-willed business man. So at the time, the idea of fighting him in court seemed fruitless. Instead, Abbie turned introspective; racking her brain in an attempt to figure out why the Lord would allow one of her children to be taken away.

Deep within her soul, however, she knew it wasn't the Lord who was responsible for such an evil thing. Underneath her feelings of confusion and betrayal, Abbie came to understand that, as is often the case, God took the blame for what were actually the devil's deeds and mankind's pride-driven, sinful ways.

Her semi-trance was interrupted by the barely audible stirrings of her infant son, Wyatt, who was noisily waking up from his nap. Abbie wiped the copious amount of perspiration from her forehead once again, then headed inside to tend to her now, one-year old son.

When she arrived in his bedroom, Abbie had an unexpected wave of euphoric joy sweep over her. Although she still felt desperate and sad, somehow, Abbie felt this small, bastion of happiness to still have one of her sons remaining in her life. In truth, her duty to Wyatt was the only thing which had kept her going for the past week.

Abbie smiled as she gazed upon Wyatt. She then proceeded to change his cloth diaper. When she was finished, Abbie returned to the sweltering front porch with little Wyatt in tow.

After a few minutes of rocking the chubby little tike on her knee, Abbie saw a tan, late model Ford Falcon approaching from the left. The Hunter house was located only a few blocks from the town square, and since their neighborhood rarely saw much traffic, she knew that something was amiss.

Abbie was well-familiar with the vehicles her neighbors drove, and this car was not one of them. The sturdily-built Falcon appeared to be brand new, and she would have likely known if one of her neighbors had purchased a new car from the local Ford dealership. That would have been big news in such a small town.

This must be a stranger, she thought.

Abbie watched the sedan with curiosity until it slowed down in front of her house and parked. The man inside the car had grayish-blonde hair in a pony tail, and appeared to be in his fifties.

Great, she thought. *Another one of those irritating hippies is going to hassle me – just when I don't need any more aggravation!*

The driver stepped out of the Falcon and smiled at her. He then approached the walkway up to the front porch. Curiously, the man stopped half-way up the path and asked, "Ma'am, would you mind if I joined you on the porch for a moment?"

"What do you want, mister?" Abbie asked. "I'm really not in the mood to hear about any of that *love-and-peace* stuff you hippies are always going on-and-on about."

The man nodded.

"Oh, I can certainly understand that," he said. "Actually I'd like to talk to you *precisely* about love and peace. But I promise it'll be none of that hippie-stuff."

"Is that a fact?" she asked. "Then what exactly do you have to say?"

"I'd actually like to talk to you about the love and peace of our LORD and Savior, Jesus Christ."

She shook her head. "I'm afraid I don't have any money to give to your church—"

"That's fine," the stranger interrupted, holding up his hands in a halting motion. "I'm not here for your money."

"Then what *are* you here for? Everyone always seems to be wanting *something.*"

The man nodded in agreement. "Actually, I'm here to help you with the reconstruction of your life."

Suspicious, Abbie asked, "How on Earth do you know anything about what's going on in my life???"

"Ma'am . . . if you'll kindly permit me to join you on the porch . . . I can explain everything."

Abbie sized up the stranger once again. He was wearing a psychedelic-colored tee shirt and well-worn blue jeans and sandals—a fairly normal looking guy—for a hippie.

He doesn't seem to be so bad, she thought. *He was also polite enough to not approach my front porch without first asking for permission.*

Abbie sighed. "I suppose it would be un-neighborly of me to not offer you a cold glass of sweet tea on such a hot day," she admitted.

"Yes indeed, ma'am. It's awfully hot today. I'd be very appreciative of that."

"So what's your name, mister?" Abbie asked. She stood up with Wyatt in her arms.

"My name is Mick," he said. The angel proceeded slowly towards the front porch.

"You're not gonna make me regret this, are you?"

"Of course not. I'm actually here to help you, Miss Abbie."

Abbie was taken aback at hearing the stranger's use of her name. "How in the world did you—?"

"Do you mind if I take you up on that iced tea now?" Mick asked as he arrived at the foot of the stairs. "I'm awfully thirsty."

Mick slowly wiped the sweat from his forehead with a handkerchief.

After looking the man over once again, Abbie felt comfortable enough to proceed. She sighed once again, declaring, "Where are my manners today? Of course I'll get you something to drink. C'mon in."

Mick walked the four steps up to the front porch as he asked, "Who is that cute little rascal?"

As they proceeded inside, a metallic *thud* sounded-off as the screen door rapidly closed behind them.

"This is my son Wyatt," she said. "He just turned one. He actually has a twin broth—"

"I know all about Caleb and the terrible thing Earl did."

Abbie stopped dead in her tracks in the middle of the small living room. She had a look of astonishment on her face. "How did you—?"

"Earl was actually sold a pack of lies by an evil fellow named Damon. Unfortunately, I'm very familiar with Damon."

Abbie thought for a moment. "Now that you mention it, Earl often spoke of a guy named Damon . . . from work."

"Damon used to work for Earl's trucking company. They made local cotton deliveries to nearby Jefferson Mills. Unfortunately for Earl, he fell under Damon's evil influence."

"You're right about that. Things sure went downhill after he hired that Damon fellow."

"Please listen to me, Miss Abbie. I'm here today to tell you what *really* happened with Earl and Caleb. I'll also explain to you how you can still serve the LORD."

She shook her head in disagreement as tears began to stream down her face. "My life is all messed up now Mick, and I don't have any idea how I'm going to get along by myself. How can I do *anything* for the LORD?"

"Even though your life has taken this unexpected turn, I can assure you that you can still serve our Father in Heaven. He specifically sent me here to see you today."

Abbie fell into deep thought for a few moments before venting, *"Do you have any idea how arrogant Earl is?"* Before Mick could respond, she continued, "He actually had the *gall* to load up my other son in his brand new Shelby Mustang GT350 like he was some kind of *hot-shot* . . . then he left me . . . apparently for good!"

"Not necessarily," Mick said.

Abbie continued her rant. "He drove outta here acting all uppity and whatnot, and all he left me with is that old Ford truck out there. I guess he thinks since he's gonna pay my bills around here, he can do whatever he wants to!"

"I really-do understand," Mick said. "But please don't forget what I just said—I'm here to explain all of this to you."

Abbie looked skeptically at Mick as she bounced Wyatt gently up and down. The baby cooed as she asked, "Just who are you anyway? Are you some kind of pastor or something?"

"No. Actually, I'm an angel sent by the LORD to help you get your life in order."

Abbie shook her head in disbelief. "Oh LORD, not today! You must be an escapee from the insane asylum!"

Mick chuckled. "Nah, I promise I'm not crazy. If you think about it, an insane person wouldn't know anything about Earl, Caleb, or Damon, would they???"

She thought for a few moments. "Then why would the LORD care about a simple, *no-account* country girl like me?"

"Abbie my friend; our Father cares about every single part of His enormous creation. In *Psalm 145:9* He says, *The LORD is good to all; he has compassion on all he has made.* So what makes you think God wouldn't notice that your husband was influenced by a demon to take Caleb and leave you all alone with Wyatt?"

Abbie looked down at the floor for a moment, then said, "Earl claims that God commanded him to take Caleb away and raise him separate from Wyatt. He went on to say his new mission in life would be to help Caleb achieve the great things the LORD has in store for him."

"Now Abbie, do you *really* think the LORD would have someone do something foolish like that?"

She shrugged her shoulders. "I guess not. It sure didn't make any sense to me. Not at all."

"Listen," Mick began, "you can get my tea in a minute. This seems to be a good time for me to read you a passage of Scripture. Believe it or not; this will actually help you whenever you think of Earl's terrible mistake."

"Well if you really are an angel, I suppose it makes sense that you'd wanna read me something from the Bible."

"You got that right. Anyway, this passage is from *Isaiah 58:11 . . . The LORD will guide you always; he will satisfy your needs in a sun-scorched land and will strengthen your frame. You will be like a well-watered garden, like a spring whose waters never fail.*"

Abbie continued to bounce Wyatt as she thought about the passage. "My pastor tells me that Earl is gonna burn in Hell for what he's done to me and Wyatt," she said. "What do you think about that?"

Mick slowly shook his head. "No. Earl's not going to Hell for what he's done. He'll only go to Hell if he doesn't repent of his sins and surrender to Jesus Christ as his Savior before he dies."

"He sure seems to think he's a good Christian," Abbie retorted.

"Unfortunately, many people think that they can 'good' their way into Heaven," Mick said. "However, they're absolutely wrong—dead wrong. Listen, why don't you go ahead and get me that iced tea now. We really-do have much to discuss. But rest assured, the LORD sent me here today to help you, and to show you the *real* truth about what's going on in your life."

"The *real* truth?"

"Indeed, the *real* truth."

Abbie looked thoughtful before nodding, but said nothing. She then turned and proceeded into the kitchen to get their cold beverages.

Mick realized that this meeting with Abbie Hunter would merely be the first of many, and that this would ultimately help to shape future kingdom affairs. He also knew that one day down the road, he would also be instructed to call upon her son Wyatt.

The angel smiled to himself, relishing the fact that he had just met another male child of the Hunter-Tsayid family. Mick had been assigned countless similar missions with Wyatt's relatives for over two thousand years now, and he never grew tired of meeting the newest members of this special family.

The angel sat down on the couch and waited for his newest student to fetch him that nice, cold iced tea. Normally he liked to drink coffee, but a cold beverage on such a hot day in a sun scorched land sure sounded awfully good to him.

PART 1

PREPARING FOR BATTLE

Heaven
October 3rd, 2010
-- Today --

"And by that will, we have been made holy through the sacrifice of the body of Jesus Christ once for all."
Hebrews 10:10

Mick sat snugly next to Abbie and Earl Hunter at the beautiful baseball park, which was located in the sprawling sports complex just outside New Jerusalem. Seated directly in front of them were some good friends and fellow fans: Candace's husband Willie and his son Menelik. The five compadres were thoroughly enjoying that afternoon's game, which was in the top of the seventh inning with the score tied. A gentle, cool breeze blew steadily throughout the entire park, providing an idyllic and comfortable setting for what was, of course, a perfect day for a game of baseball.

Before joining Willie and Menelik at the ball park, Mick, Abbie, and Earl spent the morning roaming around Agora, the largest of the regional markets in Heaven. During their visit to the colossal emporium, Abbie giggled as she caught herself once again reaching for her purse after deciding on a few items to take home. Even after all this time in Heaven, she still had to be reminded that the LORD provides every need for His children, so money is unnecessary. Every time she had that instinctive reaction, it reinforced the fact that the joys of Heaven will never cease to be overwhelming for every one of its citizens.

Heaven's initial orientation for new entrants lasted only a few weeks. However, the latter parts of the program took the new citizens of Heaven to every corner of the LORD's homeland. Earl had actually been busy traveling for the past several months, enjoying every moment of his visits throughout the LORD's vast kingdom along the way.

During their time shopping at the market that day, Abbie and Earl began discussing some of the more difficult times they had experienced when they were still down on Earth. Of course, while they were very proud of their son Wyatt and the direction he was taking in his life, they were also very concerned with the wrongful path their other son Caleb was following.

As they sat there, Mick helped Abbie and Earl by lending some perspective to their earthly lives.

"So Earl," the angel began, "Abbie and I were recently reminiscing about my very first visit with her; right after you left with Caleb back in the sixties."

Earl shook his head. "Yeah, it wasn't one of my more shining moments, was it?"

Abbie grabbed Earl's hand and said, "Sweetheart, no matter what mis-deeds someone does on Earth, the most important thing they can do is to find a true relationship with Jesus Christ before dying. My-oh-my, *you* should know that more than anyone."

"Indeed I do," Earl said. "So Mick, other than talking about how Damon deceived me by claiming he was an angel sent by the LORD, what else did you and Abbie talk about that day?"

Suddenly, the catcher from the visiting team hit a line-drive single up the middle. Willie, who was sitting directly in front of them exclaimed, *"Oh c'mon!* You can't throw fastballs to Stephen. He'll hit 'em every time!"

Mick smiled, knowing how much Willie enjoyed the healthy competition of Heaven's ball games and other sporting events.

"Well Earl," Mick said. "To answer your question, Abbie and I discussed in detail how important it was for her to raise Wyatt to love the LORD—*regardless* of how bleak her situation seemed at the time."

"It sure wasn't easy getting through those dark times," Abbie said. "I don't know what I would've done if Mick hadn't showed up to tell me the LORD still had plans for me. At that time, I was feeling pretty helpless."

"You know," Earl began, "I suppose I found it a little strange that you seemed to accept my leaving so well, Abbie. I halfway expected a protracted court battle; even way back then."

Abbie shook her head. "That's not what I was instructed to do."

"What do you mean?"

"Mick basically told me to concentrate on keeping Wyatt on his path with the LORD, and to raise him as a Christian."

"Hmmm . . . I'm curious about something Mick," Earl said slowly. "Other than the eternal ramifications, why do you think the LORD thought we were important enough to involve an angel like you in our measly little lives?"

Mick nodded at Abbie, but remained quiet.

Abbie quickly added, "Mick only told me that one of Wyatt's heirs would end up playing a very pivotal role in some future kingdom affairs. He actually said it was likely that more than one of them would be involved."

"I see," Earl said. He then looked straight into Abbie's eyes. "I still can't figure out what I was thinking when I left you."

"Earl my friend," Mick said. "I'm afraid you experienced an affliction that a lot of humans inadvertently fall into when you lived your life according to Satan's template."

"Satan's template?"

"Yep. Remember, the Earth is temporarily Satan's playground, and he shows people in both overt and subtle ways how to live their lives according to *his* ways of the world—not the LORD's."

"Mick is absolutely right," Willie agreed, looking back at them. "The devil will deftly point you towards the road to perdition by convincing you that looking after your own glory is more important than anything else in life."

"Amen Willie," Mick agreed. "Thankfully, the LORD is always in charge of all things. Isn't that right Earl?"

"He sure is," Earl said, squeezing Abbie's hand. "I know all-to-well where I'd be; that is, if it had been up to me to find my own way into Heaven."

"You got that right," Mick said. "You sure wouldn't be sitting here right now, enjoying another day in Paradise."

The top of the seventh ended with the game still tied. Everyone in the stadium stood up for the seventh inning stretch and began singing a song of glory to their LORD, Jesus Christ. This song of tribute to God was one of the major differences between baseball games on Earth and games in Heaven. Of course, none of the players that day had any of the egotistical habits which are sometimes displayed in games on the fallen Earth.

Everyone re-seated themselves after the beautiful and familiar song, and the resulting ovation. Mick and his compadres then continued with their chat.

"So Earl," Abbie said. "What was your life like after you left Wyatt and me in Georgia?"

"Work, work, and more work," Earl lamented. "I ended up selling the small trucking company I owned in Jefferson and started a new one up in Essex County, Massachusetts. After that, it was all about buying trucks, finding customers, and generating revenue."

"I see. So how did you take care of Caleb if you were always working?"

"Actually," Earl began, "Damon said he would help me in my alleged *mission for God* by finding me a suitable nanny who could help me with the raising of Caleb. Unfortunately, that's exactly what he did. The woman he chose had a really unique, old-school sort of name—Mildred Fountainhead. Anyway, Mildred ended up moving in to completely care for Caleb."

Abbie continued to hold Earl's hand to comfort him as he recounted his great mistake. "So what can you tell me about Mildred?" she asked.

"Mildred was—*and probably still is*—a key soldier in an evil, worldwide satanic cult; one which I was trying to track down until the day I died. Anyway, I'm afraid Mildred is a *real* Satanist—not one of those phonies you may have heard of. Unfortunately, Mildred's group is committed to raising disciples for the Evil One."

"Why did you trust her with our son?"

"Because I was foolish and believed that Damon was an angel from the LORD. Believe me; I had no idea I was being deceived, or that Mildred was a Satanist. There's *no way* I would've put up with that."

"I see," she said. "So how did you get along with this woman?"

"Oh, I promise you—it was strictly professional, if that's what you mean," Earl said. "I was certainly an arrogant man, but I was far from being a philanderer."

Abbie grinned, coyly. "No, silly—I know you weren't like that."

"Anyway," Earl continued, "Mildred was younger than me, and she seemed to be a nice young lady. I actually did some business with her father, who owned a small textile company in the area. As you know, hauling textiles and cotton back then was my specialty—"

Earl was interrupted as Willie and Menelik joined the rest of the ballpark's crowd in standing up and cheering loudly.

"What's going on?" Abbie asked.

"Check it out—the LORD is going to pinch-hit!" Menelik said.

During their discussion in the bottom of the seventh, two players from the home team had singled. There were now runners on first and second, with only one out.

"If we were at a ball game on Earth, some folks might say the LORD is the *ultimate ringer,*" Mick chided.

"You know, it's weird," Earl said. "I'm still getting used to the fact that Jesus participates in all of these wonderful activities up here with us. I mean; most people on Earth would be pretty surprised to see how interactive the LORD is with all of His children in Heaven."

"You'll become more accustomed to it the longer you've been here," Mick said. "Many of Heaven's newest saints are pleasantly surprised at the wonderful combination of God's vast holiness, coupled with his intense intimacy in every detail of His kingdom . . . including sports."

"You know; the folks on Earth really do need to know more about the wonders of Heaven," Abbie said. "Living their lives in the light of eternity can only serve to help them persevere."

Earl nodded, then said, "So tell me something, Mick. Why don't people on Earth know more about Heaven?"

"It's largely because Satan blinds them," Mick said. "However, that's *exactly* what the Flaming Sword Communications group is tasked with fighting against. And *oh-by-the-way,* your son Wyatt now has a book that's actually beginning to sell a few copies across the country."

"We're very proud of him," Abbie said. "And speaking of Wyatt . . . on that day you first called on me back in the sixties . . . that was actually the first day you met Wyatt, wasn't it?"

Mick shrugged. "Well, sort of. I'm quite sure Wyatt was too young to remember meeting me. But based on my historical assignments, I always knew the LORD would one day send me back down to work with him. Of course, that 'one day' was about a year ago in Seattle."

"That *was* a year ago, wasn't it?" Abbie said.

"Yep, it sure was. Right there at Pike Place Market. However, after I met Wyatt as an infant when I first met you, Abbie, I actually saw him several other times over the years; although Wyatt still hasn't realized it yet."

Abbie nodded. "I suppose that one day, Wyatt's going to be pleasantly surprised when he finds out how many times he's crossed paths with you over the years, but never knew it."

"He sure will," Mick said, grinning.

"So Willie," Earl began, changing subjects. "Can we expect Jesus to knock a home run clear onto the football field next door, or what?" Jesus took a few practice swings before approaching the plate.

Willie smiled. "We'll just have to wait and see," he said with a knowing grin. He winked at Mick, knowing that what was coming next would be a pleasant surprise to Earl.

The left handed pitcher wound up and hurled a slider towards home plate. Jesus, who was batting right handed, responded by laying a perfect sacrifice bunt down the third base line. Although He was thrown out at first base, the bunt pulled the third baseman in to field it, allowing the runners on base to advance to second and third.

"Wow!" Earl exclaimed. "I didn't see *that* coming!"

The crowd continued cheering loudly.

"It's absolutely *awesome,*" Menelik said. "Jesus always lays down a sacrifice bunt when He pinch-hits."

"Why didn't the Lord just hit one out of the park?" Earl asked.

"Because that's not who Jesus Christ is," Mick said. "The Lord has the power to do anything He wants to do, but He chose to live on Earth and sacrifice Himself on the Cross to pay the price for mankind's sins."

Earl looked thoughtful for a moment. "Well, I suppose that makes sense," he said.

"Listen, my man," Willie said as the crowd noise settled back down to normal. "The Lord has all of the power in the universe. However, He cherishes us so much, instead of creating a bunch of mindless *robots* for eternity, He chose to have *children,* who can worship, serve, glorify, and fellowship with Him forever."

"Willie's right," Mick said. "I like to point out *Mark 10:45* as a way of describing this sacrificial attribute of your Savior."

"What does it say?" Earl asked.

Mick winked. *"For even the Son of Man did not come to be served, but to serve, and to give his life as a ransom for many."*

"Sweetheart," Abbie said to Earl. "That's what the Lord is all about, dear. Instead of hitting a home run into the next dimension, He always chooses to sacrifice Himself for us—even in something as normal as a baseball game."

"That's right," Willie added. "Although Jesus Christ's batting average is around zero, it's because He only pinch-hits whenever a sacrifice is needed."

"Really?"

"Absolutely," Willie said. "Jesus *always* accomplishes His goal of sacrificing Himself for His children."

The next batter promptly delivered a line drive single into left-center field, driving in the runners on second and third base. The crowd cheered loudly as Willie and Menelik high-fived everyone around them. After the next batter popped up to the second baseman, the inning was over and the home team had a two run lead.

"So let me get this straight," Earl said. "Are you telling me that the Creator of the universe would rather lay down a sacrifice bunt than to get the glory of a game winning hit?"

"Bingo," Mick said. "Basically, he sets you up for the game-winning hit, then cheers you on when you get it. The same thing applies to His sacrifice for a person's sins."

Earl nodded. "It appears we aren't talking about baseball anymore, huh?"

"Nope, we sure aren't," Mick said. "Listen; a situation like the LORD sacrificing runners into scoring position should always remind you that He humbled Himself, even to the point of death on the Cross to save you."

"As time goes along, I suppose I'll continue to further comprehend that idea," Earl said. "It's just that understanding what Jesus did for mankind is so incredibly shocking; even more so, once you're directly in His holy presence."

"Trust me Earl," Mick said. "You'll come to love the LORD more-and-more every day for the rest of eternity. Your personal journey has only just begun."

"You know something? My life sure would have been a lot more useful to God's kingdom if I had understood the magnitude of His sacrifice a long time ago," Earl said quietly, more to himself than the others.

"So Mick, when are you heading back down to Earth?" Abbie asked.

"Very soon," Mick said. "There's a lot of stuff going on down there, and it appears that our friends will need my help."

As they continued their discussion, the snack man walked by. Mick and most of his friends took a bag of delicious popcorn. Out of the group, only Willie ordered peanuts. It amazed Earl that even though Willie no longer hated popcorn as he did on Earth, he still preferred peanuts. Personal preferences were just another one of the many unexpected blessings of life in Heaven.

Earl smiled as he realized that his own bag of popcorn was absolutely perfect—with no unpopped kernels. *Of course,* he thought. *That's what Heaven is all about."*

The game ended soon after their snack, and everyone began to make their way towards the exit. God's beloved children continued to engage in pleasant chats on their way home after another wonderful afternoon, enjoying the Lord's eternal bounty in a pain-free Paradise.

It was indeed, another spectacular day in Heaven.

Seattle, WA
October 4th

**"The house of the wicked will be destroyed,
but the tent of the upright will flourish."
Proverbs 14:11**

Candace Johnson-Richardson flipped the sign from "Closed"
to "Open" before unlocking the front door to the newest shop
in Pike Place Market—*Flaming Sword Christian Books & Novelties*.
Located in a quiet area on one of the lower levels of the Down Under
shops of the Main Arcade, the newest tenant of Pike Place Market was
now open for business on this; its very first day of operation.

Candace smiled to herself as she thought about how far she
and her group had come in only the past eight months. Since their
meetings at the Mall of America earlier that year, her life had gone in
a completely unexpected and wonderful direction. As strange as it may
have seemed to her in years past, the way she now viewed her life had

taken on a fundamental shift; one which she would have never guessed would happen in a million years: Candace was now fully devoted to proclaiming the Gospel of Christ to others. As a result, her love of the law profession had now been fully and safely tucked away in the yearbook of her memories.

Candace turned and walked towards the check-out counter in the back of the store, admiring their quaint shop along the way.

An awful lot of work has gone into this place, she thought.

Candace figured that since there were only a few aisles of books in stock, they probably wouldn't be setting any new Pike Place Market sales records on their opening day. Nevertheless, she was still very proud to be leading the Flaming Sword Communications group, and in particular, their brand new store.

When Candace arrived in the back of the shop, she moved behind the counter, which ran parallel to the front-facing of the store. She then surveyed the shop's comfortable environs once again.

Along both walls to her right and left stood floor-to-ceiling shelves, all fully stocked. On the wall to her left were numerous Bibles of various translations. On her right, the wall contained both the fiction and apologetics books. The center aisles ran diagonal to the slightly rectangular shop and dominated the center of the room; they contained a veritable cornucopia of offerings on Christian living, with one section set aside for end-times prophecy books. Various other novelties, including featured books on cardboard stands, filled in most of the empty spaces. Surprisingly, the brand new store already had a "lived-in" look to it. As the proverbial "cherry on top," the entire public area of the store already had that comfortable, old library scent. Candace found this incredibly relaxing and tranquil.

She affectionately picked up one of the books displayed on the counter to her left; one which was very important to the group's ministry. Candace was thrilled that Wyatt' first self-published book titled <u>A Walk With An Unusual Messenger</u> was now selling a few copies online, and hopefully soon, in their new store.

Candace marveled at the novel's unusual-but-symbolic cover, taking a few minutes to once again page through the flagship book of their new endeavor. She had just begun to read chapter four when Danny appeared from the back of the shop.

"What's up, dudette?" he asked.

Candace took a moment to climb out of the peaceful trance she had lapsed into. "Oh, I'm good," she said.

"Good deal."

"Hey Danny . . ." Candace began, "I meant to ask you earlier how the baby's doing this morning. Is everything okay?"

"DJ's thankfully sleeping once again. So he's fine for now."

"And how is Mi-Cha hanging in there today?"

"Our boy actually slept through the night, so Mi-Cha's feeling really well today. Thanks for asking."

"Good to hear," she said, still distracted. "Have you had a chance to check-in with all of our folks this morning?"

"I have," Danny said. "Although I must say, I'm not exactly sure what JJ is up to."

"What do you mean by that?"

"I haven't been able to get him on his cell phone yet today. Although he was kind of vague the other day when we did speak, he told me he was taking a couple of days off to go driving through the New England countryside."

"Oh really?" Candace asked, surprised.

"Yeah. He said he's been wanting to do that for a long time."

"Well, I guess there's nothing wrong with that, is there?"

"Not really; except that JJ hardly ever takes a day off. He's pretty much consumed with his ministry, you know. In particular, he really wants to find that demon named Donovan."

"I suppose you're right," Candace agreed. "Please keep in close contact with him. We both know how obsessive JJ can be. Sometimes he gets lost in his research and reconnaissance."

"Will-do," Danny said. "By the way, have you talked to my dad in the past few days?"

"I have," Candace said. "He's still getting prepared for the interview about his book on that local-access Boston TV show the day after next."

"Good deal," Danny said. "You know; I'm still getting used to all of the changes that have taken place since our meetings with Mick at the Mall of America. It's still hard to believe what the LORD has us all doing."

"You're right about that sweetie," Candace said, her thoughts once again reflecting on the past few months . . .

Shortly after their initial meetings the previous February, Mick laid down the gameplan for the entire team. Of course, this new plan involved a lot of major changes for most of the group.

It was first decided that Danny and Mi-Cha would move into Wyatt's condo in Seattle, down the hall from Miss Charlene, who was Candace's older sister. At the same time, Candace returned to Boise and sold her home and most of her furnishings. She then made the permanent move to Seattle and became Charlene's roommate.

Essentially, Danny, Mi-Cha, Candace, and Miss Charlene would comprise the northwest contingent of the new Flaming Sword Communications group. Their mission would be to not only open the book store, but also to work together as a family unit in the raising of Danny and Mi-Cha's son, "DJ," which was short for "Danny Junior." Little DJ was now four months old.

With Wyatt moving out of his condo, it was decided that he would move from Seattle and Cam would move from Jacksonville; both men relocating to the Boston, Massachusetts area together. They quickly settled into the former home of Earl Hunter in Peabody. Earl, of course, was Wyatt's recently deceased father. Candace surmised that the reason for this move was for the newly discovered father-son relationship between Wyatt and Cam to have some time to grow and mature. She was not surprised by that development.

After only a couple of months, Wyatt and Cam successfully sold Earl's old house, which had so many bad memories for the Hunter family. They then proceeded to purchase a house in nearby Methuen, not far from the New Hampshire border.

It was further decided that Wyatt would continue to write his novels, while Cam would enroll at a nearby community college and take a few courses. In an effort to further their spiritual growth in

Christ, both father and son enrolled in some online theological courses together. During all of this, Wyatt and Cam were set up to represent the Flaming Sword group in the northeast.

Heading up the southern contingent for Flaming Sword down in the state of Georgia were the unlikely duo of Moo and Bobby. Mick explained that this was necessary due to the fact that Bobby was still working on his recovery from alcohol abuse. Moo, who was a much younger man and largely a teetotaler, provided some necessary companionship and support.

After receiving his new assignment, Moo had fortunately been able to get out his apartment lease in nearby Buford. He then moved into Bobby's house in Watkinsville, outside of Athens. After getting rid of Bobby's old, run-down trailer on the family property, they proceeded to set up the main house, which Bobby inherited from his father, as the southeast office for Flaming Sword.

During their time working together, the two oddly-paired teammates settled the estate of Bobby's recently deceased father, George James. Since Bobby was George's sole heir, the two bachelors were blessed with a nice house on a large parcel of land in which to reside. Thankfully there was no loan on the property.

Moo and Bobby had actually become close friends during the past several months. The younger man was a constant companion and strong supporter for the elder, as the recovering alcoholic prayerfully worked every day towards permanent victory over his addiction. As a part of Bobby's prescribed therapy, Moo began teaching him the art of Taekwondo. Of course, this was not an easy discipline for an out-of-shape man in his late fifties to embark upon.

While all of these events were progressing, the twosome also reached out to local charities and churches as they began to build their ministry. Chief among their current initiatives was to coordinate the sourcing of supplies for a local food bank. They also started working with a local, no-kill humane society, which cared-for and trained abandoned dogs to be companions for disabled and elderly people.

The remaining members of the current roster were very much the wild-cards of the group: the father-son combo of Jacques and JJ, who unsurprisingly remained in the Philadelphia area. The second wild-card was Juan Montoya, who technically lived in southern California, but who primarily lived in his commercial truck. Juan continued to travel the country, earning a living and spreading the Gospel.

Such was the setup for Flaming Sword Communications and their group leader, Candace Richardson. Because her mind had drifted off as she ruminated over these developments, Danny had to draw Candace back to reality . . .

"Earth to Candace . . . ?"

She looked up, now out of her trance. "Sorry about that," she said.

"We were talking about how Mick has us stationed all over the country now, each of us doing several different things."

"Indeed we were," she said. "Anyway, have you made any progress on your investigations into those crooked hedge fund managers?"

"Some; but I honestly haven't gotten very far," Danny said. "But I sure am glad to get all of those computers and such out of the condo and into the back of the store. All of that stuff was getting in the way at home."

After DJ was born, Danny had been doing his work from Wyatt's former condo as he and Mi-Cha settled in. Due to the fact that the store had ample space available in the non-public area, Danny later moved all of his Flaming Sword work into the shop's back office, behind the counter, where he and Candace now stood.

"You're right about getting all of that stuff out of the condos," Candace said. "Charlene's place was also getting *way* too congested."

"Yeah, well anyway . . . I can't wait to see who our first customer is today."

Right on cue, the shop's door opened with the jingle of a little bell; in walked a pony-tailed gentleman in a brown leather jacket. Complimenting his worn-looking blue jeans and sneakers, the man wore a black "Seattle's Best Coffee" tee shirt with their old red logo.

"Well, speak of the angel!" Candace said.

"Mornin' folks," Mick said with a smile. "Can a dude get a good cup of joe around here or what?!?!"

"Hey there Mick," Danny said. "What brings you here today?"

"What—you're not just glad to see me?"

"Don't be silly," Candace said, then added, "Hey, I like your shirt."

"Yeah, I have to admit—I like the old SBC logo much better than the new one," Mick said. "Anyway, I just had an excellent latte upstairs in the market at one of the old restaurants. And *boy* was it good."

"Hey—why didn't you bring us one?" Danny chided.

"That's actually why I'm here, sport. I wanted to check-in before I went back upstairs and got you guys a coffee."

"You could've just brought us one," Danny said.

Mick shrugged. "I suppose you're right. But this will now give me a good excuse to have latte numero two when I head back upstairs in a minute."

Danny shook his head. "I should have known."

"Anyways," Mick continued, "after I get our coffees, we do have a little business to tend to. A new mission is getting ready to kick-off."

"I see," Candace said. "So what's the scoop?"

"Actually, quite a lot is fixing to go down," Mick said. "But I'll first go get our coffees before we chat. Then we'll dive into all the details of our battle plan."

"That'll work," Danny said.

"Oh, I almost forgot," the angel said. "What I also wanted to accomplish today was to become the store's very first customer."

"I see," Candace said, amused. "So what can we help you with, sir?"

Mick proceeded into a faux-pondering mode before declaring, "I think I'll take a copy of that new book on the counter. You know, the one by that dude named . . . oh, what's his name? Ah yes—Wyatt Hunter."

The angel winked as Candace nodded approvingly.

Woodstock, VT
October 4th

**"Do not take revenge, my dear friends,
but leave room for God's wrath, for it is written:
'It is mine to avenge; I will repay,' says the Lord"
Romans 12:19**

The picturesque Vermont village of Woodstock languished under the late afternoon clash between the fading daylight and the invading darkness of night. Creeping tendrils of light streaked across the sky in what appeared to be daytime's final, desperate salvo. Holding court over this battle was the sun, which perched itself atop the western horizon, appearing as a colossal orange orb, slowly submerging into an icy lake of shapeless purple clouds. Raging behind the mask of this seemingly harmonious sunset was the invisible struggle between the season's mild daytime temperature, and its daily nemesis, autumn's chilly evening.

Decorating the entire area was a palette of brilliantly colored leaves, all of which were approaching the season's optimal hue. This colossal army of foliage stood at full attention, resolute in its collective readiness for the annual exodus from their soon-to-be barren hosts. With the advent of winter only a few weeks away, the numerous red, orange, and yellow maples appeared as majestic sentinels among the rolling farmland. These colorful trees towered over a sea of placid, green grazing fields, dutifully guarding the area's precious leaf-peeping season. This beautiful community, replete with all of its amazing autumnal accouterments, provided the perfect backdrop for the ideal fall landscape.

Jacques Baugh Junior, aka "JJ," had just arrived in the village's charming downtown after driving all day from his home in Drexel Hill, Pennsylvania. During the day, he had traversed the very heart of the northeast, en route to an important meeting in this unusually idyllic locale.

He turned right off of Route 4, back onto Route 12, heading north.

The meeting which JJ was heading towards was a much anticipated conclave with the senior members of IFI; a covert group who believe in "eye for an eye" justice. He had actually been waiting for many years to meet with IFI, and as such, JJ felt the simultaneous emotions of being both nervous and excited.

After a few miles, JJ's GPS unit indicated he was very close to his destination. As he surveyed the local landscape, he marveled that amidst this bucolic backdrop sat such an important fortress for the leaders of IFI. From his research, he knew their mammoth estate was spread across one hundred acres of pristine Vermont pastures. The 10,000 square foot main house—which was his destination for this meeting—sat snugly atop a tree-covered promontory. Guarding IFI's sacred keep was a winding, one mile stretch of paved black asphalt, which was connected to a surface road off of Route 12.

Turning his old Dodge Intrepid left onto a back road, then right into the massive estate's driveway, JJ steadily tapped his hand on the steering wheel to the beat of a smooth Jazz tune by David Benoit. Over the property's entrance stood a majestic set of red-brick pillars on either side of an overhead arch. Stretching out in both directions from the archway was a well-maintained white fence, which seemed to have no end.

JJ drove slowly into the compound.

After driving over what seemed to be an endless pattern of S-shaped turns, he wound his way up the hill. Upon reaching the top, he then turned right through a tunnel of trees, which were unable to completely block the occasional, desperate shards of fading sunlight. Upon exiting the heavily treed area, the road turned northwest to his left. At that point, JJ turned off both his satellite radio and GPS unit as he made his approach towards the main house.

JJ's exhaustive research had indicated that several interconnected gravel roads throughout the property gave the cloistered keep an appearance of self-efficiency which hinted at virtual autonomy from the outside world. After making his way due north past a rolling pasture on his left, complimented by a wooded area to his right, JJ spotted the circular driveway of the main house. When he landed on the loose gravel driveway at the end of the asphalt, he pulled his car to the right and drove in a counter-clockwise fashion, making his way around towards the front of the majestic mansion. He then stopped and parked right behind a black GMC Yukon.

Still feeling nervous, JJ found himself craving a cigarette, but opted against indulging his bad habit. Being fairly well acquainted with his meeting partners, JJ was quite sure they would frown upon smoking. He knew they would consider it to be very much beneath their dignity. And due to IFI's parochial way of dealing with things, JJ didn't want to upset the apple cart; at least, not today. He felt fortunate enough to have arranged this meeting in the first place.

Just as JJ was stepping out of his car, a tall, strong-looking, slightly husky bald man appeared, seemingly out of nowhere.

"Welcome Mr. Baugh," he said. "Our group leaders have been eagerly awaiting your arrival."

The large man had light-colored, indistinct eyebrows, which gave him a curiously formidable-yet-gentle appearance.

JJ paused for a moment, slightly disconcerted. *"And you are???"*

"My name is Saul. I'm the personal assistant for both Sampson and Ezekiel; our top executives."

JJ nodded and exited the car. His hiking boots made crunching sounds on the gravel driveway as he followed Saul towards the front door; staying a few steps behind the large man.

Tall, ionic pillars of marble towered over the entry to the house, adding an ancient Greek majesty to its ambiance. Three granite steps greeted JJ at the bottom of the porch, so he quickly ascended his way up to the granite and wooden landing area.

As he moved towards the front door, JJ looked both right and left, noticing white-painted Adirondack chairs, dainty tables, and white wicker couches adorning the expansive front porch. Interestingly, the entryway to the house was inviting and comfortable. This contrasted greatly with what JJ knew was a raging sea of anger below the surface of this fallacious facade.

JJ turned back towards Saul, who had a butler-like set of mannerisms, and followed the black-suited man through the front door and into the marble-floored atrium.

Saul turned abruptly and announced, "Our leaders will meet with you in the library, to your right." He pointed the way, then stood in place with his hands folded respectfully in front of his abdomen. Before JJ could ask any further questions, Saul continued, "They're eagerly waiting for you, sir."

Saul's voice was insistent, yet calm and reassuring.

JJ nodded as he began walking through the large, rectangular front room, towards the library. As he moved forward, Victorian furnishings and wall hangings surrounded him, giving the living space a very formal appearance. For some reason, this made him very uncomfortable.

JJ continued his passage through the elegantly decorated salon. When he arrived at the dark stained double doors of the library, he looked back at Saul in order to inquire whether or not he should knock. However, Saul had already disappeared; almost like some kind of apparition. JJ sighed as he turned back towards the doors and politely knocked.

"Please come in, Mr. Baugh," an ominous voice said.

JJ proceeded through the double doors into another large parlor, covered in floor-to-ceiling book shelves. His initial impression of the masculine space was that it could have easily passed as a sitting room for one of the Vanderbilt's in the late nineteenth century. At least a dozen mounted animals adorned the walls, giving the room a somewhat unique appearance—a hunting lodge fused with an old library.

In the back of the long room was a huge stone fireplace, which was busily crackling away. Towards the middle of the library sat a circular, medieval-looking table with a dozen chairs surrounding it. This immediately drew JJ's attention.

At one end of the sturdy table—which reminded JJ of the Knights of the Round Table—sat a handsome man with long, graying black hair. On the man's left, sat a thin, muscular bald man with a wide, bushy mustache. Both men were dressed in dark suits, but no ties.

JJ proceeded to the table and stood behind the chair to the leader's right, across from the thin, mustached man. He instinctively waited for the leader's next instruction.

"Please Mr. Baugh, have a seat and make yourself comfortable," the leader said, his hand waving towards the chair. The leader's eyes remained buried in a report of some kind as he declared, "My name is Sampson. I'm very pleased to finally meet you in-person."

Sampson then looked up and gazed coolly at his guest.

JJ nodded and politely seated himself.

"Please . . . call me JJ." He looked across the table and said, "And I take it you're Ezekiel?"

"I am," the man said, curtly.

Sampson grinned wryly, and without preamble, cut to the chase. "Once again JJ, I do hope you realize just how rare it is to be extended an invitation to personally visit one of our facilities," he said.

"Of course I do. I actually—"

"And I regret the need to begin our conversation with such a dire caveat." JJ frowned as Sampson continued, "But of course, you understand that if you were to disclose anything about our organization with anyone outside of this room, it would most certainly jeopardize your physical well-being."

JJ's shoulders visibly sank. "Look Sampson," he began, "I truly respect your need for secrecy here. So trust me; I wouldn't have *dared* to meet with you personally if I didn't understand your need for absolute confidentiality. But having said that, there's absolutely *no* reason to threaten me."

Sampson shook his head, admonishingly. "It was most certainly *not* a threat, JJ. You must understand that our primary objective is to protect our founder and IFI's objectives; not to mention all of our members. For your own, personal security purposes, it's important that you understand *exactly* who you're dealing with. You see; we don't take our mission of exacting justice for the LORD lightly. Furthermore, we'll absolutely *not* allow anyone to stand in our way. So please remember; we will not tolerate anyone who betrays our confidence. Are we clear?"

"I see," JJ relented, swallowing the insult. "Like I said, we've already discussed all of this. I merely—"

"We obviously know that you've waited a long time to meet with us, JJ," Ezekiel interrupted. "But I must say; we remain disappointed that you were unable to convince Cameron Hunter to join IFI last February."

JJ held his hands up. "Whoa pal—wait right there!" he objected. "All I did was give you his phone number after my dad met with him and the rest of the group last winter. I never promised that I would intervene in his decision to join IFI—*or* stay with Flaming Sword. That was—*and still is*—his decision, and his decision alone."

"That's *exactly* what has us so concerned," Ezekiel continued. "We've been cooperating with you for all of these years on several projects, yet you've consistently resisted our overtures to join our organization, yourself. And when we discovered that Cameron had some outstanding skills that we can certainly use in the execution of our duties, you bowed out of convincing him to join us. Truthfully, I'm wondering why we're risking ourselves by talking to you here tonight in the first place."

Ezekiel quickly looked over at Sampson skeptically.

JJ shook his head. "Wait a minute! I didn't drive all this way to—"

Sampson held up his right hand to silence both men. Out of respect, Ezekiel and JJ immediately fell silent.

"JJ my friend," said Sampson. "Do I need to remind you that we've previously agreed to disagree with our differing methods of dispensing justice? We obviously have an important issue at hand to discuss. Before you try to dissuade us from what we do, I'd like to bypass any further dialogue regarding our diametrically opposed approaches to punishing evil. We've had this conversation ad nauseum, and quite frankly, I've grown weary of it."

JJ sighed. "Listen Sampson . . . and I mean absolutely no disrespect by this . . . but I'm really not interested in trying to change your minds about what you do. I actually gave up on that many years ago. We both know that you guys believe in the Old Testament ways of exacting revenge—"

"Of course, you meant to say *justice*," Sampson quickly added.

JJ paused for a moment as he looked at both men. "Yes, of course. I meant to say *justice*," he relented. "Anyway, my personal mission is to fight against Satan and his demons in the same way Jesus Christ did two thousand years ago."

Sampson folded his hands, interlocking his fingers in an attempt to suppress his anger. "If you don't mind, I'd like to ask you a question," he said.

JJ shrugged. "Be my guest."

"What do you think Jesus Christ would do if He was on Earth today? Do you *really* think He would sit-still for all of the evil you see in the news? Do you think He would idly stand by and watch today's depraved reprobates trample over everything that is good in this world?"

"I don't think Jesus would go around killing those who needed to hear his Gospel . . . if that's what your question is . . . ."

Sampson bristled at this, and Ezekiel leaned forward with an angry glare. Sampson held up a hand, restraining his right hand man once again.

"I suggest we move along to the business at hand," Sampson said. "You've come here tonight to discuss our common *enemy number one*, Caleb Hunter. Is that correct?"

"Yes it is," JJ agreed.

"Now then," Sampson began slowly, "can we agree that this human maggot needs to be dealt with before he commits any more violence in the name of serving Satan?"

"Of course," JJ said. "But I have to be honest, here. I'm a little concerned about how Caleb will be brought to justice; that is, once we've apprehended him."

Sampson grinned. "I'm afraid that Caleb Hunter's castigation will depend entirely upon who apprehends him first: You and the Flaming Sword newbie's, or those of us at IFI who wish to *properly* deal with that reprehensible villain."

JJ nodded as a wave of quixotic emotions dashed through his head. Of course, he realized that meeting with IFI was indeed, a desperate move. However, all of Flaming Sword's efforts to locate Caleb Hunter during the past several months had been unsuccessful. JJ knew that involving a cabal of vigilantes like IFI was certainly a risky endeavor. But at this point, he felt that it was absolutely necessary.

JJ knew just how much of an unorthodox move this rendezvous was, so he set up this meeting with IFI without anyone else in his group having knowledge of it. Although he had been completely honest about his whereabouts with Danny, he already regretted withholding from his friend what his actual intentions were that day.

JJ had actually been engaging in information exchange with IFI for several years now. But when he recently approached them about finding Caleb Hunter, JJ was surprised to discover they wanted to meet with him personally. He was further baffled when Sampson invited him to one of IFI's citadels up in pastoral Vermont; a location which was previously unknown to him.

JJ's primary mission was to not only bring Caleb to justice, but also to present the Gospel of Christ to him. The combination of these factors ended up overriding his common sense, so he guardedly agreed to this questionable meeting.

"I see," JJ said. "Listen, I understand that Caleb has done some absolutely horrible things throughout his criminal history—"

"Particularly against members of your little Flaming Sword group," Sampson added.

JJ nodded. "I suppose you're right about that. Anyway—"

"Doesn't it *bother* you that Caleb Hunter was responsible for the murders of Robert Harris, Willie Richardson and Cammie Spears?" Ezekiel asked pointedly. *"For God's sake*, they were Charlene's husband, Candace's husband, and Cam's mother!"

JJ nodded humbly. "Yes. It bothers me a great deal."

"Then why won't you agree to help us eliminate that piece of human garbage?" Ezekiel leveled, emphatically pointing his finger at JJ.

Sampson once again held up his hand to restrain his sidekick.

"Don't you think we should probably move on?" JJ suggested, realizing they would dash any chance of finding common ground if this current line of discussion continued.

Sampson sighed. "Very well then."

For the next hour, the three men proceeded to swap notes and review each other's respective dossiers on Caleb Hunter. Although the information exchange between them was substantial, they were still unable to settle on anything concrete as to where Caleb and his group of Satan worshippers were located. Although they were unable to attain any solid solutions, JJ was thankful that their conversation had become civil. In the end, they agreed to an ongoing exchange of intelligence regarding their common enemy.

The relaxed setting for the three men continued as Saul brought them a tray of hot tea and biscuits as they were finishing up. After fifteen or so minutes of light chatter, Sampson guided their conversation in an unexpected direction. "If it's alright with you JJ, there's something that we'd like to show you before you leave here tonight."

"Oh, and that is—?"

Sampson glanced at Ezekiel with pride. They nodded at each other with smug grins.

"Please follow me," Sampson said.

They all stood up.

Sampson led the way to the front of the fireplace at the end of the library. He continued, "We obviously invited you here tonight for something other than a mutual review of information—we could have accomplished that by simply meeting with you someplace where we couldn't be overheard. To be completely honest, we felt like it was finally time to pull back the curtain on our operation for you. Of course, that couldn't have been accomplished elsewhere."

JJ nodded as Ezekiel bent down and rolled back the 5 x 8 Oriental rug in front of the fireplace, exposing a trap door. Goose bumps instantly appeared on JJ's neck.

Sampson continued, "You see, we think it's important that you understand just how committed we are to carrying out our missions of justice."

He nodded once again at Ezekiel.

JJ watched the thin, muscular man lift the trap door, exposing a set of cold, uninviting concrete stairs, leading downward.

"Where on Earth does that go?" JJ asked, a disconcerted timbre invading his voice.

Ezekiel sensed JJ's trepidation. "Don't worry my friend," he said, wearing a smirk. "So far, we don't have any *real* beef with you."

"Don't be silly," Sampson added. "We only wish to demonstrate our substantial commitment to achieving our organizational objectives. Please, follow me."

Nervously, JJ followed Sampson and Ezekiel down the stairs, all the while looking for a way of escape, if needed.

The three men walked down thirteen steps into a surprisingly clean, well-lit concrete hallway. As they moved forward, the reverb from the sounds of Ezekiel's shoes on the cold floor paced the group. After about one hundred yards, a large, metal door greeted them. The door was painted an eerie, glossy black. From his internet research of the estate property, JJ surmised they were directly under the huge, red wooden barn, behind the main house.

Sampson gazed gravely at JJ and declared, "What you're about to see is the unattractive underbelly of what we're required to do in an effort to carry out our duties. Unfortunately for those who arrive here, their condemnation has already been decided."

"What exactly is this place?" JJ asked, perplexed.

"The room you are about to enter is where we carry out sentences."

JJ nodded, nervously.

Sampson opened the door, which creaked mightily as it gave way to an opening of semi-darkness. A dry wave of tepid air from the gloom rushed past them as Sampson turned on a fluorescent light, which began illuminating the expanse of a large room. The rest of the series of lights blinked on, as well.

The three men proceeded inside.

JJ surveyed the punishment center and found himself in a dark chamber, which sported a hardened, austere look. His first impression of the dungeon-like room was that it was surprisingly clean. As his gaze panned the room from left to right, he noticed that slate gray painted cinder blocks dominated the interior. At the far end of the large room were three prison cells, all of which were empty. Along both the right and left walls were several closed doors.

Oddly, right in the middle of the room was a black-painted, circular metal railing over a dark hole. There were a couple of desks adjacent to where they currently stood in the entryway. Several metal shelves were lined-up along the perimeter of the room, in-between the various doorways. The shelves were primarily stocked with supplies.

"Why did you bring me down here?" JJ asked, not totally convinced he wanted to hear the answer.

Sampson grinned with pride. "We merely felt like you needed a glimpse of what we *really* do—"

He was interrupted by the low wailing of a strained voice emanating from the circular black-railing in the center of the room.

"Ahhh, our *guest* has apparently awakened," Sampson added, then led the way towards the cries.

JJ reluctantly followed.

In JJ's mind, what happened next would later seem to be a completely surreal event. Ezekiel pulled a nine millimeter pistol out of his jacket and stood watch over the circular railing, opposite of where Sampson and JJ now stood. As the three men looked downwards, JJ felt a cold, dank wave emanate from the hole, which was about fifteen feet in diameter, over a dirt floor. Its walls were smooth and completely straight. He estimated that the pit was also about fifteen feet deep.

Due to the fact that Ezekiel had brandished a weapon, JJ instinctively moved his right hand near the pistol in the crook of his back, under his jacket. He readied himself for action.

Sitting in the bottom of the pit was a Caucasian man in his mid-twenties. His clothes were tattered and his red crew-cut hair accented the scraggly, intermittently grown patches of hair which masqueraded as a short beard on his square jaw. The young man was only semi-conscious. His low moaning had Ezekiel on high alert.

JJ stood in a stunned silence for a few moments before Sampson pronounced, "Presenting Mr. John Thomas. This subject has been convicted in the Court of IFI, and his death sentence will be carried out, post haste."

JJ shook his head. "Wait a minute—what did he do???"

Sampson smiled facetiously. "If you'll kindly let me finish. During the past fourteen months, this subject has murdered a total of seven prostitutes in the Richmond, Virginia area. Thus far, the local law enforcement officials—in all of their glorious bureaucracy—have failed to connect the dots. In other words, they're completely oblivious to the fact that the seven murders were committed by the same man. But due to our substantial network of resources, we were able to locate and remove this subject from the streets before he committed any more of his heinous crimes." JJ's mouth almost fell open. He was speechless as Sampson continued, "Today is the last day on Earth for this condemned man."

JJ shook his head. "But—?"

"We wanted you to witness the importance of what we actually do for the kingdom of God," Sampson added.

"So you're going to kill him . . . right here . . . right now?"

"Of course we are. The sentencing phase for this prisoner is being carried out tonight. Tell me something JJ; what on Earth did you think we did with these low-lifes?"

JJ shook his head once again. "I can't believe this."

Sampson continued, obviously amused. "We were actually hoping you'd like to participate in this subject's execution. Or, at the very least, witness this righteous act of justice."

32

The prisoner let out another groan.

"Listen; I didn't drive all the way up here for this," JJ said, pointing into the pit. "I came here to—"

"You *came* here to see if we would convert to your inadequate way of dispensing justice . . . did you not???"

JJ was thoughtful for a moment. "Not exactly."

"Of course you did!" Sampson said. "However, you needn't be concerned. You see; it was *I* who wanted to entice you over to *our* way of dispensing justice."

JJ continued shaking his head in disbelief.

"Listen guys," he began, "I believe in being well-armed for self-defense purposes—you never know when you'll have to defend yourself against the forces of evil. But the stuff you do down here isn't exactly my cup of tea. No offense, but I think it's time for me to leave."

"Very well then," Sampson said. "If you don't have the stomach for this kind of thing, then you're obviously not a good fit for our organization. However, we'd like to continue cooperating with you regarding Caleb Hunter . . . to the extent that's possible."

"I'll keep working with you in an effort to fight against God's enemies," JJ said. "But I'll *never* do anything like this."

"I see," Sampson said coolly. "Well JJ, I suppose it doesn't matter now, but as a sign-on bonus, I was planning on telling you where Donovan is."

"Donovan the demon?"

"Indeed; *that* Donovan. You know; that pesky little demon who was a contributor to your mother's death."

JJ bristled. "How do you know the whereabouts of Donovan? For Pete's sake, he's a demon!"

"Like I've told you before, our resources are substantial. Due to this, tracking Donovan has not been terribly difficult. You see; he has a particular signature of evil that he almost always leaves in his wake."

"I see," JJ said, biting his lip.

Sampson sensed JJ's frustration, so he offered up another enticement. "Oh, I suppose I can give you at least *one* little tidbit of information regarding your little Flaming Sword group."

"What do you mean?"

"I'm going to tell you an important piece of information about our involvement with an individual who was once connected to your group. And don't worry, this is completely *gratis.*"

"Gee thanks," JJ retorted.

Unfazed, Sampson continued. "Do you recall the fact that your friend Bobby was in the car that was driven by Hank Pickett? You know who I'm referring to; Hank is that little scoundrel who Damon inhabited before he intentionally killed Vanessa Hunter—Wyatt's wife and Danny's mother."

Curiosity invaded JJ's thoughts. He knew the group didn't have a firm answer as to how Bobby, who unfortunately was in the car with Hank that night, escaped the post-crash accident scene. They also had no idea what later happened to Hank—he had literally disappeared off the grid.

JJ nodded. "Yes. I'm aware of what happened that night. At least, most of it."

"Do you now? Well, please allow me to further enlighten you. You see; Damon entered Hank Pickett and did indeed crash into the Hunter's vehicle on the night in question. Soon after the accident, Damon fled Hank's body, because he believed it to be no longer useful. At that point, Mr. Pickett suddenly found himself behind the wheel of a wrecked car with his friend Bobby in the passenger seat. It appears to us that Damon's plan was for both Hank and Bobby to be caught red-handed in the crime. However, Damon made the mistake of underestimating Hank. At least, that's what we believe to be true."

"What do you mean by that?" JJ asked.

"We have surmised that immediately after the crash, Hank dragged Bobby away from the accident scene prior to the arrival of the local authorities. Fortunately for him, traffic was quiet that night, and there doesn't appear to have been any other witnesses."

"Have you considered the possibility that it was the LORD who intervened to get Bobby to safety? You know what I mean; maybe it was one of God's holy angels who helped Bobby."

"Whatever do you mean by that?" Sampson asked.

"Maybe the LORD protected Bobby somehow, because he later surrendered his life to Christ. Isn't it at least a possibility the LORD knew all along that was going to happen one day?"

"I'm not really concerned with that sort of thing," Sampson said dismissively. "Anyway—"

"By the way, how do you know all of this?" JJ asked.

"Please, be patient and listen. So when the authorities arrived, Hank apparently had already hidden Bobby nearby, only to return to the accident scene and act as a witness. We believe he then told the authorities that, *some kids took off on foot,* and that was all he saw. Not knowing any better, they took Hank's word for it. The authorities had absolutely no idea that Bobby was passed out nearby, and it was indeed his father's car that was involved in the wreck."

"If it really happened that way, I must say, that was some pretty quick thinking on Hank's part," JJ said. "But like I just said, I can't believe Hank did that all by himself. It sounds to me like God somehow intervened to protect Bobby."

"Oh, perhaps you're right," Sampson shrugged, sighing. "I cannot dismiss the idea that divine intervention is at least a possibility."

JJ nodded. "So what happened next?"

"We believe that Hank likely made a few calls and was quite efficient in getting Bobby back to his trailer that night. Hank then poured that sorry, drunken excuse of a man into his bed a few hours later. Fortunately for Bobby, he awoke the next day, blissfully unaware of what had happened the night before."

"So, that's it?"

"Of course not. The story doesn't end there. Once we became aware of Hank's transgression—"

"How again did you find out about the accident?"

Sampson lifted his head slightly, gazing disdainfully at JJ.

"I'm afraid that's a trade secret," he said. "But since you're being so persistent, I'll explain. Essentially, we had been tracking the activities of Wyatt Hunter, due to that scoundrel and Satanist, Caleb Hunter. We believe that Caleb wants to kill his brother Wyatt. You're an intelligent man, JJ. You can do the math from there."

JJ nodded. "Okay," he said. "So now I know what happened to Bobby. But what ever happened to Hank?"

"Nicely done!" Sampson declared, facetiously. "The day after the accident which took the life of Wyatt's wife Vanessa, our field agents apprehended Hank at his home and brought him here; to this very room."

"All the way from Georgia?"

"My men are well versed in how to drug and transport condemned people. Our field agents are *very* efficient. Anyway, shortly thereafter, we sent Bobby—who was Hank's only real friend—an email stating that Hank would be gone for a while. Apparently, that did the trick, because Bobby failed to ask any further questions."

"So what did you do with Hank when he arrived here?" JJ asked.

Sampson smiled widely. "Since his primary crime that night was that of theft and allowing a demon to inhabit him, we simply placed him in the pit below you, which we affectionately refer to as the *black hole*."

"What happened then?" JJ asked, already knowing the answer.

"His guilt was pronounced and his sentence carried out."

JJ shook his head in disbelief. "What do you mean? Are you telling me you killed Hank?"

"Of course we did," Sampson said smoothly. "But on that front, I do have some rather good news for you."

"Oh, what's that?"

"We actually gave Hank the opportunity to come to Christ before his sentence was carried out. And I'm pleased to inform you that he accepted Jesus before he died."

JJ shook his head once again. "You can't force someone to surrender their life to Jesus Christ—no matter how little time they still have."

Sampson had a quizzical expression grip his face. "And why not?"

"A salvation experience must come from a general changing of someone's heart. Otherwise, it's a complete waste of time."

Sampson shook his head in disappointment. "Come now; you can't be saying you're not happy we gave that vile bag of bones an opportunity at redemption out of the goodness of our hearts, are you? I must say; *Hank was very lucky to get that!"*

JJ ignored Sampson's sanctimony. "So you actually killed Hank . . . right here?"

Ignoring the redundant question, Sampson continued. "Since we typically administer punishment in a fashion similar to how the crimes are committed by the perpetrators, we found ourselves having to make an exception in Hank's case."

"Oh—why is that?"

"Because disposing of a criminal with a car wreck and demon possession was very . . . How shall we say? . . . impractical. So instead, Ezekiel simply fired three shots into Hank's head."

JJ felt his stomach turn and was quiet for a moment. "So what did you do with his body?" he asked.

"No worries. We have a state-of-the-art disposal vat behind that door to your right." Sampson pointed towards one of the doors down the side of the room. "Essentially, Hank's remains were simply processed and flushed down the drain, nevermore to be heard of—or seen—ever again."

It took all of JJ's strength to retain a calm exterior in order to make an efficient exit. Although he previously had a good idea of what IFI did with criminals, actually seeing it first-hand brought with it a sickening reality.

"Listen . . ." JJ began, "I really appreciate you letting me know what happened, but I'm afraid I must go. Do you have any objection to that?"

"Of course not—you're certainly free to go," Sampson decreed.

"Shall I leave the same way we came down here?"

"There's an entrance down here from the barn up above," Ezekiel added. "You know; for easy prisoner transfer. But yes, you may exit the same way we came in. I'll have Saul escort you out."

"Thank you."

"And we thank *you* for coming by tonight," Ezekiel said.

"Indeed JJ, thank you for your time," Sampson said ominously. "And I do hope that in the future, we'll never have the need to see you down here again. Oh, and one more thing. As an act of good faith, you can rest assured that we've pardoned your friend Bobby for his crimes. Since he is now part of your little *group,* we've graciously decided to leave him be."

JJ nodded solemnly, sickened by the veiled threat on both himself and Bobby. He turned and quickly left the punishment center. Ezekiel walked part of the way back down the hallway, until he saw JJ meet up with Saul, who escorted him upstairs. After a couple of minutes, Saul rang-in on the intercom, "Mr. Baugh has left the property, sir."

"Thank you Saul," Sampson said. "That is all."

Ezekiel grinned smugly. He absolutely loved the intimidation of others. "I'm not surprised in the least that JJ turned us down again," he said to the newest guest in the room. "However, he still may be of future use to us."

"He may indeed," IFI's founder said, wearing a sanctimonious grin.

"Anyway," Sampson added, turning towards The Founder. "Do you wish to participate in the execution of the prisoner in the black hole?"

The Founder seemed to be amused by Sampson's question. *"But of course.* Have the prisoner strapped into the gurney in room number two. I wish to slash his throat, *just* like he did to those seven women he murdered."

"Ahhh!" Sampson exclaimed. "A sentence being carried out, just like the perpetrator did to his victims. I must say, I really do get maximum satisfaction when we proceed with executions this way—just like it was done in the old days."

The Founder sported a smug grin. "That's *exactly* why I chose you to lead this group, Sampson. You truly understand vital importance of exterminating the degenerates of this world, and to carry out God's righteous vengeance. Please continue, my friend, and let me know once the prisoner is fully-prepared for his most unpleasant exit from this planet. Also, please remember, I want the prisoner to be fully-conscious for his execution. I want him to know *precisely* what the term, *eye for an eye* means."

Sampson nodded. "As usual, it will be done as you wish . . . ."

Methuen, MA
October 5th

**"Let us therefore make every effort to do what leads
to peace and to mutual edification."
Romans 14:19**

A glorious autumn sunrise greeted Wyatt Hunter as he relaxed in front of his computer, early that crisp October morning. Decked out in his normal "battle fatigues" of plaid flannel pajama bottoms and a plain, oversized black tee shirt, the desk-chair warrior complemented his morning armament with a mug of piping hot coffee. As the java's caffeine brushed away the cobwebs from his previous night's slumber, Wyatt eagerly made plans for what he expected would be a very busy day.

After tediously working on a proposed television interview for the past several weeks, Wyatt had finally secured an appointment for the next evening on a small, local-access TV station down in Boston. The program which he was scheduled to appear on featured local artists of varying kinds, including authors, musicians, painters, and the like. In Wyatt's case, he was excitedly preparing to be interviewed for his book's very first television promotion. He thought this was a great publicity opportunity.

Tempering his excitement, however, was also an uneasy feeling of anxiety creeping into his soul. This was due in large part to a recent communiqué from the TV station; something that just didn't seem right to him. His concern centered on the fact that the premise for the program had recently been amended by the program's host. Nonplussed, Wyatt continued with his normal morning routine of intermittently sipping coffee, while doing research on the internet and reading emails.

The house that Wyatt and Cam had chosen to purchase was in a quiet neighborhood between I-495 and I-93, adjacent to the New Hampshire border, and only about a mile or so from the Merrimack Valley Golf Club. The four front-facing gables of the house complemented the white painted structure, which sported glossy black shutters on the front windows. The house sat on a large unfenced lot and featured an expansive walk-out basement, which led down a hill and into a large, forested green space.

As father and son continued to settle into their new locale, Wyatt found himself totally enthralled with the basement area, where he had set up his own, personal "man-cave." Initially, he did this in an effort to create a distraction-free zone from which he could comfortably write his novels. Over the proceeding weeks and months, however, his man-cave had actually evolved into his official sanctuary from the world.

Wyatt's workspace featured a dark-colored L-shaped desk, an old comfortable "napping couch," and a fifty inch plasma television with an accompanying Blue Ray player. Oftentimes, he found himself not leaving the house for days at a time as he pecked away at his next literary work.

Subsequent to Wyatt and Cam settling on their new home, it was agreed that since Cam was younger and would likely live in the house longer than his father, he would be the one to decide on the upstairs decorating. Of course, that left Wyatt as the one-man committee

A WALK THROUGH HEAVEN & HELL

responsible for deciding upon the accouterments for his downstairs domain.

Before his move to New England from Seattle a few months previous, Wyatt had unselfishly left behind his beloved female Boston terrier named "Baby." He did this as a gift for his son Danny and daughter-in-law Mi-Cha, as well as the newlywed's infant son, DJ. Although Wyatt very much missed his canine companion, he was happy that his son's family would be able to enjoy his beloved dog.

Baby had originally been brought to the family by his wife Vanessa, who was now joyfully living with the LORD in Heaven. Because Wyatt had left Baby behind, he felt like he was actually leaving a piece of Vanessa behind with them. Not only that, but Miss Charlene was getting older, and she really enjoyed the dog's company, as well.

As Wyatt continued to key away at his computer, Cam came dragging into his basement office; his own cup of coffee in tow.

"Good morning Pop," he said, yawning.

"Mornin' son," Wyatt said, not looking up.

Cam plopped down onto the napping couch across from Wyatt's desk. "Why on Earth do you keep it so dark down here?" he asked.

"I've already told you that. It's because the peaceful setting down here allows my mind to function at its optimal capacity."

Cam shook his head. "Whatever, dad. It still doesn't make any sense to me. I'd much rather lay in the sunshine by the pool."

"Whatever yourself, kid," Wyatt said evenly, still engrossed with an online article. "By the way, did you ever get back the paperwork on your surname change from Spears to Hunter?"

"Actually yes," Cam stated proudly. "Believe it or not, that's why I dared to venture down here so early this morning."

"I see. Go on."

"I wanted to be the first one to tell you that my name is now officially *Cameron Joseph Hunter.*"

Wyatt looked up as if a cold bucket of water had been poured over his head. "Your middle name is *Joseph?*"

Cam shrugged. "Yeah, I thought you already knew that."

"Nope. Honestly, I've never thought about it before."

"Why do you ask? Is it a big deal or something?"

"No, it's not a big deal. It's just interesting."

"Why is that?"

"Because my middle name is Joseph, as well," Wyatt said.

Cam looked surprised. "Oh really?" he asked, pausing for a few seconds. "I don't suppose that's a coincidence, is it?"

Wyatt removed his hands from the keyboard for a moment and took a big sip of his coffee. "No, it's definitely *not* a coincidence. My best guess is that my mother Abbie cooked up that idea, then led your mother Cammie towards it when you were born. Of course, that's just my guess."

"Hmmm . . . I suppose you may be right. Hey, why don't we ask Mick about it?"

Wyatt shook his head emphatically. "Don't bother. I've already tried to quiz him further about the relationship between my mom and your mom."

"Really? What did he say?"

"He said it was under *DP*."

"*DP?*" Cam asked, confused. "No offense, but I don't exactly remember what that is," he admitted.

"*Divine Privilege*. Mick can't tell us everything we want to know—he can only tell us what the LORD allows him to."

"Oh, I see. I remember now."

"Anyway," Wyatt continued, "welcome to the family," he said, turning his attention back to the computer.

"Uh . . . Pop . . . since you titled this house in my name, I think my *welcome to the Hunter family* has already been established."

The room remained quiet for a few moments. Wyatt stopped tapping away at his computer once again.

"I'm sorry son. I suppose I'm a little distracted this morning."

"What in the world are you working on that's so important?"

"Well, I got this email last night from Jeanette Collins, who is the hostess for the show I'm being interviewed on tomorrow night."

"And—?"

"She told me the show will now feature another guest; joining me."

"Really? Who else will be there?"

"Some guy named Alistair McClellan. It's weird, because I was originally scheduled to appear on the show, all by myself."

"So—?"

"I've been googling this McClellan guy, and it appears he just published a book titled <u>The Modern Age of Enlightened Atheism.</u> As you can imagine, I'm a little concerned that—"

"You're concerned about walking into an ambush, right?"

"Actually, I am . . . ."

Wyatt's thought was interrupted by the sound of the doorbell. "Who in the world could *that* be, this early?" he wondered out loud.

"You got me," Cam said, yawning once again.

"Hey kid, you're a lot younger than me—hop to it, please."

"Huh?"

"Go get the door, dude."

"Oh okay . . . sorry. . . ."

Cam got up from the couch and headed upstairs. Wyatt interrupted him, "By the way, why are you so darned tired?"

"I had a late date with Maria down in Boston last night."

The doorbell rang once again.

"I see," Wyatt said thoughtfully. "Anyway, please go see who has their knickers in such a twist this morning. I'm gonna *scream* if I hear that doorbell ring one more time."

"Take it easy Pop—I got this," Cam said, proceeding upstairs.

After a few moments, Wyatt could hear him unlock the door; then the sound of jingling. This signaled the door-chain being unhooked.

Barely audible, Wyatt could hear Cam say, *"Hey, it's my favorite angel!* How's it going, Mick? What're you doing here so early?"

Wyatt grinned and shook his head. His attention then returned to the computer. He wanted to figure out what McClellan's book was all about.

It took a few minutes for Mick and Cam to make their way downstairs. When they appeared, Wyatt blurted, "What took you guys so long to make it down here???"

In his deep-but-friendly voice, Mick retorted, "I'm afraid I can't face you and your *sparkling personality* unless I first have a cup of joe," he joked. The angel held up his mug to emphasize the point. "And Cam here was kind enough to hook me up with some java before we entered this dimly-lit paradise of yours."

A smirk swept across Wyatt's face. "Wow, we haven't been blessed with your presence for a whole two weeks now. To what do we owe this honor?"

Mick grinned. "Oh, I just wanted to rub it in a little about that whoopin' I put on you boys when we played golf a couple of weeks ago while we were discussing some Kingdom business."

"Oh c'mon—get outta here!" Wyatt said. "You've played a *lot* more golf than me over the years. That's cheating as far as I'm concerned."

Mick simply shrugged. Wyatt looked over at Cam for support, but his son held up his hands, indicating a neutral position.

"Oh, I get it Cam," Wyatt continued. "You're not gonna rock the boat because of how well Mick has helped you with your fantasy football team this year, are you?"

"That has *nothing* to do with it," Cam shot back. "Mick is only a *consultant* for my team—nothing more."

"Don't you mean *mascot???*"

Cam grinned. "You're just saying that because my team's name is the *Angels*, aren't you?"

Mick withheld a grin as he sipped his coffee, but said nothing.

Wyatt's eyebrows narrowed. "Whatever. I still think y'all are cheating," he chided.

"Oh—why is that?" Cam asked innocently.

"Because you're still in first place with a pretty big lead. That's why."

"Hang on a minute," Mick quickly added. *"Cam* isn't the bonehead who passed on Tom Brady at the beginning of the second round— you are."

"That's right Pop," Cam agreed. "I simply snapped him up when you didn't pick him. As you well know, he's already thrown for a pile of touchdowns this year. I'm afraid that's on *you*—not me and Mick."

"Yeah, yeah, yeah," Wyatt said. "I'm just glad we don't gamble any money in this league. If we did, I'd be losing—big time."

"How true," Mick said. "Gambling can be very destructive, anyway. I strongly recommend against it."

Wyatt nodded, then scratched the back of his shaved head. "Anyway," he continued, "to what do we owe the honor of this early morning visit, Mick?"

"Well partner, not to get too serious or anything, but we *really* need to talk about your impending interview tomorrow night."

Wyatt bristled with curiosity. "Oh yeah, why do you say that?"

"I just think you need to be prepared for the unexpected. I'm afraid you may be walking into a Christian-bashing ambush."

"Cam and I were just—"

"But don't worry," Mick interrupted. "I've got some good Scripture to prepare you with."

"I'll be more than happy to crack a few heads if anyone gets out of line," Cam joked.

Mick shot Cam an admonishing look. "Cool it, dude. You and I *both* know it took you almost *two weeks* before you told the rest of the group about your little interlude with those bozos at IFI last winter. You haven't forgotten about *that,* have you?"

Cam held up his hands, defensively. "Whoa, Mick! We've already talked about this," he objected. "I've already apologized several times. I also promised that I'd never—"

"Take it easy, partner," Mick interrupted. "I was just giving you a little reminder about how to fight against evil—with the Truth, prayer, and obedience to the Word of God."

"I know, I know," Cam said.

"Please remember fellas," the angel continued, "I'm only the assistant coach on the sidelines, signaling in the plays from the LORD. *You* guys are the players on the field; *you're* the ones who can either follow the LORD's plays, or audible on your own."

"So in this football analogy, does that mean the LORD is the head coach?" Wyatt asked.

"Of course not, dopey! The LORD actually owns *everything*—the stadium, the team, the uniforms, the cheerleaders, the cameras . . . you get the picture. It's *His* game and only *He* can call the shots. Your jobs are to simply follow God's lead."

"I suppose you're right," Wyatt said wearily. "But seriously, can you give me any *real* insight into what I'll be dealing with tomorrow night?"

"Indeed I can, dudemeister," Mick said. "Let's start off with a short passage in the book of *Proverbs*. This will actually be easy to keep in the forefront of your mind as you walk into this potentially loaded-gun situation."

"What, are you saying I'm a numbskull and can't remember a longer passage of Scripture?" Wyatt chided.

"Don't be such a knucklehead and listen up . . . *Proverbs 26:4* says . . . *Do not answer a fool according to his folly, or you yourself will be just like him.*"

"Hmmm," Wyatt mumbled. "If I remember right, verse number five after that seems to say just the opposite. But I also know that both verses are talking about discernment regarding the difference between trivial arguments, and genuine dialogue on important matters of faith in God."

"Correctamundo," Mick said.

"Anyway, do you think the other author who they just added to the show—Alistair McClellan—will try to debate me tomorrow night or something? That's kind of what I've been sitting here thinking about."

"Not necessarily. What I'm saying is this: You need to realize that some unbelievers in this world will try to appear intellectually superior to you, because you believe in an unseen God. On the other hand, others will genuinely wish to engage you in a real, meaningful discussion about their concerns. In the case of the first example, that's essentially the current bread-and-butter play which Satan uses to blind humans; it's actually a really old subterfuge the evil ones have a real penchant for using."

"What do you mean by that?"

"Satan and his demons deceitfully attempt to elevate mankind's perception of human intelligence to a significantly higher level than what it actually is. When they're successful in doing so, a person's need for an alleged *Creator* or *God* seems totally unnecessary. Or rather, it seems below their intelligence."

"I see," Wyatt said.

"So if you stoop down to their level of condescending rudeness, you're essentially playing by Satan's rules. I'm afraid the LORD can't help you if you're not running the plays from His playbook. That's the Bible, you know."

"Is dad supposed to just sit there and take a bunch of baloney from this guy, or what?" Cam asked.

"That's not what I'm saying," Mick said. "Christians should always stand up for the LORD, thereby standing up for them self—"

"And—?" Cam interrupted.

"Please—let me finish. I need to give you one more Scripture. This will be a complement to the overall gameplan for the interview tomorrow night. After that, it'll be my treat for a round of golf today. That way, we can talk about this situation in a much more . . . How shall I say this? . . . *Competitive setting.*"

"I don't think we'll have time for a full round today," Wyatt said. "I haven't been hitting the ball very well lately, and it might take me all day to finish eighteen holes."

"I've noticed," Mick said, grinning. "Anyways, we'll just play the front nine today if you want. No problem."

"Hey Mick," Cam began, "not that I'm trying to digress or anything, but since you and I first met on a golf course earlier this year, I've been wondering how long you've actually been playing the game. What's the deal?"

The angel stroked his grayish goatee. "Oh, let's just say that I'm pretty familiar with the old course at St. Andrews over in Scotland."

"Really?" Wyatt asked. "How long have you been playing there?"

"Oh, only for about six hundred years or so. . . ."

"For real?!?!?" Cam asked, incredulous.

Mick wore a sly grin. "Ask yourself this, fellas—why do you think neither of you has ever beaten me on the golf course?"

"Ah-ha!" Wyatt said. "So tell me; have you had missions to Scotland in the past? Or, have you just boondoggled your way to playing the old course?"

"C'mon, dude. You know that angels are *always* on a mission," Mick said. "Anyway, I suppose I can tell you this: I spent some time a few centuries ago with some of your ancient relatives who lived in nearby Dundee—across the bay from St. Andrews. Actually, I got to know these folks pretty well. We did some mighty battles against demonic evil together."

"I see," Wyatt said. "So, you didn't just make up a reason to go play golf, huh?"

"Of course not—that's *not* how angels roll. Everything we do is for service unto the LORD."

"It must be really cool to have done all of those things throughout history," Cam said. "I mean, you've been all over this world, I'm, sure."

"Indeed I have," Mick agreed. "Listen guys, once you've made it out of this chaos down here on Earth, you'll be amazed at how your perception of reality will change; that is, once you're in Heaven with Jesus."

"How so?" Cam asked.

"Now I know it's probably difficult for you to imagine this right now, but in Heaven, your outlook on all of the wonders of the LORD's incredible creation will be *immensely* intensified. As a result, you'll no longer be thinking in finite terms."

"What do you mean by that?" Wyatt asked.

"Like I said, everything you observe and enjoy in creation will drastically change. Now then; this not only includes what the LORD has directly created, but also what He's guided mankind to create for Him. Basically, your entire outlook will take on a much more relaxed and comfortable pace. In other words, it won't amaze you to play awesome golf courses for hundreds of years, because you'll be exploring and enjoying God's vast kingdom for all of eternity."

"That's interesting," Wyatt said quietly. "I also look forward to when you can tell me more about your missions to see my ancient relatives."

"I'm sure I'll find some time soon to fill you in on some of that," Mick said. "Anyway, the other passage we need to talk about for tomorrow night is in *2 Timothy 2:23 . . . Don't have anything to do with foolish and stupid arguments, because you know they produce quarrels.*"

"I'm familiar with that one," Wyatt said. "But that's a lot easier said-than-done when you're being called *stupid* by a bunch of God-haters."

"I get that," Mick said. "I really-do understand how you feel. But remember; you need to just wait and see how things unfold in the interview tomorrow night. In other words, don't let your preconceived notions steer your attitude. Instead, you need to allow the Holy Spirit to guide you."

"I suppose that makes sense," Wyatt agreed.

"Anyway, why don't you boys go get dressed so that we can hit the links? We'll finish up this discussion whilst I put another whoopin' on you golfing novices."

Wyatt chuckled. "I suppose that'll work."

"After that," Mick continued, "we need to go have some awesome New England clam chowder somewhere."

"Gosh Mick, you and your stinky seafood," Wyatt bemoaned.

"Go on now, dude. Let's get moving."

Wyatt and Cam then proceeded upstairs to get ready for the day. As they did so, the blue collar angel sipped his coffee, deep in thought. Mick sensed that the showdown with Caleb and Damon was now moving into the starting gate, so he prayed earnestly for God's guidance in their upcoming battles.

Watkinsville, GA
October 5th

**"Because he himself suffered when he was tempted,
he is able to help those who are being tempted."
Hebrews 2:18**

An array of puffy cumulus clouds dotted the southern skyline, appearing as pure white gobs of cotton splotched across a brilliant blue backdrop. Autumn was late arriving in northeast Georgia that year, and a surprisingly warm day greeted the oddly-paired ministry squad within the ranks of Flaming Sword Communications, Chul Moo Kim and Bobby James.

After receiving their new assignments from Mick several months before, "Moo" and Bobby methodically began their ministry work. As a starting point, God had chosen two primary areas for them to focus on: assisting local food shelters and supporting local humane societies. During that time, they also processed the James estate through probate.

Between themselves, they had a tongue-in-cheek nickname for their first ministry assignment: "Food and Fido." It gave both men a huge amount of satisfaction when they saw how much the local community embraced their support. Their initial assignments served them well in getting established as a ministry resource in the area.

To that end, Moo and Bobby spent much of their time sourcing dry food goods for needy families, as well as contributing to a large, local food bank. They also worked closely with local animal shelters, helping a large number of homeless dogs in getting placed with loving families and into service visiting the elderly.

As he chilled-out in his room that day, Moo busily wailed away on his beloved Fender Stratocaster. The young Taekwondo instructor always enjoyed playing along to his favorite guitar hero of all time, Stevie Ray Vaughan. Moo had worked up quite a sweat during the current jam session, busily cranking out some bluesy riffs as he played along to the song "Cold Shot" on his I-pod. Through the wall of music, he heard an insistent knock at his bedroom door.

"It's about time," Bobby said, greeting his roommate as Moo opened the door. He handed the wannabe rock star a hot cup of coffee. "You must've not heard me through all of that loud guitaring and such."

"Ah—the coffee dude finally arrives!" Moo declared. He turned off the music and put his guitar on its stand. "I thought you said you were gonna make a fresh pot an hour ago."

"Sorry, dude. I actually forgot all about it."

"Not to pry or anything, but what were you doing?"

"Oh, just checking some emails and doing a little Bible study."

"I see. Hey, did we ever get a response on our suggestion from that pastor over in Winder?"

"Yeah, we sure did," Bobby said. "He was on a mission trip to Haiti and just got back. That's why we didn't hear from him for a few days."

"Oh, okay. So what did he say about our idea of starting a food pantry at their church?"

"He's all for it. He also liked the idea of the 'coupon club' for the ladies at his church. He actually liked it quite a bit."

"Good deal," Moo said. "The concept of using the couponic prowess of some of those folks to build a church food ministry should work really well."

"Couponic prowess?" Bobby asked, confused. "What on Earth is that?"

"Of course—*of or relating to coupons . . . .*"

Bobby shook his head. "No offense partner, but you're starting to sound just like Wyatt with all those fancy words you make up."

"Thank you, my good man."

"Anyway, I honestly don't know a whole lot about the coupons thing," Bobby admitted. "But if the church can lead at least a dozen or so people in its congregation to obtain some good deals on groceries for folks who need food . . . well then . . . that'll be a really good thing to do."

"You got that right," Moo agreed. "We should probably try to meet with that pastor sometime this week—"

The ringing of the doorbell interrupted their conversation.

"Paper, rock, scissors to see who gets it!" Bobby said quickly. After a three count, Bobby laid out a flat hand to represent paper. Moo put out his fist to represent a rock, signifying his loss. "Nailed you again," Bobby cooed. "Now then; go get the door."

Moo shook his head and stomped towards the front door, his coffee in tow. As he prepared to unfasten the locks, the doorbell rang once again. *"Just a minute!"* Moo said. He then mumbled to himself, *"all right, all right,"* before opening the door.

Standing before him was a handsome African-American man who sported faded blue jeans and a non-descript, thin black sweater. The stranger politely said, "Greetings Moo, my name is Ebenezer—but my friends call me *Ben.*"

Moo's instincts clicked on at the mention of his name by a complete stranger. His fists instinctively flexed as his mind emptied and he prepared for a potential assault.

"Who are you???" he asked, skeptically.

"No worries, my friend," Ben said. "I'm an angel who works with Mick. He sent me here today to chat with you and Bobby."

Ben had medium-dark skin to compliment his somewhat muscular build. The angel had piercing, dark eyes and a slight African accent. This latter part added a layer of curious reassurance to his persona. Ben's head was shaved clean and he sported a close-cropped mustache and goatee, giving the visitor an appearance that was casual-yet-classy.

By this time, Bobby arrived at the front doorway and stood behind and to the right of Moo.

"Listen," Moo began. "How do I know—?"

Ben gently interrupted, "Like I was just saying . . . Mick sent me here today to—"

"So how do we know you're really an angel?" Bobby interrupted.

Moo quickly added, "And like *I was saying,* how do we know that Mick sent you? If you know anything about our ministry, you'll also know that attacks from demons are very likely to cross our path."

"Ahhh, very good," Ben stated warmly. "*1 John 4:2* says, *This is how you can recognize the Spirit of God: Every spirit that acknowledges that Jesus Christ has come in the flesh is from God.*"

Moo continued to wear a skeptical look. "Even the devil knows Scripture," he said. "Heck, I'm sure that Satan knows it better than most Christians do."

Ben grinned once again. "Jesus Christ is the eternal Son of God, sent by the Father to be born of the virgin Mary. He was the descendant of King David, and in the flesh, He willingly became the Savior of the world by dying on the Cross. Jesus is the only way to Heaven for eternity with God our Father. He died for your sins and was physically resurrected. Jesus loves you more than you can ever know. He is your Father and my Father, and He reigns supreme in the universe. Satan is His mortal enemy, and we must *all* fight against the Evil One and his minions of demons until the LORD returns for His final victory. So, how does that work for you?"

Moo looked back at Bobby and nodded, obviously impressed. "C'mon in, Ben," he said.

Ben smiled broadly as he stepped across the threshold. "By the way, in Hebrew, Ebenezer means *stone of help.*"

The angel proceeded into the living room.

"Does that mean you're here to help us, or what?" Bobby asked.

"Indeed I am Bobby," Ben said. "Especially you."

A quizzical look passed over Bobby's face.

Moo quickly asked, "Hey Ben, before we get started, can I get you something to drink?"

"Ahhh yes! A cup of joe would be very nice. I drink mine black."

Moo nodded before disappearing into the kitchen.

"Let's have a seat," Bobby said, nodding towards the living room.

"Thank you, my friend," Ben said.

Bobby and Ben made themselves comfortable. They engaged in some minor chit-chat about the unusually warm fall day, before Moo returned with Ben's coffee, anxious to hear what the angel had to say.

"So tell me Ben," Moo began, "do you work directly with Mick?"

"I do," Ben said. "I'm actually part of *The Dozen.*"

"Ah-ha!" Moo said. "I've been wondering when we'd meet another one of you guys."

"I see what you're saying," Bobby added. "We've only met a couple of Mick's group so far."

"Actually," Ben began, "you've previously met four of the original members—I'll make number five for you. That is, if you're keeping count."

Bobby looked deep in thought. "Let's see . . . Mick makes one . . . and Jimmy and Ruth make it two and three. . . ."

"And let's not forget that Damon was originally part of their group," Moo added.

"Yes, he certainly was," Ben agreed. "But since Damon's banishment many years ago, we have remained eleven-strong."

"So what's the deal with Damon?" Moo asked. "What happened?"

Ben looked thoughtful as he began his explanation. "I'll need to go back in history to properly explain Damon's shenanigans. You see, the LORD originally placed the twelve of us together so we could serve His beloved creation—especially mankind. As you know, people were made in God's image. And we—His holy angels—are merely humble servants of our LORD."

"So how long ago did this happen?" Bobby asked.

Ben gently shook his head. "I'm afraid that falls under Divine Privilege, my good friend."

Moo nodded. "But it's true that Damon was originally part of your group, right?"

"He was," Ben agreed, nodding. "Before Satan was booted out of Heaven, along with the angels who chose to follow him—*like Damon*—we were a very close-knit group of twelve who had a special set of tasks in serving God."

"And Mick was your group leader, right?" Bobby asked.

"Again, yes. He still is, by the way."

"If I remember right, Mick told us that Damon resented not being the leader," Moo began, "and that's pretty much the reason why he rebelled against God and chose to follow Satan."

"That is also correct," Ben said.

"Technically," said Moo, "I suppose Satan's name was Lucifer back then, right?"

"I see that Mick did a good job of explaining things when he visited each of you," Ben exclaimed. "Yes, Elon's sin was the mistake that all of the rebellious angels made when they followed Lucifer. It's largely driven by the same sinful sentiment which also plagues every normal human being who has ever been born into this sinful world of yours; or rather, this world of Satan's."

"Who is Elon?" Moo asked, confused.

"Oh, I'm sorry," Ben said. "Elon was Damon's original heavenly name before he rebelled. Elon is a name which actually indicates 'oak tree' in Hebrew. And that's what the LORD thought of Elon when He named him—that he was as strong as oak."

"I see," Moo said. "So Lucifer and Elon turned into Satan and Damon after they got kicked out of Heaven; all of this because of their sin of pride against God. Isn't that right?"

"That is correct. But actually my friends, pride is the root of *all* sin."

"What do you mean by that?" Bobby asked.

Ben sighed. "The sentiment behind pride always starts like this: *I deserve*—you can fill in the blank from there. Coincidentally, that's the *precise* moment where someone begins to believe they can make their own decisions about what they should or should not have; or what they should or should not do."

"That's interesting," Moo said. "Please go on."

"The decision about what a person should or shouldn't have is often made without consideration of our Creator's wishes. It's basically an entitlement mindset that may or may not line up with the LORD's will."

Moo nodded. "So you're saying that the sin of pride is the turning *towards* oneself and *away* from the LORD?" he asked.

"That's correct. Unfortunately, all humans are born into this prideful world of Satan's; his evil influence is very powerful."

"So when does pride enter the scene with humans?" Moo asked.

"Unfortunately, all humans have inherited a prideful sin nature from Adam and Eve," Ben said. *"Romans 5:12* tells us that sin entered the world through Adam. Truthfully, pride can easily take hold and assault your entire soul. Ultimately, prideful sin will snake its way throughout every thought you have. And if you're not careful, pride will completely overtake you and turn you away from the LORD and towards yourself."

Bobby and Moo were quiet for a few moments as the angel's words sank in.

Moo broke their brief silence. "So, let's see if I've got this straight. Elon/Damon decided he should be in charge of your group, and when he didn't get it, he rebelled and followed Lucifer and one-third of all the angels in Heaven's mass-exodus many years ago?"

"That's correct. Of course, we didn't call ourselves *The Dozen* or *The Dirty Dozen* back then. We've actually had many different monikers over the centuries. But we've remained eleven-strong during all this time."

"So why didn't the LORD replace Damon when he was kicked out of Heaven?"

"Ah yes, an excellent question!" Ben said. "Throughout the Bible, the LORD has used twelve as a very special number. In some cases when one of the twelve has been removed—perhaps as a reminder of the fallen world you live in—sometimes God replaces the missing member. In other cases, He leaves it at eleven—at least for some time."

"Why is that?" Bobby asked.

"God probably leaves it that way for a while as a reminder of the tragic consequences of rebellion before His Holy Throne."

"You mean, you don't know for sure?" Bobby asked.

Ben smiled. "As angels, even though our missions are to serve the LORD and His Creation, we're not privy to *all* knowledge. Only the Most High God knows all things."

After a few moments of thought, Moo added, "You know; that eleven-thing sure sounds familiar to me. After Christ's resurrection, the eleven remaining apostles met with Jesus before His ascension into Heaven."

"They sure did," Ben said. "If you have a Bible handy, let's take a look at a passage at the end of the gospel of *Matthew*."

Moo grabbed the Bible on the coffee table and flipped to the New Testament. "Where to, Ben?"

"*Matthew 28:16-20,* my friend."

"You got it . . .

> *"Then the eleven disciples went to Galilee, to the mountain where Jesus had told them to go. When they saw him, they worshiped him; but some doubted. Then Jesus came to them and said, 'All authority in heaven and on earth has been given to me. Therefore go and make disciples of all nations, baptizing them in the name of the Father and of the Son and of the Holy Spirit, and teaching them to obey everything I have commanded you. And surely I am with you always, to the very end of the age.'"*

"Very good," Ben said. "After Judas Iscariot hung himself, there were only eleven of the original apostles remaining. You see, Judas betrayed Christ, just as Damon betrayed the LORD. We have always believed the LORD never replaced Damon so it would remind us of the consequence of his rebellion against God."

"Hmmm," Moo thought out loud. "There are eleven remaining members of The Dozen angel group, and eleven remaining original apostles in this Scripture. That's very interesting."

"I'm glad you see the connection," Ben said. "What's also interesting is that later on, the LORD added to the eleven apostles, just as He's also added to our group of angels who do missions on Earth."

"I thought you said there were only eleven of you guys left," Bobby said.

"There are, my friend. But we also work *very closely* with several other groups of angels who also perform missions on Earth."

"What do you mean?" Bobby asked. "Will we be working with more than one group of angels?"

"Oh yes," the angel said. "We actually work very closely with a group of deep cover angels who are charged with long-term infiltrations into evil situations. We also work with numerous other angel groups."

Moo looked thoughtful for a moment. "These deep cover angels almost sound like undercover cops."

"In a manner of speaking, they are," Ben said. "In particular, we're currently involved with a deep cover angel who is working on an important job that's under heavy demonic influence."

"For real?" Bobby asked.

"Oh, yes. This situation is connected very strongly with what's going on with those of you in Flaming Sword."

"So what is it?" Moo asked.

"I'm afraid I can't disclose anything further about that situation right now. However, we believe the whole thing is about to boil over."

"Wait a minute!" Bobby said. "How can a deep cover angel hide himself from a demon? I thought you guys all knew each other in Heaven before Satan was banished; at least, that's what Mick told me."

"That's a very astute question Bobby," Ben said. "Don't forget the fact that the LORD is omnipotent. If He wants to lay His protective hand over a deep cover angel in order to conceal them as being part of the heavenly hosts, then our powerful Father is certainly able to accomplish that."

"I see," Bobby said. "I suppose that makes sense . . . ."

"So Ben, tell us what's really going on, here," Moo said. "I'm sure that Mick didn't just send you down here to hang out, drink coffee, and talk about Damon with us today."

"Your instincts are correct," Ben said. "I need for both of you to be prepared to travel on a moment's notice. There are some very important events unfolding up in Wyatt's neck of the woods in New England, and this will necessitate your involvement and assistance."

"Really?" Bobby asked. "Are we leaving today?"

"I'm actually not sure yet," the angel said. "All I can tell you is to be prepared to fly to Boston on a moment's notice. I believe the LORD will need you to deploy very soon, so please get ready. Fortunately, you don't have any pressing engagements with your current ministry work."

"I see," Moo said. "Do you have anything else for us?"

"Unfortunately, I do," Ben said, solemnly. "Satan has unleashed a legion-demon from his personal arsenal. It's very likely that this demon will become a problem for either our friends—*or us*—to deal with."

"Are legion-demons any different than Damon and the rest?"

"Unfortunately, they are," Ben said. "This particular legion-demon is named *Geyotteream*. I'm afraid he is the vilest of the vile."

Bobby had a chill sweep across his soul. "What makes this demon so bad?" he asked.

Ben's expression turned very serious. "Legion-demons are, to use a human term, Satan's top henchmen. The Evil One typically deploys them only when he's engaging in a *serious* campaign against God. The thing that's so difficult about humans having to deal with legion-demons is that they're *incredibly* powerful. Once a legion-demon has entered and overtaken a human body, it's rare for them to allow the human to survive afterwards; that is, once they've made their exit."

"Why is that?" Bobby asked

"Legion-demons are perhaps the mightiest of all demons, except for Satan himself."

"This doesn't sound too good," Bobby lamented. "I'd sure like to know more about them."

"Please relax Bobby. I'm not here to scare you. I'm actually here to help you in the next step of your ministry. Since you have both had ample time to get settled into your new living situation, I believe the real battles in your important missions will soon begin."

"I sure am glad you're here," Bobby said.

"And I'm pleased to help," Ben said. "But before I leave today, I need to cover one last thing. Now Bobby, I must tell you this—you're doing an excellent job in your ongoing recovery from alcohol abuse. The LORD is most pleased with your progress."

"Really?" Bobby asked. "Thank you."

"However, it's important you realize this battle will be with you until you enter Heaven to be with the LORD one day. Please also know that your addiction should not define you, and it's certainly *not* a disease. It's actually an affliction of sin; which is something the LORD has given you the ability to overcome through the power of the Holy Spirit."

"Hey, I think I'm staying on top of this thing pretty well—"

"Don't get me wrong," Ben interrupted. "Although you've done an excellent job thus far Bobby, you must know that Satan will attempt to use this weakness against you. Satan and his demons generally know each individual's soft spot for sin, so you must continually prepare yourself for assaults from the evil ones."

"Why are you telling me this now?"

"It's because the first significant mission for those of you in the Flaming Sword group is about to begin, and Satan will undoubtedly try to attack each of you in your weakest areas. Mick sent me here today to specifically speak with you, Bobby, because your role in the unfolding Kingdom affairs is very important. Remember, my specialty is being a *stone of help,* and I'm often called on to work with those who struggle with addictions."

"Are you like my guardian angel or something?" Bobby asked.

Ben chuckled. "Of course not! Those in the guardian group generally do not take on human-like bodies when they carry out their God-commanded missions like I do. They actually manage their affairs from the heavenly realm."

"I see," Bobby said. "So are you here to help prepare us or something?"

"I am," Ben said. "Once again, please remember what I said when I first arrived here today. Ebenezer means 'stone of help', and I'm here to help you in your specific ministry within Flaming Sword."

"What else do you do?" Bobby asked.

"Like I said, I work very closely with those who battle with addictions," Ben said. "But you needn't worry Bobby. I've had a lot of experience with this kind of thing."

"Welcome aboard, Ben," Moo said. "It'll be our honor to work with you."

Bobby nodded and Ben smiled.

Cape Elizabeth, ME
October 5th

**". . . those whose teeth are swords and whose jaws
are set with knives to devour the poor from the
earth and the needy from among mankind."
Proverbs 30:14**

Swirling winds arrived as noisy marauders on a cool, foggy night, ushering in an intangible sense of deep malevolence. The winds swayed in concert with the rolling ocean as the dense soggy air permeated everything in its path. Although the nor'easter which was causing the bad weather was well off shore, its effects were pronounced in this normally quiet, southern Maine town.

The massive house being used for this month's meeting of Sunagōgae Satana, or the "Synagogue of Satan," as is referenced in *Revelation 2:9,* was perched atop a rocky bluff overlooking the raging sea. The jagged coastal rocks adorning the east side of the house served as cymbals on the angry storm's drum kit; constantly receiving blasts of grayish, white-capped seawater from the wrathful Atlantic Ocean.

In a deeply reflective moment, Damon continued to gaze through the bay windows of the large house facing the sea.

This is my night, he thought.

As the western side of the dark storm pelted the rocky coast with irregular blasts of rain, the incarnation of Evil seemed to be making its irreverent entrance upon the area.

A boom of thunder suddenly rumbled the walls. As it did so, a baleful sneer slipped onto Damon's face. This was definitely the demon's kind of night—restless and angry.

To Damon, the noise from the winds and sea sounded very much like a symphony from Hell. And he, of course, was the conductor. Savoring the moment, the sharply dressed demon sipped on a glass of single-malt scotch whiskey; his psyche devouring every iota of what he perceived as his tremendous power and influence.

This is going to be a great night – my night of glory, he thought.

The maestro of the storm was now prepared to make his speech to the assembled group—this evil synagogue—so he lustfully gulped his last swig of liquor from an ornate Waterford tumbler. As the booze burned its way down his throat, Damon gently set the glass down with a mild *clink* on a nearby white marble end-table; its contents emptied.

Damon had actually grown quite fond of this primary meeting house, which was located off of Shore Road, not far from Portland. Indeed, he had many good memories of the group's numerous human and animal sacrifices in this place over the years.

Although the demon greatly detested the Christian's Bible, deep within his thoughts, he did enjoy one particular ode to his master—Satan—in *Ezekiel 28:14* . . . *"You were anointed as a guardian cherub, for so I ordained you. You were on the holy mount of God; you walked among the fiery stones."*

Unlike the other alleged satanic cults, the members of Sunagōgae Satana worship a supernatural god named Lucifer, now called Satan. *The Servants,* as they often call themselves, was an ode to their master. Due to the intense dedication they have for their god, The Servants view the other false Satan-worshippers as nothing but clowned-up, gothic "posers." They felt this way because many of the other alleged followers of Satan typically don't believe in a supernatural "god" at all. Instead, they believe in a "god within." In other words, them self.

Ironically, this particular satanic lie—that humans have a god within them self—was one of Damon's favorite demonic deceptions on mankind. *How can any human believe that creation was formed and evolved from nothing?* the demon thought. *Nevertheless, if we can keep humans focused on themselves, then we win! If we can keep people away from Jesus Christ, then our job is accomplished. It really doesn't matter how it's done.*

Of course, Satan and his demons don't need for someone to believe in them at all. The Evil One and his wicked army merely desire for someone to avoid knowing their mortal enemy—Jesus Christ. To that end, The Servants eschewed those imposter groups—the alleged Satanists—who don't believe in any kind of supernatural presence. To the true worshippers of Satan, a' la The Servants, the misguided Satanist groups were nothing but narcissistic, disingenuous atheists in disguise. *At least the normal atheists are honest,* Damon thought. *They don't believe in any kind of supernatural presence – and they don't pretend that they do.*

Because of the regular presence of powerful demons like Damon at their meetings, The Servants have a passionate, fervent faith in Satan. Damon's demonic counterpart and frequent partner-in-crime, Donovan, had already escorted the meeting's attendees down into the Holy Chamber below the house from the inside entrance, which was located in the kitchen-patio area.

I do believe it's finally show time, Damon thought.

The demon donned his dark-gray, London Fog rain coat and placed it over his wool, two-button, navy-pinstripe Armani suit. He walked over to the back door made of checkerboard window panes, opened it, and stepped out into the furious night.

Buttoning up his overcoat, Damon stepped down three wooden steps onto a stone and grass patio. The flat cobblestones were spread wide and long, with soaked grass choked in-between them. The demon's

Italian leather shoes sounded-off as they smacked against the wet stones as Damon made his way towards the belligerent sea.

Gazing towards the end of the cobblestone promontory, the livid ocean stood as a tortured canvas, appearing as if it was the absolute end of the Earth. Distant thunder crackled once again as lightning flashed across the watery horizon. The downpour suddenly whipped a sideways blast against Damon's face. He quickly blinked his eyes and removed the annoying rain.

When he arrived at the end of the pathway, a series of two-foot high bushes adorned either side of him, framing a rocky crevasse below. The zigzag pathway through the covert passage was lit by an occasional solar light. This provided just enough illumination so as to avoid being in total darkness. As Damon descended the pathway, a splash of seawater crashed nearby, drenching a salty spray all over his coat. Some of the seawater sloshed across his mouth, summoning with it a cold, salty kiss. Now fully annoyed with the incessant soaking, he continued his descent. *Perhaps I should've gone through the kitchen-patio entrance like the others did,* he mused to himself.

Damon descended through six consecutive zigzagged paths, finally arriving at ocean level. To his left was the tumultuous sea, which persisted with its vehement objection to the evil conclave in the process of taking place. Turning to his right, back towards land, he proceeded into a tunnel-like cave, which stood both ten feet high and wide.

The walls of the cave were surprisingly smooth, with darkness shrouding its outer reaches. As Damon continued walking inland towards the firelight ahead, the only sounds were that of the angry ocean behind him, and the subtle splash of mini tide pools of seawater under his shoes. As he neared the end of the tunnel, the floor was drier. The only sound in the cave, now, was a constant *drip-drip-drip* . . . .

Upon reaching the end of the partially man-made tunnel, Damon turned right at a torch-lit opening. He then proceeded into a rough-hewn, stone hallway. The salty air was slowly replaced by a musty odor as the demon walked in a slightly ascending fashion through four more narrow stone hallways—left—then right—then left—then left again. All of the hallways were dimly lit by torches, so Damon took his time, anticipating the power of his triumphant entry into the worship chamber.

As he approached the end of the final hallway, the increasing illumination and chanting levels signaled that he was close to his destination. When he stepped into the opening at the rear of the worship chamber, Damon was directly under the main house above. When the red-hooded ushers near the mouth of the chamber saw him approaching, they proceeded to bow their heads in deference to the powerful demon.

Damon surveyed the entire expanse of the room, which was five feet down in a large pit. Covering the majority of the floor area was a group of about one hundred people; all sporting various, brightly colored clothing.

The regular members of The Servants wore red cowls. They stood in the back of the chamber, just below where Damon was perched. The next higher level of leadership further into the chamber wore gold; they stood beyond the red group, closer to the altar of sacrifice. The special few members in emerald stood in the very front, directly under the altar.

The emerald group reported directly to the Grand Master, who was the only one worthy of wearing the purple cowl. This signified that he or she was of the highest order for a non-possessed human. Within The Servants, wearing the purple cowl was a tremendous and highly coveted honor. Damon nodded his approval of the assembly ahead of him, then began descending the stone steps, towards the main floor below.

The worship chamber was originally used during war time in the eighteenth and nineteenth centuries as a secret storage area for supplies. The tunnel connection to the ocean was later blasted out by the grandfather of Nelson Pritchard III; the latter of whom is the current owner of the property. Pritchard's grandfather, the first Nelson Pritchard, was once a Grand Master of Sunagōgae Satana.

The evil which had taken place over the years in this Hell-like dungeon was enough to make a normal person's skin crawl. The chamber itself was huge—approximately fifty yards wide and long. At the far end of the cavern, towards the right, was the elevated altar area. Chiseled in stone directly above a plain stone altar was the cunning logo of The

Servants—a large *S.S.* comprised of intertwined serpents; obviously representing their group, *Sunagōgae Satana*. The symbolism of "S.S." reflects what The Servants feel was the wrongful fall, but future ascent, of their god Satan and his future kingdom.

The fall was the beginning of what they believe was Satan's unrighteous banishment from Heaven, as described in *Ezekiel 28:11-19*. This is when Satan's earthly rule began. The ascent is what they believe will be Satan's ultimate taking of the earthly throne via the future worldwide religion of the Antichrist, which is referenced in *Revelation 2:9*. Essentially, the primary mission of The Servants is to help Satan overcome the Antichrist's predicted demise to Jesus Christ in the book of *Revelation*.

The Grand Master of The Servants stood proudly in front of the altar. Another man in a tunic of sorts stood to his right. The low murmur of chanting fueled the adrenaline of all of the participants as a growing fervor within the chamber continued to rise. Both men eagerly awaited Damon's arrival from the other side of the cave.

When Damon reached the bottom of the stairs at the rear of the chamber, members of the congregation took his overcoat; then began bowing as they cleared the way for their important visitor. This greatly excited Damon. As the congregants formed a pathway through the sea of evil humanity, Damon savored the chamber's uniquely familiar ambiance from this spot—the floor of the cave.

The choking humidity in the room was due to the dozens of fire torches, combined with the moisture from the nearby sea. There was a very slight layer of smoke and incense, which only barely covered the appalling smell of rotting flesh. The tomb-like, claustrophobic atmosphere throughout the room summoned with it an indescribable sense of blood lust and terror.

Upon reaching the other side of the room, Damon ascended to the altar area, where the Grand Master, his guest, and the congregation all bowed to the night's featured speaker. Damon then shook hands with the demon named Donovan, who under his tunic inhabited a dark-haired, olive-skinned man with a thick black beard.

Damon then greeted the Grand Master. As he turned to look down upon the sea of hooded figures, the Grand Master suddenly held up his right hand. Immediately, the chanting in the room abruptly ceased.

Damon's gaze panned the entirety of the room as a blanket of pin-drop silence ensued for a few moments. Due to the intense quiet, the soft flicker of the numerous torches throughout the chamber now collectively sounded like a roaring forest fire. The light from the torches also seemed to be dancing in concert with the dank heat and foul stench in the foreboding atmosphere.

Damon then spoke . . . .

"Good evening, our beloved members of the Synagogue of Satan— our Servants and our friends. Donovan and I welcome you to this very important meeting tonight—one in which we will explain to you *exactly* what we plan to do with those Yahweh-serving miscreants in the new Flaming Sword Communications group. As you well know, Donovan is responsible for our repeated attacks on the Baugh family, and I-myself am responsible for attacks on the others—the families of Hunter and Johnson. Now then; before we proceed tonight, I'm going to ask our Grand Master to recite our Ten Great Truths. As usual, I'll ask you all to repeat the words with him. Grand Master—the floor is yours."

Slowly, the Grand Master removed the hood of his purple cowl, and the face of Caleb Hunter emerged. Mumblings of approval swept throughout the chamber.

"My friends," Caleb began, "let us now bow in prayer to our master, Lucifer. Out of dignity and honor for our god, we will recite his Ten Great Truths . . . ."

After a few moments, the entire room began to chant:

> "**One** . . . Lucifer was Yahweh's second in command, full of wisdom and perfect in beauty.
>
> **Two** . . . Yahweh anointed Lucifer and gave him prominence in creation.
>
> **Three** . . . Yahweh wrongfully punished Lucifer because he was exercising his benevolent leadership and desired to be

appreciated for his kindness. Lucifer righteously deserves our worship.

Four . . . *it was unrighteous for our master to be banished from Yahweh's holy mountain.*

Five . . . *it was wrongful for his angels to be banished along with him.*

Six . . . *Yahweh abdicated his power on Earth. It is now our world and he will not take it from us. Earth will always be our domain.*

Seven . . . *Yahweh is a great liar.*

Eight . . . *we are the ones who care about humans—not Yahweh's son Yeshua. We desire for all people to fulfill their every dream.*

Nine . . . *Yeshua—Jesus Christ—is our mortal enemy. We must prevent others from knowing his lies.*

Ten . . . *we will prevail in the end. We will defend our homeland at any cost. We will not surrender our eternal home. We will destroy our enemies."*

When they were finished, a deafening silence resumed for a few moments. Then Caleb said, "Master Damon, I turn the floor back to you."

"Thank you, Grand Master," Damon said. "Very well done. My friends; tonight's first announcement is one of great importance. As you know, my direct report spirits who are always in attendance with me have abandoned their previous hosts. The reason for this is due to my new orders for an upcoming battle. Therefore, Chas and Blake are actually now with me, inside the man you see before you . . . ." There was a mumbling of excitement in the crowd. "I'm pleased to announce to you that Chas and Blake have now been ordered to enter two of our members in attendance here tonight. As you all know, this is an *extremely* high honor. After the new hosts have submitted their bodies for habitation here at the altar of sacrifice, they will be entered by Chas and Blake for service unto our god. After that, I'm pleased to announce, they will join several of us on a holy mission of execution. *Yes, you heard me right.* The time has finally come for us to overcome our previously failed attempts to execute Wyatt Hunter."

Grand Master Caleb grinned and nodded with satisfaction. He had been waiting for this moment for decades now, and could barely contain his excitement. Knowing this, Damon turned back towards Caleb, wearing an evil sneer. They both nodded at each other, approvingly.

Damon continued, "And to ensure that our mission is successful, we have been granted a rare honor, indeed. Our master has graciously allowed us the presence of one of his personal angels . . . ." Damon paused as an excited murmur rippled throughout the crowd. "The angel *Geyotteream* is in charge of a legion, and I'm pleased to inform you that he is here with us tonight."

The fervor in the room vaulted into a crescendo. Since only members of the emerald group were eligible for habitation, several of them busied themselves with predictions as to who would receive the honor of being entered by Chas and Blake. The gold and red groups had never seen one of Satan's legion-demons, so they all bristled with anticipation, as well. The room was absolutely charged with evil electricity.

Damon's sneer intensified as he continued. "My dear friends . . . please call to order. We have much to discuss tonight." The chamber slowly fell back to quiet once again. "Now then; prior to the commencement of the honored ceremonies tonight, and as a prelude to our mission of execution of Wyatt Hunter, we must pay homage to our god, Satan. Grand Master, please bring out the sacrifice."

Caleb raised his right hand and waved towards two of the red-hooded thugs behind him. The two guards disappeared into a dark opening in the wall to the right, behind the altar. They re-emerged only a few moments later with an older, chubby man with a thick gray beard. The man was bound and tied. He appeared to be waking up from a drug-induced state of euphoria.

As several of the guards hoisted the man onto the huge granite rock—which primarily served as their altar of sacrifice—the legion-demon Geyotteream appeared from an opening behind them, on the congregation's left. The crowd began to sway and chant in ever-increasing murmurings. When Geyotteream reached the edge of the elevated worship area, the congregants dropped to their knees and worshipped him.

71

Emanating from the demon was a sulfuric foul stench more appalling than a hundred sewers heated to boiling. Unlike other demonic possessions, the presence of six thousand demons jammed into one human being was so absolutely repugnant to the laws of nature; the result was nothing short of other-worldly. The malodorous funk began to spread outwards in all directions.

Geyotteream stood six feet, two inches tall and was incredibly strong. A sickening amber slime covered his entire body, and his clothes were in tatters. As much as his assigned handlers within The Servants tried to contain Geyotteream, the legion-demon continually frustrated their efforts by tearing his clothes and continually cutting himself with stones.

During the past few days, the demon had already utilized sharpened stones to carve his front teeth into serrated triangles, giving him the look of a hungry shark. This was very much disconcerting—even to the worshippers of Satan. Of course, the most unpleasant chore for The Servants was trying to tolerate Geyotteream's odor; the repugnant aroma of Hell itself.

The soon-to-be sacrificial bearded man was placed onto the altar and chained down on his back, looking upwards. His arms and legs were fastened in a way which placed him spread-eagle; he was completely unable to move his body—only his head. When the man finally realized what was happening, he began to scream.

The legion-demon grinned, enjoying the fear-induced reverie. His triangular jagged teeth were yellow, brown, and crusty as he licked his dry, chapped lips. Indeed, Geyotteream was pleased to offer a sacrifice to his god, Satan. He was also ravenously hungry, and would very soon feed on the sacrifice before him by drinking the blood of one of God's image-bearing children.

Blood. Yes—that was the only thing acceptable for a powerful demon like Geyotteream to feed on. The demon would not be forced to feed on the blood of an animal that night, as was often the case. No, he would feed on the blood of a human being—a thoroughly disgusting creature made in the image of Jesus Christ. A human sacrifice was the only thing that would quench the demon's unwavering thirst.

A few moments later, bound on the altar of sacrifice, the bearded man's spirit suddenly left his body as a nine-inch dagger was driven into his beating heart. An instant later, Geyotteream proceeded to feed his current human host-body by plunging his jagged teeth into the dead man's neck and drinking the blood of his rapidly departing life.

Heaven
October 6th

"Blessed are those who find wisdom,
those who gain understanding,"
Proverbs 3:13

T he environs surrounding the central library in Heaven were bustling with their usual activity that morning as Abbie and Earl Hunter enjoyed a relaxing stroll. Along with a fellow citizen named Patrick, they gradually made their way towards the massive entrance to the largest collection of books in all of creation.

The three friends earlier had lunch near the center of New Jerusalem, ultimately entering the library campus via the garden gateway. This particular path was adorned on both sides with lush, colorful plants and trees, which visually exploded with the glory of God. Every single color in the light spectrum was represented in the palette of carefully placed botanical works of art, giving the area a complete and utter sense of serenity. Although Patrick was a regular visitor to the central library and its surrounding campus, Abbie had only been there once before, without him. This was Earl's maiden voyage.

With the building's massive rotunda in clear view, they approached the stone stairway entrances, which led upwards onto the library's main level. Earl gazed at the dual staircases on both the right and left, which were made of a creamy, off-white marble. Standing prominently on the ground area in-between the zigzagged staircases was a simple wooden Cross. This was Heaven's constant reminder of Jesus Christ; from which all good things come.

Earl, Abbie, and Patrick ended up choosing the stairway on the left, which ascended to a large, grassy area directly in front of the elegantly-columned entrance to the library. The perimeter pathways around the manicured fields of grass were made of gold, which framed the two lush green fields into parallel rectangles; both highlighting the central pathway into the library's entrance. They made their way through this area, towards the steps leading up to the rotunda, then entered the library.

Once inside, they approached the circular greeting desk, which was centered under the steeply vaulted dome. As a relatively new citizen of Heaven, Earl was constantly mesmerized with the meticulous artistry and craftsmanship in all of Heaven's architecture.

Patrick and Abbie arrived at the front desk's greeting committee, while Earl staggered behind them, gazing upwards at the top of the dome.

Earl found himself totally enchanted with the depicted story of Elijah being taken up to Heaven in *2 Kings 2:1-11*. The breathtaking artistry of both the chariot of fire and horses of fire in the passage was amazing. He continued to survey the story painted across the dome as Patrick and Abbie engaged one of the greeters at the desk.

"Good morning my friend," Patrick said. "How're things today?"

"It's Heaven, Patrick," the lady behind the desk said, shaking her head in jest. "This is pretty much the only home you've ever known. So of course, things are wonderful."

Patrick smiled. "Thanks, Sassy. I can always count on you to give me a hard time," he joked.

"That's my job," she said. "Well, aren't you going to introduce us?"

"Sure thing," Patrick said, looking towards Abbie. "Abbie, this is my friend Sassy; Sassy, this is my earthly mother, Abbie."

"Oh great!" Sassy said. "It's so nice to finally meet you Abbie. I've been bugging Patrick to bring you here for quite some time now."

"Same here Sassy," Abbie said. "I've actually been here once before, with some other friends. Anyway, it's nice to finally meet you as well."

"And who is this gentleman?" Sassy asked, nodding towards Earl.

Earl, now out of his daze, was heading towards the desk. He was amused by the banter he was hearing.

"Oh, I'm sorry," Abbie said. "This is Earl. He's Patrick's earthly father."

Earl approached the desk. "Well hello there, Sassy. I've been very much looking forward to meeting you. Patrick has been telling me since I arrived in Heaven that I needed to come see you folks."

Sassy grinned. "Oh he did, huh?"

"He sure did," Earl said. "Patrick told me that you and he entered Heaven around the same time; forty some-odd years ago."

"That's correct."

"He also said that y'all became great friends due to the fact that you both spent so little time on Earth."

"That's also true," Sassy agreed. "Since Patrick was your first child who Abbie lost during pregnancy two years before your twin sons were born, he was ushered immediately into the presence of God."

"Yeah," Earl said. "Abbie and I were so completely heartbroken when Patrick didn't survive, we never even considered the fact that he might have been brought into the Lord's presence. I suppose that's true for you as well, huh Sassy?"

"It sure is," Sassy agreed. "I didn't survive until childbirth on Earth either—just like Patrick. Several years later, when both of my earthly parents were killed in a tragic car wreck, their joy was overwhelming when I was present at their greeting committee upon their arrival in Heaven. I must say, it was absolutely incredible; our reunion, that is.

What was also amazing is that my folks immediately knew me, without even having to be introduced! It was really an awesome moment."

"Actually, all of Heaven's reunions—and even the first time introductions—are absolutely incredible," Patrick added. "When my mother Abbie arrived a couple of years ago, our first meeting was one of her biggest surprises."

"It was absolutely wonderful!" Abbie said.

"Yeah, it was the same thing for me when I arrived a few months ago," Earl said. "So tell me folks . . . since I'm kind of new at living in Heaven and all . . . does the Bible actually state whether or not children are taken directly to Heaven—particularly if they don't live very long on Earth?"

"Not specifically," Patrick said. "But there's a good hint given by King David in the Old Testament."

"Oh really? Where is that?" Earl asked.

"It's in *2 Samuel 12:23*," Patrick said, then nodded at Sassy.

Sassy quickly paged through a colossal Bible, which was situated on the greeting desk.

"So," she began, "Let's see what the greatest bestseller of all time has to say . . . ahhh here it is . . . *But now that he is dead, why should I go on fasting? Can I bring him back again? I will go to him, but he will not return to me.*"

"You see," Patrick said. "King David had just lost a child, and he knew he would not see his son again on Earth. But in his heart, David knew he would indeed see him in Heaven one day; of course, after he died, himself. Anyway, the one thing we need to remember, here, is that all people are judged through Jesus Christ."

"Ohhhh," Earl said.

Patrick continued, "Jesus wants people on Earth to read their Bibles for many reasons; not the least of which is to find solace when tribulations occur in their lives. Although the Bible doesn't specifically spell out every detail of every thing that happens—as is the case in this example—God gives people the opportunity to know Him and His wonderful gift of *Hope* through the Bible. So in this case, that passage gives people great hope about what occurs in situations like what happened to Sassy and me when we died on Earth so young."

"Why do you think it happened that way?" Earl asked. "I mean; both of you not surviving on Earth."

"I'm afraid that's under DP—Divine Privilege," Patrick said. "Of course, the LORD later gave you guys twin sons—Wyatt and Caleb—my earthly brothers."

"He sure did," Abbie said. "And speaking of that . . . Sassy, we're here today to do some family research. This is actually one of the last assignments from Earl's orientation agenda as he gets acclimated to Heaven. We're just here to help him."

"Well in that case, *welcome to Heaven's central library folks,*" Sassy proclaimed, officially. "This is where all of your earthly works which were not burned up, arrive for their eternal cataloguing. It's also where God has placed all historical information so that we—His beloved children—can continue to pursue our knowledge of Him in our eternal home—"

"Whoa there," Earl interrupted. "What do you mean by our *earthly works which were not burned up?*"

Sassy nodded, understanding that Earl was still learning about the LORD's kingdom. "What I'm talking about is from *1 Corinthians 3:13* which says . . . *their work will be shown for what it is, because the Day will bring it to light. It will be revealed with fire, and the fire will test the quality of each person's work.*"

"Oh I see," Earl said. "So that means the works which a Christian does for the LORD while on Earth will survive into Heaven; while those things not done to His glory are burned up?"

"Exactly!" Sassy said.

Earl nodded. "So the good works that do make it to Heaven are available right here—at the central library?"

"For the most part, that's correct," a new voice said, approaching from the left. "Hi folks. My name is Ed. I'm the angel who runs this place."

"Hey Ed. It's good to see you again," Patrick said.

Patrick then proceeded to introduce Abbie and Earl. As he did so, several cats entered the desk area.

Abbie grinned. "Hey Ed; are those your cats?"

Ed shrugged. "What can I say? We like cats around here."

Sassy giggled.

"You know," Abbie began, "a lot of people on Earth really love their pets. But since the Bible doesn't directly say whether God restores them in Heaven, confusion seems to reign on this subject down there."

Ed sighed, his calm-but-strong mannerisms giving him a quiet confidence. "Just because some folks on Earth think the LORD isn't powerful or loving enough to restore someone's pets; *doesn't* mean it's true. All of these cats you see here are the passed pets of Sassy's earthly parents—who, by the way, are regular visitors to our library."

"How true," Sassy agreed.

"So," Ed continued, "when someone on Earth says that mankind is God's crowning achievement in creation, they'd be well-advised to also include the not-so-small fact that God loves every single part of His creation . . . including His animals. For Pete's sake, everyone here in Heaven knows that!"

Abbie nodded. "So why do you think people on Earth love their animals so much?"

"Oh, that's easy," Ed said. "It's because God's powerful and loving fingerprints are all over His creation. Of course, this includes His animal kingdom. If you ask me, people on Earth tend to love their pets because not only do they see God's divine handi-work, but also, the animal kingdom didn't originally sin. As you know, it was *mankind* who succumbed to sin in the Garden of Eden. The animal kingdom was then *subjected* to Adam and Eve's original sin against its will. By the way, that's in *Romans 8:20.*"

"So tell me this," Abbie said. "Why are we able to understand and enjoy the animals in Heaven so much better than we could down on Earth?"

"Oh, that's another easy one," Ed said. "Let me see now . . . how does our friend Mick say it? Oh yeah, *RYB, dude!* Read your Bible."

Abbie chuckled. "Yeah that seems to be Mick's favorite saying."

"Anyway," Ed continued, wearing a grin. "You don't have to go very far in the Bible to understand that Adam's original relationship with animals was very significant. In *Genesis 2:18-19,* God brought to Adam all of the animals, because He wanted Adam to have suitable helpers. Adam then named every one of them. Of course, the LORD then made Eve from Adam, because the animals weren't quite enough for him."

"That's very interesting," Earl said.

Ed nodded. "Therefore, due to the LORDS' great love and power, God restores mankind's relationship with animals in Heaven in a similar fashion to what was originally intended on Earth—before original sin. Hence, your relationship with God's animals is significantly better than it was while you were still on Earth."

"I see," Earl said.

"You know, that's the really sad thing," Ed continued. "People on Earth should give God a little more credit for being a loving and giving Father. Just because the Bible is silent on the pets-in-Heaven issue; *doesn't* mean God isn't loving enough—*or able enough*—to restore your little friends in His eternal paradise."

"That's pretty neat," Earl said.

"Anyway," the angel continued. "I suppose you all are here to do some research into your family lineage, right?"

"We sure are," Patrick said. "I'd actually like to take my folks down to the wing of family records. We have a lot of books to pore over as we trace our lineage back to ancient biblical times."

"Be my guest," Ed said. "You know where you're going, right?"

"I sure do," Patrick said. "And if you don't mind, I'd like Sassy to join us."

"Sure thing," Ed said. "Since all work in Heaven is done to the glory of God, I'll be happy to cover the greeting desk for Sassy."

Patrick, Earl, Abbie, and Sassy all proceeded down one of the long hallways towards their research area. The massive central library continued to stay busy with its usual activities, while Ed-the-angel, along with the plethora of meowing cats, tended to the greeting desk area, assisting all of Heaven's saints.

It was indeed, another spectacular day in Heaven.

Boston, MA
October 6th

**"No man chooses evil because it is evil;
he only mistakes it for happiness,
the good he seeks."
Mary Wollstonecraft**

Mid-morning arrived in beantown as a piercing beam of sunlight knifed through a small slit between the curtains in the beautiful suite at the Marriott hotel on Long Wharf. As the golden ray invaded the slumbering face of Ian Thompson, the weary man's eyes opened on another day in a life which he truly despised.

Staring straight upwards, Ian was unable to focus his eyesight on anything specific. Unfortunately, however, he remembered enough about his raucous activities of the previous night to know he had partied until dawn. Due to his ever-growing feelings of incredible self-loathing,

Ian had actually grown to detest all hotel rooms—the usual locale for his unbelievably sinful, self-centered lifestyle.

Ian attempted to focus his vision on the ceiling's details above him. However, everything remained blurred. He then blinked several times in an attempt to push back the haze of another drug and alcohol induced hangover. Unfortunately for him, the first of his senses which functioned normally was his sense of smell. Since the odor in the room was not pleasant by any standards—in fact, it was absolutely repulsive—his stomach turned queasy.

Ian sighed in frustration as the vile smells of sour booze, vomit, and stale smoke comprised his morning's greeting committee; their presence summoning in him a wave of pure and utter disgust. To Ian, these things were like a team of unwelcome bill collectors, incessantly banging on his front door in an attempt to call-in their overdue debt. He sighed once again as he sat up; his eyesight finally able to focus.

In his bed were three female groupies, all ardent members from the local chapter of the fan club for Ian's band, *Vampire Dawning*. Although his band had been recording and playing together for over two and a half decades, they had neither attained mainstream status, nor critical acclaim. Undaunted by this, the band's public image of predatory violence and blood lust had nonetheless grown to a near cult-like status among those obsessed with the fantasy of vampires and their evil ways.

Vampire Dawning's music was a foreboding combination of heavy metal chops, infused with lyrics which bordered on an insane obsession with the mythical vampire lore. Touring mostly in Ian's native U.K. early in their career, the band later expanded by playing venues across the rest of Europe. Ultimately, they found themselves with a growing fan base in the United States, so they began touring America about ten years ago. Unfortunately for Ian, who was the lead singer and bassist for the band, wherever he went, his self-idolatry followed right along with him.

Vampire Dawning currently found itself with a vibrant following of hard rockers, gothic outcasts, and bloodsucking wannabes on several continents. Although Ian had never felt any remorse over the money he had made from his fan base, the truth was, he had grown to detest the band's ardent fans—every twisted one of them.

Ian stealthily slid his tall, slender body from in-between the gaggle of unclothed, vampire-loving groupies, quietly making his way towards the restroom. He paused for a moment in front of the large mirror in the bathroom area, staring at his own, naked body for a few moments. As he did so, he felt like he was viewing a complete stranger.

Who is this fool staring back at me? he thought, shaking his head in disgust.

Gazing back at Ian from the mirror was a man in his late forties, who looked more like a man in his sixties. His long, stringy black hair was greasy; mostly from the incessant sweating on stage the night before. The bags under his eyes looked like small overlapping layers of fat; only serving to accentuate his pallid British skin tone. Ian shook his head sadly, feeling that he was looking directly at the reflection of a condemned man.

Due to his haggard appearance, Ian felt very much like death warmed over. Deep within his feelings, he no longer wanted to live another day; at least not another day in his ridiculous band and the evil nonsense they sang about. *I simply cannot do this anymore,* he thought remorsefully. *Today has to be different, but I have no idea what to do.*

Vampire Dawning had played to a full house in a large, local club the night before. Although their current agent, a man named Chris Derwyn, wasn't in attendance for their gig, Ian knew he would be pleased with the substantial revenue they had generated.

Of course, Ian Thompson didn't care very much about money anymore. He had actually blown most of his past income on drugs, booze, and a debauchery-filled lifestyle. Prior to that morning, the only thing he really cared about was his next cocaine high; or, of course, another bottle of Jack Daniels.

Feeling an almost overwhelming need for a cup of coffee and some fresh air, Ian decided to do something different than his usual routine of sleeping until mid-afternoon. To that end, he proceeded to take a refreshing shower before getting dressed. He then prepared to leave his tomb-like hotel room.

As Ian moved towards the door, he surveyed the sad scene: his room was completely filled with the hung-over bodies of vampire groupies and a couple of his band mates. Since he had spotted a Starbucks inside the hotel when his entourage had checked in the previous day, he thought about getting a grande vanilla latte. The thought of some fresh coffee caused him to quickly make his exit.

Ian headed downstairs.

Feeling an unexplainable sense of urgency, Ian was grateful there was only one other person in line ahead of him at Starbucks, just finishing up. He quickly placed his order. When the young barista named Tony handed him his jumbo cup of java, Ian mumbled his gratitude, "Thanks, mate." He then proceeded outside the north entrance of the hotel, hanging a right, towards a comfortable park bench.

The day was overcast and cool, with an occasional gusty breeze. The fresh air pleased Ian as he sat down and prepared for a time of deep, personal reflection. *I don't think I can live another day like this,* he thought. *Something has to change, but I have no idea where to start.* Sipping his extra hot latte, he began an introspective journey, deep into his psyche. . . .

Ian's thoughts gravitated towards his numerous failed relationships, estranged children, immaturity with money, and his praising of violence against the weak. All of these unpleasantries and more sprinted through his mind. And then there was the lifeblood on which he fed, fueled by his daily lust; a longing, desperate desire—the hunger to feed his addictions. As much as he was sickened by Vampire Dawning's fans, who actually think of vampires as something to admire, he had to admit that he longed for drugs and alcohol much like the mythical vampires crave blood.

Ian shook his head in disgust as he pondered his empty life. *Where did the past twenty five years go . . . ?* he thought. For a few minutes, he sat sipping his coffee, now trying to empty his mind of these haunting specters of failure. As he casually gazed towards his left, Ian noticed two men walking towards him.

His first thought was that he hoped they weren't fans of his outrageously foolish band. He wasn't in the mood that morning to put on his public persona by acting like a tough, vampire-like rocker. Ian was actually unsure if he could ever play music with his band ever again. A quarter-century of lying about who he really was had emotionally worn him down. That, plus he was really tired of putting on makeup and fangs before going on stage—things that completed his lie to the world.

Of the twosome approaching his bench, Ian noticed that the man on the left was obviously of Hispanic origin. He was short, a little chubby, and had a few streaks of gray in his otherwise jet black hair. His companion on the right had a somewhat austere look and was thin, with unkempt, hair. The thin man on the right exhaled a puff of smoke, then flicked his cigarette away as they approached.

They sure don't look like my typical fans, Ian thought. He then mentally prepared himself as the Hispanic man spoke.

"Good morning, Ian. My name is Juan . . . and this is JJ. We were wondering if we could borrow a few minutes of your time this morning."

"Look mate," Ian said. "I had a rough night last night, and I'm not really in the mood to sign any autographs this morning. So if you don't mind, I'd appreciate it if you were on your way—"

"Ian my friend," JJ interrupted. "I can assure you that we're not in the least bit interested in an autograph. No offense."

"Oh???" Ian asked, surprised.

"I'm afraid not," JJ said. "We're actually here to assist you with your life's transition; that is, if you'll allow us to help."

"How on Earth do you know anything about me???" the singer blurted.

"Whoa there, partner," JJ said, holding up his hands in a defensive gesture. "All we're here to do is to present you with the real truth about how things work in this world. I promise you; we only wish to help."

Ian started to yell at JJ and Juan, but something held him back; he thought better of it.

"So who are you guys, anyway?" he asked, in a calmer voice. "Are you some kind of paparazzi or something?"

"Of course not," JJ said. "Those fools only wish to glamorize your celebrity. Our desire is to show you the way to Jesus Christ; the One who is the *real* Truth in the universe. To be completely honest, we couldn't give a rip about your celebrity—or your band for that matter."

Ian looked thoughtful for a moment as the boldness of JJ's comments began to sink in.

"Are you blokes some kind of religious nuts or something? If so, then please don't waste your time with me. I gave up on religion a long time ago."

JJ and Juan looked at each other and nodded. JJ then spoke, "Yeah Ian; so did we. *Religion* is something we both detest."

The rock star gazed suspiciously at JJ and Juan for a few moments. It occurred to him that these two odd strangers showing up today could in no way be a coincidence. However, he remained quiet for a few moments, gathering his thoughts.

Ian then felt strangely driven to turn the conversation around, so he asked, "Tell me something, guys. Why has God waited all this time to reach out to me? I mean; if you knew only *one-tenth* of the terrible things I've done with my life, you'd absolutely retch. These days, I can't go a single day without my fixes. Not only that, but I stand on stage, singing songs about sucking the blood of the innocent—*blah blah blah*. The truth is; I'm nothing but a humongous pile of rubbish."

"Of course you're not," JJ said. "To God, *all of us* are unfit for being in His presence—that is, until we surrender to Jesus Christ as our Savior. In the grand scheme of things, that's the only thing that really matters."

Ian was quiet for another moment, then said, "Look guys . . . I have no idea how you found me here today, but I do appreciate your effort. The truth is; before today, I would've cussed both of you from one end of this park to another for mentioning anything about God or Jesus. But today, I'm feeling like . . . actually . . . I'm feeling like putting this ludicrous life I live behind me. The problem is, I was just sitting here, not understanding how to go about doing so."

Juan and JJ both nodded.

"We understand," Juan said.

"Listen," Ian continued, "for most of my selfish life, I've believed in a good and loving God. The beautiful things in this world have demonstrated His presence to me many times over. But as I look back on it, I suppose I thought it was easier to do whatever I wanted to do to please myself. And at this point in my wretched life, I'm fairly certain that the God of the universe wants nothing to do with a complete reprobate like me."

"That's simply not true," Juan said. "But if you don't mind, I'd like to ask you a question."

Ian shrugged. "I suppose that'd be alright."

"If you died today, what do you think would happen to you?"

"Hmmm," Ian mumbled. "I suppose that I'd cease to exist . . . or something. Who knows? To tell you the truth, I haven't really given it much thought."

"Really?" Juan asked. "Why is that?"

"Oh, I don't know. Perhaps it's because I try to live for each day and enjoy it for what it is. You know what I mean—that whole carpe diem—*seize the day,* thing."

Juan nodded. "There's nothing wrong with that. Each of us should indeed, *seize the day.* However, instead of claiming it for ourselves, we should seize it for the LORD. Our time on Earth is pretty short, you know."

Ian shrugged and stared towards the nearby waterfront. "Perhaps you're right, mate. This whole thing I'm doing—this ridiculous life I'm living—sure isn't working."

"To demonstrate the truth of what Juan just said," JJ added, "I have two passages to share with you from the book of *Matthew 6.* This was when Jesus was giving his Sermon on the Mount. May I read them to you?"

JJ was already retrieving his Bible from an inner jacket pocket.

"Sure," Ian said. "Knock yourself out."

JJ took a few moments to flip to the first passage. "The LORD's Prayer in *Matthew 6:11* says . . . *Give us today our daily bread . . .* Jesus goes on to say a little bit later in *Matthew 6:34 . . . Therefore do not worry about tomorrow, for tomorrow will worry about itself. Each day has enough trouble of its own.*"

Ian nodded. "I have to admit, fellas, I'm not very familiar with the Bible. So if you don't mind, can you please dummy that down for me?"

"Certainly," Juan said. "Jesus, in His own words, tells us in both passages a similar sentiment—to indeed seize the day. However, God wants us to seize it—*and* submit to Him daily. In truth, if you want to live a joyful life, every person must depend on the LORD for everything. And I mean *every thing.* You see, no one understands human nature more than our Creator; the LORD Himself. God knows that our natural, sinful nature always leans towards self-dependence. However, He greatly wants us to reject that worldly way of thinking."

"But I was always taught to depend on myself and to *look out for number one,* all of my life," Ian said. "What's wrong with that?"

"You absolutely should look out for *number one,*" JJ added. "However, for all of our lives, we've been lied-to about who *number one* really is."

"What's that supposed to mean?"

"*Number One* is Jesus Christ—not ourselves. Our being *number one* is a gigantic lie, perpetrated by the devil and his fallen angels."

"Hmmm," Ian mumbled. "The devil, huh?"

"Indeed—Satan himself," JJ said.

"You know," Ian began, "I used to think that Satan was like that typical cartoon character. You know the one—where the cute little bugger is dressed in a little red outfit—"

"Let me ask you a question," Juan interrupted. "God gave us the entire world and everything in it. What did Satan ever give us?"

"Hang on there, mate," Ian said. "I was trying to tell you that I used to think the devil was only metaphorical; that laughable little red devil with a pitchfork. But last week, after our gig in Albany NY, I overheard our agent—a man named Chris Derwyn—talking to one of our roadies about Satan."

"Really???" JJ asked, his investigative instincts clicking on. "Do tell."

Ian nodded. "Yeah, well it was actually very odd; their conversation, that is."

"How so?"

"Chris and one of our regular roadies . . . I think the lad's name is Randy. Anyway, they were both pretty drunk backstage after the show.

Well, they were so smashed; they must've not realized I was relaxing on a big comfy couch nearby, within earshot. So as I sat there, I heard Chris talking about having to go to some kind of odd-sounding, secret meeting up in Maine last night."

"What's so strange about that?" JJ asked.

"Well it was—" Ian began, but quickly halted his thought. "Hey, do you know what? I don't mean to be abrupt or anything, but do you mind if we take a little walk through this lovely park? My legs are getting stiff, and the exercise might help me wake up."

"Sure thing," JJ said, and Juan nodded.

Ian, Juan, and JJ proceeded to walk through Christopher Columbus Waterfront Park, which was adjacent to the hotel. As they walked, the three of them continued their chat.

"Like I was saying," Ian began, "our agent, Chris Derwyn, has always been a secretive sort of fellow. So when I heard him tell the roadie about this meeting he was going to attend, I thought it was very strange."

"Go on," JJ said.

"It was odd because Chris never misses one of our shows."

"I see."

"Well, it sounded to me like . . . well . . . maybe I should just shut up. The both of you are going to think I'm nuts or something."

"No-no-no!" JJ said. "Please continue. This is very important."

JJ looked over at Juan and nodded.

They previous day, Juan and JJ were given a mission by Mick via Candace and Danny. By no small coincidence, both men were not far away from each other in the New England area. After receiving the call from Candace, Juan and JJ quickly met up at a local truck stop to discuss their mission to go see Ian Thompson the next day.

As they visited, JJ advised Juan that he was also in the area to pick up on the investigation regarding the possible whereabouts of the Satanists in the area. JJ knew that if he discovered where the Satanist group met, he would likely locate Caleb Hunter—the enemy of their ministry.

"Anyway," Ian continued, "our agent Chris . . . because he was drunk and all . . . blabbed on about how Satan is the *real* god of this world. I mean, he went on-and-on about how much of a scoundrel that Jesus Christ is, and how much Satan is the god who offers all the fun. Truthfully, it sounded to me like he was trying to recruit this Randy fellow to join his devil-church or something."

"That's very interesting," JJ said. "Did he say where they were meeting up in Maine?"

"Hmmm," Ian mumbled. "No, he didn't actually say where the meeting was. But he did say it was about two hours north of our gig here in Boston; somewhere up in southern Maine. So I suppose your guess is as good as mine. Anyway, why are you asking me these questions?"

JJ shrugged. "Oh, let's just say that the ministry we work for has a significant interest in finding those particular Satan worshippers."

"Oh—what ministry is that?"

"Flaming Sword Communications. Our goal is to spread the Word of God among the various media sources and outlets, and to fight against Satan's lies."

"I see," Ian said. "Well, let me tell you this . . . all of these ridiculous vampire-wannabe fans of ours are a bunch of twisted idiots. They actually think that it's *cool* and *tough* to vamp-out and act like predators. The truth is, they live their lives in a total fantasy world."

Juan nodded. "Not only that, Ian, but let's not forget the fact that the whole vampire mythology evolved from the biblical truth about demons. So in essence, when someone portrays themselves as a vampire, they're actually emulating a demon."

Ian stared off into the distance as they continued to walk through the park. He then said, "I suppose you're right, mate. For all of these years, I felt like this vampire nonsense was merely a clever ruse to make money. Unfortunately, I never considered the fact that it might be detrimental to someone's soul."

JJ nodded. "Not to change the subject guys, but there's been something bothering me about the throngs of vampire books coming out these days."

"Oh yeah, what's that?" Ian asked.

"If you really think about it, many of them have taken the idea of evil and glamorized it."

"How so?" Ian asked.

"Think about it," JJ said. "Vampire books used to be about good versus evil—and there was generally no question that the vampires were evil. But today, these vampire characters are actually being subtly glamorized. It appears to me that the subject of evil has been pushed into a gray area of *good evil* and *bad evil.*"

Ian nodded. "That's actually very interesting. Please go on."

"Essentially," JJ continued, "the subject of evil in these books has been turned into a world of gray; in other words, there are *good vampires* and *bad vampires.* So, let me tell you this straight out—there is only one kind of evil, and that's *evil-evil.*"

"Hold on mate," Ian said. "I'm not sure I'm following you."

"What I mean is this," JJ said. "There is absolutely *zero* good in vampires. Or, what I'm really trying to say is this: there's absolutely nothing good whatsoever in glorifying demons—vampires—or whatever. Period. End of story."

"Ahhh, I see," Ian said. "You know, I was both angry and amused when I saw that one of those ultra-popular series of vampire books was delving into romance with vampires to the point of having vampire babies. Admittedly, I was mostly torqued about it, because my band promotes nothing but tough, mean vampires. So when all of this vampire-baby rubbish hit the scene, it actually diminished what we're selling to our fans."

"I suppose that makes sense," Juan added.

"Anyway," Ian said. "Tell me this—how did you guys know I'd be open to chatting with you about God today? Like I said; on any other day, I probably would not have been so accommodating with you fellas."

Juan smiled and said, "Oh, let's just say the Lord does have His mysterious ways."

"What do you mean?" Ian asked.

"Maybe an angel from God told us that you'd be having an epiphany this morning about your life."

Ian stopped walking for a moment. *"Are you serious???"* he asked.

JJ shrugged. "Let me ask you this—is it really important how we knew to come see you? Or, is it simply a blessing that we showed up here today?"

Ian shrugged. "The latter, I suppose. But tell me this—if God is so powerful and good, how come he allows us to do the things we want to do—which sometimes includes doing the wrong things? I mean, couldn't He simply snap his fingers and we'd all drop to our knees and obey Him?"

"That's a fair question," Juan said. "But if the LORD were to remove our ability to freely choose Him, then our relationship with God wouldn't really be *love,* would it? In other words, if He forced us to love Him, how could anyone think that's real love?"

"I suppose I'm with you," Ian agreed. "But what about all of the sins we all do? Is this Satan character to blame for those?"

"Absolutely not," Juan said. "At least not completely. Satan and his demons merely inflame the sinful urges in us—they don't create them. In other words, people are responsible for their own rebellion against God by sinning. *James 4:7* says . . . *Submit yourselves, then, to God. Resist the devil, and he will flee from you* . . . As far as I'm concerned, that passage says we must all fight against the devil by resisting our self-centered urges. Tell me Ian; is any of this making sense to you?"

"Hmmm . . . ." Ian mumbled. "Like I said earlier, if it was any other day before today, I would've yelled obscenities at you fellas that would have melted your ears. But today—and I really can't explain why—but I felt my heart open to God for the first time ever. Well, perhaps I'm just open to hearing more about Him."

"It sounds to me like you're ready to put your old life-style behind you for good," JJ added. "So allow me to be blunt: are you ready to walk away from those terrible songs you sing? Are you ready to start a completely new life in Christ?"

Ian sighed. "Perhaps so; but I do have a lot of questions for the both of you. But before we dig into some of those, I want to first answer Juan's question from earlier."

"Which was—?" Juan asked.

"You asked me what Satan ever gave to me, right after you said that God gave us the world and everything in it."

"I sure did," Juan said. "I'm glad you remembered."

"Well my friend, here's the answer: This Satan apparently showed me a pack of lies that living for myself was the only path to true happiness. I suppose you could say, when I opened my eyes this morning, the realization finally hit me that my self-obsessed lifestyle was never going to give me the joy I've always longed-for in my heart. At that point, my heart finally opened to hearing more about God. But to be honest; I've never really had a conversation like this before. Ever."

They all stopped on the path, right next to a beautiful tree.

"Listen Ian," Juan said. "*Luke 12:34* says . . . *For where your treasure is, there your heart will be also.* So the obvious question is this—are you ready to finally give Jesus Christ a chance—I mean, a *real* chance? I know you'll be pleasantly surprised at how much you'll learn about the LORD. That is; *if* you'll give God an open heart and open mind to work with. You've already said that you found no treasure in the wicked world of sex, drugs, alcohol, and singing about vanquishing the weak. So tell me Ian, will you give Jesus Christ a fair shot at winning your heart? What do you say?"

Ian looked down for a moment and then said, "What do I say? *I say I still have a lot of questions.* Before I met you guys today, I knew a major change in my life was needed. I simply cannot spend another minute in this repugnant lifestyle of mine. Although my band mates will probably be upset with me for leaving them, they'll eventually get over it. To be honest, I think they've been half-way expecting my exodus from the band. Everything we do has been bothering me for quite some time now, and I know they must have sensed it."

"Good deal," JJ said. "Listen; I need to make a quick phone call back to our ministry headquarters. In the meantime, Juan will go ahead and tell you about two things to consider as we answer your questions about Christ."

"Oh yeah? What are these two things all about?" Ian asked.

"The first thing is a nearby Christian rehab facility that we recommend you check into very soon—like today."

Ian nodded, hesitantly. "Perhaps you're right."

"The second thing is this," JJ said. "God gave you some wonderful musical abilities, and you shouldn't abandon them just because you're considering a relationship with Jesus. In fact, I have some friends who work for Warrior Instruments down in Georgia. They can show you some of their beautiful handiwork—anointed, hand-crafted instruments which bring glory to God. And by the way, their basses are absolutely outstanding!"

"That's interesting, mate. I never thought about continuing with my music."

"I really think you should," JJ said. "Juan and I actually saw some of your show last night."

"Really?" Ian asked. "That's rather odd."

"Not really," JJ said. "Let's just call it *research*."

"I see," Ian said. "Anyway, first things first—you go make your call. While you're doing that, Juan can continue answering some of my questions about God."

"You got it," JJ said. "Please excuse me . . . ."

JJ walked several yards away from Juan and Ian. He then pulled out his cell phone and called Danny at the group's book store in Pike Place Market.

After a few rings, Danny answered. "Hello?"

"Hey there dude. This is JJ."

"What's up, JJ? It was good talking with you yesterday—after your day off. Candace and I were a little worried about you."

"Gotcha. Listen, is Candace in the store yet? I know it's early out there, but I need to speak with both of you."

"She sure is. Do you want me to put her on the speaker?"

"Absolutely."

"Give me a minute," Danny said. After placing JJ on hold for a few moments, Danny opened the line again with a mild crackle, "Okay— you're now on the speaker . . . Candace is here with me . . . so what's up? How did your meeting with Ian Thompson go?"

"It's still going on. Actually, it's going much better than Juan or I expected."

"Good deal," Candace said.

"Listen guys, I need you start working on something for me—like right away."

"Oh really? Is Jacques okay?" Candace asked. "We're more than happy to help, but you often have him do your research."

"He's fine. It's just that Jacques is at the doctor right now."

"No problem," Danny said. "So what do you need us to do?"

"We may have caught a real break here. It seems that the agent for Ian's band may be connected with the Satanist group we've been searching for here in New England; the one connected with Caleb."

"Wow—really?" Candace asked. "Please go on."

JJ lowered his voice, emphatically speaking into his phone. "Please listen to me. I can give you the details about this later on; after Juan and I are through with helping Ian today. What I need for you to do is this: Please start checking out the area which is about two hours north of Boston—up in Maine. From what Ian said, my best guess is that the Satanists are located somewhere around Portland. I'll be busy with Ian for a little while longer, so I can't do any research right now."

"We got your back, JJ," Candace said. "Go ahead and see if you can get Mr. Thompson into rehab. If he tries to go back to those people in his band, they probably talk him out of leaving."

"You got it," JJ said. "Juan and I will call you back this afternoon; after we're through. But rest assured, we'll be heading up I-95 towards Maine as soon as we're finished."

"No problem," Danny said. "But you need to first stop in Salem to pick up Moo and Bobby on your way up there."

"Really?" JJ asked. "That's awesome—we're gonna need some extra feet on the street, doing some reconnaissance. When did they fly up here?"

"Late last night," Candace said. "One of Mick's crew—an angel named Ben—called on those boys down in Georgia yesterday. Shortly after that, the orders came down for Ben to fly with Moo and Bobby from Atlanta to Boston last night."

"Yeah. I'm familiar with Ben. So what are they doing?"

"The three of them got up early and scouted out that empty warehouse property that Caleb Hunter bought in Salem earlier this year. I actually just spoke with them a little while ago. Unfortunately, they've come up with nothing solid so far."

"So they're in Salem right now?"

"Moo and Bobby are. I think Ben should actually be close to you guys down in Boston by now."

"Why is that? What exactly does Ben do?" JJ asked.

"His specialty is helping those with addictions. Bobby told me that Ben was heading down to join you guys in your chat with Ian Thompson. He should probably be—"

"I think he just arrived," JJ interrupted, noticing a well-built, African American man already chatting with Juan and Ian. "You know," he continued, "these angels sure-do come in handy."

"Indeed they do," Danny said. "It must be that *messengers-of-God* thing. I'm just glad they're on our side."

"Amen to that, bro," JJ said.

"You be careful, honey!" Candace said.

"You know I will. I'll talk with you guys later."

JJ hung up, then proceeded to light up a cigarette. He needed a moment to gather his thoughts before re-joining the others. JJ had been waiting for a break like this tip from Ian for quite some time now. He took a long drag of his cigarette as his mind focused on finding the shifty Caleb Hunter—their enemy number one.

A short time later, the angels and saints in Heaven rejoiced as Ian Thompson—with the assistance of Juan, JJ, and a "cool bloke" named Ben—surrendered to Jesus Christ as his Savior. Of course, Ian had no idea that the "cool bloke" joining them that day was actually one of God's holy angels.

But of course, another day down the road, Ian Thompson just might discover the true significance of his unexpected meeting that day.

PART 2

WYATT'S WATERLOO

Boston, MA
October 6th

**"For the message of the cross is foolishness to those who are
perishing, but to us who are being saved it is the power of God."
1 Corinthians 1:18**

The largely austere confines of the ancient WKJE public access
television studio bristled with activity, as the latest taping for
their weekly artist series entered its final preparations. The host for the
program, Jeanette Collins, gently closed her eyes as a makeup artist
named Coco completed the signature ensemble for his favorite client.

Jeanette had once been the lead news anchor on several local
northeast newscasts, including gigs in Albany, Hartford, and ultimately,
New York City. However, as she approached her late forties, time had
overtaken her ability to outrun an aging appearance; apparently along
with her ability to connect with a younger audience—at least that's what
her former studio executives had implied.

Although Jeanette was now in her early fifties, she was still a beautiful woman by most standards—blonde and petite, with an effervescent smile and quick wit. Sadly though, most news stations perceived her as simply being washed-up. Almost on a daily basis, Jeanette cursed "the universe" for her situation, and she often racked her brain on how to retain a youthful appearance. Deep down, below the many layers of her gargantuan ego and pride, she knew the sun had already set on the glamorous part of her career. This realization always summoned with it extreme frustration and an almost furious anger.

Several years before, Jeanette had been on top of the world when she was a co-anchor in the Big Apple. Back then, she felt like she had it all—the million-dollar apartment, the substantial clothes allowance, and the fanfare of exposure to millions of people watching her every day on television. All of these things contributed to a lifestyle in the spotlight with tremendous fame and power, and she had absolutely cherished every single moment of it.

But about a year ago, there had been an unexpected fall from grace when Jeanette lost her highly coveted position. Unfortunately, she now found herself with the only gig she could find when her lucrative contract expired—a bottom-rung television studio like WKJE. To Jeanette's way of thinking, this studio was clearly below her standards. She felt like "The Fates" had been incredibly unfair to her.

Nowadays, due in large part to her precipitous fall from fame, her lifestyle had become a bit of a runaway train. Contributing to this were her nonstop sexual escapades, binge drinking, occasional drug use, and even the occasional trip to Atlantic City to gamble away that week's paycheck. All of these things contributed to Jeanette living perhaps the most unfulfilling lifestyle anyone can possibly engage in—one of complete worldliness and the resulting abject desolation.

Tonight would be her revenge, however, and she felt like nothing could now stop it. In fact, her plan was just about to enter the starting gate. Although she didn't originally plan it that way, Jeanette had actually lured some idiot Christian fiction writer named Wyatt Hunter to the show from one of the northern suburbs. Her plan was now to expose him for the fool he really was.

Yes indeed, she felt utter exhilaration at the prospect of knocking an obvious novice like Wyatt Hunter from his high horse. She really detested those Christians; what, with all of their ridiculous rules and all. No, she didn't have any time for their ancient nonsense. In her mind, Christianity was only appealing to unenlightened simpletons.

Tonight's the time for some payback to the universe, she thought.

Going back several weeks, and after many delays on her part, Jeanette had finally relented and scheduled the surprisingly persistent Christian writer. Of course, she originally found this interview to be an absolutely sickening prospect. But later, a brilliant epiphany entered her mind: to show her viewers what an ignoramus Mr. Hunter was, and to demonstrate just how outdated Christianity had become. To that end, Jeanette had pulled off a real coup d'état by securing a subsequent appointment for the same show with a well-educated professor from Great Britain to join Wyatt Hunter; a scholar who would most certainly make mincemeat of a miniscule, self-published Christian writer.

During her brief research on both Wyatt and his scholarly adversary, Alistair McClellan, Jeanette discovered what she felt was the ideal set-up for her goal: to point out just how ignorant those science-hating Christians were. She had been incredibly fortunate that not only was McClellan in town for a book signing of his own at some kind of atheist or free-thinker convention, but that he was also available and eager to participate in the upcoming show. In briefly reviewing the respective backgrounds of each individual, Jeanette's journalistic instincts were absolutely screaming that the intellectual McClellan would clobber his foolish Christian counterpart with relative ease. This would undoubtedly make for a great show—one which just might get her some national attention . . . if she was lucky.

Jeanette bristled with anticipation as she pictured Wyatt Hunter's face in a short while. That is, his disappointment when he realizes that his stupid book isn't the focus of their interview that night. She found the prospect of this to be absolutely delicious.

No, Jeanette had something more interesting to present to her largely secular audience, and tonight would be part of her payback. She planned to demonstrate to those simple-minded Christians, who love their wonderful "God" so much, just how wrong they were. Indeed; she would resurrect her career by evolving into a tough-nosed, hard-hitting reporter who certainly won't take any bunk from a fool who believes in an after-life, let alone an "all powerful" God. That kind of foolishness was only for the unenlightened; those whose simple minds needed a crutch like Christianity to get them through their simple lives. Jeanette certainly didn't need any of that kind of nonsense—she was obviously well above their intelligence.

Jeanette politely waved off Coco and stood up in preparation for her entry into the studio area. The makeup would just have to do for now. Unfortunately, her dank dressing room was at the end of a dark, cinder-block hallway, right next to a unisex restroom. *What did I ever do to deserve this?* she thought, grabbing her notes and heading towards the stage's interview desk to review her plan of attack. It was almost show time . . . .

****

Mick, Wyatt, and Cam entered the WKJE studio reception area, which was located in the Back Bay area of Boston, not far from Fenway Park. The stone-clad building was at the end of an older, normal-looking street, which appeared as if it could easily pass for a neighborhood in the early nineteen-hundreds.

Old brownstone buildings dominated the surrounding area, lending itself to the charm of a bygone era. Interestingly, the old studio seemed to have had prosperity flower all around it; avoiding WKJE in an oddly deliberate manner. The narrow street on which the studio was located dead-ended into a concrete border, which fronted a fenced area adjacent to I-90.

Several years ago, the studio's previous owner added extra insulation to the building to minimize the incessant noise from the busy interstate nearby. Unfortunately, it had never been fully effective.

Once inside the front door, Wyatt led Mick and Cam straight towards the reception area, where a sliding window greeted them.

An attractive college-age young lady with striking red hair slid the window open.

"How may I help you gentlemen this afternoon?"

Due to the fact that the receptionist was a real looker, Cam quickly took the lead. "Hello there. My name's Cam Hunter, and this is my father, Wyatt Hunter," he said, nodding towards his dad. "We're here for the taping with Ms. Collins tonight."

Quickly sizing up the threesome, she replied in a thick Bostonian accent, "And this other gentlemen is—?"

"Howdy ma'am," Mick said. "I've been retained to represent Mr. Hunter in his . . . *spiritual affairs* . . . ."

"I see. Please have a seat. The show's producer will be right with you."

"So what's your name, young lady?" Mick asked politely.

"I'm Daphne."

"Daphne—as in the Scooby Doo cartoon?" the angel asked.

Daphne tried to hold back a grin, but failed. After a few moments she said, "I suppose my parents had a good sense of humor."

Mick nodded and winked. The visitors then took a seat in the unimpressive waiting room.

Covering the perimeter of the small reception area were partially stained cloth chairs, which were saddled with stainless steel armrests topped with faux wood. In the center of the room was an old coffee table, which was covered with an array of worn-out magazines. Wyatt picked up a "Sports Illustrated" that was over two years old. He began to slowly page through it.

After sitting quietly for only a few minutes, the show's producer opened the door adjacent to the reception window.

"Mr. Hunter, we're ready for you now," she said.

"Thank you," Wyatt said.

The producer was short, very thin and wore thick, horn-rimmed glasses. Her grayish brunette hair was pulled into a very tight pony-tail, which complimented her gray sweater and charcoal slacks.

"By the way, my name is Barbara," she said.

"Hello Barbara," Wyatt said, shaking her hand. "It's nice to meet you."

She nodded politely and turned back towards the interior of the studio. Wyatt, Cam, and Mick all followed Barbara down the narrow hallway. After turning right, they proceeded down another long corridor, which ended at a doorway. She showed her three guests inside the small room.

"This is where you'll be staged until we call you for the taping," she said. "Please make yourself comfortable. A makeup technician will be in shortly to prepare you for the show, Mr. Hunter."

Barbara then politely excused herself.

Cam and Mick both sat down on the brownish tweed couch, while Wyatt assumed the barber-style chair adjacent to it, awaiting his makeup job. Mick then prepped his student with a serious tone.

"Listen Wyatt, I'm afraid I have to leave here soon, so—"

"Why are you leaving now?" Wyatt asked, perplexed.

"Please let me finish," Mick said. "I'm getting the initial call to go back to Heaven, so I'm going to blast out of here in a minute."

"What do you mean by, *initial call?*" Cam asked.

Mick thought for a moment, mentally digging through his arsenal of analogies.

"Cam my man, it's sort of like the two minute warning in pro football. I know that I'll be leaving here soon, so we need to wrap things up."

"Oh okay," Cam said, nodding.

"Anyways Wyatt," Mick continued, "please remember what I've told you over-and-over since yesterday morning about how to conduct yourself during the onslaught of hatred you *may* be encountering."

Wyatt nodded.

"By the way," Wyatt said. "Thanks for sticking around after our golf match yesterday. Cam and I really enjoyed hanging out with you last night and today."

"No problem, dude. I was really surprised that my orders were to stick around for a whole day and a half with you fellas. Not that I'm complaining."

"I see," Wyatt said. "Anyway, I fully understand the lessons you've shown me, and I'll do my best to represent the Kingdom of God."

"Just remember," Mick said. "Showing the love of Christ is the most important thing you can do, so make sure to, *be Jesus to the world*. If you get all ticked-off and start cussing and whatnot, the viewers will probably not see the King of kings who you worship."

By this time, Cam had meandered over towards the counter adjacent to the small sink area in the back of the room. "Hey, they left us some grub to nibble on," he said.

Wyatt turned around and asked, "They did? What do we have?"

"Let's see . . . we have some cheese and crackers . . . also some of that summer salami . . . ."

"Cool," Wyatt said. "Hey Mick, do you want a little snack before you go—?"

When Wyatt and Cam turned around, Mick had already disappeared, back to Heaven.

Cam shrugged. "I guess not."

Wyatt shook his head. "I hate it when he does that."

****

A studio staff member soon thereafter visited Wyatt and prepared him for the show. Wyatt was then led into the small studio area. Greeting him were several technicians, all bustling about in a chaotic trance. Already stationed in the hostess spot on the stage was Jeanette Collins. Seated across the round interview table and to her right was the other guest for the show, Alistair McClellan. After receiving an encouraging pat on the shoulder from Cam, Wyatt proceeded over towards the hostess, stepping onto the slightly elevated stage.

Jeanette greeted Wyatt as if he was her long-lost brother, heartily shaking his hand while wearing a joyous smile. Wyatt found this to be a little disconcerting. On the other hand, McClellan presented himself as a polite British gentleman; proper and respectful. Wyatt was far more comfortable with this.

After they sat down, Jeanette rambled through some formalities about how the taping would proceed, and that she would ask both of them questions about their books. She also said that during her questions, she would delve deeper into any issues which she felt her viewers would find interesting. Jeanette encouraged her guests that it was certainly okay if they wanted to ask each other questions about their respective books.

Although both authors nodded their understanding, Wyatt thought he detected McClellan holding back a smirk.

The surreal situation now had Wyatt feeling strangely transported into another time. As his instincts clicked on, he suddenly pictured himself on an ancient arena dirt floor, surrounded by screaming, bloodthirsty Romans who were calling for the lions to be released.

Boston, MA
October 6th

"Hell is empty and all the devils are here."
William Shakespeare

Why don't these demons realize that I'm Caleb Hunter, Grand Master of the Synagogue of Satan? Honestly, I've had to wait *way* too long for this moment. It really seems unfair. I don't think it's asking too much for Damon to show me a little more respect for my position as their earthly human leader.

Anyway, the time has *finally* come for me to drink from the cup of my long-awaited revenge. I can't believe the time is actually here! Although I'm not sure how everything works in this battle between God and Satan, I'm sure glad it's time to send my disgusting brother Wyatt to his long overdue grave. It'll sure be nice to never see his fat, ugly face ever again. I've been spying on him for years, and I'm pretty sick of it.

You know, I'll actually be doing that idiot a favor. When I kill Wyatt, he can go spend as much time as he wants on his knees, worshipping a false god like Jesus Christ. For some odd reason, that really seems to be his kind of thing. *Whatever!*

Suddenly, I catch a whiff of sulfur.

"C'mon Damon," I say. "Why does Geyotteream smell so bad? He and the others are in the van behind us, but I can *still* smell him."

"With all due respect Caleb," Damon said. "Do I need to remind you once again that all of your incessant complaining makes you look like a weakling? Our job is much bigger in this world than the occasional, unpleasant duty. Do I make myself clear?"

I sigh and say, "You do."

"Very well then," Damon said, obviously annoyed. "After Wyatt and Cam make their exit from the studio, we'll ambush them. At that point, you can finally have your moment of glory when you plunge that special, ancient dagger right into your twin brother's heart."

"That's awesome," I say. *"I can hardly wait."*

"So, my friend, it seems that your moment of truth has finally arrived. Now that it's here, *can I expect an end to your constant complaining???* I've been listening to your whining for decades about wanting to kill Wyatt, and quite frankly, I've grown weary of it."

"Yes sir, I'm very happy," I say, all the while stroking the nickel and ivory handle of my nine-inch dagger.

"Good. I'm glad we're clear on this."

"So what about Mick?" I ask.

"What about Mick!!!" Damon shot back. "If he's still with Wyatt and Cameron, we'll sick Geyotteream on him . . . capiche???"

"Yes sir," I say.

"You've come a long way in your development as our supreme human leader Caleb, but you must learn some patience if you're going to effectively serve Satan. Our master will absolutely *not* tolerate those who are disobedient."

"I understand that," I say. "By the way, I'm not clear on why it's taken so long for me to have permission to kill Wyatt. Can you please explain this to me again?"

Damon sighed heavily, then with a restrained politeness said, "How many times have we been through this before, Caleb? Do you not realize what an honor it is to be elevated to Grand Master? I mean; aside from your other duties for us."

"I know, but—"

"Listen to me!" Damon insisted. "I've explained to you before that the raining down of our judgment on the human race must go through a certain process. As a part of your ongoing training, it's been necessary to share with you the Christian's playbook—*their silly little Bible*. Now then; you absolutely *must* remember this—reading their outrageous Scriptures is *not* something I enjoy very much."

"Why is that?" I ask.

"Because their lies make me sick to my stomach!"

"Whoa Damon," I say. "I know we've been through all of this before. It's just that I don't understand why we can't do what we want to do. Their God did put us in charge here on Earth, did He not?"

Damon sighed again, then calmly said, "That's not the point."

"Then what *is* the point?" I ask.

"Listen . . . if you really want to go through this once again—*you* can read about it in their silly little book of rules. I don't have the stomach for it tonight."

"Fine," I say. I reach over and pull the enemy's playbook—their stinking Bible—out of my glove box. I then flip to a section which I've hi-lighted from my warfare studies as a teenager.

You know; I remember so well how Damon taught me how to defeat God's people in my biblical studies as a young lad. What's interesting though, is that I've always found it a little disconcerting how difficult it is for Damon to read some of the Christian Scriptures. The truth is, if we don't read the Christian's Bible, then how in the world are we supposed to understand how to defeat them?

Anyway, I look over at Damon and ask, "Are you okay?"

"I'm fine Caleb," Damon said. "But if I must listen to this nonsense once again, it won't be uttered from my lips."

"I understand," I say. "Alright . . . here we go . . . it's in *Job 1:12* . . . *The Lord said to Satan, 'Very well, then, everything he has is in your power, but on the man himself do not lay a finger.' Then Satan went out from the presence of the Lord."*

Damon shrugged. "That one actually doesn't bother me very much."

"Why is that?"

"Because it only shows our master in dialogue with his enemy."

"Yeah," I say. "But doesn't it also show that God is in charge?"

"How dare you blaspheme Lucifer!!!" Damon shouted.

Oops, I guess I went too far again.

"I'm sorry," I say. "I don't mean any disrespect." Damon waves me off with his hand. "Anyway," I continue, "the other passage I don't quite understand is *Luke 22:31,* which says . . . *'Simon, Simon, Satan has asked to sift all of you as wheat."*

"Don't you dare quote that passage to me, you idiot!" Damon yells, pointing his finger in my face. He looks really hacked-off.

"What's wrong with that one?" I ask.

For some reason, Damon looks like a big chicken drumstick bubbling in oil; he's obviously angry. Then, in an amazingly calm voice, he said, "My dearest Caleb . . . we're certainly permitted to study the Christian's Bible as a way to fight against the enemy. However—and I've told this to you many times before—*we do not quote their Scriptures where Jesus Christ himself spoke.* Have you forgotten your training already?"

I hold up my hands in a stop motion. "Listen master; I've followed every single thing you've ever asked me to do. I've executed the enemies connected with these Flaming Sword losers over the years; I've studied all of the warfare materials you've given me; and last-but-not-least, I killed the former Grand Master of our group so I could take charge. So please . . . if you don't mind . . . give me a little credit here—"

"Let me remind you, Caleb, that *you* executed the previous Grand Master because of your *own* ambitions," Damon said. "If you'll remember, it was because of your other critically important duties for The Servants that you absolutely *insisted* it was your unquestioned destiny to become our Grand Master."

"Perhaps you're right," I say, shrugging. "But my predecessor is partying in Hell right now. In fact, I'm sure he's being heralded as a hero at this very moment. That doesn't sound so bad to me. Actually, I think I may have done him a huge favor by taking his earthly life."

Damon gets this smug expression on his face. "How right you are, my son," he said.

"Anyway," I say, "it's just that I don't really understand everything about our missions against God's people. In all of my years of training, this is something I still don't get."

"It's actually very simple," Damon said. "Basically—and I mean no disrespect here—but humans are merely God's failed experiment. After our master was wrongfully banished from God's holy mountain, those of us angels who aligned with Lucifer were also subjected to Satan's process of attacking humans. The passage in Job you just read only shows a small part of that process."

"So once again, how does this process work?" I ask. "Like I said, I thought we were in charge down here on Earth."

"I'm afraid the actual process is a little beyond what you humans can comprehend," Damon said. "To boil this down for you; those of us angels in Satan's army must go through a certain permission process to carry out our attacks on the human race."

"Just like Satan asked Jesus for permission to sift Peter?" I ask.

Damon nodded. "It's more complicated than that, but your crude synopsis is not far off the mark."

"Then why do so many of my fellow humans listen to us instead of listening to God?" I ask. "Although, I must admit, sometimes it seems like we just can't get through to some people."

"It's our job to simply tell humans that Satan's way of this world is a free ticket to being released from the suffering and sacrifice of being a Christian. All we must do is to demonstrate that there is indeed a way to avoid being told everything you *really* enjoy is a sin—that's what their God constantly tells them."

"I get that," I say. "If I'm not following my own ways or committing what Christian's call *sin,* then I'm not really having any fun, am I?"

"How true, my fine young student," Damon said.

"But tell me something chief," I say. "Why am I any different then the rest of the human race?"

Truthfully, I already know the answer to this. I just love to hear Damon say it.

"Ahhh Caleb . . . you're like my own son. You were chosen when you were born to become the cornerstone of our future plans. *You are indeed, very special to Satan and myself.* We've determined that your destiny is to fulfill a very special purpose in helping our master to attain full worship as the unquestioned ruler of this world. Even the Christian's silly little Scriptures admit that Satan will ascend to his earthly throne one day."

"Oh, you're talking about the book of *Revelation* . . . yeah . . . but doesn't the Bible also say that Satan will ultimately be defeated by Jesus Christ Himself? How in the world are we going to stop that? If we have to go through this mysterious permission-process for attacking humans, then what's to stop Jesus from carrying out the rest of their prophecy?"

"Please don't forget," Damon said. "Many of the prophecies in their silly little Bible haven't taken place yet. They're merely God's wishful thinking."

"Yeah, but isn't it also true that their past biblical prophecies have *always* ended up happening? What's to stop the future ones from also coming to pass? As you know, their Bible emphatically states that things don't seem to bode very well for us in the end."

Instead of getting angry, Damon simply said, "Don't you worry for one single moment about that, my friend. Our master has *no* plans to lose to God in the end. Your job is to simply help Satan ascend to his earthly throne; one on which he so rightly deserves to sit. Please trust me on this and let us worry about all of the details."

"Hmmm," I say. "I suppose that makes sense." Damon glares at me with his typical, smug grin. "Anyway," I continue, "how long will our enemies be in this dump of a studio?"

"Oh, I don't know," Damon said. "I think they're probably just getting started. It could be an hour or so. Perhaps less."

"Oh, okay," I say. "By the way, I've been meaning to ask you about that atheist-dude who Wyatt is apparently debating. Is he on our side?"

"Of course not," Damon said. "At least not directly. I've told you before that atheists claim to not believe in any kind of supernatural presence whatsoever. To tell you the truth, many of today's atheists are no different than the Pharisees back in the time of Jesus—they're both under our influence, unawares."

"What do you mean by that?" I ask.

"Our mortal enemy—Jesus Christ—rebuked the sanctimonious religious authorities of His day. You know, the ancient Pharisees and Sadducees. In fact, their apostle Paul was actually a Pharisee himself; that is, until Jesus confronted him on the road to Damascus and stole Him from our ranks."

"I understand that part," I say.

"Anyway," Damon continued. "As it relates to Christianity, as you well-know, our attacks on mankind center on two primary areas: Number one is keeping people away from any kind of religious beliefs at all—like with the atheists. And number two; if they must worship Jesus Christ, we simply need to pump-up their religious fervor so that when they do profess to believe in Him, they become prideful and boast of their holiness. In that case, they're not much of a threat against us. In other words, their overly religious and sanctimonious attitudes—just like the ancient Pharisees—will keep them from serving Jesus Christ. In the end, that's all we really care about."

"That makes sense to me," I say. "Either way, Satan wins, right?"

"That's correct."

"To zero-in on the atheists," I say, "I don't quite understand how they account for the origin of life. Do they really believe that all of life randomly evolved without a creator? How can anyone fall for a massive deception like that???"

Damon has a satisfied grin on his face. He's obviously proud of the way our little ruse of Evolution has corrupted mankind and given them an excuse to not follow God.

"Oh yeah," Damon said. *"There is that . . . ."*

Boston, MA
October 6th

"The lady doth protest too much, methinks."
Shakespeare's *Hamlet* (act III, scene ii)

The studio lights blazed overhead, causing a scarcely discernible layer of perspiration to appear above the makeup on Wyatt's shaved head. Although he was desperately trying to avoid it, Wyatt found himself to be nervous. In fact, he was very nervous. He actually had butterflies in his stomach, and the saliva in his mouth ran dry. Without a doubt, this anxiety was a completely unexpected development, because Wyatt thought he was fully prepared for this interview; both mentally and spiritually.

Across the table, Wyatt heard the barely audible voice of the show's producer speaking through Jeanette's earpiece say, "Thirty seconds, Jeanette."

She nodded.

A few moments later, the camera man used a silent *three-two-one* count, then pointed at Jeanette. It was finally show time. Or in Jeanette's mind, it was *show-down* time.

"Good evening Boston, and welcome to another episode of 'Our Neighborhood.' I'm your host, Jeanette Collins. Tonight, we're honored to have two distinguished authors here to speak with us about their recently published books. To my immediate right, we have Alistair McClellan, who is actually from the U.K. Doctor McClellan is in town this week promoting his book, The Modern Age of Enlightened Atheism. Also joining us tonight is a local Christian novelist, Wyatt Hunter, who hails from the Methuen area. Gentlemen . . . welcome to the show!"

Both McClellan and Wyatt mumbled, *thank you.*

"Let's begin tonight with the distinguished Alistair McClellan," Jeanette said. "Doctor, would you please tell us a little bit about your history, and how you came to write your book. It sounds very interesting."

"Very well," McClellan said. His accent was mostly Scottish, with a British tinge; it was very professorial. He was only in his mid-fifties, but looked somewhat older due to his thick gray hair and round, wire-rimmed glasses. McClellan was dressed in a brown tweed sport jacket, which lay nicely over his medium frame.

He continued, "I have a PhD in environmental micro-biology from the University of Aberdeen in Scotland. I also have a number of undergraduate and masters degrees from other universities throughout Europe. However, micro-biology is the true passion of my life."

"I see," Jeanette said. "So tell me; how did you come to write your book? What drove you to put your thoughts to pen and paper, so to speak?"

She smiled. Wyatt cringed inwardly.

"I'm afraid my story is rather dull," McClellan said. "After many years of study at the university, and after wrestling with my own spiritual identity since I was a teenager, I finally concluded that the whole story of Jesus Christ in the Bible was likely nothing but a huge myth, perpetrated by the religious establishment . . . ."

"Do go on," Jeanette encouraged.

"My education in the biological sciences led me to conclude that religion is largely for the uneducated masses. Furthermore, I cannot find any real proof for the Christian's claim that a poor carpenter from ancient Palestine was the unique son of God. To me, it's nothing but a simple yearning of the unenlightened mind. Honestly, I wish it wasn't so, but that's the conclusion at which I've arrived. And truthfully, the more I've discovered in the area of science through my studies, the more I've come to realize that the concept of any kind of supernatural presence like God was likely not possible; or at the very least, the whole idea is impractical and *definitely* not knowable. Like I said, I see the whole religious kit-and-kaboodle as wishful thinking—created entirely by ancient people and carried forward by those throughout history who don't really care about true scientific knowledge."

"I see," Jeanette said. "So, is it fair to say that you believe in Evolution as the driving force behind life?"

"At this point, I have no choice but to believe that. So yes."

"Okay then," Jeanette continued, turning towards Wyatt. "Mr. Hunter; can I assume you have a differing opinion on this matter . . . ?"

This was Wyatt's moment of truth, and he found it hard to believe it had arrived. Jeanette's cowardly attempt at an ambush truly sickened him. But for the past year, Wyatt had worked very hard to eliminate his disgust at those who he considered to be God-hating bigots. He knew that Christ's way was to embrace that fact that true believers in the LORD will be hated for following Jesus. He also knew that the Gospel of Truth is something that is utterly offensive to the prideful human spirit. Having sympathy—not angst—for the unsaved had become very important to Wyatt, and he continually worked to improve his attitude on this subject.

On the other hand, Wyatt also knew that the concept of Christ-like humility in no way included being pushed around. To the contrary; one of his favorite phrases, *meek ain't weak,* entered his thoughts. Of course, this had to be tempered with love and concern for the eternal destination of all people. To Wyatt, this was not an easy balancing act.

As all of these things vigorously swam laps in his mind, Wyatt found himself no longer nervous. Instead, he felt strongly-convicted, positive-minded, and anxious to tell the Truth. Wyatt sensed the pronounced presence of the Holy Spirit in his heart, so he knew he was ready to properly do battle. He sighed and caught his breath for a moment as his soul invisibly grabbed the sword of the spirit—which is the Word of God, and the Truth of the Gospel of Jesus Christ.

"Ms. Collins . . . with all due respect . . . you invited me here tonight to speak about my first novel, <u>A Walk With An Unusual Messenger</u>, did you not? I really didn't come here to engage in a debate over the existence of God."

Uh-oh, Jeanette thought. This was an unexpected development. She had been convinced that the element of surprise weighed heavily in her favor. However, this didn't sound like Wyatt Hunter was surprised one single bit. From all of her years in journalism, Jeanette knew that if you catch someone off guard when asking probing questions, you'll more than likely put them on the defensive, and therefore quickly find out how they really feel.

"I see, Mr. Hunter," she said, clearing her throat.

Before she could continue, Wyatt said, "Jeanette . . . I really have no beef whatsoever with the esteemed Dr. McClellan here. To tell you the truth, I really don't have any problem with *anyone* who doesn't believe in, or who questions the existence of God. In fact, those who don't know Jesus Christ as their Savior are actually the ones who have ultimately inspired me to continue with my writing."

Oh boy, Jeanette thought. *How can I possibly redirect this conversation so I can slam-dunk this Christian idiot?*

"I understand, Mr. Hunter," she said. "By the way, may I call you Wyatt?"

"Please do."

"Wyatt . . . I'll admit this; the theme for tonight's show did go through a slight change once we discovered that Dr. McClellan was available to join us. We just thought that—"

"You just thought that you could bring in an atheist with a doctorate to tear me to shreds???" Wyatt asked, pointedly.

"Wyatt my good man," McClellan interrupted. "Right off the bat, I can see that you're understandably feeling somewhat picked-on. So if it's okay with you, I'd like to offer you an olive branch. Do you mind?"

Wyatt shrugged. "I don't mind at all."

"First off," McClellan continued, "I'd like to assure you that I'm unlike most of my non-deist contemporaries who typically take on a much more *combative* approach to sharing their opinions on the non-existence of God."

"I appreciate that, Dr. McClellan," Wyatt said.

"Please, my good fellow; call me Al."

"Thanks Al," Wyatt said.

Jeanette cringed, ever so slightly.

Not only had her ambush on Wyatt Hunter gone irrevocably off the rails, but her other guest had actually taken the reins on engaging him in dialogue before she wanted him to. At this point, however, she decided to let the interview follow its own path. Trying to pull it back to the original plan would likely make her appear foolish and manipulative.

"Please go on gentlemen," she said. "I think our viewers would enjoy hearing both of your valuable perspectives."

"Very well then," McClellan said. "If you don't mind, Wyatt, I have some questions I'd like to ask of you. But first, I'll give you a wee-bit of my history."

"That'll work," Wyatt said.

"For whatever reasons, the religious people who have haunted my spiritual history have been unable—*or unwilling*—to engage me in an honest discussion about my concerns—"

"Listen Al," Wyatt interrupted. "I have no problem with an honest discussion. What I refuse to do is get into an argument with someone who wants to condemn my belief in Jesus Christ—which is the most important thing in my life. And to tell you the truth, I feel that life is *way* too short to waste my time arguing with someone who doesn't have any intention whatsoever of listening to my testimony—or to my answers to their questions and concerns. Does that seem reasonable to you?"

"It certainly does," Al agreed. "Well . . . not that I'm trying to take over Jeanette's job of asking the questions, but why don't you tell us about your own background?"

Jeanette fell into a false smile which hid a torrent of frustration and anger boiling just below the surface of her professional facade. Although she very much wanted McClellan to directly engage Wyatt Hunter, it was certainly not like this. *They almost seem to be having fun together,* she mused to herself. If her producer even so much as uttered one single word through her earpiece, Jeanette was afraid she would pull out a chainsaw and chase both guests around the stage.

"Sure thing, Doctor Al," Wyatt said.

McClellan grinned. "Just plain ole 'Al' will work for me," he said.

Wyatt nodded. "Okay Al. My story is also a very simple one. My wife died a couple of years ago in a car wreck, and of course, I've struggled with tremendous grief because of it. So about a year ago, while I was walking through Pike Place Market in Seattle, I got this idea to write a story about God. You know; like Jesus and I having a little chat as we walked through the market. Anyway, in my mind, the idea continued to evolve. But instead of me having a chat with the LORD in the story—which is something most anybody would want to do—I chose to utilize an angel character instead."

Obviously amused and somewhat captivated, Al asked, "So why did you do that? Choose an angel, that is."

"Because it's my belief that no one currently on Earth will see Jesus Christ until He returns to claim what is His. It's not that Jesus *can't* come to Earth; I just cannot find a biblical reason why He would."

"I see," Al said. "Of course, I don't believe in angels any more than I believe in an unseen God. But I must say; the premise for your book is very charming."

Al had downloaded Wyatt's book onto his Kindle the day before, and he actually took the time to read it. Inexplicably, he thoroughly enjoyed the little story about an angel and a regular guy walking through Pike Place Market, talking about their God.

"Anyway, my book is all about using the subject of spiritual warfare to draw the reader closer towards the Bible," Wyatt said. "Of course; the Bible is where I believe all of life's answers are."

"So based on all that you've said," Al began, "can I safely assume that you reject the idea of Evolution?"

"I reject the idea of Evolution as the driving source of power in life. It's a scientific fact that species do evolve; but only within their own *kind*. What I thoroughly reject is the theory that all things in life evolved from a single, *common ancestor*. In my heart, the LORD is the origin of all life, not the personification of natural selection over billions of years. No matter what way you slice it, that flawed thought process embraces utter randomness and assigns it godly powers. As I observe all things in life, I don't perceive anything random whatsoever."

"I see. So, what are your overall feelings about science?"

"Actually, I *love* science," Wyatt said. "But I also think that science should be neutral. To me, science should be all about the seeking of evidence and facts—not the furthering of any kind of anti-God agenda."

"I'm not sure I'm following you on that," Al said.

"Let me back-up and say that intellectually, science is the key to opening the door to knowing God for many people. While I don't fall into that category—I'm guided more by my heart with faith—I acknowledge that people have differing needs in what they seek during their journey towards either knowing or rejecting the LORD during their lifetime."

"I see," Al said. "So what do you think about the claim in my book that religion is for the uneducated masses? I hate to be so blunt about it, but that's the conclusion at which I've arrived. Unfortunately, at this point, I see no other choice."

"Honestly, I'm surprised that a level-headed man like yourself would embrace such a claim," Wyatt said. "In my opinion, the problem with academia in general, is that it's become too highly-secularized. And to be perfectly frank, it's apparent to me that many of those who reject the LORD seem to be overly impressed with their own intelligence; present company excluded."

"Hmmm," Al mumbled. "Before I respond, I'd like you to expound on what exactly you mean by that. Do go on."

"I'm a pretty basic guy," Wyatt said, "and I like to keep things simple in my mind. Let me put it to you like this: whether people realize it or not, most of the world's population falls within the same category of intelligence."

"And that is . . . ?"

"Most of us have IQ's which are south of Einstein, but north of Forrest Gump."

Al chuckled.

"What I mean is this," Wyatt continued. "It's obvious that some of us are more intellectually gifted than others. In each of our cases, I'm quite sure that your IQ is much closer to Einstein than that of Forrest Gump. And while I'm at it, I'll also admit that my own IQ is probably closer to Forrest Gump than Einstein. Anyway, the problem, in my opinion, lies with the fact that within the intelligentsia, people tend to elevate human aptitude and knowledge to a level much higher than what it actually is. The truth is, there are very few Einsteins in this world, and perhaps just a few Forrest Gumps. Like I said, I believe that most of us reside between those two polar-opposite boundaries . . . so to speak."

"I think you may be vastly short-selling the evidence in the evolutionary process, my good man," Al said. "While I'll admit there are a few things about Evolution which remain a mystery to me, it still offers a much more satisfying explanation about life on our planet than some random mythical musings from one little book. No offense intended."

Wyatt nodded. *This man is relatively considerate, honest, and seems to be level-headed,* he thought.

"How about this, Al?" he asked. "I'll reel off a few of the litmus-test questions which many of the nouveau atheists of today have a penchant for leveling at believers in Jesus Christ. You can then tell me what you think. Alright?"

"Certainly. Do go on."

Wyatt caught his breath for a moment. "I believe that many intellectual-types do this test in an attempt to call Christians stupid;

or to somehow mitigate our opinions. Anyway, after I've said my piece, you can be the judge."

"That's fine with me," Al said.

Jeanette continued to smile at the camera, but remained quiet.

"I had a discussion one night with a professor several years ago, and he asked me some interesting questions," Wyatt said. "And it didn't take me long to figure out that he was actually trying to test me. Okay, here goes with the questions. Number one: is Evolution false? No offense Al, but you just started off with this question, yourself. Number two: how old is the Earth? If you so much as entertain the assertion—*as I do*—that the Earth is only thousands of years old instead of billions, then you're nothing but an idiot in their eyes."

"I see," Al said. "Please go on."

"Number three," Wyatt continued, "is about the highly politicized global warming. If you so much as question this subject at all, then you're automatically branded a right-wing whacko and should be discredited. Four, was there really a world-wide flood? Not just a local flood, but a *world-wide* flood. And finally, there's number five—and this is a big one—do you really believe that Adam and Eve encountered an actual serpent in the Garden of Eden? Those, my dear friend, are among the most often-asked questions by atheists to Christians."

"I see," Al said. "So what are your answers to these questions?"

Wyatt breathed in deeply once again before responding. He really hoped that Al wasn't simply playing games with him.

"That's easy, Al. I've already given you my answer on Evolution—which certainly exists, but is *not* all-powerful. I find it to be an interesting point and agree with the assertion that the Earth is only several thousand years old instead of billions, but I'm not worried about it either way—God is in charge and the Bible is one-hundred percent correct. I also think that God is in charge of the weather, not man; and there was most definitely a *worldwide* flood. Last but not least, if the Bible said that Satan showed up in the Garden of Eden as a serpent, then I believe it. Who am I to question the Creator of all things?"

"I'm not sure I agree with—" Al began.

"And one more thing," Wyatt interrupted. "Then I'll shut up and let you talk. I've run into a lot of intellectuals who only consider a person to be intelligent if they agree with their positions. Do you know something? I have absolutely *no* idea what happened to spirited dialogue and polite disagreement in this world, but I sure wish we could get back to those days."

Al nodded and paused for a moment.

"Wyatt my dear chap . . . believe it or not, I very much appreciate your opinions on this matter. Although I disagree with many of your assertions, I'm unlike many others who either question or do not believe in God—and I'm *certainly* not angry about my position. That's actually what prompted me to write my book."

"I've noticed that your approach is unique among many of the skeptics of today."

"However," Al continued, "I must admit, when I evaluate whether God exists or not, I feel that we must go down to the foundation of the issue. When I do that—and I've ardently studied this for decades now—I simply cannot find any proof of God's existence. To tell you the truth, I wish that I did indeed have the faith to believe in an unseen and unproven God as you do. Admittedly, there's a part of me which cannot picture how creation occurred without some thing or some one behind it all. But alas, at this point, I cannot make that leap of faith and believe in an unseen God."

"It almost sounds like it might not take much for you to agree with Anselm's ontological argument that God's non-existence is absolutely inconceivable."

"Not exactly," Al said. "While I'll admit that Evolution doesn't have all the answers, neither does religion."

"And that's *precisely* my problem with Evolution," Wyatt said. "A great claim like Evolution must have an accompanying requisite of great evidence. Irrespective of how ardently believers in Evolution wish it weren't so, the fact is, there are some crushing deal-busters in their argument."

"Such as . . . ?"

"First and foremost," Wyatt began, "let's concentrate on the big-picture items—like nothing in our physical world can account for something coming from nothing. In other words, nothing can arise by chance; that is, according to all known natural laws of science. So in order for someone to believe in Evolution with its great claims, there absolutely *must* be a solid foundation. Absent of that, why should I believe the spotty evidence to back up Evolution's lofty claims?"

"I see," Al said. "And I suppose you're implying the lack of evidence in the fossil record?"

"I am," Wyatt said. "But I'm also talking about the lack of explanation of where the matter itself came from. And while we're on the subject, where did the origin of life come from? I know you must be familiar with the theory held by some evolutionists that space aliens seeded life on Earth billions of years ago, right?"

"Yes of course; I'm familiar with it."

"So is nonsensical *science fiction* like that really easier to believe than an all-powerful God who made us in His image?"

"I think you may be misunderstanding my position a bit," Al said. "Although I do indeed spend part of my book, <u>The Modern Age of Enlightened Atheism</u>, on some of the science which allows for the strong *possibility* of Evolution, unlike most of my contemporaries, I don't have any anger towards religion—or those who practice it."

"I see—"

"By the way, have you, perchance, read my book?" Al interrupted.

"Uhmmm," Wyatt stammered. "I actually haven't had the time to."

Al winked. "Well my friend; I'm proud to say that I found the time to read your book yesterday."

"Gentlemen, I think it's wonderful when guests do that kind of thing," Jeanette added.

Wyatt and Al ignored her.

Blushing, Wyatt said, "I'm honored."

"I actually have a couple of questions about your book," Al said. "And one of my questions is about *demons.*"

"What would you like to know?"

"Do you really believe in the assertion that evil spirits—or demons as your book refers to them as—are possessing people today to carry out evil deeds?"

"I do," Wyatt said. "However, demons aren't the source of all evil. *Human sin* is what separates us from God—our own, foolish personal pride. That's why Jesus had to die on the Cross to atone for our sins. It was the only way."

"I see. I must admit; there are two lingering things about biblical Christianity which have always bothered me."

"Oh—what are they?"

"The first thing I've had trouble reconciling is that the God of the Bible's Old Testament seems so utterly cruel. The other thing is that it often seems like Christians severely dislike science—which is the passion of my life."

Wyatt knew he had to be very careful, here. He already regretted being a bonehead by neglecting to read Al's book—or at least part of it—before the interview tonight. Since he saw 'atheism' in the title, he had assumed that Al was like so many of the hateful atheists of their time. To the contrary, Al seemed like he sincerely wanted someone to explain the Christian faith to him in a straightforward way.

Wyatt nodded. "Why don't we start with the 'God of the Old Testament' issue?"

"That's fine with me. So what say-you?"

"To understand God in any way whatsoever, you must do this one, critically important thing. If you neglect to do this one thing, then you'll possibly never have any real understanding of the LORD; unless, of course, He personally intervenes . . . ."

"Please go on."

"It's actually very simple—you *must* look at the events on Earth from *God's* perspective. Not our own. In this case, if you don't look at the events in the Old Testament through the prism of the LORD's perspective, it's quite easy to see a stern, unloving God."

"Please elaborate on that . . . if you don't mind."

"Certainly. Let's look at The Exodus, for example. The LORD delivered the Israelites from slavery in Egypt, and while they were still in the wilderness, they began to worship idols. Now let's think about that for a moment. What if you were standing in God's shoes? What if you did everything to help your people, but they continued to betray you by *doing things their own way.* Tell me; would you tolerate such nonsense?"

Al sat quiet for a moment, staring into his clasped hands. He then said, "I'll need to ponder that question before I can properly answer it."

"I'm glad to see that you're not going to simply shoot me down with rhetoric and tell me I'm a religious nut," Wyatt said.

"Of course not," Al bristled. "There's simply no need for that sort of rubbish in a fair-minded discussion."

"Might I also suggest, Al, that you read the books of Genesis and Exodus—I mean *slowly* read them. I think you just may find some answers to your burning questions. That is; if you open your heart and mind and begin looking at things from God's perspective."

"Wyatt my dear man; I've read the entire Bible all the way through on at least five separate occasions in the past. I'm not sure how a sixth time will be any different."

"I understand. But this time I'm suggesting you read it *slowly*— without trying to race through it. You also might consider reading it with a completely clear state of mind. If you read the Bible in conjunction with an open heart and open mind, you just may see God's Holy Word in a different light. Please remember; putting yourself in someone else's shoes is perhaps the best way to understand them. In this case, I suggest you try looking at the events in the Bible from God's perspective. You see; if you only look at things from the human experience, you'll probably and *incorrectly* see a cruel and capricious God."

"I will indeed consider your suggestion," Al said.

"I have a couple more things for you to consider while you're at it," Wyatt said. "If you look closely at the science vs. religion issue, you'll see that Satan—*the Evil One*—has clearly switched sides."

"Now you *really* have my interest!"

"It breaks down like this . . . many centuries ago, Satan used the religious establishment to persecute scientists. It's as if the church was terrified that any scientific discoveries would disprove God's existence, thereby crushing their fragile faith. Well, it seems pretty obvious to me; that type of thinking shows a *huge* lack of faith on their part."

"Indeed," Al agreed.

"However, in modern times today, Satan has flipped to the side of science, which is currently inundated with men and women who flippantly dismiss and persecute those who believe in God. This switching of the sides is *exactly* how Satan works. Throughout history, he'll often play both sides against each other in order to serve his own evil purpose."

"And what purpose is that?"

"To keep people away from the only true pathway to everlasting joy with Jesus Christ. Satan doesn't care who you worship; just as long as it's not Jesus."

Jeanette quickly added, "Gentlemen, I'm afraid we're almost out of time tonight. Do either of you have any closing comments?"

Al nodded, a huge grin invading his face.

"My esteemed fellow author—Mr. Wyatt Hunter—has passionately shared his opinions on the existence of God. For that, I am most grateful that he didn't get in my face and judge me. You see, I'm most assuredly *not* an atheist. At least, at this point I'm not. I'm actually much more of an agnostic—meaning I feel that belief in an unseen God—since he apparently cannot be proven beyond the shadow of a doubt—is unknowable to us. Therefore, I have many doubts about him. I am also a great lover of science. Now then; I wouldn't go so far as to call science my *religion,* but I will say that it satisfies my mind about the order of the universe much more completely than my heretofore knowledge of God."

"I see," Jeanette said. "And Mr. Hunter . . . ?"

Wyatt cleared his throat. "God is the master scientist, and I know that He loves it when we discover Him through His incredible creation. Let me also say that I absolutely *detest* religion. To me, religion is an artificial blanket which mankind lays over our souls in an attempt to understand or please the LORD. To my way of thinking, we don't need religion—*we need Jesus Christ.* The LORD is more than sufficient, and He loves us more than we can possibly know.

"I'd also like to add that Evolution has now become very much like a religion to many of today's unbelievers. There's no question in my mind that it has replaced Christianity as the religion of the public school systems here in the United States—and I suspect for most of the world, as well. In my opinion, Evolution is actually a belief-based system which merely has consequential evidence—not evidential proof. The manner in which each person views the world and its creation is also how we view Evolution.

"But let me also add this: the idea that Evolution is the source of power in the universe is an unmitigated trick by Satan; it's a gigantic ruse. No matter how hard atheists try to make it so, Evolution cannot explain the objective moral values that human beings possess. Micro-biology can't do it, methodological naturalism can't do it, and space aliens seeding life on Earth billions of years ago won't get you there either. The simple answer in this case is the best answer: only believing in a transcendent, loving, creator-God can explain all of these things.

"And one last thing," Wyatt continued, "*Psalm 14:1* says . . . *The fool says in his heart, 'There is no God.' They are corrupt, their deeds are vile; there is no one who does good.* So if I agreed with those who reject the LORD, then we'd *both* be wrong. Nevertheless, it has been a great blessing today to have met Al; a genuinely honorable man who shows respect, even though we have differing opinions."

"On that note, I'm afraid we've run out of time, gentlemen," Jeanette said. "We'd like to thank both of you for sharing a little bit about your respective books, as well as your well-thought out opinions." She turned towards the central camera. "So for all of us here at 'Our Neighborhood,' we wish you a very pleasant evening."

"Cut," the technician said. "That's a wrap."

Boston, MA
October 6th

"Wolves and lambs can enjoy no meeting of the minds."
Achilles in *The Iliad*, by Homer

"That was absolutely *amazing*, Pop!" Cam said, beaming. After gathering their belongings, Wyatt and Cam relaxed in the studio's dingy dressing room for a few moments after the show's taping. "That thing went down *sooo* much better than either one of us expected," he continued.

"It sure did, son," Wyatt agreed. "But I sure felt like an idiot when Al said he had read my book, but I hadn't even thought about reading his."

Cam nodded, acknowledging his dad's faux pas. "Listen; are you about ready to blast out of this nasty ole dressing room? And for that matter, this whole studio kinda gives me the creeps."

"Yeah son, I'm ready to go. But this place isn't so bad. I've actually seen much worse."

"I hear ya," Cam said. "Anyway, are you hungry?"

"Son . . . as you gaze upon my husky physique . . . I'll ask you to utilize deductive reasoning to determine the answer to your question."

"What's that supposed to mean?"

"Of course I'm hungry, dude!"

Just then, a knock at the door interrupted them.

"C'mon in," Wyatt said.

In walked Alistair McClellan.

"Hey there, Al. I'm glad you—"

"Hello Wyatt," Al said heartily. "I just wanted to bid you a proper farewell."

"It's good to see you. I'm glad we have a moment to talk outside the interview stage."

"Hear hear!"

"Although I must say; at first I thought you were here tonight to ambush me with some of that hatred you see against Christians these days. No offense."

"None taken. Unfortunately, I think that was Jeanette's plan all along. That's one of the reasons why I wanted to stop by and chat with you for a moment. I wanted to tell you that I understand where you're coming from, my friend. And I do hope you understand my perspective, as well."

"I certainly do," Wyatt said. "By the way Al, this is my son Cam."

"It's nice to meet you, young man," Al said, extending his hand. Cam shook it heartily.

"Listen Al," Cam said. "Dad and I are fixing to go get something to eat. Would you care to join us?"

"I wish I could, Cam," Al said. "But I'm afraid I have a previous engagement with some of the fellows at the convention I'm in town for."

"I see," said Cam. "So tell me; you seem to be quite conciliatory in your non-belief in God. How are you being accepted at the convention?"

"To be honest, it's a little unpleasant at times," Al said. "Due to the fact that I'm not constantly angry at Christians, some of my colleagues do indeed give me a difficult time. They're actually quite argumentative about my moderate approach. For example, during a break this morning, I had a colleague allege that I was a *disgrace* to the atheist community."

"Really???" Wyatt asked.

"I'm afraid so. Unfortunately, I had to be verbally forceful in pointing out to him that I wasn't an atheist at all; I'm an *agnostic* who feels that it's important to have respectful dialogue with the Christian community, as well as those who follow other religions. As you well know, these *nouveau atheists*—as you so aptly refer to them as—are quite the ornery lot. They even shout me down when we're in private conversations about some of my concerns regarding Evolution."

"It's funny Al; it seems that you have to deal with radical unbelievers in the same way I have to deal with many radical so-called believers."

"In what way is that?"

"Well," Wyatt began, "just as I infer a guilty indictment of the radical positions that some of the atheists have, the same angry fervor exists among many religious people who claim to know Christ as their Savior. I actually think of them as nothing but modern-day Pharisees and Sadducees in disguise."

Al was quiet for a moment. "If we're being completely honest here, I must admit something to you . . . ."

"Oh, what's that?" Wyatt asked.

"I'm afraid there were a number of judgmental religious people in my past who inadvertently pushed me away from the faith I had in God as a lad."

"Hmmm," Wyatt mumbled. "I don't think you should feel like the *Lone Ranger* on that front. To tell you the truth, I'd rather sit in a room with a hundred polite atheists than one religious nut."

Al chuckled. "Listen," he said. "I think we have much to talk about, my friend. But to properly engage me on the subject of whether God exists, I'd like to ask you to go ahead and read my book before we begin our deliberations."

"Actually, Cam and I were just discussing that," Wyatt said. "You don't have any copies of your book handy, do you?"

"As a matter of fact I do," Al said cheerfully, pulling a copy from his shoulder satchel.

"You'll sign it for me of course . . . right?" Wyatt asked.

Al gazed at Wyatt with a professorial expression and said nothing. Instead, he pulled out a beautiful fountain pen and began signing the book.

Cam grinned, adding, "Hey Pop; I think Dr. McClellan just gave you his stock *disappointed look* he gives students when they ask him dumb questions."

Al stopped signing the book for a moment as he chuckled. "As you Americans like to say, *I'm busted.*"

After signing, Al blew lightly on the autograph page, drying the ink.

"I actually wasn't through making my deal with you Al," Wyatt said. "I'll tell you what; I'll begin reading your book tomorrow, and if you'll kindly provide me with your email, we can regularly keep in touch."

"My thoughts exactly."

"But before you go, I'd also like to recommend another book or two by one of my favorite authors. I have a few copies at home, and I'll be more than happy to mail you one . . . if you like."

"Oh . . . what books are they?" Al asked.

"Are you familiar with any of the books by Lee Strobel?"

"Yes, of course. I've heard of him."

"In particular, *The Case for Christ* and *The Case For A Creator* might be of interest to you. Lee was once a huge skeptic, but upon conducting his own, lengthy investigations, he discovered the truth in Jesus Christ. His perspective is quite valuable for many reasons; not the least of which is that he has a sincere respect for those who have genuine questions about God."

"Hmmm," Al mumbled. "I'll tell you what; I'll see if I can download those books onto my Kindle. If so, I'll be sure to check them out. At the very least, I'll treat them as research for my next book."

"Great," Wyatt said. "So you don't want me to mail you a copy to your home in the U.K.?"

"Thank you, but no," Al said. "I can download those books in a matter of seconds. Why then, should you go to all the trouble of mailing a printed copy all the way to my home in Dundee, Scotland?"

"You live in Dundee?" Wyatt asked, clearly surprised. He remembered Mick telling him the day before about one of his ancient relatives being from Dundee.

"Indeed I do," Al said. "A fine place it is; albeit a little chilly most of the year."

"A friend recently told me that our ancestry also traces back to Dundee," Wyatt said, winking at Cam. "Wouldn't it be weird if we discovered that my relatives actually knew your relatives?"

Al nodded. "It seems unlikely, but certainly possible. Anyway, let's do keep in touch via email. And if you ever do decide to hop across the pond to Scotland, please let me know. I'd be honored to be your tour guide."

Wyatt and Cam both heartily shook hands with Al, bidding him goodbye. Wyatt had a strangely odd, but overall good feeling that he'd be seeing Alistair McClellan again before too long.

As their new friend departed the dressing room, Cam said, "Are you about ready to roll, Pop?"

"I sure am. I love you son."

"I love you too, Pop."

****

After his enjoyable visit with Wyatt and Cam, Al quickly sought out Jeanette's dressing room. He needed to tend to some unfinished business with their host that night. After a studio worker directed him to the correct door, Al politely knocked. A few moments later, Jeanette yanked open the door.

"Ms. Collins . . . do you have a moment please—?"

"*What do you want???*" she shouted.

"I see no reason to be hostile," Al said. "I merely came here to—"

"You absolutely *ruined* my show tonight," Jeanette interrupted. "What kind of atheist are you anyway?!?!?"

"Madam . . . I'm not one who takes kindly to negative discourse. It's obvious that you neglected to do your research on my book, because I'm not an atheist at all. I'm more of an agnostic."

Jeanette stood in the doorway, trying to compose herself. She was still in her professional stage clothing, but smelled of liquor.

"Okay Dr. McClellan . . . or Al . . . or *whatever* you call yourself. Then tell me something; why on Earth do you have the word *atheism* in the title of your book if you're not an atheist???"

"Because *atheism* is the buzz word of choice for today's readers, Ms. Collins. The whole point of my book is *not* about radical atheism. Although I do not currently possess a belief in God, the fact is, many of today's atheists are nothing short of purely arrogant and incredibly rude. They say outrageous things to Christians in tidy-but-nasty little sound bites, and most of you in the media seem to bask in their hateful reverie."

Jeanette sighed loudly and visibly held out her hand in an attempt to regain her composure. "I see, Dr. McClellan. But don't you think you could have—"

"No," Al interrupted. "I don't think I could have made you do a proper job of vetting your guests tonight. That, by the way, is *your* job, is it not? *You're* the host of this program, are you not? It seems to me that if you had paid attention, you'd have discovered that my book is largely centered on restoring a sense of dignity to our differing opinions with Christians . . . as well as those who follow other religions."

"*How dare you* question my journalistic talents, you arrogant bas—"

"Madam—how dare *you* attempt to use profanity with me!" Al said. "I absolutely will *not* stand for it. It's not *my* fault you didn't read Mr. Hunter's book. And it's not *my* fault you neglected to at least read the synopsis of my own book on Amazon. It seems to me, you were so determined on discrediting Mr. Hunter, you absolutely lost your good senses concerning the show tonight."

Jeanette looked down at the floor for a moment. "I think we're done here."

"Indeed we are," Al said. "Good day, madam." He then turned on his heels and headed towards the studio's front exit.

****

Wyatt and Cam opened the creaky metal door to the studio's rear exit. Proceeding down several metal-grated steps into a dark alley, they discovered it was illuminated with only a single street light at the other end of the building. It was mostly pitch-black that night, with the nearly full moon playing hide-and-seek behind a thick cloud cover.

Wyatt had chosen the rear exit because it allowed them to avoid passing by Jeanette's dressing room, or speaking to any of her staff. He had no intention of speaking to that woman ever again.

"Yo Pop," Cam said. "It's kinda creepy back here. Maybe we should've gone out the front door instead."

"Nah, we'll be okay," Wyatt said. "Besides, I have a retired Marine by my side. What can possibly go wrong?"

"Don't say that, Pop. I've been in some of the worst firefights when I was least expecting it."

They quickly rounded the northeast corner of the building and headed west, towards the street. The northern alley ran parallel to I-90, slightly above them. Adjacent to the alley was a narrow dirt field, which was bordered by a successive string of large concrete barriers, now on their right-hand side. They continued towards the car.

"Yeah son, perhaps you were right about going this way," Wyatt said. "Anyway, we need to have a conference call with the others in our group tomorrow. We're simply not making any progress in finding Caleb. There's *got* to be something else we can do to find him."

Wyatt gazed up towards I-90 as the incessant *clickity-clack* of cars zipping over an expansion joint on the nation's longest interstate grabbed his attention. Suddenly, as a feeling of utter alarm swept over him, Wyatt instinctively turned and looked at Cam to see if he was okay.

"Uhhh . . . Pop . . . take a look straight ahead," Cam said, grabbing his father by the arm. Wyatt stopped in his tracks as he focused on the ghastly sight moving straight towards them, about twenty five yards away.

On point, standing in the middle of a V-formation was Damon. A taller, rather ghoulish-looking man stood directly behind the demon, but it was difficult for Wyatt and Cam to see him. At both the back-left and back-right of the formation were two men who neither Cam nor Wyatt recognized. A step closer than those two on the right was a foreign-looking man with a thick black beard.

But it was the man who was on the opposite side of black-beard which caught both Wyatt's and Cam's attention. This man was on their left, slightly behind Damon. His appearance was unmistakable in that he looked just like Wyatt. In fact, he looked identical to Wyatt.

Caleb.

The entire demonic V-formation was aimed straight at Wyatt and Cam. Both men knew this couldn't be good news. There was no time to call law enforcement for help, and there wasn't anyone in the studio who could assist them quickly enough—even if they wanted to. It was simply a matter of father and son versus a battalion of pure demonic power.

As if on cue, the dark clouds parted and a wide beam of bright moonlight illuminated the desolate arena below.

The demons moved closer.

The newfound luminescence made the attack formation appear even more formidable than it did at first glance. Although the goon behind Damon was still difficult to see, Damon appeared to be balefully cold and menacing; almost vampiric.

And then there was Caleb.

Wyatt's identical twin was much thinner than Wyatt, sporting an austere, muscular look. His scraggly goatee was several inches long. This was only the second time that Wyatt had seen Caleb's appearance; the first time was in a photo earlier that year.

The demons moved closer.

Cam stepped in front of his father, but Wyatt moved quickly back to his son's left side. Father and son looked quickly into each other's eyes. They knew a battle was upon them. No words were necessary.

Wyatt began to stare directly into his approaching brother's dark eyes as the constellation of evil closed in. Oddly enough, the first thought that popped into Wyatt's head was that this had to be the first time he and Caleb had actually eyeballed each other since they were infants. And of course, that didn't count. As far as Wyatt knew, Caleb and he had not been in each other's proximity since their early days back in their hometown of Jefferson, Georgia.

"Well hello there Damon," Cam said suddenly. "It's an absolutely *lovely* evening for a stroll, wouldn't you say?"

The demonic provocateurs were now within a few yards of Wyatt and Cam, having come to a complete stop. The two men in the back of the demonic formation visibly flinched at hearing Cam's sarcastic words. They were furious.

"Oh, I just thought it was high-time we made a proper introduction," Damon said casually. "My spiritual son Caleb wanted *sooo* much to finally meet his long-lost little brother."

In lieu of any further retorts, Cam spat noisily on the ground in the space between them.

"*That's not a very nice way to greet someone,*" Damon hissed. "My dear companions Chas and Blake are now engaged with brand new hosts since you last saw them at the Mall of America, Cameron." He pointed towards his back-left and back-right. "In particular, Chas has something he wants to *personally* discuss with you; since you assaulted him in such an unprovoked manner."

Without further preamble, Cam darted forward. Wyatt's instinct was to restrain his son, but as he followed behind Cam, he knew it was rumble time. Of that, there was no doubt.

Cam quickly surmised that when you're greatly outnumbered, the wisest thing to do was to take out the leader. If he did that, the others might lose their steam. But before he could reach Damon, the lead-demon stepped behind the strange-looking goon, who previously stood behind him.

At first glance, this didn't bother Cam. If this guy was Damon's primary henchman, he'd be glad to take him out—then pound Damon's head into the ground.

As he neared Geyotteream, the demon's foul stench fired repugnant, aromatic arrows into Cam's sense of smell; the entire area now reeked of burning sulfur. Just as Cam planted his left foot to anchor a sweeping side kick on the demon, he got a fleeting glimpse of Geyotteream's jagged, triangular teeth. This prompted an unexpected pang of primal fear, surging throughout Cam's entire soul.

While Cam engaged Geyotteream, Donovan, Chas, and Blake converged on Wyatt. Although Wyatt was able to land successive blows on both Donovan and Chas, the three demons quickly overwhelmed the author with a barrage of punches to his abdomen and face. Wyatt landed on the ground and was quickly subdued by his attackers.

In the meantime, Cam had landed numerous punches and kicks on Geyotteream. To his astounded dismay, his substantial offensive seemed to have little effect on his opponent. Cam then backed up a step, hopped to the side, and performed a spinning kick to Geyotteream's hip and kidney area.

Nothing. No effect whatsoever.

Unfortunately, it was now the demon's turn. Quickly stepping towards Cam, Geyotteream took the butt of his palm and sent a crushing, lightning-quick blow straight into his forehead. Cam took a few steps backward, dazed.

This was trouble.

By now, Chas, Blake, and Donovan had completely pinned down a defeated Wyatt Hunter. Wyatt wasn't much of a fighter, and three powerful demons on top of him was clearly an overmatch for his limited pugilistic skill set.

This was more trouble.

Geyotteream then backhanded Cam with a mighty swipe, sending him sprawling onto the ground. The legion-demon then held Cam down with the strength of six thousand demons. Regardless of what a magnificent warrior Cam was, Geyotteream's superior strength was nothing short of other-worldly. An amber slime from the demon oozed onto Cam's neck as Geyotteream pinned Cam firmly to the ground. It was as if the former Marine was nothing but an infant to the horrific demon.

Things then got quiet.

Very quiet.

The attacking force of demons turned towards Damon, awaiting his next order.

The demonic assault team's leader sauntered over towards Cam, then moved back near Wyatt. Damon truly relished this moment. Twice before, he had tried to kill Wyatt Hunter. And after his embarrassment at the hands of Cam at the Mall of America the previous February, he was now ready to revel in this savory moment of revenge.

"You humans are pretty useless when those stupid angels like Mick aren't around to defend you, huh???" Damon asked. Silence continued. "Yeah, I thought you wouldn't have much to say about that," he bragged.

I'm gonna kill you, Cam said through Geyotteream's vice-like grip on his neck.

"You idiotic humans don't get it, do you?" Damon shouted. "If you take away my current flesh-suit, then I'll simply choose another one that suits my needs. So you see; you *cannot* defeat me!"

"Lord Damon," Caleb began. He had quietly been standing off to the side, waiting for the situation to be secured. "May I now have permission to carry out Wyatt's execution?"

Damon's glare moved away from Cam and back onto Wyatt.

"Of course Grand Master. This is *your* moment of truth. Please proceed."

Caleb stepped forward and stood over Wyatt with a menacing grin adorning his gaunt face. Wyatt continued to struggle against his assailants; thus far, to no avail.

"To my little brother Wyatt . . . for years now, you have attempted to steal our family name from me, just like that foolish Jacob did in your wretched Bible. Indeed, he deceitfully stole Esau's birthright."

Being the ever-loving student of the Bible, Wyatt was surprised at how quickly his mind connected the dots about Caleb's claim. As he pondered *Genesis 25:23-27*, Wyatt knew his brother was partly correct. Caleb was indeed just like Esau in that he was marginally the first born; they were also both rugged and very much cherished by their father.

On the other hand, Wyatt was the second born of the twins, just like Jacob. Also similar to Jacob, Wyatt wasn't rugged at all. But rather, "he was content to stay home among the tents." That sure sounded like something like an author would rather do. Wyatt was also similar to Jacob in that he was beloved by his mother.

"For your many years of serving Yahweh, I am pronouncing you apostate," Caleb continued, "and I'm now here to carry out a death sentence upon you. Do you have any final words?"

"Actually I do," Wyatt said.

Cam groaned as he struggled once again to free himself from Geyotteream's control.

Wyatt continued. "In the story of Jacob and Esau, didn't Esau end up forgiving Jacob for his deceit?"

"Oh, so you *do* admit you tried to steal my birthright as the spiritual leader of our family?"

"Not exactly," Wyatt said. "And to be honest, I don't think this example is a good one for you to compare to our situation, because *God* is the One who chose Jacob. But for argument's sake, if I somehow did steal your birthright, are you going to show me forgiveness in the same way Esau did for Jacob?"

"Jacob never deserved forgiveness, you idiot!" Caleb yelled. "And unlike Esau in your silly Bible, I've not only vowed to kill you for many years now, I will indeed carry out this sentence. I absolutely will *not* bow to your pressure or your lies! I will *never* forgive you for following God instead of Satan. You have been deceived."

Is today my day to meet Jesus? Wyatt wondered. *Can it be that I'm about to be in His very presence?*

"Please listen to me Caleb. Are you afraid that you—as the elder brother—will have to serve me, the younger brother as the Bible says in the story of Jacob and Esau? If so, you have absolutely nothing to worry about. All I really want to do is to write my stories and live peacefully."

"Just as we struggled in our mother's womb together," Caleb said, ignoring Wyatt, "so it is that you and I have found our way to become two different nations here on Earth. You serve Jesus Christ and I serve Satan. I'm obviously more powerful than you, and this world will always know that it is *I* who brought fame to the Hunter family name."

"But—"

"And as for you, I suggest you prepare to die . . . ."

Caleb stepped towards Wyatt, who in turn wrestled against his demonic restrainers; once again to no avail. Damon grinned with delight. It was finally time for his enemy to die.

Caleb stood over his brother, his legs straddling each side of Wyatt. He then mumbled something in an unintelligible language as he slowly raised the nine-inch dagger into the air.

"It's all for you, master Satan," Caleb declared, then launched the dagger downward towards the location of his savory target—Wyatt's beating heart.

Boston, MA
October 6th

**"Do not forget to show hospitality to strangers,
for by so doing some people have shown
hospitality to angels without knowing it."
Hebrews 13:2**

With a flash of lightning and a crackle of thunder, an angel suddenly appeared out of thin air. Although this member of the heavenly host was seemingly unconventional—a tall, slightly husky, bald white man in a black suit and black sweater—the angel looked both serious and determined. Adding a curious wrinkle to the angel's sudden emergence from the heavenly realm was the interesting clash between two attributes of his physical appearance: his oddly indistinct eyebrows and furiously powerful demeanor.

The angel had strategically landed in the center of the current melee wielding an immense majestic sword, directly over his head, pointing towards Heaven. As brilliant pinpricks of fiery flashes surrounded the perimeter of the mighty weapon, Wyatt found himself more surprised at the angel's sudden manifestation than the dagger looming over him.

Events then seemed to move in slow motion as Caleb drove the dagger downwards, towards Wyatt's heart. Fortunately for the author, the angel's sudden appearance brought with it an immediate and pronounced distraction to the attack.

Undeterred, Caleb did indeed hit pay dirt as he drove the dagger into Wyatt's chest. Blood splattered Caleb's legs, as well as the three demons restraining Wyatt. However, the dagger missed Wyatt's heart by a wide margin. Due to his experience with previous executions, Caleb knew that he had definitely missed his mark. He quickly pulled the dagger out before preparing for another blow.

The angel quickly took action.

Instead of racing to Wyatt's rescue, the angel surprisingly moved to his left and swiftly swung his mighty sword through Geyotteream's grip on Cam. Suddenly, Cam felt the legion-demon's grip on him loosen, so he quickly pushed the smelly demon's body off of himself.

To Cam's surprise and dismay, Geyotteream's body fell to his right, while his slimy, pungent head fell to the left. He quickly surmised that the mighty angelic warrior had severed Geyotteream's head with a single stroke of his magnificent sword.

Cam quickly got to his feet.

At the sight of this, the three demons on top of Wyatt became terrified and subsequently released their grip. The entire lot of attackers then began sprinting towards the street. This included Damon and Caleb. As the departing wannabe death squad made their hasty exit, Cam darted towards the angel, who was now standing protectively over Wyatt.

But instead of pursuing the fleeing demons, the angel said to Cam, "We must immediately get him to the hospital. The dagger missed his heart, but he's still losing a lot of blood. Help me get him to your car, and I'll accompany you to the emergency room."

The angel then placed his mighty sword on the ground next to them. It quickly disappeared.

"Wait a minute," Cam said. *"I know who you are!"*

"Hello again Cam," the angel said in an even tone. "Can you grab your dad's feet? I'll pick him up by his shoulders. Let's do this quickly."

Cam obeyed the angel's command. As they swiftly shuffled towards the street, the angel and Cam could hear the sound of screeching wheels as the demonic assailants sped away in their vehicles.

"Shouldn't we chase after them?" Cam asked.

"Don't worry about that," the angel said. "We've got it covered."

"How—?"

"I'll explain it later. Let's keep moving."

They arrived a few moments later at Wyatt and Cam's vehicle, then gently laid the ailing Wyatt in the back seat. The angel then said, "I'll drive."

Cam tossed him the keys before hopping into the passenger seat. As they sped off, Cam reached his left hand into the back seat area, covering his father's wound with a jacket. Wyatt remained unconscious and was obviously in shock. At this point, the dire nature of his condition began to sink in with Cam.

As they sped eastward through the Back Bay streets of Boston, Cam looked at the angel, somewhat incredulous.

"Before I start asking questions," Cam began, "I suppose I should show some proper manners and say—*Hello Saul.*"

"Hello Cameron."

"Gosh, I haven't seen you since last February up in Salem."

"Indeed. I'm sorry to be seeing you again under such dire circumstances."

"What on Earth are you doing here?" Cam asked. "I thought you worked for those idiots at IFI. And oh-by-the-way, how did you show up out of nowhere?"

Saul grinned as he shot a quick look at Cam. He then returned his gaze to the street in front of him.

"I think you know the answer to that question," Saul said.

"Wait a minute – *you're an angel?*"

"Since we're definitely *not* in a super-hero movie," Saul chided, "what else would I be?"

"But I thought you were Sampson's assistant . . . or chauffeur . . . or butler . . . or whatever. So what's the deal?"

"I'm what you might call a *deep cover angel,*" Saul said.

"A what?"

"I'm a deep cover angel. My duties are primarily those of long-term infiltrations into evil scenarios. Of course, those around me are completely unaware that I'm one of the heavenly hosts."

"Really?" Cam asked. "Why do you go into deep cover?"

"Oftentimes, certain evil situations dictate the necessity of having one of God's representatives directly in the middle of the muck and mire. Truthfully, I'm often the first one on the scene of a situation which will ultimately be defeated by the LORD. So whenever I receive a new mission, I also know that it's actually the beginning of the end for whatever evil is taking place in that situation."

"I see. But why do you have to remain anonymous?"

"Because it would ruin all the fun if everyone around me knew who I was, wouldn't it?"

Cam shook his head. "Was that a joke or something?"

"Or something," Saul said. "Anyway, how's your father doing back there?"

Cam still had his hand over Wyatt's wound, which was bleeding heavily. Fortunately though, it didn't seem to be getting any worse. As Cam remained hopeful to get his father to the hospital in time to save his life, he also realized he still might lose his dad. The pain of this was inconceivable, so Cam's attention quickly shifted gears.

"Where are we heading?" Cam asked.

"Massachusetts General," Saul said. "We're not far away. Hang on."

When they screeched to a stop at the Emergency Room entrance, medics quickly helped Wyatt onto a stretcher and into the hospital. The E.R. doctor quickly diagnosed Wyatt's injury as serious, so she told Saul and Cam they would be rushing him directly into surgery. With that said, they were instructed to sit-tight in a nearby waiting room. The doctor advised them that she would provide an update as soon as she could. Saul and Cam then found a quiet spot in a corner, where no one else was present.

"Okay, it's time for some *real* answers," Cam demanded.

"Very well then," Saul said. "Please proceed."

"First off; how are we gonna track down Damon and the rest of those scumbags?"

"I'll get to that in a minute," Saul said. "But please; try to show a little patience, my friend. I've always failed to understand why you humans are always trying to control everything around you. Don't you realize that our heavenly Father is in charge of everything?"

"Oh, c'mon Saul—quit being so evasive."

The angel shrugged. "Alright Cam—have it your way. Here's the scoop: I'm here because Mick is currently stationed in Heaven on another assignment. That's why he had to suddenly leave you and Wyatt back in the studio tonight."

"But I thought our group was Mick's primary responsibility."

"No sir," Saul said. "Serving the Lord is every holy angel's primary responsibility. But you're correct in that the Flaming Sword group appears second on Mick's priority list; only behind serving God."

"And—?" Cam asked, impatient. "That still doesn't tell me why you're here."

"Hmmm . . . it appears that Mick hasn't informed your group about this yet. But I suppose now is as good a time as any to bring you up to date."

"Up to date with what?"

"You see," Saul continued, "Mick and I are assigned to the same basic operations group of angels. Some of those in our various groups remain in Heaven, while others—like Mick and me—we spend a lot of our time down here on Earth. As I'm sure you know by now, all angels have specialties."

"Yeah . . . go on," Cam said impatiently.

"Mick oversees our overall team as the head of The Dozen. The angels in The Dozen are basically the management group which oversees the specific duties which those of us in the related angel groups perform. So as a support group of The Dozen's missions, my assignments are typically centered on infiltrating evil human groups. In other words, when Mick's group needs an *undercover cop,* so to speak, he sends me in."

"That's interesting," Cam said. "But I'm still not getting why God needs you to do this."

"God doesn't *need* anything from *any* of us—humans *or* angels. Our loving Father merely allows us to participate in his ultimate victory over evil. This is quite an honor, you know."

Cam was quiet for a moment, taking in the angel's words. "So how does this whole thing work? You know; like how do you get your assignments and whatnot?"

"As the general in charge of God's army," Saul began, "Michael the arch-angel provides our orders from the LORD. So when God wants something done, Mick and I get together and coordinate the battle plan. This typically includes sending me into the middle of the enemy's camp. And trust me; the evil humans and demons involved never have any idea that I'm an angel . . . or their enemy . . . until, of course, it's too late for them."

"So what other evil groups have you infiltrated in the past?"

"That'll actually take a while to explain. But I will give you one example, so you can better understand my current role. Fair enough?"

"Fair enough, I suppose," Cam said, shrugging.

"Let's see . . . I spent virtually the entire campaign of World War II in Nazi Germany, in deep cover. You see; Hitler and all of his malicious henchmen—*especially Heinrich Himmler*—were unquestionably Satan-directed, occult-obsessed, Jew-hating lunatics. So both myself and many other angels were deeply involved throughout the entire prelude, during, and aftermath of the Great War."

"So like; what did you do?"

"I stayed in the background in a similar way I now do with IFI. Most notably, I did stints as a seemingly *nobody* staff member at the concentration camps. In particular, I spent a significant spell at Dachau."

"Wow," Cam said. "But I thought Mick said you guys only work in the United States. Is that true?"

"Yes, of course that's true," Saul said. "But we worked hard during WW2 in Europe because of some of your relatives."

"Really?"

"Yes, absolutely. I'm not sure how far Mick has gone into this with you guys, but the primary responsibility for our particular group throughout history has been to oversee, protect, and mentor the Hunter family. Oh, and also the Johnson family—Candace's relatives."

"I guess that doesn't surprise me," Cam said. "Dad also told me that we have Hebrew lineage in our family line; though at this point, I don't know a whole lot more than that."

"Actually, that Hebrew lineage is also true for Candace and Miss Charlene. Anyway, the important thing for you to know is that Mick, myself, and many other angels have been working with the descendants of your family for many generations now. While it's true that our efforts are currently geared towards the United States, the reason is because that's where most of you now reside."

"I see. So why are you currently stationed at IFI?" Cam asked.

"It's because they're highly mis-guided in their efforts to serve the Lord," Saul said. "Based on your interesting conversation with Sampson back in February—when you and I first met up in Salem—I think you'll quickly see what I'm saying is true."

"I think you're right—"

"You see," Saul continued, "a few years ago, the Lord knew the destinies of both IFI and those of you in the new Flaming Sword group would one day be crossing paths. So in preparation for the events which are now taking place, I was folded into the IFI group to keep an eye on them. What occurred tonight was merely one of the many things that will happen as these events play out."

"So tell me something," Cam said. "Do you have to stay on top of things or something while you're undercover at IFI?"

"Essentially yes," Saul nodded. "I'm also in place, just in case the Lord desires to call me into immediate duty. When that happens, I'm already briefed and on the spot, ready to take action . . . like tonight."

"So what happened tonight?"

"Like I said, Mick is on another assignment back in Heaven right now. Since the leaders of IFI are scouring New England looking for Caleb and his Satanist group, I was all alone at our home base over in

Vermont. So, just a short while ago, I got the call to go back to Heaven. I then briefly appeared at Bob's office at the Flaming Sword portal, just before coming back down to Earth to assist you and your father."

"So this Flaming Sword-thing is real, huh?" Cam asked.

"Indeed it is," Saul said. "It's basically the barrier between absolute perfection in Heaven and utter sinfulness on Earth. But yes, it's real."

"So who is Bob?"

"Bob is an angel who manages the portal activities. When I bounced back to Heaven and briefly saw Bob, I immediately came back down to Earth—*armed with my sword*—to take out that disgusting legion-demon named Geyotteream."

"I see," Cam said. "So what about the demon's body? What are we going to do about that? That dude was both powerful and disgusting."

"We also have that under control," Saul said.

"How so?"

"For some time now, we've been working with someone in the U.S. government who helps us out with these types of situations."

"Like cleaning up Geyotteream's torso and severed head?"

"Exactly," Saul said.

"So how does that work?"

"Cameron . . . you were a Marine, were you not?"

"What does that have to do with—?"

"It's about the power of your government. We have a special person in the FBI who helps us with the aftermath of some of these spiritual warfare battles. Basically, things like this are kept under wraps so that human lives can play out and eternal decisions made without undue influences."

"Go on," Cam encouraged.

"There's not much more to it than that," Saul said. "Our man in the FBI is always on the job. He has virtually unlimited resources, including some very dedicated contractors at his disposal. So when we need his help, we receive it. Since our friend is a completely autonomous source at the bureau, he doesn't have a lot of red-tape to deal with. Like I said, he also has some very special government approved contractors to assist him."

"I see. So when are you going to send this G-man in to clean up the mess outside the studio?"

"That's already been taken care of," Saul said. "Bob was dispatching another angel to get with our FBI friend when I descended back to Earth to help you and your father."

"Oh, okay," Cam said. "I guess that makes sense. So why did you have to kill the man who was hosting Geyotteream?"

"First and foremost, it's because I was instructed to," Saul said. "The host for Geyotteream was actually a sadistic murderer who's always evaded prosecution. I'm sure that's why Satan chose him to host one of his favorite legion-demons. That's kind of a big deal within the hierarchy of Hell."

"Don't you feel any remorse for lopping-off Geyotteream's head?"

"Not really," Saul said. "You don't think that's the first time I've been dispatched to send that demon back to wherever he came from, do you?"

"Uhmmm," Cam stammered. "To tell you the truth, I haven't really had that much time to think about it."

"If you really want to study what the Bible says about a legion-demon, I suggest reading *Mark 5:1-20.* You'll discover that although Jesus did allow the formerly demon-possessed man in that passage to live, it was so he could tell others what Jesus did for him. In tonight's situation, that wasn't going to happen."

"Alright, I get that," Cam said. "So what are we going to do about chasing after those scumbag demons and Caleb? They're not going to get away with this, are they?"

"That's also under control," Saul said. "An angel named Ben is assigned to that task. He was in town earlier today, working with Juan and JJ. Also, Ben, Moo, and Bobby flew up last night from Georgia. They were actually in the Salem area first thing this morning, checking out that old warehouse I took you to last February with IFI. Remember that?"

"Of course I do," Cam said. "That's the property that Caleb bought earlier this year. Unfortunately, we haven't been able to uncover anything further on it."

"I suggest you keep looking," Saul said.

"Anyway," Cam said. "It's interesting that when we met last February, I had no idea you were an angel who worked with Mick."

"Yeah, we don't usually tell people who we are," Saul said.

"I see. So, are Ben, Moo, and Bobby chasing after those demons?"

"They're on their way," Saul said. "Earlier this afternoon, Moo and Bobby were dispatched back down to Boston to join Ben. They were all told to wait for their next assignment here in town, which we now know is to pursue Damon and company back to their headquarters. I understand that it's not very far from here."

"I suppose I won't bother asking you how they know where Caleb and Damon are going," Cam said, thinking out loud.

"God has it under control."

"So what about Juan and JJ?" Cam asked.

"They were working with a new client named Ian Thompson this morning. By now, that's all been taken care of. Because of that, Juan and JJ were freed-up to assist the others. I believe they're already up near the enemy's hideout."

"Oh boy," Cam said. "And as for our crew following the demons; Heaven help those who run-up on Moo. With his martial arts skills, that boy is a one-man wrecking crew. He and I had a chance to spar over the summer, and let me tell you, he's not one to mess around with."

"I suspect that's precisely why he was brought up here," Saul said.

"Anyway," Cam began, "so what's next?"

"We're here, Saul," a nearby voice said.

"Hello Jimmy. Hello Ruth," Saul said. "Good to see you."

"Jimmy and Ruth???" Cam asked. "What are y'all doing here? Is this some kind of angel convention or something?"

"We're taking over for Saul," Jimmy said. "He's got to get back to his undercover work at IFI. We don't want Sampson and Ezekiel to become suspicious."

"Wait a minute," Cam said. "Saul and I are having a really good chat—and I was finally getting some answers!"

Jimmy shrugged and nodded at Saul's chair. The angel was gone. "I don't dig when you angels do that," Cam said, shaking his head.

"Nevertheless," Jimmy said. "Ruth and I are here to handle a couple of situations."

"Such as–?"

"First and foremost, Ruth has already spoken to the medical staff about your dad. We've been assured they'll keep us posted as to Wyatt's condition. Ruth is mostly here to support you, so stick close to her."

Cam nodded.

"And secondly," Jimmy continued, "we have a little bit of a situation that I'm here to personally deal with."

The angel nodded towards the entrance to the waiting room.

There, standing in an obvious daze, was the pale-faced expression of Alistair McClellan. Cam waved him over.

"Listen," Jimmy said. "I'll handle this—it's what I do."

Jimmy stepped over and intercepted a visibly shaken Al by guiding him out of the waiting room.

"Where are they going?" Cam asked Ruth.

"They're probably just going to take a little walk through the hospital and chat," Ruth said.

"How did Al know we were here?" Cam asked.

"Al witnessed the events that happened outside the studio."

"He did???"

"He sure did. Right after you and Wyatt bid him goodbye, Al had a few unkind words with the show's host, Jeanette Collins."

"I'm not surprised to hear that."

"After Al told her off, he exited via the front door of the studio."

"Oh, I see," Cam said. "Al must've heard all the commotion from the street. The attack from Damon and Caleb came from the side of the building."

"That's right," Ruth agreed.

"This must be a huge shock for him. Al must've seen the whole thing: the attacking demons; the angel Saul appearing out of nowhere with a big ole sword; the sword disappearing back to Heaven after the demon was beheaded . . . ."

Ruth nodded. "And I have a strong feeling that after Jimmy explains all of this angel and demon stuff to him, Al just may abandon his doubts about the existence of God."

Cam nodded. "I think you're probably right about that . . . ."

Heaven
October 7th

**"The heavens declare the glory of God;
the skies proclaim the work of his hands."
Psalm 19:1**

Under a radiant setting on the outskirts of New Jerusalem, Mick sat comfortably on a sturdy wooden bucket inside a huge red barn. Seated in front of him on a semi-circle of hay bales was a group of special citizens, who were carrying on a discussion with the angel regarding God's enormous universe. All of those in attendance were related to various members of both the Flaming Sword Communications and other groups working together on Earth.

Included in the audience was one of Mick's favorite citizens and dear old friend—the venerable Chung-Hee Kim. Chung-Hee was Mi-Cha and Moo's paternal grandfather, making him the father of Chin-Hwa; Mi-Cha and Moo's father.

Also in attendance were JJ's mother Francine, Cam's mother Cammie, Miss Charlene's husband Robert, three old friends of Mick named Stack, Bill, and Ronnie, and Wyatt's first dog Scout—who sat in-between Wyatt's parents Abbie and Earl. Last but not least, the audience was blessed with several relatives of Juan Montoya.

"By now, of course," Mick began, "all of you have been through both phases of your tour of Paradise. Actually, some of you did that a long time ago. Anyways, what I want to emphasize with you today is that this incredible place called Heaven is *not* our eternal home. As you should remember, you were taught in Heaven's initial orientation the important promise in *Revelation 21:1-4,* which talks about a new heaven and a new earth, and God living with His people. As of now, you're all enjoying the LORD's home in Heaven, so you already have a taste of being in His holy presence—"

"So what will this new heaven and new earth be like?" Earl interrupted.

"Let me begin to answer that question by reciting to you a passage in the book of *Psalms,*" Mick said. "Let's see, it's in *Psalm 147:4 . . . He determines the number of the stars and calls them each by name . . .* Now then; none of us really knows the entire magnitude of what the LORD will do at the end of this age. But let me assure you, it isn't a small thing by any stretch of the imagination."

"It sure doesn't sound like it is," Earl said. "When I was still on Earth, it was estimated that the number of stars in the universe was over seventy sextillion—that's a seven followed by twenty-two zeros. Based on what you just said, God knows every single star by name."

"Indeed He does," Mick agreed. "But I must say; that estimated number of seventy sextillion is actually *way* too low."

"It certainly is," Chung-Hee chimed in. "But when you add into this discussion *Psalm 8:3 . . . When I consider your heavens, the work of your fingers, the moon and the stars, which you have set in place,* it's pretty hard to see a small God. Wouldn't you say?"

"I agree Chung-Hee," Mick said. "But I'll add to what you said with the following passage . . . *Exodus 15:11 . . . Who among the gods is like you, Lord? Who is like you--majestic in holiness, awesome in glory, working wonders?* The bottom line is this: we serve an awesome God, my friends. His power is limitless. Let me point out that it's *mankind* who tries to pull the LORD down to their level so they can understand Him. Of course, that's not even close to reality."

"But I don't understand," Earl said. "When I was growing up, the religious leaders never talked about God in this great big way. It almost seems as though they worshipped a miniscule God who can't do very much at all. Am I missing something?"

"No Earl," Mick began, "you're not missing a thing. To be brutally honest, the problem on Earth throughout the ages is that religious people often make faith in God very boring. Oh, they drone on-and-on with rituals about how much they love God and all, but like I said, they often spend a lot of time trying to bring the LORD down to their tiny, human level of understanding. They say things like, *God doesn't really care about something as insignificant as which team will win the game.* But of course, God *does* care. Actually, He very much cares about every single thing—both big and seemingly small—in His vast creation. He cares about the smallest of microscopic quarks, up to the uncountable number of stars in the sky. It's all by Him and for Him. You know; we're all pretty fortunate in that we get to join the LORD in His eternal work my friends. Wouldn't you agree?"

"I absolutely agree," Chung-Hee said.

"Listen folks," Mick continued. "Essentially, the Bible is the treasure map to Heaven for all people on Earth. Those who spend their time trying to put the LORD in a neat little box in order for them to comprehend His powerful ways are really missing the whole point. Let me ask you this: which one of you would feel compelled to worship a tiny little God who was limited in scope?"

The barn remained silent.

"I thought so."

"So what's your point, Mick?" Earl asked.

"My point is this: all of your relatives and friends who are embroiled in battle on Earth right now are doing so due to their *faith.* You see; it's easy to have faith once you've seen how incredible our home in Heaven is, first-hand. But for those who show great faith in the LORD before they come to Heaven—just like all of you did—well now, that's pleasing to the LORD in a great big way."

"*Hebrews 11:6* says that it's impossible to please God without faith," Chung-Hee added.

"Absolutely," Mick said. "All of our friends on Earth who are doing battle need to keep another particular Scripture in mind as they tell the world about the wonders of knowing Jesus Christ. The passage I'm talking about is *1 Corinthians 2:9 . . . However, as it is written: 'What no eye has seen, what no ear has heard, and what no human mind has conceived'—the things God has prepared for those who love him—*"

"That's so true," Chung-Hee agreed. "I tried very hard when I was still on Earth to imagine how magnificent Heaven was. Although I did the best I could, I discovered a feeling of complete serenity here in Heaven I could just barely imagine while I was still on Earth. When I entered Heaven on that glorious day, it was as though a huge weight had been lifted off of my shoulders."

Mick nodded. "The weight that was lifted off your shoulders was your sin and rebellion against the LORD . . . ."

The angel then went quiet for a few moments, staring down at the floor of the barn. When he finally spoke, he said, "I'm sorry, my friends. I've just been called to another assignment near the Flaming Sword terminus. I'm afraid I must leave you now. Chung-Hee, would you mind taking over for me?"

"I certainly will, Mick. You go take care of what you need to handle for our LORD. I'll continue with today's curriculum."

It was indeed, another spectacular day in Heaven.

Lake Geneva, WI
October 7th

**"When you work the ground, it will no longer yield its crops
for you. You will be a restless wanderer on the earth."
Genesis 4:12**

Peter R. "Pete" Canon sat at a small table near the doorway of the
Olympic Family Restaurant in lovely Lake Geneva. Located on
Main Street in this utopian Midwestern town, Pete was certain that
the other patrons in the restaurant were oblivious to the fact that a
reformed-but-dangerous man was in their midst. As usual, Pete was
there to make sure their idyllic town remained both quiet and safe.

Although he was still in the middle of performing a not-so-covert
surveillance, Pete was enjoying the environs of this comfy joint. It
very much reminded him of the numerous diners in his home town of
Baltimore. Since it was mid-morning, most of the other patrons were
enjoying various breakfast items, from syrupy pancake dishes to savory

egg platters. Unfortunately for Pete, he had endured quite a long night back east in Boston. As a result, his appetite hungered for one thing, and one thing only—lots of coffee.

Having spent most of his forty-eight years either in the FBI or preparing for it at college, Pete had become accustomed to long hours when cases collided or overlapped with one another. Last night's and this morning's duties were a perfect example of the spontaneous, lonely, and unplanned lifestyle he lived due to the nature of his unique job.

Pete had used his opportunity late last night to catch a few zzz's on his flight from Boston to the Chicago area. With his unpredictable job duties, he actually slept whenever he had the chance. When he arrived on the outskirts of the Windy city, Pete and the local Chicago crew drove up to Lake Geneva.

Once again, and for what seemed like the gazillionth time, Pete said a prayer of thanks on how much he was blessed to travel via his privately-funded jet to investigate the various religious phenomena he was tasked with researching. Having to utilize commercial airlines for what he got involved in would undoubtedly make his job virtually intolerable.

The chore of cleaning up the mess from when Saul took down the legion-demon in Boston the previous night had been fairly routine. Pete actually didn't arrive on the scene in Boston from his home-base in northern Virginia until his local affiliates had already done the dirty work of erasing the brief battle's evidence. Although there had been ample blood on the ground, a severed head, and a headless corpse to deal with, the three-man crew which handled the situation had done their normal bang-up job. Fortunately, there were no loose ends.

At least, this time there weren't.

Pete's interesting FBI career dated back to the mid-eighties. At that time, he had just graduated from both college and the FBI's academy. It was then that a friend introduced him to an elderly, multi-billionaire philanthropist named Bill Hainey. Hainey, of course, was now deceased. But before he passed away in the early nineties, he had invested a substantial sum from his personal fortune on the Two Seals Warriors; a covert society of believers in Jesus Christ and the true message of His

Gospel. The generous funding of the Warriors was very much Hainey's gift to the world.

The Two Seals Warriors continue to operate as a clandestine network of associates who Pete works with on various paranormal religious phenomena. The network he now cooperated with is actually descended from the original members of this covert society of dedicated stewards. Pete's work with the Two Seals group represents an ongoing, completely unique relationship in U.S. history.

The cooperation between what is now the U.S. government and the Two Seals Warriors dates back to the late sixteen hundreds; around the time of the Salem Witch Trials. It was during that colonial period in America when several operatives of the Two Seals emigrated from Britain to the Massachusetts Bay colony. There, they began their work in the new world of ensuring that the ongoing battles between angels and demons who are engaged in spiritual warfare stayed out of the mainstream news and historical accounts.

The prime directive of the Two Seals has always been to remain in the shadows. This is necessary due to the fact that notoriety in the ongoing battles between good and evil is something which must never be glamorized. The reason is because God generously gives all people the ability to choose Him or not, so any undue influences must be neutralized; unless, of course, it is specifically ordained by God. As a group specifically anointed by the LORD—assisted in part by His holy angels—the Two Seals Warriors have always ensured that the covert group's prime directive is honored.

As technology has progressed at such a rapid pace during the past century or so, the ranks of the Two Seals Warriors has experienced a commensurate increase. Their division within the United States now has a network which covers all fifty states, as well as all U.S. territories. Occasionally, groups of Two Seals Warriors work together with their foreign brothers and sisters in other parts of the world.

Pete's primary duties—with the substantial assistance of the Two Seals Warriors—is to investigate extraordinary religious events, assist the angelic forces who fight against evil, and to keep the battles between angels and demons out of the public domain. To Pete's way of thinking, this last task was the critically important one. It was also the one on which he spent most of his time.

The man who originally recruited Pete into the FBI was his mentor, father-figure, and dearly departed friend, Stack Hanson. Stack was an old Cold War veteran who was the Director of Religious Anomalies for the bureau. When Pete was in his early twenties and fresh out of the academy, Stack personally recruited him by first introducing him to Bill Hainey.

Pete was honored to be drafted into this small but specialized division within the bureau. He was only 23 years old at the time, and in his new job working for Stack, Pete was able to move about the country on a private plane, just like he was Fortune 500 CEO. This, of course, was due in large part not only to the generosity of Bill Hainey, but also to his predecessors and successors.

"Can I freshen up your coffee, hon?" a waitress asked, startling Pete out of his daze.

"Sure thing ma'am," Pete said.

He once again gazed over at the man they were currently pursuing—Spiro Soubilis. Spiro sat by himself in the back of the restaurant, heartily chowing down on his breakfast.

Pete had really caught a break the night before when his office in the DC area contacted him while he was en route to Boston to oversee the battle's aftermath. By tracking an old credit card previously used by Soubilis, Pete's assistant was able to pinpoint their long-desired target as being in the Lake Geneva area. This was a huge stroke of luck.

Since Spiro's ouster as Sampson's right-hand man at IFI a few years ago, the Two Seals Warriors had been ardently pursuing Soubilis. The reason for this was because they were very much hoping to learn more about the mysterious IFI group by apprehending him. Any information they could extract concerning IFI's activities would undoubtedly be valuable to the efforts of the Two Seals and their initiatives. Although Pete truly detested the means by which IFI executed their vigilante duties, he did admire their abilities and overall efficiency. He also admired IFI's ability to remain anonymous—much like the Two Seals Warriors.

Over the years, Pete and his group had been regularly keeping tabs of IFI as best as they could. On the surface, it seemed as though IFI was carrying out God's righteous judgment on the wicked. But upon further review of the teachings of Jesus Christ in the Bible, Pete knew that vengeance belonged to the LORD; not any man, woman, or group.

The real value of apprehending Soubilis was due to his knowledge of IFI's leader Sampson, as well as the man who replaced Spiro as Sampson's right-hand man, Ezekiel. A few of Pete's duties over the past couple of decades had been to oversee the clean up of the messy aftermath of IFI's vigilante activities. Obviously, Pete was anxious to learn more about them.

The Two Seals squad leader outside the restaurant suddenly spoke into Pete's earpiece, "We've got the exits covered, sir."

Pete nodded inwardly, then folded the newspaper he had been using as a ruse. He then got up and proceeded towards the table where Soubilis was located. Since there was no one else sitting near his target, Pete sat down at Spiro's table, directly across from the dark-haired, olive-skinned Greek man who was in his mid-forties.

"Good morning Spiro," Pete said.

"Mornin', Pete," Spiro said, without looking up.

This bewildered the agent. Pete thought the element of surprise would have worked in his favor.

Spiro continued, "I suppose you're here to take me away for an interrogation, huh?"

"First and foremost, I'm here to ask you some *questions,*" Pete said.

"So what if I don't want to answer them?"

"Oh, I believe you will. Trust me, you will."

"I see."

"So . . . how do you know my name?" Pete asked.

"Do you think so little of my previous tenure at IFI that I'd be unaware of who you and the Two Seals Warriors are?"

"Wait just one min—"

"By the way," Spiro interrupted. "I know that the *Two Seals* reference doesn't have anything to do with the Navy Seals. So tell me; what does it actually stand for? I've always wondered about that."

Uh-oh, Pete thought. *This was unexpected.*

"I'll get to that later," Pete said. "Listen Spiro; I realize you're no longer a part of IFI. But what those mis-guided men are doing is *very* dangerous to the kingdom of God. They think they're serving the LORD by exterminating evil. But what they're really doing is serving Satan, unawares."

"And I suppose you think I'm too stupid to realize that?" Spiro asked pointedly. "Why do you think I left IFI, Pete???"

"I understand—"

"No you don't!!!" Spiro said, raising his voice. A couple of other patrons looked around in curiosity.

Pete held up his hands in surrender. This calmed Spiro down.

"Please—let's don't make a scene," Pete said.

Spiro sighed heavily. "I'm sure you're probably not aware of this," he said. "But those psychos at IFI executed my wife Beatrice a few years ago. So trust me; I know first-hand just how evil they are."

Due to the fact that Pete only knew sketchy details about Spiro's life, he was completely unaware of this tragedy.

"Please go on," the agent said.

Spiro's eyes were now misty. "At that point, I realized all of IFI's *missions of justice,* as they like to call them, were nothing but sanctimonious lies . . . ."

"I see," Pete said. "I agree with you. Please continue."

"They killed my wife Bea because she somehow figured out something nefarious was going on behind the scenes at IFI," Spiro continued. "Although I'm not exactly sure what she discovered about them. Anyway, when Sampson told me he had instructed Ezekiel—*my own right-hand man at the time*—to execute Bea for treason, I went absolutely nuts. You see; Sampson, in all of his self-centered arrogance, actually thought I would accept his decision to kill my wife. *Can you believe that???*"

"That is surprising, indeed."

"Anyway, after I was fortunate enough to escape from IFI, I've been very much like a wandering ronin from ancient Japan."

"What do you mean by that?" Pete asked.

"When IFI killed Bea, I knew it was murder. Pure and simple, murder. I also knew that if I didn't flee from them, I'd end up dead myself. It was then that I fully realized something absolutely terrible: when Sampson had ordered me to execute all of those criminal scumbags *in the name of Jesus* over the years, it was also murder. There's no getting around that. Anyway, since the time I left IFI, I've been on the run, trying to do a few good things as I wander from town to town. I figured that helping some folks along the way was the only way for the LORD to forgive me for what I had done."

Pete shook his head. "Don't you realize that Jesus Christ's atonement on the Cross was complete? The magnitude of what He did should be enough to bring you to your knees in awe—not wander around trying to play super hero."

"But—"

"Trust me Spiro; you'll never be able to impress the LORD with your own goodness—*or* your acts of goodness—unless you're following His commands. You see; Jesus is primarily concerned that you drop your pride and surrender your life to Him. That's first and foremost."

"I don't know," Spiro said. "Maybe you're right. I've been kinda thinking the same thing here lately."

"You know; your story almost reminds me of Cain in the book of *Genesis*," Pete said. "In *Genesis 4:16,* Scripture says . . . *So Cain went out from the Lord's presence and lived in the land of Nod, east of Eden.*"

"You may be right," Spiro said. "I really-do get the sense that I live in Cain's land of Nod, because I feel like I've been banished for my own sins. So in this apparently feeble attempt to atone for my own stupid mistakes, I wander around, doing good deeds and righting a few wrongs in these small towns I travel through, hiding from IFI."

"So that's it?" Pete asked. "Instead of eliminating evil psychopaths and general reprobates for IFI, you now wander around, trying to do good deeds?"

"Well yes. That's basically what I do. During the process, I write my own psalms, which are often poetic. I also spend quite a bit of time studying the word of God. Since my family's heritage is Greek, I like to study the ancient New Testament manuscripts, which as you know, are written in the original language of my people. The Greek language, of course, has had some changes over the last nineteen centuries, but it's not enough so that I can't relish the original writings of the Apostles."

"Did you say that you write your own *psalms?*" Pete asked.

"I write *some* psalms, not *the* Psalms," Spiro said. "They're basically my way of apologizing to the LORD. Although I never took-out one single person who wasn't already an extremely dangerous criminal, it was nevertheless wrong."

"I see. That's very interesting."

"Wanna hear some?"

"What—one of your psalms? Uhmmm, sure . . . ."

Spiro pulled out and opened a beat-up composition book that looked very much like a mad scientist had been scribbling in it.

"Here it is," he said. "This one is all about joy:

> *"Joy is not an outward expression, like happiness pretends to be,*
> *It's an inward feeling, filling your heart with glee.*
> *Joy is like a state of being, not a fleeting emotion,*
> *It's an ongoing journey; a never-ending ocean.*
> *Joy cannot come from the world, it can only come from the Lord.*
> *But the Great Liar will try to steal it,*
> *With his sorrow, deception, and sword."*

"Actually, that's not too bad," Pete said.

"Thanks, Pete."

"But tell me something, Spiro. How could an experienced man in covert ops like yourself make such a rookie mistake by utilizing a previously-known credit card? Of course, that's how we found you today. Do you really need traveling money that badly?"

Spiro grinned and nodded. *"To understand who you are, you must first understand who made you."*

"Meaning?"

"I use that expression to help others understand that if they want to have any chance at all of understanding themselves or the LORD, they *must* look at their life from God's perspective. In other words, how can anyone understand human nature if they don't truly understand who made them?"

"I'm still not—"

"C'mon Pete," Spiro said. "You're better than that! I used that credit card so you *would* find me here today."

"Hmmm," Pete mumbled.

"So as it relates to my warrior skill-set," Spiro continued, "to understand who I am, you must understand who made me."

"And that is—?"

"The Army Rangers and the CIA. Oh, and let's not forget all of my years working for a cabal of evil, secretive men like those clowns at IFI."

"I see. So just to be clear, what exactly are you telling me?"

"With today's technology, only a desperate *idiot* would have used that old credit card."

"I see," Pete said.

"Listen; I've known about your cooperation with the Two Seals Warriors since your first years in the FBI," Spiro said. "I believe knowledge and experience are the most valuable earthly commodities. So as a result, I'm always pursuing them. C'mon Pete, how do you think I've been able to evade Sampson for the past few years since I jumped ship?"

"I was actually wondering—"

"How about this?" said Spiro. "For both of our benefits, I'd like to lay all my cards on the table. Like right now. Is that okay with you?"

"Sure thing. Please go on."

"The bottom line is this: I'm absolutely *sick* of being on the run. During the past few years, all I've basically done is to help old ladies across the street and tell teenagers to stay away from drugs. Although Sampson and Ezekiel don't have the necessary experience to effectively hunt me down, I'm fed-up with cheap hotel rooms and fast food. What I really need is another purpose in my life—a more significant one."

"So Sampson and Ezekiel still want to kill you, huh?"

"*Of course they do,*" Spiro said. "Joining IFI is unquestionably a life-long commitment. Or rather; it's like joining a cult. If someone tries to leave the IFI cult, the potential threat of exposure is always eliminated."

"I see. So instead of beating around the bush, why don't you just tell me what it is you really want?"

"It's actually very simple," Spiro said. "I want to be part of a family again; one which *really* does good things for God. In other words, I want to be part of a group *unlike* IFI. Essentially, what I want to do is serve the LORD. Not my way—*God's* way. I want to be more like . . ." he paused, "I want to be *just* like the group serving in the *Two Seals Warriors*."

Pete nodded. He quickly understood that Spiro didn't give up his whereabouts to make any magnanimous statements, and he most certainly wasn't caught by surprise. He knew there was another reason.

"I see," Pete said. "So in essence, what you're really telling me is, *you want a job,* right?"

"I do," Spiro said. "And if you're kind enough to introduce me to the Two Seals leadership, I'll strongly recommend that as our first job together, we take down IFI. It's well-beyond time for someone to put a stop to the things they do. I can help us get that done."

Pete sat quietly for a moment. He knew that the Two Seals squad leader outside had been listening to the entire conversation with Spiro, via their surveillance equipment. The squad leader named Harold quickly made his recommendation.

"Do it, Pete. Don't hesitate. With Spiro's vast experience, he'll be a *huge* asset to us. After all of our research, I sincerely doubt he's toying around with or deceiving us. My gut feeling is that he's being straight-up."

"Well now," Pete began, looking directly into Spiro's eyes. "I suppose that—"

"And one more thing," Spiro continued, "While we're at it, let's also take down that nest of vipers who're running Sunagōgae Satana— the Synagogue of Satan. I've always believed that the most important mission for all true Christians is to fight against their satanic lies. I think we both know they're the *real* enemy."

After a few moments, Pete shrugged and extended his hand. "Welcome aboard, Spiro."

Boston, MA
October 7th

**"In the last days, God says,
I will pour out my Spirit on all people.
Your sons and daughters will prophesy, your young men
will see visions, your old men will dream dreams."**
Acts 2:17

Cam's mild snoring now marked the cadence of the exhausted warrior's vigil outside his father's room at Massachusetts General Hospital. For the time being, no visitors were allowed admittance to Wyatt's room due to his condition. Ruth the angel sat placidly next to Cam, casually reading a magazine. Across from Ruth and Cam sat the angel Jimmy, along with his also-sleeping companion, Alistair McClellan. Both angels had nothing remaining on their agenda for this mission, except to watch over their human clients as they caught some shuteye.

Right after Wyatt's surgery the night before, the doctor estimated that he only had about a 50-50 chance of surviving, mostly due to his substantial blood loss. Although the dagger had fortunately missed Wyatt's heart, it had certainly done some damage to several blood vessels. The doctor advised them that the next several hours would likely tell the tale. Wyatt was currently in a coma.

Cam obviously received the news of his father's grave condition and the possibility of his passing with great sadness. Wisely turning to his only solace, Cam prayed incessantly during the night for Wyatt's full recovery. He finally fell asleep, right before dawn.

Al's night had also been quite tumultuous, bordering on the surreal. One minute he was on a local-access television program, preparing to return to an atheist convention to sign books and debate his contemporaries; the next minute he was witnessing an intense battle between an angel and some demons. Then, after covertly following Cam to the hospital, another angel named Jimmy had dealt his doubts about God an emphatic and crushing defeat with their interesting walk through the hospital. Undoubtedly, this was an eventful night for Alistair McClellan as well.

Everything continued to be quiet as the angels sat-tight, with nothing else to do but wait. Jimmy and Ruth's orders were to stay in place on Earth until Wyatt's destiny was determined. Unbeknownst to Cam and Al, however, Wyatt's comatose condition in the next room began to take on a significant change.

Instead of remaining in a hazy, dreamless state during his coma, Wyatt Hunter proceeded into an experience the LORD only utilizes on occasion—a vision within a dream. As his mind slowly moved from an indistinct series of random thoughts into a lucid vision, Wyatt's mind began to materialize with him standing in front of a twelve-foot wooden door.

This is strange, Wyatt thought. Instinctively, he knocked.

"Do come in," a barely audible voice said.

The large door appeared quite sturdy, as if it was guarding an important castle. Wyatt was surprised, because he could definitely feel the slight cracks in the wooden door on his knuckles as he knocked. The metal of the ornately decorated knob also felt cold to the touch as he turned the handle, which made a pronounced *clink* as the door opened.

He proceeded inside.

Curiously enough, Wyatt was still wearing his hospital gown. As his mind continued to come into clear focus upon his entry, everything around him seemed to slowly take on more detail. He continued to gaze around the room until the voice who had invited him inside spoke again. "I'm over here, Wyatt."

Wyatt looked around a large, elegantly appointed office, which looked very much like a small library. Volumes of old books stood floor-to-ceiling around the perimeter of the room, creating a quiet and peaceful setting. Towards the middle of the room sat an ancient wooden desk, with more books stacked on top of it. On the wall directly behind the desk was one of the most beautiful, rustic, river-stone fireplaces Wyatt had ever seen. To no surprise, there was a gentle fire crackling away.

Sitting behind the desk was a man with jet-black hair and a short, nicely trimmed beard. He was dressed simply in an off-white tunic of sorts. Wyatt guessed that he must be in his early forties. The man continued to write something in a large journal, which Wyatt estimated to be about three feet long by two feet wide.

"So who are you?" Wyatt asked.

"Hello Wyatt. My name is Bob."

"I see. So where am I, Bob?"

"You, my good friend, are in the beginning phase of a vision from the LORD, delivered by His holy messengers."

"His holy what?" Wyatt asked. "Where are we, Bob?"

"Don't you remember anything that happened last night?"

Wyatt fell into deep thought for a few moments. "Yeah, I suppose I remember some of it," he said. "I remember Caleb standing over me . . . and I remember some dude with a sword appearing. After that, I don't remember much else."

"I see," Bob said. "Well, that doesn't surprise me. You see; Caleb stabbed you in the chest outside the television studio in Boston. You were actually very fortunate, because the angel with the sword arrived just in the knick of time."

"That guy with a sword was an angel?"

"He sure was."

"I see. Anyway, where again did you say I am?"

"You're actually still in the hospital, down in Boston. Like I said, instead of you experiencing a series of listless dreams, the LORD is giving you a vision, delivered by His holy angels."

"Oh I see. So you're also an angel, huh? I get it now."

"Good. By the way, can I get you anything to drink?"

Wyatt shrugged. "Well, like what? Is it possible to have a proper cup of coffee in a dream like this?"

Bob grinned. "If Yahweh can create the entire universe out of nothing by simply speaking it into existence, don't you think it'd be pretty easy for Him to give you a vision within a dream that somehow seemed real?"

"Uhhh . . . yeah . . . I suppose. But what's all this supposed to mean?"

"Wyatt my friend, let me first grab your coffee," Bob said. "We have a few things to talk about, and it may take a spell."

"That's fine with me," Wyatt said, shrugging.

Bob proceeded to an area in the corner of his office. The pouring sound of coffee into a cup made Wyatt's mouth water.

Sensing Bob's next question, Wyatt said, "I'll take it black, please."

"Very well," Bob said. He proceeded back towards Wyatt. The angel then said, "Please . . . take a seat." Bob nodded at one of the chairs directly in front of his desk.

Wyatt sat down.

Bob handed Wyatt his coffee, which was in a yellow cup on a white saucer, accompanied by a small metal sword lying on the saucer's side. The little sword was obviously for stirring the coffee. Wyatt took a sip of his heavenly nectar and was amazed at how wonderful it tasted.

Before either Bob or Wyatt could say anything, there was a sudden knock at the door, behind Bob's desk, on Wyatt's right. Wyatt had entered Bob's office from the opposite side of the room.

"C'mon in," Bob said.

To Wyatt's surprise, Mick entered the office.

"Hey there Bob," Mick said, "And hey there *dude!*" he added, nodding at Wyatt.

Wyatt was dumbfounded. "What in the world—?"

"Well Wyatt," Mick said. "It seems that our little friendship has just kicked up another notch."

"What do you mean by that?"

"Think about it. I've already seen you several times on Earth in a human-like body. But I always told you that my imperfect body on Earth was only temporary when I'm down there."

"Uh, yeah . . . I'm with you so far."

"Angels like Bob and I are also utilized by the Lord to deliver messages in dreams and visions. Last year, when we had our little chat in Pike Place Market, you remember that I delivered a vision to you from the Lord regarding Vanessa being in Heaven . . . right?"

"Of course," Wyatt said. "I'll never forget it."

"Well, today, you're in a coma in a Boston hospital. And to be perfectly honest with you, Bob and I aren't really sure if you'll be proceeding on into Heaven, or whether you'll be recovering and staying down on Earth."

"Hold on, here. Are you saying you have no idea if I'm gonna die from my wounds?"

"That's correct Wyatt," Mick said. "We really don't know that yet. Don't forget; although we're clearly different than humans, angels are also finite. As a result, we can only know the future if God tells us."

"I see."

"Anyways, we're actually here to chat with you about some stuff today. That is; until we get the word if your work on Earth is finished. If it is, of course, you'll be joining us in Heaven for eternity."

"Uhhh Mick . . . this is really weird."

"What do you mean—?"

"This entire scenario," Wyatt interrupted. "Angels appearing to me in a dream—really?"

"Why not?" Mick asked, pointedly. "Listen; I haven't had to drop this on you for quite a while, but *RYB Dude!"*

"Oh, c'mon," Wyatt said. "What now?"

"Hey Bob; can you help us out here?" Mick asked.

"Certainly," Bob said. He closed his large journal, then opened the most ornately decorated Bible that Wyatt had ever seen. "It's right here at the beginning of the New Testament," he continued. *"Matthew 1:20* says . . . *But after he had considered this, an angel of the Lord appeared to him in a dream and said, "Joseph son of David, do not be afraid to take Mary home as your wife, because what is conceived in her is from the Holy Spirit."*

"But I'm just a nobody," Wyatt objected, "and Joseph was the Lord's earthly father. Why in the world would Jesus want to send me a vision in a dream?"

"God's will reigns supreme, dude-ster," Mick said. "The more you grow in your love of the Lord, the more you'll come to realize that God is sovereign over everything in creation."

"I suppose you're right about that. But once again; why me?"

"Let me ask you a question—does it really matter *why* the Lord called Bob and I to appear to you today? Isn't it more important that you focus on what He wants you to hear—instead of trying to figure out all of His mighty ways?"

Wyatt shrugged. "Yeah, I guess that makes sense."

"So anyways—"

"By the way," Wyatt interrupted, "what's up with your outfit?"

Mick grinned. Both angels were wearing similar tunics.

"We don't exactly engage in fashion shows up here," Mick said.

"I see. So you and Bob are really speaking to me from Heaven, huh?"

"Yep. We sure are. I've actually been back here since I popped out of the studio with you and Cam last night."

"Oh, okay. Anyway, it's just kinda weird seeing you in that tunic. I'm so accustomed to seeing you in a leather jacket and jeans. It's really strange seeing you outside of your earthly, *dude-ful* ensemble."

"I get what you're saying," Mick said. "But the truth is; there's a reason why I often wear leather jackets while I'm down on Earth."

"And that is—?"

"It's an ongoing reminder that a lamb—*the Lamb of God*—had to be slain to pay for mankind's sin. In *Genesis 3:21,* God allowed the use of animal skins for clothing. Since then, the LORD's wonderful animals—which were originally intended to be mankind's helpers—have been subjected to God's curse against their will."

"So what does that have to do with you wearing a leather jacket on Earth?"

"Admittedly, it's true that as angels, Bob and I will never fully understand the salvation process that humans experience. However, all of creation was subjected to God's curse on mankind due to original sin. So as a consequence, when I'm down on Earth, the after-effects of that curse often come into play."

"Like what specifically?" Wyatt asked.

"Like animal skins being used for clothing and animals being used for food—the latter of which was the case with the angels in *Genesis 18:7.* You remember that—where the pre-incarnate Jesus had a meal with Abraham and two angels, right?"

"Oh, I see. A calf was slaughtered for that meal. Hey, not to change the subject or anything, but what's behind that door you just came through?"

"Unfortunately, what's beyond that door is not a part of your vision," Mick said. "Remember—you're still on Earth right now, and your body is still alive. Bob's office is actually located at the edge of Heaven, so you're not really here. Like we said, this is merely a way for the LORD to present us to you in a dream."

"So how exactly does this work? Did you say you're in Heaven, and I'm still on Earth?"

"How this works is actually under D—"

"Yeah, yeah, I know," Wyatt said. "It's under DP, right?"

"That's correct," Mick said. "Divine Privilege."

"So is this some kind of heavenly *virtual reality* or something?"

"In a manner of speaking, yes," Bob said. "If humans can come up with some pretty neat virtual realities on Earth, *just imagine* what the Creator of the universe can conjure up."

"I see," Wyatt said. "So I guess you guys aren't gonna tell me what's behind that door in Heaven, huh?"

Mick looked at Bob, who simply shrugged.

"I see no reason why I can't at least tell you about it," Mick said.

"Cool. So out with it."

"That door in Heaven is actually what we call the *Employee Entrance* to Bob's office. What that means is that only angels can enter that way. Now then; *theoretically speaking,* if you were actually here in Heaven and left Bob's office through that door, you would see an absolutely gigantic city at the edge of Heaven—the Flaming Sword terminus . . . ."

"Go on," Wyatt said.

"Oh, let's see . . . there are magnificent buildings . . . lots and lots of activity . . . and many angels who are stationed in the area."

"Oh yeah, like who?"

"All of the angels who perform the greeting and guiding of new citizens into Heaven, for one. Also, mission-oriented angels like me are stationed near the Flaming Sword portal."

"Why is that?"

"It's so that when we receive our missions to go down to Earth, we're able to quickly descend into battle."

"Oh. So what about Bob, here?"

Mick shook his head. "Bob is an angel who rarely leaves Heaven. He's basically responsible for what takes place here at the edge of Heaven, so I guess you could say he's sort of like the mayor of the area."

"Oh, okay," Wyatt said. "So here's an odd question—are there any animals in this area of Heaven?"

"Of course there are," Bob said. "Animals are all over the place up here. You see, animals often represent emotional markers, so to speak, in a human's life. It's sort of like when certain songs remind you of different eras of your own life. Anyway, those songs always evoke the emotions you had during those times. Well, since the LORD lovingly enjoys restoring His children's beloved pets—*because He truly loves you*—it only makes sense there would be animals throughout all of Heaven, doesn't it?"

"Of course!" Wyatt said. "That makes perfect sense."

"Remember," Bob said. "The LORD loves his animals, also. He made them on Day Six of creation—the same day He made mankind."

"I see," Wyatt said. "That's pretty cool. Actually, it's *very* cool!"

Cape Elizabeth, ME
October 7th

"With foxes we must play the fox."
Dr. Thomas Fuller

After cobbling together a countless audience of dismal gray clouds over the inauspicious battlefield below, the largely overcast day found itself lazily gazing upon the Maine coast. Standing watch under the somber skyline was the ancient Portland Head Light; a majestic old lighthouse which towered as a pure-white beacon of hope among the crashing waves of satanic evil nearby. The lighthouse was perched atop the eastern tip of Ft. Williams State Park, directly on the ocean.

Fortunately, there weren't many visitors to the old fort that morning, so it was very quiet. Juan and JJ stood at the far end of a grass and gravel parking lot, waiting patiently in the light fog for the arrival of their fellow soldiers—Moo, Bobby, and the angel named Ben. Both men leaned up against JJ's old Dodge Intrepid as they chatted.

After ushering Ian Thompson into a quality Christian rehab facility the previous afternoon, Juan and JJ's mission was to then relocate to the Portland area to begin the search for Caleb and the Satanists. Although they were originally dispatched to pick up Moo and Bobby in Salem along the way, due to Ben's subsequent instructions, their plans had changed.

After JJ and Juan arrived in the Portland area the previous day, they were forced to sit-tight and wait for their next assignment. This greatly frustrated JJ, who was known to be impatient when he wanted to get something done. However, he had no choice but to await further instructions in a nearby budget motel.

JJ finally received a call from Bobby the previous evening and was advised that Moo, Ben, and he were en route to the area. Because they weren't planning on staying in the same motel due to their late arrival, Bobby went on to say they would meet with Juan and JJ at Ft. Williams State Park in the morning, where the team would discuss their next plan of action.

"When did you say the other guys are arriving?" Juan asked JJ.

JJ took a long drag of his cigarette, then exhaled. "Should be any minute now," he said.

"I see. Tell me something JJ; when are you going to give up that stinky habit, my friend?"

JJ shook his head. "I hear you, dude. Listen; nobody knows better than me how much I need to give up smoking. I need to do it not only for the benefit of my own health, but also as an act of worship to the LORD. I have to admit though; it's not been an easy road."

"Whoa—take it easy," Juan said, holding up his hands in a halting motion. "I was just busting your chops."

"Oh, I know," JJ said. "But I also know that smoking is a terribly bad habit which brings *zero* glory to God."

"I'm with you. Hey; I actually used to smoke myself, so I very much understand where you're coming from."

"Really? You smoked?"

"Sure I did. Of course, that was before Cecelia and I got married. Yeah, that was way back in my rowdy days as a teenager."

JJ took a deep breath. In his many dealings with Juan over the past few years, this was the first time his friend had mentioned anything about his family. To JJ's bewilderment, Juan had always been evasive about the details of his life whenever it came up in conversation. Since he wanted very much to know more about Juan's family, he decided to proceed gently.

"So where is Cecelia nowadays?" JJ asked. "No offense, but you don't seem to want to talk about your family very much."

"I suppose you're right" Juan said, then went quiet for a few moments. "Well, I suppose it won't hurt to tell you a little bit about them, huh?"

"No, it won't hurt a bit. So what's up Juan? You know you can talk to me, right?"

"Of course I know that. It's just that I'm afraid my story is a rather sad one."

"I'm sorry to hear that. But why are you so hesitant?"

"Since I'm convicted that the remaining purpose in my life is to encourage others towards Christ, I don't often bring up the terrible thing that happened to my family. You see; I'm not looking for sympathy from the world. Truthfully, I'm only comforted by the promise of a joyful eternity with Jesus Christ and the ultimate reunion with my wife and children in Heaven one day."

"I see," JJ said. "Please go on."

"I really don't know how to tell you this, other than straight out."

"Please, don't hold back. I'd really like to know."

Juan sighed. "My wife and three children were murdered several years ago in a drug-cartel hit gone wrong."

JJ's mouth inadvertently fell open in surprise. His guess had been that Juan had experienced something from the garden variety of tribulations, such as Juan's wife had left him for another man. He sure wasn't expecting this.

"Wait a minute—what gang?" JJ asked. "What happened?"

"It wasn't a gang-thing; it was a professional cartel assassination. It happened several years ago in Southern California."

"Why did they go after you wife and children? I mean; were you involved with drugs or something?"

"No, of course not!" Juan said. "It's actually much simpler than that."

"So what happened???"

"I'm afraid the assigned hit-squad made a mistake. They were actually gunning for another man named Juan, who lived near us in Carson, California. Apparently, that particular cartel had a beef with this other Juan fellow, so they mistakenly eliminated my family, thinking it was the other guy's family."

JJ shook his head. "Unbelievable. So your wife and three children are really gone?"

"I'm afraid so. However, I'm very much comforted by the fact that they're all with Jesus Christ right now—at this very moment."

"Man, I have no idea how you can get up each morning and be as cheerful as you are. I mean; I love the LORD and all, but if that had happened to me, it would've shaken my world to the core."

"Truthfully, it almost killed me in many ways," Juan admitted. "But instead of blaming the LORD for what happened, I ultimately came to realize the truth about the situation."

"Oh—what truth is that?"

"I figured out that the combination of Satan's evil influence *and* prideful human sin—*those* were the culprits behind why my family was killed."

"How did you figure that out through all of your grief?"

"I realized that blaming the LORD for what happened to my wife and children was very much a worldly trap."

"What do you mean by that?"

"Blaming the LORD for what happened to my family is the same ole song that's been sung for ages now," Juan said sadly. "You know how this goes—something terrible happens, and somehow the LORD gets put on trial because of it. *Sheesh!* I've never been able to figure out why God gets blamed for the evil things that happen in this world. Why don't people put the blame where it *really* belongs—with human sin and demonic influence that coaxes people towards evil and pride? That's where the blame for a tragedy belongs."

"That makes sense to me," JJ said. "But I'm not sure most of the world sees it that way."

"I'm afraid you're right. They sure don't."

"Anyway, did you say your wife was named Cecelia?"

"That's correct."

"So what are the names of your children?"

Juan smiled broadly. "Our eldest was my son, Juan, who was only ten years old at the time. But before you ask, *no*—I didn't call him 'JJ' for *Juan Junior*—similar to why you're called 'JJ' for Jacques Junior."

JJ chuckled. "I gotcha. That was before we met, anyway."

"Now then; my middle child and our youngest were both daughters. Their names were Isabella, who was six, and Lourdes, who was only three. My little Lourdes was the absolute apple of my eye."

"Lourdes was only three, huh?" JJ asked. "What a terrible shame."

"I'm afraid so. Anyway—"

Just then, a dark blue Hyundai Santa Fe noisily turned onto the gravel parking lot and slowly began rolling towards them, crunching sounds leading the way.

"That must be them now," Juan said.

"It sure *better* be them," JJ warned.

Instinctively, JJ reached behind himself and touched the revolver cradled in the crook of his back, under his jacket.

When the SUV got close enough, JJ spotted Bobby in the driver's seat. He then relaxed. After pulling up beside them, Ben, Moo, and Bobby proceeded to exit the vehicle.

Ben grinned widely, heartily declaring, "Greetings JJ and Juan. It's good to see you again after such a short time!"

"Good morning to *you*, Ben," JJ said.

Ben shook hands with JJ and Juan before introducing Moo to both men. Bobby had already met JJ the previous February down on Martha's Vineyard, so they were familiar with each other. However, Bobby had previously not met Juan in-person, so they heartily shook hands.

Once everyone said hello, the chatter died down. JJ then looked at Ben and said, "Okay Ben, what information do you have for us? I'm chomping at the bit to get an update from you. What's going on?"

"I see," Ben said. "After our meeting with Ian yesterday down in Boston, instead of heading back to Salem, I received my instructions to stay in town."

"Yeah, I already knew that," JJ said. "I was originally supposed to pick-up Moo and Bobby in Salem before driving up this way."

"Indeed," Ben said. "But in the afternoon, after you and Juan left for Portland, I asked Moo and Bobby to meet me down in Boston."

"So how did you guys get down there?" JJ asked, looking at Bobby.

"It was really easy," Bobby said. "All we had to do was take the train from Salem down to the north station in Boston. From there, we hopped on the 'T' over to the Marriott on Long Wharf. They actually have a subway entrance right in front of the hotel."

"Why did you meet at the Marriott?" JJ asked. "That's where Juan and I first met Ian yesterday."

"I'll get to that in a moment," Ben said. "But first, I'm afraid I must inform you that our friend Wyatt was attacked last night by Caleb, Damon, and a few other demons on the west end of Boston. Currently, Wyatt is in the hospital in critical condition."

"Those scumbags attacked Wyatt last night?" JJ yelped. *"Why didn't someone tell me what was going on???"*

"Just take it easy JJ," Ben replied calmly. "Things are merely playing out as they are supposed to. Please don't forget the fact that our jobs are to be warriors for our King, Jesus Christ."

"Meaning?"

"It's very simple," Ben continued. "Jesus Christ is the only One who can decide when people are to be apprised of certain situations."

JJ shrugged. "I guess—"

"So what's our situation today?" Juan interrupted.

"Like I was saying," Ben said. "I had Bobby and Moo take the train down to the hotel, where we waited for further instructions."

"What happened next?" Juan asked.

"After Wyatt was on the way to the hospital last night," Ben began, "I was given simultaneous orders to take Bobby and Moo up to a hotel near the New Hampshire-Maine border after our business was finished. When we awoke this morning, we drove the rest of the way to meet with you here today."

JJ nodded. "I learned from Ian yesterday that Caleb's group is likely around this area."

"One of their primary meeting places is indeed very close by," Ben said. "And we'll soon mount up and go confront Caleb and those evil demons."

"So how did you discover where Caleb was?" JJ asked. "I knew from Ian telling me about a conversation he overheard that Caleb's group was in this area. How did you know exactly where it was? Did the LORD give you some heavenly wisdom or something?"

"Actually, no," Ben said. "At least not this time."

"Then how did you know?"

Ben grinned. "Let's just say that I was given divine instructions to pay a *little visit* to Ian's band manager, Chris Derwyn, last night. Soon after I greeted him, Mr. Derwyn was actually quite accommodating with telling me everything he knew about Caleb's local meeting house."

"Oh—why was he so accommodating? Did you rough him up or something?"

Ben laughed heartily. "Oh, no! Let's just say that those of us who are angels are sometimes required in certain situations to demonstrate our more . . . How shall I say this? . . . *Glorious* side."

"What do you mean by that?" JJ asked.

"It's all in the Bible my friend," Ben said. "When an angel announced the birth of Jesus to the shepherds, he showed part of his true heavenly appearance—which is reflective of the glory of the LORD Himself. Are you familiar with the Christmas story in the Gospel of *Luke?*"

"I see what you're saying," Juan added. "I used to read that passage to my children on Christmas Eve, so I know it by heart. Let's see, it's in *Luke 2:9 . . . An angel of the Lord appeared to them, and the glory of the Lord shone around them, and they were terrified.* Is that what you're alluding to Ben?"

189

Ben nodded enthusiastically. "Very nicely done, Juan!" he said. "So as you can see, angels are sometimes called-on to demonstrate our true, glorious appearance to humans. People tend to respond very strongly when we do that."

"Wait a minute Ben," JJ said. "I thought you're specialty was ministering to those with addictions."

"It is indeed."

"Then why are you doing all of this warrior-stuff?"

"Let's just say that angels are often required to be multi-taskers. When our King Jesus Christ asks us to do something, we simply do it."

"I see," JJ said. "So did you go to the hotel where Chris Derwyn was staying and scare the living daylights out of him?"

"In a manner of speaking—yes," Ben said. "Ian's band was staying over for another night at the hotel, so I paid a little visit to Chris in his room. And believe me; when I asked him where Caleb's group was located, he was initially quite rude and tried to slam the door in my face."

"What happened next?" Juan asked.

"I simply made my way inside his room. When Mr. Derwyn started cussing me out for barging inside, I showed him I was not in a mood to listen to any of his unpleasant objections. Once I flashed him my true heavenly appearance, he quickly began confessing *exactly* where the Satanist's meeting house was."

"Hmmm," JJ mumbled.

"Once I had that information, I left Chris all alone to figure out what had just happened. At that point, I gathered together Moo and Bobby, before we began driving north. And before you ask, we didn't go any further because my instruction was to only relocate for the night."

"I see," JJ said. "I guess that makes sense. So anyway, what's our plan today? Are we going to storm their headquarters and take Caleb prisoner?"

"Good question," Ben said, then turned to the others in the group. "We need to understand that our encounter today will likely bring forth the need to physically defend ourselves against demonic forces. But our primary mission is to present the Gospel to Caleb Hunter."

"Why are we bothering to do that?" Bobby asked. "Isn't this Caleb a total loser or something? I mean; he's murdered a bunch of folks, right?"

"Indeed he has," Ben said. "But as we look at Caleb from an eternal perspective, we must remember that God is in charge. It is not for humans or angels to judge someone's eternity; but rather, we must all proclaim the Gospel of Jesus Christ. Let me recite to you *2 Peter 3:9 . . . The Lord is not slow in keeping his promise, as some understand slowness. Instead he is patient with you, not wanting anyone to perish, but everyone to come to repentance.*"

"C'mon Ben," JJ moaned. "I was hoping to turn that scumbag over to the FBI. I actually work with an agent named Pete who has been looking to apprehend Caleb. Are you saying we're actually going to present the Gospel to that little dirtbag?"

"Of course we are," Ben said. "After we do that, we can get your FBI friend involved to bring Caleb to justice. But for now, our orders are to proclaim the Truth of the Gospel to him."

"Do you think he'll actually listen to us?" Moo asked.

"Over the years, I've seen many evil men turn from their wicked ways," Ben said. "But once again; our job is to present the Truth to Caleb. Beyond that, none of us—angel or human—have any say over what happens. That, of course, is God's job."

Boston, MA
October 7th

"Join with me in suffering, like a good soldier of Christ Jesus."
2 Timothy 2:3

"Tell me something guys," Wyatt said. "I'm having a good time chatting with you and all, but what are some of these things you wanted to discuss with me? If I've learned anything by now, it's that angels don't just hang out and talk with people without having a specific purpose in mind. No offense, but you guys always seem to be on the clock . . . so to speak."

Bob nodded. "I suppose Wyatt's right. We really should proceed with our agenda. Hey Mick—do you want to go ahead and get us started?"

"Sure thing Bob," Mick said. "Wyatt my friend, let's begin today with something very familiar; something we've talked about many, many times before."

"Oh, what's that?"

"Original sin in the Garden of Eden."

"Oh c'mon," Wyatt said. "Haven't we covered this enough during the past year?"

"Obviously not," Mick said coyly, and Wyatt shrugged. "Anyways, I want you to think about something. Imagine this: picture walking into a great big Toys-R-Us toy store with Danny when he was a youngster, and no one else is with you. Can you imagine how excited Danny would be? I mean, think about all of those toys and whatnot. How awesome would that be for a kid?"

"Pretty awesome I suppose."

"Anyways, I want you to also picture this store as being fully stocked with toys—absolutely filled to the brim. Are you still with me?"

"Of course."

"Now then; I want you to imagine that Danny would be completely alone in this store—no other kid would be there to possibly take any of the toys he wanted. And because he was all alone, he could pretty much take his time and *really* enjoy himself. Do you have a mental picture of this?"

"I do," Wyatt said.

"Good. Now I want you to also picture how much Danny appreciates you as his loving father. In fact, you care so much about him that you gave him this wonderful toy adventure. Not only that, but you also care enough about him to warn him about the one toy in the middle of the store that would be harmful to him if he played with it. In fact, this toy would be *extremely* harmful. Are we still good here?"

"We are."

"So," Mick continued, "there Danny is; having a good time playing with all those toys. And you, his loving father; you're as pleased as you can be at seeing him enjoy the fruit of your hard work."

"I'm afraid I know what's coming next," Wyatt chided.

"Anyways, the next thing you know, you come walking into the toy store and you see Danny acting ashamed. Of course, you know what he's done, but you ask him anyway. Your beloved son then tells you he's betrayed you by listening to your mortal enemy who had slithered into the store. You see; Danny could have resisted listening to your enemy, but he didn't. As a result, because he played with the one toy you lovingly asked him not to, you must punish him—that's the only thing a loving parent would do. Danny disobeyed you, and actually betrayed you to your enemy in the process. So he deserves to be punished for his rebellion against your goodness and generosity."

"Let's see," Wyatt said. "So in this analogy, this forbidden toy is like the tree of the knowledge of good and evil in the Garden of Eden. Therefore, I must punish Danny by banishing him from the toy store, where he'll have to struggle outside its doors in the rebellious land beyond. He must struggle to survive in this land, which is fraught with danger and death."

"You see there, Bob?" Mick began, "I told you Wyatt was a sharp cookie."

Bob nodded.

"Cute," Wyatt joked. "That's obviously a depiction of the story of mankind as told in *Genesis 2 & 3,* with a little storytelling thrown in."

"It sure is," Mick said.

"I might even be wise enough to make the application," Wyatt said with a grin. "As descendants of Adam and Eve, all humans are born with this sin nature, which is the desire to do things our own way instead of God's way."

"Right on, dude."

"So why are we covering this?" Wyatt asked. "Whenever we get together, it seems like we keep coming back to this same subject."

"It's because for you to really understand just how dreadful your sin and rebellion against the LORD is, we must keep coming back to this essential foundation."

"Yeah, but—"

Mick held up his hands. "Please bear with me, dude. You see; the tendency of human nature while you're still on Earth is to drift away from doing things God's way, and into doing things your own way. The most effective means to avoid this self-centered tendency and to stay on the LORD's path for you is to continuously *repent.* When you submit yourself to Jesus Christ on a daily basis through prayer and the reading of His Holy Word in the Bible, you greatly increase your chances of staying focused on God, not yourself."

"But I repented of my sins many years ago," Wyatt objected.

"That's not what we're talking about," Bob added. "True repentance isn't merely the moment when you repented of your sins."

"Then what is *true repentance?*" Wyatt asked.

"If you've decided to repent of any sin or sins, every step from that point forward is affected. In other words, you need to acknowledge the areas where you're easily tempted. As a result, you must continuously *turn away* or *change direction* away from your own ways, and into Christ's way. That's what true repentance is. In other words, it's not a one-time thing. But rather, it's an ongoing living process of making sure you don't drift into a sinful direction again."

"Well," Wyatt began slowly, "I hear what you're saying and all. But it seems to me that overall *repentance* often takes on a much milder definition to people than what you're saying here."

"That's true, dude," Mick said. "And that's because getting on your knees and asking Jesus for forgiveness of your sins—*although extremely important*—is much more than simply an altar call. It must also be accompanied by a significant changing of your heart, which in turn, affects every step you take from that point forward. In other words, you must also turn away from your own sinful, rebellious ways to live your life according to the LORD's way."

"Don't get me wrong here," Wyatt began, "because I'm glad you emphasized this with me. But why is this so important that you've appeared to me in a dream?"

Mick looked at Bob, then back at Wyatt. "Wyatt my friend," he said. "You probably haven't realized this yet, but your book writing is much more than just telling stories about an angel who chats with people like a regular dude and uses lots of Scripture."

"What do you mean by that?"

"The central theme in your first book—and very likely all of your future books—is not just telling stories using the theme of spiritual warfare. All of that angel and demon stuff is secondary to your main theme."

"Then what am I writing about?" Wyatt asked, confused.

"The LORD's intended central theme of your books is actually the condemnation of the never-ending furnace of destructive human self-centeredness. You see, human narcissism is the cancer of your soul, and you absolutely must combat it every single day. No matter how much you love the LORD, as long as you're still living on the fallen Earth in your cursed bodies, you'll have to combat the human tendency to put yourself at the center of the universe. And believe me; human self-centeredness is *not* simply a cancerous tumor that you can control or remove on a one-time basis. Instead, it's a rapidly spreading disease which will overtake your entire soul and spirit; that is, if you let it."

"I see," Wyatt said. "As I'm mulling this over, it does seem that since my first book, you've slowly been moving our discussions away from a simple story of a guy like me meeting an angel in Pike Place Market."

Bob nodded as Mick continued. "That was merely the original plan. God has always intended for the underlying theme of your books to be focused on the ongoing spiritual war against human self-centeredness . . . as well as demonic forces. Like I said, all people who have ever been born—with the exception of Jesus Christ—have been born with Adam's sin nature, which is a type of flawed spiritual genetics. God simply chose you to be a soldier who tells the world just how destructive it really is."

"That's very interesting," Wyatt said. "Do you have any contemporary examples of human narcissism?"

"I sure do," Mick said. "How about all of that *bucket list* nonsense?"

"*Bucket List*—as in the movie?"

"That's the one."

"What's wrong with the movie?"

"There's nothing wrong with the movie," Mick said. "It's actually pretty good. The problem is the *theme,* which centers on a prideful human wish list. Essentially, a bucket list is basically some cleverly disguised human narcissism."

"How did you arrive at that conclusion?"

"Think about it. The whole idea of a bucket list is that people now dream up all the stuff they want to do before they die. At first, it sounds pretty cool. But you need to remember this: *all* human self-centeredness sounds absolutely wonderful to the human spirit and soul. But what sounds good to the human spirit and soul is often utterly offensive to the spirit of the LORD."

"Why is that?"

"Because it focuses your attention on yourself; often to the exclusion of the LORD's plans for you. To tell you the truth, the idea of a bucket list is nothing but a covert trick of . . . *wait for it* . . . the devil."

"Ahh, I see. So you *really* don't like the idea of a bucket list, huh?"

"Actually, in a way, I do," Mick said.

"How so?"

"Don't you realize the LORD already has an *eternal* bucket list for you? In the case of a true Christian, God's bucket list covers not only what you'll do on Earth, but also what you'll do for eternity when you arrive in Heaven . . . and ultimately on the new Earth."

"Oh c'mon Mick," Wyatt said. "Don't you think you're being a tad *holier than thou?*" he challenged. "Having a bucket list seems pretty benign to me."

Mick had a disappointed look pass over his face. "Hang on there, Wyatt. Being *holier than thou* is for religious fools. I'm an angel of the Most-High God, so religion is something I've never been interested in. In fact, most of what I do centers on guiding people *away* from religion and *towards* Jesus Christ."

"Listen, I'm sorry if—"

"Over the course of our long relationship," Mick interrupted, "you should know better than that. I'm only interested in telling you the Truth so you can share it with others through your writing."

"I see."

"And one more thing," Mick continued, "if anyone is interested in what a real bucket list is—*God's bucket list for you*—they should check out *Ephesians 2:8-10.* You see; God has already designed good works for each of His children. I'm afraid that all other so-called bucket lists are centered on worldly pleasures."

Wyatt sat quietly for a few moments. "What did you mean by our *long relationship,* Mick? I've only known you for about a year."

Mick looked over at Bob, who simply nodded once again.

"Wyatt my friend, I've actually known you for a lot longer than the past year."

"What are you talking about? I don't rememb—"

"Allow me to give you a little history," Mick said. "I actually went to see your mother Miss Abbie; right after your father Earl fled with Caleb and left her all alone with you."

"Oh I see," Wyatt said. "So am I finally going to get some answers about your relationship with my family? If so, I've been waiting on this for a *loooong* time."

"Yes indeed Wyatt, now is finally the time."

Cape Elizabeth, ME
October 7th

**"You cannot drink the cup of the Lord and the
cup of demons too; you cannot have a part in both
the Lord's table and the table of demons."
1 Corinthians 10:21**

Making their way through thick vegetation while skirting various property lines along the rocky coast, Ben and the others carefully made their way from the park to the outskirts of the Pritchard estate. During their relatively short trek, the fog had noticeably thickened; summoning the appearance of a walk through the shadow of death.

Moo and Juan opted not to carry any weapons for their confrontation with Caleb. On the other hand, Bobby and JJ decided to carry firearms, just in case they needed them. All of the human warriors knew their job was to primarily present the Gospel to Caleb, regardless of his response.

They were also prepared to arrange for his arrest. But just in case, JJ and Bobby were prepared for the worst.

As they crested a small, tree-lined promontory directly north of the Pritchard house, Ben held up his hand in a halting motion. The beautiful house was now in clear view, not far away. Interestingly, by this time, the fog around the house had somewhat subsided.

"Before we make our entrance," Ben began, "we need to observe the comings-and-goings of the house for a short while."

"That'll work for me," JJ said, reaching for the pack of smokes in his jacket pocket.

Ben proceeded to stand watch for the group, intently gazing at the Pritchard house. In the meantime, Moo and JJ found large rocks to rest on. Bobby and Juan then plopped down across from them on a fallen tree.

"So, Moo," JJ began, taking a drag from his cigarette. "I understand that you're well-versed in the area of self-defense. Did I hear correctly?"

Moo shrugged. "Yeah, I suppose that's a fair statement. I'll admit that I can handle myself pretty well."

"That's good to know," JJ said. "You never know what these demonic scumbags will try next. Let's not forget the fact that they tried to kill Wyatt last night."

"I understand," Moo said. "I know we've got to be careful this morning. But tell me something, JJ. From our emailing back and forth, I got the impression that you're against violence. Am I right?"

"Actually, I am. But there's a big difference between being prepared for a potential attack, and seeking revenge through violence."

"That makes sense," Moo said. "Of course, Mick has told us over-and-over that our jobs are to use the Word of God as our primary weapon."

"I certainly agree with that," JJ said. "If I didn't feel that way, I'm sure I wouldn't be involved with you guys at Flaming Sword."

"Good point."

"However," JJ continued, "I also believe in being prepared to defend myself against the demonic forces of evil. While I'm definitely against being a vigilante and killing others who *are* evil, I also know that I'm at risk when confronting evil and/or demon-possessed people. So basically, I believe in being prepared."

"No problem," Moo said. "So Juan," he continued, "what's your story, my friend?"

"I'm just an old, over-the-road truck driver," Juan said. "It's a difficult job that's often under-appreciated and sometimes dangerous, but I still enjoy the freedom of driving all over the country. It actually gives me a chance to spread the word of God through the many people who I meet out on the road; especially at lonely truck stops."

"So what's the story with your family lineage?" Moo asked. "Where are they originally from?"

"As you know," Juan began, "Christians are spread all over this world. For me; my family heritage goes all the way back to fifteenth century Spain. At least, that's as far as I've been able to trace it so far."

"Really?" Moo asked. "That's pretty cool. Have you done much research on your family beyond how far back they go?"

"I certainly have. First off, I think we all know that the United States is a melting pot of many, many nations from all over the world. It almost seems like the Lord planned it that way on purpose."

"I agree with that," Moo said.

"And I also know that your Korean heritage is one that's rich with dedication to Christ," Juan added. "In fact, Korea is one of the top countries in the world for sending out missionaries, is it not?"

"That's my understanding," Moo agreed. "I'm proud of that."

"As well you should be," Juan said.

"So Juan; what's your family's story as it relates to Spain? What have you discovered? Anything interesting?"

"Actually, I discovered something very unexpected," Juan said. "My ancestors were affluent Jews. That is; until the Spanish Expulsion in 1492."

"Really?" Moo asked. "I just saw a history program about the Spanish Expulsion not too long ago. If I remember right, the Jews were persecuted and thrown out of Spain about the same time Columbus was commissioned to sail towards the new world."

"That's right," Juan said. "My family left Spain and emigrated to Portugal. Later on, they became Christians. Of course, the Spanish Expulsion is a very sensitive subject for the Jewish community."

"It sure is," Moo said.

Juan nodded. "But I also know that Jesus Christ came to free the entire world from the shackles of sin—for both Jew and Gentile. *Galatians 3:28* says . . . *There is neither Jew nor Gentile, neither slave nor free, nor is there male and female, for you are all one in Christ Jesus.*"

"Amen to that," JJ added. "Hey Ben; is there anything going on over there?"

"Not yet. It appears very quiet."

"That's what worries me," JJ bemoaned.

"Worry-not my friend," Ben said. "We have the power of Jesus Christ empowering our mission. Therefore, we *ultimately* cannot lose. Only those who reject God's powerful message will end-up losing."

"Of course, you're right," JJ said. "But I still like being armed."

"Ahh," Ben exclaimed. "Let me remind you of a passage from King David. *1 Samuel 17:45* says . . . *David said to the Philistine, 'You come against me with sword and spear and javelin, but I come against you in the name of the Lord Almighty, the God of the armies of Israel, whom you have defied.'*"

"So what're you saying?" JJ asked.

"I'm saying you should never share the Gospel with your physical weapons in the forefront. You must use the *word of God* against your enemies, and only use force if you're defending yourself or the life of another person."

"I think we all know that," JJ said.

"But I must remind you once again of our mission," Ben said. "Trust me; I've been leading God's children into battle for quite some time now."

"That's a big 10-4," Bobby added. "We hear you, Ben."

"Thank you, Bobby. As God's image-bearing children, you must always remember that if you want to honor the LORD, you cannot do things Satan's way of the world—you must do things God's way. In the end, for all people, it's either God's way, or Satan's way."

"Amen brother," JJ added.

"Anyway," Ben said. "With that in mind, it's time for us to make our move towards the house. As you humans like to say, *it's time to rock and roll!*"

Boston, MA
October 7th

**"He had a dream in which he saw a stairway resting
on the earth, with its top reaching to heaven, and the
angels of God were ascending and descending on it."**
Genesis 28:12

"So what exactly do you have to tell me?" Wyatt asked Mick. "No offense, but you always seem to be feeding me information in small doses. When we first met last year, I found that to be a little frustrating. But now—since I'm on the verge of death and all—am I finally gonna get the big picture about my family's history?"

"What can I say?" Mick said, shrugging. "As a loyal messenger of the LORD, I can only give you information as He instructs me to. And believe me; God knows exactly what you need to know—*when* you need to know it. It's not like I'm trying to be a great big *dud* by holding out on you."

Wyatt chuckled. "I see. Anyway, what say-you about my family?"

"Let me start off by elaborating on what I just mentioned concerning your mother Abbie. Like I was saying, I first called on your mom right after your father fled with Caleb to Massachusetts."

"Why did you go see her then? I mean; I'm sure she needed some emotional counseling and all, but why my mother Abbie? She was really just an ole country gal who went through a difficult time . . . wasn't she?"

"Actually, no. Abbie was much more than that. To tell you the truth, God has a specific purpose for *everyone* in His kingdom—whether they realize it or not. The problem is; too many people don't pay close enough attention to what God calls them to do. In this case, Abbie definitely answered God's call to service."

"That's cool."

"On the other hand, your father Earl was the one who was committed to serving his own ego and pride. That's why he took Caleb away from you and your mother. Of course, he had a little help from a lying *serpent* named Damon."

"I see," Wyatt said. "More *Genesis 3* references . . . as if I haven't heard enough of those already."

"Whatever dude. Anyways, Abbie was an incredibly loyal servant who spent the rest of her life serving the LORD; that is, after I visited her way back in the summer of 1967 . . . while you were still in diapers . . . ."

"Gosh Mick, you're on a roll. Please don't stop now."

Mick grinned. "We actually started Abbie off pretty slowly. Her first mission was simply focused—to raise you as best as she could in a Christian home, with only the modest income she received from Earl. Of course, this wasn't always easy on Abbie. However, she mentored your spiritual growth and did a great job of guiding you towards the LORD."

"You know," Wyatt began, "I always wondered why mom didn't ever get remarried. To be honest, it always seemed rather odd to me."

Mick nodded. "First off, Abbie never stopped loving her husband. It wasn't her fault that Earl was so full of self-aggrandizing pride that he listened to Damon and his lies. After your dad left with Caleb, I had a long visit with her at your old family home in Jefferson, Georgia."

"Wait a minute," Wyatt said, surprised. "Now that I'm thinking about it, did I meet you back then? How old was I?"

"It was right around the time of your first birthday," Mick said. "And yes, we did meet . . . sort of."

"What do you mean by, *sort of?*"

"Think about it dude," Mick began, "you were only a toddler. Ergo, you were much more concerned about your own poopy diaper than who the pony-tailed stranger in your living room was."

"Oh," Wyatt said chuckling. "I didn't think about that."

"Anyways," Mick continued, "after you graduated from high school, Abbie moved from your home in Jefferson, back to her home town of Jacksonville, Florida."

"She sure did. You know something? I never really understood why. That is; until I met Cam last February."

Mick nodded again. "At that time, since you had not yet met Cammie, you were obviously unable to introduce her to your mom."

"True."

"Abbie's job was to befriend Cammie while she was still pregnant with Cam. This, of course, happened after you and Cammie broke up, and Cammie had also moved to Jacksonville. Anyways, Abbie's job was to help Cammie; sort of like a spiritual guardian. What's funny is that Cam still remembers some of his times with your mom when he was little."

"That's right," Wyatt said. "I remember when we talked about this back in February at our meetings at the Mall of America."

"Correctamundo," Mick said. "But the truth is, even though Cammie was later advised that Abbie was actually your mother, she never knew your mom was being directed by an angel. That's me, of course."

"So Cammie thought it was all some kind of coincidence, huh?"

"Yep. She sure did."

"I see. So looking at the big picture, are you telling me that after I started attending college at UGA, my mom went on a mission to

Jacksonville to *later* serve as some sort of guardian or overseer for my soon-to-be pregnant ex-girlfriend Cammie?"

"That's correct. After you became an adult, Abbie dedicated herself to whatever new missions the LORD had in mind for her. In this case, she ended up moving into an apartment next to Cammie's mother. A couple of years later, Cammie moved back home. She soon thereafter gave birth to your son Cam. However, your mom was instructed to not reveal why she was really there. Like I said, it was all an allegedly *big coincidence.*"

"I see. You know; this is whole thing is kinda weird."

Mick shrugged. "I've told you on many occasions that there's no such thing as a coincidence in the kingdom of God."

"I suppose that's true."

"Anyways, after Cammie was murdered by Caleb when Cam was but a wee-lad, Abbie was instructed to cease all communication with Cam."

"Why? Doesn't that seem kind of cruel?"

Mick looked at Bob. They both shook their heads.

"Listen Wyatt," Mick said. "You ought to know by now that none of us knows all of the LORD's reasons for why things happen. You just have to trust Jesus on things like that."

"What does all of this mean as it relates to Cam?"

"Psalm 119:71 says . . . *It was good for me to be afflicted so that I might learn your decrees."*

"Oh. Are you saying it was *good* that mom stopped overseeing Cam after Cammie was killed? He ended up spending time in foster homes, you know."

"Of course I know that," Mick said, shaking his head once again. "But when are you going to learn that God's reasons for these things happening aren't always understandable—or even discernable—by *any* of us?"

"Hmmm," Wyatt mumbled. "Anyway, Cam's situation almost sounds like it was some kind of spiritual calisthenics."

"I suppose it was," Mick agreed. "His youthful tribulations were actually a big reason why he's become the strong person he is today."

"I see what you're saying. In the end, Cam ended up being okay, despite the difficulties in his growing up."

"He sure did."

"I hear you Mick. But c'mon; I sure wish I'd have known of my other son down in Jacksonville all those years. It sure would've been nice if mom had told me about him."

"You know she couldn't do that," Mick said. "Her instructions from the LORD were quite clear to not disclose anything to you. That wasn't an easy thing on her behalf either, you know."

"Yeah, I suppose you're right. Well anyway . . . no matter what, Cam turned out to be a good kid. In fact, he turned out to be an *awesome* young man."

"Look, Wyatt. Neither Bob nor I know why Abbie wasn't permitted to help Cam when his mom died—that's under Divine Privilege."

"There you go with that DP stuff again."

"*But of course,*" Mick said. "In the end, God always had a plan to bring you and Cam together; on His time—not yours."

"And I suppose you're right about that last Scripture on affliction," Wyatt continued. "You know; the idea behind that passage may be the biggest irony in a human's life."

"What's that?"

"*Proverbs 27:17* says, *As iron sharpens iron, so one person sharpens another.* In my opinion, our tribulations can be used in a similar way to make us stronger. Not to use a bad pun, but to me it's *ironic* that we-humans must go through so many difficulties in our lives to become closer to Jesus."

Mick shook his head. "Don't you mean, *to be just like Jesus???*"

"I suppose you're right."

"Don't forget that Jesus Christ doesn't ask His children to go through anything that He-Himself didn't go through. That's an incredibly important thing to remember. You suffer just like He suffered. Ultimately, Jesus overcame pain, suffering, and death, just like you will when you die."

"Speaking of me dying," Wyatt said. "Do we have any word about that yet?"

"No, not yet," Bob added. "We're still in a holding pattern."

"I see," Wyatt said. "It's pretty weird, but I really don't feel any apprehension about possibly dying."

"As well you shouldn't," Mick said.

"So tell me something," Wyatt continued, "I get the fact that over the years, unbeknownst to me, you gave my mom missions to serve the Lord. But why do you keep coming down to Earth to see me? It seems like you're always—"

"It seems like I'm always going back-and-forth from Heaven to Earth, just like Jacob saw in a dream???" Mick asked pointedly.

"I never thought about that."

"The reason I do this is because your family has always been on the undercard of the major events happening in God's kingdom. As a result, I stay pretty busy."

"What exactly do you mean by, *undercard?*"

"Like I told you before," Mick said. "You fellas in the Tsayid-Hunter family have been around since early biblical times. But unlike Jacob—who was later named *Israel* by God Himself—your ancestors weren't in many of history's headlines. God actually chose your family to be involved in many historical events, but rarely in the spotlight."

"That's pretty cool. As you know, I do love history."

"Listen dude; just wait until you see the historical shows we have at the magnificent theaters here in Heaven. It'll absolutely blow your mind. Oh, and you'll also love the numerous markets here in Heaven. They're very enjoyable to take a little walk through."

"For real?"

"Absolutely," Mick said. "But getting back to the historical shows; unlike the incomplete accounting of historical events you're accustomed to hearing about on Earth, God's recounting of history is absolutely *complete*—with both the headline-makers *and* those who weren't."

"I see. So getting back to Jacob . . . my foolish brother Caleb was actually rambling-on about Jacob and Esau; that is, right before he stabbed me."

"That's because he knows the Bible better than most Christians," Mick said. "Followers of the Evil One are actually required to study the

Bible. Anyway, it's unfortunate for Satan's followers, but they already know how the story on Earth ends."

"Then why do they keep fighting against God?"

"It's because they're under Satan's evil influence, which is to do things their own way, not God's way. To be honest, when people and demons do that, they really don't think too much about the fact that the Bible has already condemned them due to their rebellion."

"So what about the Jacob and Esau thing?"

"First off; we know that Jacob was the father of the twelve tribes of Israel. Of course, that was a pretty significant calling."

"It certainly was."

Mick sighed. "Wyatt my friend, since we haven't heard if you'll recover and stay on Earth or not, what I'm about to tell you is only a small part of an evil grand scheme that Caleb is involved in. So if you end up staying on Earth, you'll probably only be permitted to allude to this story in one of your upcoming novels."

"What are you talking about?" Wyatt asked.

"Caleb tried to kill you because he's had an evil idea drilled into his head since he was in diapers. You see; Damon took your brother away from his godly mother with the help of your father Earl; all in an attempt to set-up Caleb to become the father of a nation of disciples of Satan. That's why Caleb droned-on about the Jacob and Esau story."

"I'm still not with you."

"Let me see if I can help," Bob chimed in, and Mick nodded. "You see, Wyatt, Caleb has it stuck in his head that unlike Esau in the Bible, he'll absolutely *not* allow you to steal what he believes to be his birthright to be the father of a growing nation of Satan . . . the *Synagogue of Satan.*"

"The Synagogue of Satan? I know that's written in *Revelation* somewhere. But what's Caleb so worried about?"

"You're absolutely right," Bob said. "*Revelation 2:9* and *Revelation 3:9* make mention of this evil *synagogue,* which will attempt to replace the worship of God during the end-times in Israel and beyond. But in order for there to be a worldwide religion, it follows that there *must* be actual human beings—essentially high priests—who will lead and promote the worship of Satan. In other words, this religion will be of the Antichrist."

"I've always been confused with what those passages mean," Wyatt said. "But what I really don't get is this: why does Caleb feel like I'm a threat to him?"

Mick looked seriously into Wyatt's eyes and said, "It's because Damon has always told Caleb that you would try to steal his birthright to be the father of this future group of loyal Satanists—just like he thinks that Jacob stole Esau's birthright to be the father of Israel. Of course, they're forgetting the fact that *God* is the One who ordained Jacob, not Esau. Anyway, Caleb is simply trying to eliminate his misperceived competition."

"Wait a minute," Wyatt said. "To be a father of that magnitude, don't you have to sire many children?"

Bob and Mick looked at each other and nodded.

"Now you've hit the nail on the head, Wyatt," Mick said.

"What do you mean by that?"

"I suppose there's no easy way to tell you this, but over the years, Damon and his henchmen have provided for Caleb a twisted network of several hundred women to impregnate. Their overall intent has been to have them birth a huge army of useful human lackeys—*like Caleb*—who are willing to serve Satan, *without* the need for them to be demon possessed. In essence, this will allow the demons to grow their army organically; it will also free-up the existing army of demons to do their evil work elsewhere."

"But—"

"Hang on," Mick continued. "A few of these impregnated women are actually Caleb's wives and concubines. Unfortunately, however, most of them are essentially treated as human slaves. Now then; these women are usually discarded—*in other words killed*—later on, after they give birth, and after their child is a little older. Even worse is that these selected women are literally located all over the face of this planet, and in virtually every nation. And trust me when I tell you this; Caleb has been a *busy little bee* with getting all of these women pregnant, thereby cranking out future soldiers."

"What kind of women did you say are being chosen?" Wyatt asked, perplexed. "I'm not quite getting it."

Mick sighed. "They generally select destitute women who have no money. The demons then lie to them by claiming they'll take care of the woman financially, once the child reaches a certain age. They tell them it's kind of like a bonus. These women get to live fairly comfortably while the child is growing up, so their suspicions are few. Anyway, a demon possessed nanny is always assigned to watch over each child, even while the mother is still alive. Once the mother is out of the picture, the nanny essentially becomes the surrogate mother. Believe me; it's a horrendously evil situation."

"Get outta here!" Wyatt bemoaned. "I must be on morphine in my hospital bed. Did you angels just tell me that my evil twin brother is spawning an army of future soldiers for Satan; most of it through female human slaves???"

Bob shrugged. "As odd as it may sound, yes. That's an accurate synopsis."

"You guys are nuts!" Wyatt said. "Do you mean to tell me that all of this stuff has been going on for all of these years, and I was completely oblivious to it?"

"Yes indeed," Mick said. "Your father began to figure out Caleb's plans before he died; although he wasn't completely sure. Of course, nowadays, Earl is in Heaven with the LORD . . . as well as Miss Abbie."

"Well . . . not to digress . . . but are mom and dad back together in Heaven?"

"Yep. They're back together in the *children of Christ* sense," Mick said. "But of course, they're not husband and wife. Those were merely their temporary earthly roles. Relationships in Heaven aren't limited like that. In fact, heavenly relationships are actually much deeper and involve a much more pure version of love."

"C'mon guys," Wyatt said "What am I supposed to be doing about all of this?"

"Nothing yet," Bob said. "If you do indeed remain on Earth, you're going to be moving into the background in order for your sons Danny and Cam can take over. Your grandchildren are actually the ones who'll be playing the most pivotal roles later on."

"Great," Wyatt said. "The Hunter family tradition will be centered on my sons and grandsons chasing around Caleb and his evil offspring. That's sounds just wonderful."

"Don't be such a nitwit," Mick said. "It's an incredible honor to be asked to serve the LORD during such treacherous times. Danny, Cam, and their sons will continue to serve God; as have most of the men of the Hunter family throughout the ages."

After a few moments, Wyatt said, "Wait a minute. What about my Uncle Billy and Cousin Frank? They're also named Hunter."

Mick nodded. "Billy, of course, is your dad's younger brother, and Frank is his only son—your cousin. I hate to be the one telling you this Wyatt, but Frank has been involved in the Hunter *family missions,* so to speak, for quite some time now. Although I must say, Frank is pretty much a specialist—"

"Isn't Uncle Billy too old to be chasing around demons?"

"Nowadays, Billy is semi-retired," Mick said. "And Frank Hunter is now leading that particular part of the family responsibilities."

"Unbelievable," Wyatt said, then trailed off. After a few moments, he looked at Mick and said, "By the way, why didn't you tell me that Alistair McClellan was not one of those hateful nouveau atheists? He was quite level-headed, you know. Actually, I got the feeling that he and I will become friends. That is; if I remain on Earth."

"Wyatt my friend, with all due respect, you're being a real *knucklehead.* Listen to me; I was sent to prepare you the other day so that you'd be ready to deal with Jeanette Collins—the show's host. *She's* the one who's the real God-hater, not Al. I never said that Al was the enemy, because I knew he wasn't. And oh-by-the-way, Al has now been called into kingdom service, so he's not even an agnostic anymore. In fact, he's outside your hospital room with Cam right now, praying that you'll survive."

"Really? I must admit; I was pleasantly surprised when Al was so level-headed about the debate Jeanette was trying to draw us into."

"You and Al's family actually go *way* back," Mick said. "But that's a story for another day. I will, however, say that if you get a chance to go see Al in his home-town of Dundee, Scotland, you need to do so. There's a lot of cool history for you to discover there."

"I see," Wyatt said. "So what other little gems do you want to reveal to me today? I mean; I'm still a captive audience and all."

"Well let's see," Mick mumbled. "I've popped-in and visited you many, many times since I first saw you in Abbie's arms in 1967. Of course, before now, you were under the mistaken impression that our first encounter was a year ago at Pike Place Market."

"I sure was. That was our first official visit, but I was completely unaware that we had seen each other before."

"Throughout the years," Mick continued, "I've actually made numerous cameo appearances in your life. To me, it was kind of funny, because each time, you had no idea what was going on."

"Yeah, yeah, whatever," Wyatt bemoaned. "Anyway, can you give me an example?"

"Sure. There was the one time I was a cook at a diner-style restaurant when you, Danny, and Vanessa stopped there on your way home, after a show. Another time, I actually sat behind you at a football game at Sanford Stadium in Athens, Georgia. But of course, you weren't paying me any attention."

"For real? You sat near me at a Dawgs game?"

"Yep. That was back when you were still dating Cammie."

"Wow," Wyatt said, whistling.

"But I must say; my saddest encounter with you was when I was overlooking the accident scene when Vanessa was killed by Damon. There I stood, watching your life change forever. Back then, I knew for sure I'd be seeing you again. But at the time, I just didn't know when."

"That's weird. So you were at the accident scene, huh?"

"I certainly was," Mick said.

"Why?"

"I was there to guide one of our friends named Pete to get Bobby and Hank out of the way. As you now know, Damon had departed

Hank after the wreck, and we didn't want Bobby to get caught-up in the situation."

"Gosh, I sure wish you could have visited me that night. I'm sure it would've helped."

"Me too dude," Mick said. "Oh, and I almost forgot to tell you this one, little tidbit: do you remember when we had breakfast at The Athenian restaurant in Pike Place Market when we had our first official visit in Seattle last year?"

"Of course I do."

"Do you remember our waitress named Ruth?"

Wyatt fell into deep thought for a few moments.

"Wait a minute!" he said, suddenly excited. "Was she the same Ruth—*the angel*—who joined our meetings at the Mall of America a few months later in February?"

Mick nodded. "Yep."

"Wow. So our waitress that day in Seattle was also an angel!"

"But that's not all," Mick said. "When you first walked into the Seattle's Best café that morning, Jimmy and Ruth were sitting at that table, across from the register. Of course, I was sitting at the red-tiled counter, waiting to lay some of my angelic wisdom on you."

"I remember them being there now," Wyatt said. "They actually left the café, right before you and I started chatting."

"Indeed," Mick said. "Let me also tell you that one of our baristas that morning was named Sally. So guess what? Sally is also an angel, but she actually works for another angel group."

"Oh—what group is that?"

"She works for a deep cover group who specialize in ministering to the homeless," Mick said. "And Seattle has plenty of those folks."

"Good LORD! You angels must have been surrounding me all of my life . . . or so it seems."

"We actually have been, Wyatt," Mick said. "We have indeed."

Cape Elizabeth, ME
October 7th

"Every soul a battlefield . . ."
Rush
the song, "Cygnus X-1 Book 2"

A cacophony of crashing waves greeted the five warriors as they carefully marched along the rocky coastline. Without delay, they made their way from the surveillance spot north of the Pritchard house to the northeast tip of the property. The boisterous sea combined with the intermittent fog provided a nice cover for the group, giving them both a sight and sound advantage. Although Ben continued to lead the way for the others, his demeanor had now shifted from jovial and engaging, to one which was fiercely focused on the mission at hand.

After the group made their way over a huge, tilted flat rock, Ben held up his hand, halting the others. They were in single file by now, with Moo directly behind Ben, followed by Bobby, Juan, and finally, JJ.

Because they were currently below the horizon level of the house, Ben felt comfortable in stopping their progress. He knew that unless there was a guard standing at the edge of the estate's promontory overlooking the sea, no one could see them.

"Which way do you think we should go?" Moo asked. "Should we approach the house through the back of the yard, or continue along these rocks?"

Ben was silent for a few moments. When he spoke, his words were frighteningly deliberate. "I sense the presence of death nearby."

"What do you mean by that?" Moo asked.

"I sense there must be some kind of entrance to the house from down here . . . along the ocean . . . ."

"Are you sure?" JJ asked from behind.

Ben said nothing, but began walking along the rocks once again. The others followed.

After about a hundred feet, Ben saw the carved out opening of the outside entrance to what he instinctively knew was a worship chamber for Satan. The angel looked around at the others behind him with a steely gaze, which had invaded his pitch-black eyes. The four human soldiers knew there would be no more jocularity until this mission was over.

"This place is black with death," Ben said stoically.

"What do you mean by that?" JJ asked. "To me; it just looks like some kind of underground entrance to the house, which is nicely camouflaged behind the rocks facing the ocean. This is exactly what we need for a quiet entrance."

"This is no ordinary entrance," Ben said. "Trust me my friends. This place has seen many abominations of God's creation. I can sense it very strongly."

"So you've never been here before?" Moo asked.

"No, I have not. Angels only know what God tells us."

The angel abruptly turned on his heels and silently led them towards the mouth of the cave. Once inside the smooth-walled cavern, the crashing waves echoed like the sea within a tin can. As they moved inland, the oceanic din slowly faded into the background.

The floor was not flooded due to the current low tide, so the sounds of their shoes on the rock-filled, muddy floor of the cave were largely muffled. As the five-some continued to march into what seemed like the entrance to Hades-itself, Ben eerily said, *"Isaiah 57:20 says . . . But the wicked are like the tossing sea, which cannot rest, whose waves cast up mire and mud."*

The others looked at each other and shrugged.

"So how far inland do you think this cave goes—?" JJ asked, changing the subject.

"Shhh!" Ben said sharply. He then whispered, "No more words are to be spoken unless it's an emergency."

Everyone nodded.

Once they arrived at the back of the cave, Ben noticed a metal grate on the rock wall with an unlit torch perched above its opening. No fire was currently lit. The angel felt like this was good news and that they stood a good chance of catching their enemies by surprise.

Ben nodded his approval to the others.

JJ pulled out three pocket flashlights, which he had brought from his amply-stocked trunk of supplies. Ben took one, JJ kept one, and Moo snagged the third one. As the three switched the flashlights on, the shroud of eerie darkness at the end of the cave suddenly disappeared.

With their new-found illumination, they made their way to the right, through a hallway chiseled out of the rocks. The hallway then abruptly turned left before leading the group through another right-hand turn. After two more left-hand turns, the hallway straightened out and became wider. After another fifty feet, the group gathered at the entrance to the worship chamber.

Fortunately, there were a few scattered, dimly-lit electric wall lamps around the perimeter of the rocky dome. This eliminated the pitch-black darkness to an acceptable degree. Ben turned off his flashlight, then signaled the others to do the same.

"This place reeks of evil," Ben whispered to the others, who were now in a circle around him. "Unspeakable things have taken place down here."

"I can certainly see why," JJ whispered. "This house of horrors is completely isolated from the outside world. These Satanists can pretty much do anything they want to down here."

"Precisely," Ben said. "And believe me—they have."

"What in the world is that symbol on the wall across the room?" Bobby asked.

Ben replied, "The *SS* on the wall behind the rock altar stands for *Sunagōgae Satana,* or the *Synagogue of Satan.*"

Bobby slowly nodded. "Oh, so that's what these idiots call themselves, huh?"

Ben surprisingly cracked a grin. "Yes Bobby, they certainly do."

The group made their way down the stone steps onto the chamber floor. Ben continued to lead the way, but he was moving cautiously. JJ brought up the rear of the group, holding his hand on the pistol in the crook of his back.

When they reached the far side of the chamber, they ascended the stone steps up to the altar. Everything in the room remained eerily quiet, save for the sounds of their shuffling shoes on the rocky floor.

Ben motioned for JJ and Juan to check out the stone-framed doorway to the right, while he and Moo checked out the doorway to the left. The four men spread out while Bobby remained in the altar area.

As Bobby's vision panned the surrounding walls of the chamber, he noticed what appeared to be a barely visible indentation in the wall to his left. The apparent dark opening stood directly in one of the corners of the square chamber. It appeared to be unusually wide, so he moved over to investigate.

As Bobby neared the area, he realized it was indeed a large opening. As he reached the point where he was standing directly in front of it, he saw a wide set of stone stairs leading upwards. The stairs were set at a relatively flat angle. Bobby thought this was rather odd. To him, it almost seemed as if the stairwell was designed for many people to enter and exit the chamber from somewhere above.

Probably the main house, he thought.

Suddenly, Bobby heard gradual footfalls coming down the stairs. Sensing trouble, he stood still; frozen in his tracks. He quickly whirled around and looked at the doorways into which the other four had ventured.

Nobody was within eyesight.

Bobby didn't dare risk calling out to the others, so he moved to the right-hand side of the stairway opening and leaned-up against the wall. As he stood there with his hand on the pistol, Bobby thought it was rather odd that the sounds from the approaching steps would cease for a few moments, and then ensue. As he snuck back over to the opening and peeked around the corner, he saw why.

A gradual illumination of the stairs continued to build with each starting-and-stopping of the mysterious footsteps. It became obvious to Bobby that someone was lighting torches on each side of the walls of the stairwell.

It was too late for Bobby to run back over to where the others were, so he needed to make a decision on what to do—and he needed to make it fast. Having spent most of his life hanging-out with sinful reprobates, Bobby had acquired some good instincts on how to deal with worldly situations.

Bobby pulled out his pistol and pointed it towards the ceiling. Simultaneously, he slinked along the stone wall, securing a dark spot to hide. He then waited. When the visitor emerged from the stairwell, Bobby brought his pistol to bear, but remained quiet.

The man who lit the torches was all alone. He had thinning gray hair and was only of medium build. He was dressed simply in khakis and a navy blue sweater. Once again, Bobby looked quickly towards the area where the others were scouting. Fortunately, they had remained quiet and had not yet re-emerged into the worship chamber.

Bobby's instincts clicked-on as he realized he would have to handle the situation by himself. He quietly moved towards the man, who seemed preoccupied with staring out into the worship chamber. It was as if the man sensed something was amiss.

When Bobby was close enough, he held the pistol to the man's head and quietly declared, "Don't move—or I'll pull the trigger."

The man didn't seem surprised as he slowly raised his hands in the air and said, "I'll cooperate. There's no need to harm me."

"Good," Bobby said, intermittently looking in the direction where his compadres were scouting. "What's your name, pal?" he asked.

"My name is Nelson Pritchard. I'm the owner of this house."

"Don't you mean to say this, *death chamber?* It reeks of rotting flesh down here."

"With all due respect sir, we live in the United States of America. I'm allowed to sacrifice animals to my god if I wish to. My constitutional rights give me the ability to freely worship as I please."

Bobby softened a little. "That's not the point—"

"Tell me something stranger; why are you here? Why are you threatening me on my own property?"

"First off, I'm not intending to *threaten* you. I just happened to wander in here from the entrance on the ocean—"

"You failed to answer my question. Why are you—"

"I heard that a guy named Caleb Hunter lives here, and I have a message for him."

"Who???" Pritchard asked innocently.

"You know who!" Bobby leveled.

"Listen sir—" Pritchard began, then suddenly wheeled around on Bobby. With amazingly fast reflexes, Pritchard knocked the gun out of Bobby's hand and pushed him to the ground. But instead of lunging towards Bobby's gun to retrieve it, Pritchard brandished his own handgun.

Bobby saw Pritchard's pistol come into clear focus—an old German Luger. For a moment, he admired the weapon, which was used during both world wars in the previous century. Bobby knew the Luger was much more than just a handgun—it was the familiar sidearm for Hitler and his officers in Nazi Germany. Anything to do with Hitler always made Bobby uncomfortable.

"So how do you like my beautiful weapon?" Pritchard sneered, pointing it directly at Bobby. "It's beautiful; is it not?"

"I suppose it is," Bobby mumbled.

"You know; my father used this very weapon on many of the inferior races in World War II—especially the Jews. You see; although our family is actually Welsh, my father sought out and ultimately became a member of the Nazi party in the 1920's. Yes indeed; I'm proud to say that Papa fought for Hitler in the Great War."

"Why would he want to do that?"

"It's actually very simple," Pritchard said. "The Nazis were trying to accomplish what our blessed group *also* wants to accomplish."

"Oh yeah, what's that?"

"Elimination of all Jews from the face of this planet. In the case of the Nazis, I guess you could say we had common goals."

"Whatever."

"So tell me something; what's your name mister, *about-to-die?"*

"Uh . . . Bobby James."

"I see," Pritchard said. "No offense Bobby, but I don't tolerate intruders on my property—*especially* those who infect our blessed worship chamber."

"Wait a minute, dude. Has it occurred to you that maybe I'm just here to join your group? Maybe I was just kidding about Caleb."

"People don't *join* us Bobby. They're hand-selected by Satan and his army of powerful angels to raise up the army of the millennium— Armageddon's Army. So basically, *I know you're lying!"*

Bobby quickly tired of listening to Pritchard. Feeling like he had nothing to lose, he said, "I love Jesus Christ as my LORD and Savior, and Satan deserved to get kicked to the curb by our God Almighty. *And by the way, you're an absolute scumbag!"*

Pritchard chuckled haughtily, then raised his Luger and pointed it squarely at Bobby. "And you, sir, are about to die . . . ."

Before Pritchard could pull the trigger, Bobby heard the thunder of what sounded like a giant hammer being dropped to the ground from Heaven above. The reverb off the wall echoed mightily throughout the entire chamber as the shocking earthquake of sound pounded the thin air. When Bobby looked up, he saw Pritchard staggering backward, holding his forehead. Even in the relative darkness, Bobby could see blood trickling over Pritchard's fingers.

Someone had shot him in the head.

The sound of racing footsteps from Bobby's left created a pulsating echo. Within a matter of seconds, Pritchard had fallen to the cold stone floor, and Ben and the others were standing in-between him and Pritchard.

"What happened?" Bobby asked, obviously stunned.

"That dude was about to pop you," JJ said. "So I shot him first."

"That's a pretty good shot in the dim light," Bobby said.

"The light from the stairwell sure helped," JJ said.

"You'll be okay Bobby," Ben said, extending him a hand, helping him get to his feet. "But we must hurry upstairs. We'll soon have company, and we don't want to lose Caleb."

"What about Pritchard?" Bobby asked, brushing himself off.

The five men looked over at the bloody man on the ground. Pritchard's eyes remained open, but it was obvious he was dead.

"He is now on his way to a very bad place," Ben said. "In fact, he's going to the very place he asked for. But I'm afraid Mr. Pritchard isn't being greeted with quite the wonderful party he was expecting."

"I hate to break up this little chit-chat," JJ added, "but we need to get going."

Ben nodded.

JJ led the others up the nearby stairwell. The torches showed the way up thirty steps onto a large flat landing area. A second ascending stairwell then abruptly changed directions back on itself, leading upwards. The five men continued to climb.

After quickly moving past the second landing area, they arrived on an enclosed, rectangular patio of sorts. There were closed doors on each of the walls of the patio, which was obviously some kind of socializing area. At this point, the group began to sprint across the room. JJ and his pistol led the way. Bobby now brought up the rear, grateful that he had retrieved his own gun before they began their ascent into the house.

When they arrived at the other end of the room, they slowed down as JJ cautiously pushed his way through double doors, which had circular windows at eye level. To his surprise, he found himself standing in a large, beautifully appointed kitchen. He motioned for the others to join him.

By now, Bobby had made his way to the front. He and JJ crept through the kitchen, one on each side of an elongated marble-topped island-sink area. Ben and Moo followed behind JJ and Bobby, so Juan was now in the rear, by himself.

As JJ and Bobby peeked outside the kitchen into a massive formal dining room, an unexpected, sickening resonance assaulted their ears. The distinctive sound reminded them of a carving knife being plunged into a pumpkin during autumn. A grotesque gurgling reverb then followed as someone's breath of life began to escape.

When they whirled around, they were greeted with the horrific specter of Juan being held around the neck by an intruder; a tall, muscular man. To their shock and dismay, the man had just driven a dagger into Juan's back. The expression on their friend's face was one of absolute terror.

JJ and Bobby quickly leveled their weapons at the attacker.

"Who are you???" JJ shouted.

"None of your business, you Christian pig!" the man yelled back.

Ben calmly held his hand over JJ's gun. "I will handle this," the angel said slowly.

JJ momentarily lowered his weapon. Bobby followed suit.

As the others looked on in amazement, Ben now had a stunningly beautiful sword in his hand. He held the mighty weapon in front of himself in a statement of pure and utter power.

"Where did that sword come from?" Bobby asked.

Ignoring Bobby, Ben began to issue commands, which each man immediately obeyed.

"JJ, raise your weapon once again and keep it trained on this demon," the angel said. "He is going nowhere."

"Who *is* he?" JJ asked.

"The demon's name is Chas. He is inhabiting this man."

The angel moved closer.

By this time, Chas had released Juan, who slumped onto the floor. To the great sadness of his friends, Juan appeared to be almost dead. Ben moved closer as Chas held up his bloody hands in surrender. The demon was obviously frightened.

"Hey—is that the same Chas we encountered at the Mall last February?" Bobby asked. "I mean; how many demons named Chas can there be?"

"Chas is inhabiting someone else today," Ben said calmly, continuing towards the demon, his sword leading the way. "Bobby, you need to follow Moo into the house and find Caleb before he escapes with Damon and Donovan. These demons will do anything they can to protect the progenitor of their evil army. Go now!"

Moo and Bobby made their way through the dining room and into the main parlor of the house. They stood in the two-story entryway for a few moments, trying to figure out which direction to go. Suddenly, the unwelcome sound of squealing tires caused them to race towards the front door.

After barging their way outside, Bobby and Moo saw a large Mercedes filled with four people speeding away, down the tree-lined driveway.

Their hearts sank.

Before they could go and report the bad news that Caleb had gotten away with his demonic mentors, five thugs suddenly jumped them from both sides, knocking Bobby's gun onto the driveway. Bobby's head hit the ground, staggering him for a few moments.

Unfortunately for the attackers, Moo sprang into action.

In what appeared to be nothing less than an old Bruce Lee movie, Moo quickly deployed an array of kicks and punches, devastating the attacking crew of demonic provocateurs. Moo had no idea whether the men were inhabited by demons or not, and he certainly didn't care. A foot to the face would most assuredly stop either one.

And it did.

In less than a minute, Moo had broken an array of knees, elbows, and noses on his assailants. They all lay on the ground, either unconscious or moaning in agony over their injuries. Moo then helped Bobby off the ground; who once again visually located his gun, then retrieved it.

By this time, Ben and JJ arrived on the front porch of the house, where they found Bobby training his gun on the defeated attackers.

The inhabited man who had just stabbed Juan was now being held at gunpoint by JJ.

"What happened to him?" Moo asked. "He looks like he just had the living daylights scared out of him."

"The demon named Chas is no longer in this man," Ben said. "And he will spend the rest of his life in prison for his attack on Juan. He is a member of the satanic cult which meets in this terrible place."

"So what happened to the demon named Chas who inhabited him?" Bobby asked. "Did one of you cast him out or something?"

"Ben said a prayer aloud," JJ said. "He asked the LORD to remove the evil spirit out of this man. As I stood there watching, the LORD drove the evil spirit out of him. And I have to say, it was probably the most amazing thing I've ever seen."

Boston, MA
October 7th

"give thanks in all circumstances;
for this is God's will for you in Christ Jesus."
1 Thessalonians 5:18

"So outside of these lovely surprises," Wyatt began, "what else are we supposed to be talking about today?"

"What, isn't it enough to just learn some cool kingdom secrets?" Mick chided.

"Actually, it's all good if you ask me," Wyatt said. "All except that part about Caleb spawning a nation of Satan's disciples. That part kinda creeps me out."

"Understandably so," Bob added. "The thing about Caleb you really need to understand is that he's been trained to fight against those who he thinks may prevent him and his enormous ego from remaining the father of Satan's growing army."

"What a scumbag," Wyatt said. "He's also murdered some important family members of our group; although I'm still not sure why."

"We kinda touched on this back in February," Mick said. "But let's go ahead and take a look at the big picture, here. Caleb was ordered by Damon to murder Miss Charlene's husband Robert, Candace's husband Willie, and Cam's mother Cammie. He did this over the years because Damon was effectively trying to discourage both yours and Candace's families from serving the LORD."

"What do you mean by *discourage* us?"

"Think about it; Damon greatly discouraged two members of Candace's family with both herself and Miss Charlene losing their husbands. But as importantly, Damon tried to send one of you Hunter men—*your own son Cam*—into total despair by murdering his mother when he was very young."

"I see," Wyatt said.

"After someone experiences a tremendous loss, if they concentrate on how much they've been hurt instead of looking forward into God's eternal kingdom, they're often unable to find true joy in life. When this happens, their pain is so intense that it's nearly impossible for someone to see God reaching out to them. But the truth is; the LORD always wants to comfort and love-on His people. It's the demons like Damon who will do all they can to make you blind to God's love in times of sorrow."

"I suppose that makes sense," Wyatt said.

"Listen," Mick continued. "You and I both know that everyone only gets one shot at life on Earth. Of course, Satan knows this also. That's why he does as many things as he can to distract people; to make them less likely—or at least less effective—in both knowing and serving the LORD."

"Can you give me an example of that?"

"Sure thing. Let's continue with what happened to Candace, Miss Charlene, and Cam. When each of them lost their loved ones, they were obviously hurt very deeply. But through it all, they never stopped loving the LORD. In other words, they didn't blame God for what happened. Instead, they knew that Jesus Christ was the only One who could lift their loved ones from physical death into eternal life in Heaven. Well, at least Cam figured that out later on, when he was a little older. Anyway, as a result, instead of blaming God for what happened—like many people end up doing—they blamed the *real* villains—human sin and demonic influence."

"Oh, I see what you're saying."

"And let's not forget about Satan's great lie of reincarnation," Bob added. "Like Mick just mentioned a moment ago, a human only gets one shot at life on Earth. And the ramifications of your decisions have eternal consequences—either good or bad. So as a result, Satan sows his lies all over your world, trying to deceive people. It's almost like he's an evil farmer spreading manure over a huge field, hoping his lies will grow."

"Wow, Bob. That's kinda gross," Wyatt joked.

Mick chuckled. "Listen here dude; there are some wise words from Jesus in the Gospels that apply here. Actually, it's in *John 8:44 . . . You belong to your father, the devil, and you want to carry out your father's desires. He was a murderer from the beginning, not holding to the truth, for there is no truth in him. When he lies, he speaks his native language, for he is a liar and the father of lies.*"

"I see," Wyatt said. "Satan being the ultimate liar makes sense to me. But let me ask you guys a question: why does the LORD let Satan roam around spreading his evil and lies? Listen Mick; I know we've talked about this many times before, but it's hard to comprehend why God isn't putting an end to all of this evil, *right now.*"

Mick sighed. "Dudemeister, you're forgetting something very important about the LORD; something very fundamental about your life on Earth."

"And that is—?"

"Jesus won't force you to love Him. If He did, that wouldn't be true love at all. Remember; after the LORD extinguishes all evil, it'll be forever gone. *Poof!* A distant memory. So in the end, the LORD has *already* promised He'll exterminate all evil. However, it won't happen until all of His holy plans and promises have been fulfilled. And let's not forget that human evil exists in the first place due to—"

"I get it," Wyatt interrupted. "Adam and Eve's original sin."

"If you keep going there, I'll keep giving you the same answer."

"I gotcha. I suppose you're right."

"Anyways, until Jesus returns to execute His prophesied final plan to end all evil, you need to remember that Satan and his demons will concentrate their efforts to deceive you into a compromised life of sin. They also have the bodies of the wicked to utilize in physical attacks by entering a host."

"So demons still have access to the current, fallen Earth to test, sift, and hassle the LORD's children, right?"

"That's correct. And oh-by-the-way, this is also *precisely* where I'm going to lay on you the third and final *RYB dude* for your training sessions."

"Seriously?" Wyatt asked. "I mean; wasn't two RYB's enough?"

"Obviously not," Mick said with a grin. "But you need to know that it all fits in with the master plan."

"Oh yeah, what master plan is that?"

"I'm getting there Wyatt, so chill. Anyways, let's do a quick review, starting with the first and most prominent RYB: *Read Your Bible.* If you don't read the Bible, you'll be woefully unprepared to battle Satan. Of course, that's not a real good idea."

Wyatt nodded. "Absolutely."

"Now then," Mick continued, "the *second* RYB which I told you about back in your training sessions at the Mall of America was this: *Recognize Your Blessings.*"

"I remember that," Wyatt said.

"Good. The progression of the three RYB's is quite natural, and they follow each other in succession. In the case of the second RYB, it's difficult for someone to recognize their blessings if they're not first reading their Bible."

"I agree," Wyatt said. "The way of the world will only convince us that whatever we have is *not enough*. In other words, if we don't understand the LORD's way of living our life according to the Bible, we likely won't be able to recognize our blessings. If we follow Satan's temptations and live according to the ways of the world, we'll always end up wanting more than we have."

"On the other hand," Mick began, "if you study the Bible and follow its ways, recognizing your blessings is a natural by-product. At that point, your heart is changed to one of gratefulness for what you *do* have, instead of having contempt for what you *don't* have."

"This is nothing new to me," Wyatt said. "Please go on."

"Essentially, the Bible teaches you to focus on the LORD, not yourself. Once your focus is on Jesus Christ, gratitude is a natural result."

"Like I said, I'm with you."

"Good deal," Mick said, nodding.

"So," Wyatt began, "once someone has started studying the Bible, then recognizes their blessings, where does this mysterious third RYB fit in?"

"The third and final RYB for your lessons is simply this: *Reach Your Brother.*"

"Ah-ha!" Wyatt said. "I thought it might center on telling others about the LORD."

Mick chuckled. "I can see your official *angel training* sessions have been pretty effective, Wyatt."

Bob grinned at this.

Wyatt shrugged. "I suppose they have. What can I say?"

"Listen my friend; the progression of the three RYB's also dovetails nicely with the overall mission of the Flaming Sword Communications Group."

"Oh yeah—how's that?"

"The first RYB—Read Your Bible—is connected with *Matthew 22:37*, which says, *Jesus replied: 'Love the Lord your God with all your heart and with all your soul and with all your mind.'* In order to love Jesus Christ, you simply *must* study His revelation to mankind in the Bible. It's just that simple."

"That makes sense," Wyatt agreed.

"The second RYB—Recognize Your Blessings—is connected with a subsequent passage in the same chapter. *Matthew 22:39* says, *And the second is like it: 'Love your neighbor as yourself.'* You see; once you're able to recognize your blessings from the LORD, you don't become jealous of your neighbor and what they possess. Therefore, you end up *truly* loving your neighbor as yourself."

"This is actually coming together nicely," Wyatt said.

"Hang on to your hat, Wyatt, 'cause here comes the third RYB and its Scripture: 'Reach Your Brother' is tied to *Matthew 28:19,* which is the Great Comm—"

"I get it," Wyatt interrupted. "The Great Commission!"

"Yepper, that's correct," Mick said. "The passage actually says, *Therefore go and make disciples of all nations, baptizing them in the name of the Father and of the Son and of the Holy Spirit.*"

"That's pretty cool," Wyatt said. "And all this time, I never knew you had a bigger plan on all this cutesy RYB stuff . . . ."

Just then, there was a knock at the employee entrance door. Bob, Mick, and Wyatt all looked at each other.

"That must be our answer about Wyatt," Bob said calmly.

"Listen Wyatt," Mick said quickly. "No matter what happens, you have Jesus on your side. So whether you die and proceed into Heaven, or if you still have work to do on Earth, Jesus is always with you."

"I understand," Wyatt said, feeling surprised at how quickly he became nervous as he waited for the answer.

****

Back in the hospital, Cam, Al, Ruth, and Jimmy had been joined by Wyatt's cousin Frank. Wyatt had not seen Frank since Vanessa's funeral a couple of years earlier. As they all sat waiting, the doctor exited Wyatt's room and approached them with the news on his prognosis.

"Hello folks," Dr. Bridget Andrews said. "I finally have some news on Mr. Hunter."

"So what's going on?" Cam asked nervously.

"As you know, Mr. Hunter sustained some damage to his chest cavity. Although the knife fortunately missed his heart, he actually did lose a lot of blood. For most of last night, I was—"

"Please cut to the chase," Cam interrupted. "Is dad gonna make it?"

"Actually," Dr. Andrews continued, "he's made some pretty dramatic improvement. A couple of hours ago, I had my doubts about whether he was going to pull through it. But I'm happy to report to you that just now, as I was checking-in on him, Mr. Hunter had made some almost unbelievable progress. In fact, I just saw signs that he'll be waking up soon."

"*Really???*" Cam asked, almost in tears. "So is dad really going to make it?"

"It appears so," Dr. Andrews said. "Nurse Hendricks is in there right now. She'll notify you when it's safe to go in and see him. But you can only go in there for a few minutes."

"Thank you, ma'am!" Cam said excitedly. "I don't know how I can ever thank you enough."

Cam stood up and hugged the doctor, and everyone else shook her hand, thanking her.

Dr. Andrews then departed to make her other rounds.

****

Bob stood up and walked over to the employee entrance door to his office and answered it. After the angel opened the door only half-way, he spoke to another similarly attired angel for a few moments. He then returned to his desk. During the interim, Mick looked downwards and said nothing.

"Well Bob, what's up?" Wyatt asked.

"I'm pleased to advise you that your job on Earth isn't finished yet Wyatt," Bob said. "You'll be making a fairly quick recovery. In fact, it'll appear somewhat miraculous to the medical professionals."

"*Who-hoo!* So, is this now going to end my dream with you guys?"

"I'm afraid it is," Mick said.

"You know; I've actually enjoyed myself," Wyatt said. "But I'm still not clear on why you were dispatched to appear to me today."

"If you think about it," Mick began, "we've covered a bunch of important information with you in this vision. But I still have a couple of parting instructions for you. That's how these dreams and visions work, you know."

"I see," Wyatt said. "Before you give me my parting gifts, so to speak, I have to admit something; I'm a little disappointed that today isn't the day I'm going to enter Heaven."

"That's interesting," Bob said. "Why is that?"

"I was kind of getting excited about the possibility of seeing Vanessa and my parents, not to mention, my dog Scout."

"I understand," Mick added. "And believe me; your family in Heaven is very proud of what you're doing with both your writing and with the new Flaming Sword group. But I'm afraid that today isn't the day for you to be forever reunited with them. You obviously still have some work to do down on Earth."

"Yeah, I'm feeling strangely ambivalent about the whole thing," Wyatt said. "Oh well, there'll certainly be another day for our reunion."

"They'll all be at your greeting committee when you arrive in Heaven one day," Bob said. "One of our jobs at the edge of Heaven is to coordinate that kind of thing. I promise that I'll pay extra attention to your arrival when the time comes."

"Thanks Bob. I won't forget that!"

"As you get older, Wyatt," Mick said, "you'll discover that your fear of dying and going to be with Jesus slowly diminishes."

"Why do you think that is?" Wyatt asked.

"It's because as you get older, the people who you love and care for on Earth begin to die—one-by-one. For older folks who know Christ, you end up realizing one day that you have far more of your loved ones in Heaven than on Earth. So your desire to still live on Earth slowly declines, year-after-year. That's actually one of God's great kindnesses to His children who are chosen to live longer lives on Earth."

"So what about those who die before they're old?" Wyatt asked. "Like what about Vanessa? She died at a relatively young age."

"Of course, it's very difficult on the folks who remain on Earth when something tragic like that happens," Mick said. "But have you ever considered the fact that in Vanessa's case, Earth's loss was Heaven's gain?"

"Hmmm . . . I suppose you're right."

"Conversely, since you're not joining us in Paradise today, Heaven's loss is very much Earth's gain."

"Wow Mick—thanks," Wyatt said sincerely. "I'm not accustomed to you being so mushy and all."

Mick nodded. "I do have one last instruction from the LORD for you, Wyatt. Until just now, I didn't know if you'd be staying on Earth or not. But now that we have our answer, I need to share this with you. Bob and I are fixing to go, so I need to tell you this without further ado."

"What is it?"

"After you're recovered—which I believe has been ordained to be a quick process—I want you to move from the Boston area back to Seattle."

"Why???"

"Your move to the Boston area earlier this year was only intended to be temporary," Mick said. "It was primarily designed for you and Cam to spend some time together, and for you to buy that house for him."

"I see."

"But things have now changed. The LORD wants you to go back to the place you love more than anywhere else. You need to go back to Seattle."

"I do miss the Emerald City," Wyatt said. "But why do I *need* to go back there? Also, where will I be staying? There's really not enough room for me back in my old condo. Danny, Mi-Cha, and DJ don't have much room as it is."

"The LORD already has that covered," Mick said.

"How so?"

"On behalf of Flaming Sword Communications, Miss Charlene has recently secured a modest home across from downtown Seattle on Bainbridge Island. That's where you'll live."

"Really?"

"Yep."

"I really like it over there," Wyatt said. "I used to take the short ferry ride over to Bainbridge all the time."

"Well dude, it's now going to be your new home. Don't worry though. Like I said, we've already had Miss Charlene place a down payment on a house, which will be absolutely perfect for your future writing. In fact, the closing papers are due to be signed very soon."

"I see. So what about Cam?"

"Good question," Mick said. "Cam loves you more than you can know, and the time you've had together during the past several months has been a great healer of his soul. However, Cam is still a young man, and he'll get married one day and have his own family."

"That makes sense," Wyatt said. "But I don't think Cam is very serious about dating right now."

"Actually," Mick began, "Cam has become pretty serious about this young lady named Maria who he's been dating for a little while. In fact, it seems that Cam has already fallen in love with her."

"What do you mean?" Wyatt asked. "Cam has only mentioned her on occasion to me. I don't think he'd become serious about a woman without telling me more about her."

"That's actually been his dilemma," Bob added. "Cam is afraid that you'll feel abandoned if he starts his own family."

"Of course I won't," Wyatt said, then remained quiet for a few moments. "Well, I suppose I can understand where he's coming from."

"Listen Wyatt," Mick said. "You and Cam have had a great time being together for the past few months. But as you've just figured out, that house in Methuen is for him and his future family. You and Cam will continue to work together at Flaming Sword, but your personal job will be to remain in the background, writing your novels. Cam's job will be taking-on a much more active role."

"I see," Wyatt said. "I suppose that makes sense. It's weird; I've been moving around a lot lately. I sure hope this will be my last move."

"I'm pretty sure it is," Mick said. "Oh, and one more thing . . . your new house on Bainbridge Island is on a street called Patmos Lane. Pretty interesting, huh?"

"What—am I being exiled to the island of Bainbridge, just like the Apostle John was exiled to the island of Patmos back in the first century?"

"Exiled? Certainly not," Mick said. "You're merely being placed in a situation which will be conducive to your future work for the LORD. Think of it as a very pleasant and peaceful mission on the island of Bainbridge."

"And what work is that?" Wyatt asked rhetorically. "Will I continue to write novels about a rough-looking, coffee-guzzling angel who uses the word *dude* far too often?"

Mick chuckled. "Something like that. I'll see you down on Earth again sometime soon."

With that, Wyatt's vision within his dream abruptly ended.

****

Wyatt's eyes blinked several times as the various people and objects in his hospital room slowly came into focus. Leaning directly over him was the welcoming face of his son Cam, who was grinning from ear-to-ear. Suddenly, as if the overture of a concert's opening piece had just begun, Wyatt felt a numbing pain in his chest.

He winced.

As the comfort of his vision from the edge of Heaven fled from Wyatt's thoughts, the sudden sadness of remaining on a painfully fallen Earth jolted the author back to reality:

> *No matter how much I love my family and friends, I really don't want to be back here after all,* he mused to himself.

Wyatt's attention then focused on his wife Vanessa in Heaven, and his pain sharpened. He had been so very close to seeing his beloved wife once again, so his disappointment of remaining on Earth began to settle in.

However, quickly realizing that he still had work to do, Wyatt gave a big thumbs-up to Cam and the rest of his friends in the room: the angels Jimmy and Ruth, his son Cam, Alistair McClellan, and very curiously, his cousin Frank.

"Frank???" Wyatt asked. "What're you doing here?"

Wyatt gazed upon his cousin, who was about as regular-looking as he could be—medium height, medium build, and sandy-gray hair.

"I actually have a lot to discuss with you Wyatt," Frank said. "And I'm glad now is finally the time you get to know who I really am . . . and what I do."

Wyatt nodded. "So how are—?"

"Listen Pop," Cam interrupted. "I'm afraid I have some terrible news."

"What can be more terrible that my evil twin brother trying to kill me last night?" Wyatt joked. "Is it worse than that?"

Cam nodded. "I'm afraid so."

"So what is it?"

"Juan was killed a little while ago in a raid on the Satanist's compound up in Maine."

"Oh-no! What happened? Why was Juan up there?"

"I'll explain all of that to you a little bit later," Cam said. "I'm afraid we're not allowed to stay in your room for very long. You really need to get some rest."

"I see," Wyatt said. "That's *terrible* news about Juan. But what about Caleb?"

Cam sighed. "I'm afraid he got away. Sometimes it seems like we'll never catch him."

PART 3

THE DICHOTOMY OF ETERNAL LIFE

Heaven
October 7th

**"But about the resurrection of the dead—have you
not read what God said to you, 'I am the God of
Abraham, the God of Isaac, and the God of Jacob'?
He is not the God of the dead but of the living."
Matthew 22:31-32**

After slumping to the kitchen floor, searing pain enveloped Juan's entire body as he languished in an oozing puddle of his own blood. Although he could faintly hear the voices of his friends in the room, they seemed to be slowly floating away. As Juan lay with his left check on the cold, tiled floor, the warmth of his blood quietly slithering outwards looked very much like a swath of dark red paint being brushed onto an evil painter's canvas.

Death was near.

The ripple effect of the unexpected dagger plunging into his back only moments ago immediately touched off a tsunami of terror throughout his soul. Due to the severity and depth of his injury, Juan knew the after-effects of this attack was undoubtedly a once in a lifetime event. The magnitude of the serrated steel tearing into his temporal flesh left no doubt in his mind—this was his last day on Earth. Although part of him felt totally helpless, Juan also felt unexpectedly serene.

Moving quickly through his peripheral vision, piercing beams of brilliant light began to descend upon Juan, gradually encircling him in a caring way, as if preparing him for a long-awaited journey. The gentle light felt warm, calming, and inviting. Although he felt a pronounced sense that his body was very close to physical death, Juan also felt a simultaneous and increasing peace.

After only a few more moments, with his eyes gaping wide open, Juan took his last breath on Earth.

The brilliant light continued to expand all around Juan as he felt the powerfully recognizable love of the LORD infuse His entire spirit and soul. Through the haze of this shockingly unique event, he knew the next phase of his ultimate glorification by Jesus Christ was abruptly upon him.

Juan sensed that the rapidly unfolding events were following a carefully planned script, when seemingly out of nowhere, *1 Corinthians 15:37* suddenly entered his thoughts . . . *When you sow, you do not plant the body that will be, but just a seed, perhaps of wheat or of something else.*

That's interesting, Juan thought. *The Word of God is falling upon me at my death . . .*

The blanket of light had now completely enveloped Juan in what he now knew was a comprehensive, loving embrace. As if on cue, a rounded, luminescent hallway of light then materialized in front of him. To Juan, it appeared as though it was some sort of inter-dimensional doorway.

Although he was completely lucid and well-aware of his surroundings, Juan also felt as if he was being moved into a uniquely restorative dimension. Simultaneously, he felt the steely, physical reality of the deadly dagger flee from his soul as a general lightness of spirit completely replaced the terror of his earthly body's severe affliction. As his pain completely dissipated, Juan felt like a struggling animal which was calming down after having just been rescued out of a giant quagmire of death-summoning quicksand.

He felt tremendous relief.

For many years now, Juan had contemplated this poignant event in a Christian's life—to pass from earthly death into eternal life with Jesus Christ. He always wondered what this singular moment of leaving behind one's life on Earth would be like. Without exception, he very much considered this to be the absolute nexus of truth for every single human being who has ever lived—the events which unfold immediately upon one's death. Now suddenly, Juan was experiencing this unique event; a moment which he had certainly not anticipated when he awoke that morning in a nearby budget motel.

As his brand new journey from earthly chrysalis to heavenly butterfly continued its progress, in a simultaneously sudden and gentle action, Juan felt the presence of two angels at his side. As if on cue, another Scripture fell upon his thoughts . . . *Luke 16:22* . . . *The time came when the beggar died and the angels carried him to Abraham's side. The rich man also died and was buried.*

"Hello Juan, and welcome to your eternal home," the angel on his right said, gently touching his arm. "My name is Atoggishem. Your other escort is Logault."

"Did I just die—or am I somehow dreaming?"

Atoggishem smiled. "By placing your faith and trust in Jesus Christ, you have now moved out of Earth's current cesspool of sin. Although your temporary earthly body has now died, your spirit and soul remain in Christ."

"I see. This is pretty weird . . . but very cool."

The angel nodded. "You will now continue into the next phase of your eternal fellowship with the One who reigns supreme—Yeshua."

"How wonderful!" Juan exclaimed. "This light is *sooo* beautiful."

Atoggishem smiled once again.

Juan looked around in all directions and quickly understood that he was being carried from one dimension to another on what seemed like an effortless ride on a moving sidewalk. The starry sky above appeared as a lustrous canopy over his unique voyage, providing a backdrop of absolute magnificence as he traveled through the brilliant hallway of light.

"Are you surprised to be heading towards Heaven?" Atoggishem asked.

"No, of course not," Juan said, surprised at the unexpected question. "It's just strange that this moment is finally upon me. I sure wasn't expecting it today."

"Yeshua is merciful in that He brings you home to be with Him when your job on Earth is finished. Of course, only the LORD knows when that time is."

"Are you referring to *John 14:3?*"

"I am indeed," Atoggishem agreed.

John 14:3 gently settled into Juan's thoughts . . . *And if I go and prepare a place for you, I will come back and take you to be with me that you also may be where I am.*

Juan looked to his left. "Logault; do you speak, my friend?"

Atoggishem answered instead. "Logault is the one who is sharing the Scriptures with your thoughts. To accentuate his duties, he does not speak as we escort the LORD's children into Heaven. Only I will speak with you during this brief journey."

"Oh, I see."

"Logault's name is actually inspired by the Greek term for *word*, which is *logos*," Atoggishem said. "And you will soon discover that everything in Heaven is imbued with the Holy Word of God; starting with this triumphant entry into Paradise."

Psalm 119:105 . . . *Your word is a lamp for my feet, a light on my path* entered Juan's thoughts. Now that he knew where this was coming from, Juan smiled at Logault.

The angel bowed his head in acknowledgement.

The spectrum of light continued to intensify as the weight of what felt like a thousand elephants being lifted off of Juan's shoulders continued. As such, he felt an indescribable sense of peace as his journey into the dimension of God's home continued its march forward. Once again, a Scripture fell upon Juan's thoughts. This time, however, the passage felt as though it was an official announcement from the angel Logault:

> *Hebrews 12:22-24 . . . But you have come to Mount Zion, to the city of the living God, the heavenly Jerusalem. You have come to thousands upon thousands of angels in joyful assembly, to the church of the firstborn, whose names are written in heaven. You have come to God, the Judge of all, to the spirits of the righteous made perfect, to Jesus the mediator of a new covenant, and to the sprinkled blood that speaks a better word than the blood of Abel.*

At this, the newest citizen of Heaven rejoiced. "Tell me Logault," Juan began. "What more do you wish to share with me about the wonders of God's Holy Word?"

The answer came quickly into Juan's thoughts, *Romans 15:4 . . . For everything that was written in the past was written to teach us, so that through the endurance taught in the Scriptures and the encouragement they provide we might have hope.*

Atoggishem then spoke, adding, "Hope is an amazingly unique gift from the Lord," the angel said. "And eternal Hope with your Savior Jesus Christ—completely devoid of any pain or suffering—is precisely what the Lord has in store for you."

They continued moving through the incredible brightness.

"It's funny," Juan said. "I feel like I'm in the process of moving into the heart of the Lord. I mean—*right into His very heart.*"

"Actually, that is precisely what is happening. You see; when someone genuinely surrenders their life to Jesus Christ, you spiritually enter His heart. At that point, you essentially move from spiritual death into everlasting life. Later on, after you physically die, the rest of you moves away from the cursed land and into His permanent presence."

Juan nodded. "I mean; I can feel the LORD's healing . . . I can feel an even stronger conviction of my sins on Earth . . . I can feel the LORD's loving forgiveness . . . and I can feel the absolute confirmation of every word and promise in the Bible. This is amazing!"

"My dearest Juan," Atoggishem said. "Your personal trail of tears has ended at death's door. Pain and suffering are now behind you forever. This escort into Heaven now awaits all who place their faith and trust in Jesus Christ. You must remember though; God is merciful in that your pain and suffering on Earth is only temporary."

"It's a little odd," Juan began, "but I feel so differently now."

"Of course, that is natural. You're now making a permanent move from fallen to restored; from broken to perfect. This is due to your loving relationship with Jesus."

Juan smiled. "I always knew I was an imperfect sinner, but it feels even more pronounced now. At the same time, I feel an even stronger sense of awe at being forgiven for my past rebellion against the LORD; you know, for my arrogance and pride."

"Even though you were a repentant sinner on Earth," Atoggishem began, "when you enter the LORD's home in Heaven, you've been released from your imperfect body—which is merely the seed of what will be. Therefore, both your rebellion *and* the magnitude of the LORD's forgiveness are greatly accentuated when you arrive here. Of course, this is also quite natural."

Once again, Logault sent a Scripture to Juan: *Romans 14:12 . . . So then, each of us will give an account of ourselves to God.*

"I see," Juan said. "I know there will soon be a day for that."

"Jesus paid the complete price for your sins on the Cross," Atoggishem said. "And very soon, you will experience many wonderful things because of this. But you must not worry—your sin is now a thing of the past. Yeshua knows all things, and He loved you enough to have taken the complete punishment for you."

The brightness intensified to an almost blinding level, when suddenly, the two angels and Juan slowed down. Simultaneously, the magnitude of the blinding light became less difficult for Juan to view the wondrous things around him. As his gaze panned the area, Juan saw a vast kingdom unlike anything his mind on Earth could have ever imagined.

They began to stroll ahead.

"It looks so real!" Juan said.

Every single thing around him seemed to be utterly vibrant, exploding with the love and complete serenity of being in the home of Jesus Christ. This included the colossal things—like stars, planets, moons, and galaxies hovering overhead—as well as many small things which lie ahead, like trees, plants . . . and even animals.

On a rolling hill in the visible distance, Juan gazed upon a radiant Holy City—the heavenly Jerusalem—in all of its magnificent brilliance. The city absolutely sparkled; showing through the horizon as the shimmering jewel of this undying kingdom.

Juan was absolutely mesmerized.

"The LORD's creation continues to happen every day on Earth," Atoggishem said. "It happens with every single person, animal, and even every insect that is ever born. You see; Yeshua is aware of every minute aspect throughout the entire canvas of His Creation. But that is not all. Jesus Christ, along with His redeemed children, are simultaneously building, creating, and celebrating in Heaven together, every moment of every day. The difference is; things here never decay and they never die."

"Although I really can't explain this," Juan began, "this place gives me a renewed sense of what things actually should be."

"As well it should," Atoggishem said. "Heaven is an Eden-like restoration for all that once was . . . all that now is . . . and all that ever shall be."

"I can't believe I'm finally seeing this first-hand!"

As if on cue, another gift from Logault entered Juan's thoughts . . .

2 Corinthians 12:3-4 . . . And I know that this man—whether in the body or apart from the body I do not know, but God knows—was caught up to paradise and heard inexpressible things, things that no one is permitted to tell.

"You're absolutely right Logault," Juan said. "People on Earth would find it impossible to know how it actually feels to be released from their imperfect flesh. Moments ago, I was terrified as I died. Now that I've been transported past my earthly death, I really wish it had happened a long time ago. Is it strange to feel that way?"

Logault shook his head.

"This wonderful place awaits all who call out to Jesus Christ," Atoggishem added. "All He asks in return is your faithful love. You see; Jesus only shares His heart and his home with those who He has an actual relationship with."

"That's the part I never understood down on Earth," Juan said. "How can anyone reject the LORD's love? To me, it seems irresistible."

Atoggishem and Logault both nodded their understanding.

Juan and the angels continued walking towards the end of the path, which culminated at a circle of light not far away. Heaven's newest citizen could still see the New Jerusalem on a hill in the distance, somewhat above him.

"There are many who reject Yeshua," Atoggishem said, "because they hear and believe the subtle lies of Satan. The Evil One will convince them it's the *sinners* who enjoy all the glory, and that there is no punishment in Hell for rejecting Jesus. If someone focuses all of their attention on them self, then this deception can take hold deep in their soul. At that point, Satan's lies make perfect sense. But below their pride, they always know the real Truth about Jesus being sovereign."

"I agree with that."

"In the end, those who reject the LORD's invitation to spend eternity in Heaven . . . well then . . . Jesus merely gives them their wish."

They continued forward.

"What's that area over there, down below us?" Juan asked.

"That is a great chasm or gulf which is set in place," Atoggishem said. "For the time being, it is visible on the edge of Heaven. But only in the distance."

Logault sent another Scripture to Juan: *Luke 16:26 . . . And besides all this, between us and you a great chasm has been set in place, so that those who want to go from here to you cannot, nor can anyone cross over from there to us.*

"So what's the deal with this chasm or gulf between us?" Juan asked.

"On the other side of the chasm is the place reserved for those who reject the LORD's invitation to experience eternal joy," Atoggishem said.

"It looks so far away . . . down below us . . . but I can still see it."

"That's because your eternal eyesight is almost at full strength now. While you lived down on Earth in your temporary body, your vision was greatly diminished. During that time, you actually lived in utter darkness, unaware. But by now, I'm sure you've noticed that the light in front of us has slowly become easier for you to view . . . has it not?"

"It sure has. But let me ask you another question. On the other side of that divide below us . . . I suppose that's Hell . . . right?"

"Actually no," Atoggishem said. "That realm is Hades, which remains the waiting place for people who will ultimately be judged at the Great White Throne Judgment at the end of this age. After the final judgment, the devil and his angels—along with the people who aligned with Satan's ways of the world—will go to Hell. This is known as the second death."

Logault offered another Scripture to Juan: *Matthew 25:41 . . . Then he will say to those on his left, 'Depart from me, you who are cursed, into the eternal fire prepared for the devil and his angels.*

"I see, Juan said. "Those in Hades right now must be very sad."

Atoggishem nodded. "They're experiencing the burning pain of being eternally separated from their Father who loves them. They also live every day in view of the eternal fire further below them. That horrible lake of fire is their eternal destination one day, so their sadness is beyond compare."

The two angels and Juan arrived at what appeared to be another gateway of light. The warmth and benevolence emanating from this doorway gave Juan a sense of absolute excitement; like a child waiting to storm into Disney World, just before its doors open for the day.

"What is this?" Juan asked.

"This is the end of the Flaming Sword and the gateway to Heaven," Atoggishem said. "The LORD placed this Flaming Sword barrier between fallen mankind and His home in Heaven after your parents, Adam and Eve, sinned. But by placing your faith in Jesus Christ, you have now regained permission to be in the presence of the Most High God."

"This is *sooo* exciting!" Juan said.

Atoggishem nodded. "As you walk through this doorway, you will be stepping into the next phase of your eternal fellowship in the presence of Jesus Christ the King. However, this is as far as we will take you today. Another escort awaits you on the other side."

Juan nodded. "Thank you Atoggishem . . . and thank you Logault."

Both angels nodded and turned back towards the darkness from where they had just brought him. Juan found it odd that the bright hallway of light he had just proceeded through now seemed far less shocking to his vision. At this, Juan knew his days of living in darkness were behind him forever.

As he looked forward, Juan paused for a moment. He experienced the amazing feeling of his senses becoming more vibrant and aware of every single thing around him. Juan looked down at his right arm and confirmed that he still had a real body, albeit a spiritual one. Although his new body was different than his earthly body, interestingly, it was still similar in surprising ways.

At this point, Juan knew he had just gone through the first major renovation of his body—the temple of the Holy Spirit. Although his new body was vastly superior to his earthly one, it was still somehow incomplete. Due to his biblical studies, Juan knew that there would one day be a final resurrection of the dead at the end of this age.

But in the meantime, Juan rejoiced at his incorruptible new body.

He moved forward.

Every single sense was on full alert as Juan passed through the gateway of light. He was now able to see everything with a surprising clarity. As he landed on the other side, he felt completely renewed and restored.

On the other side, Juan was greeted with an absolutely incredible vista—the Flaming Sword terminus at the edge of Heaven. The more subdued dark blue, purple, and sea-green colors from the previous side of the doorway were instantly replaced with vibrant yellows, oranges, reds, and every other bright color in the spectrum of light.

In fact, it was amazingly bright.

Framing both sides of the pathway in front of him were magnificent buildings of varying sizes. An almost countless number of angels bustled about the area, giving the edge of Heaven the appearance of a stress-free Grand Central Station. To his right was the incredible Tree of Life, which wound its way throughout the entirety of God's kingdom.

The Tree of Life is absolutely magnificent in its simplicity, he thought.

Juan stood there for a moment, his eyes following the direction of the seemingly ordinary path in front of him. He noticed that it ultimately wound its way through a heavily forested area. The pathway then gradually ascended up the hill on which the heavenly Jerusalem was perched. His heart leapt at the idea of soon entering the great city.

Another angel on Juan's right gently touched his right arm. "Welcome Juan. My name is Kuynipper. I'll be the escort to your greeting committee."

"Hello Kuynipper. Did you say my *greeting committee?*"

"Of course. Separation from loved ones is something that only happens on the fallen Earth. In God's eternal home, sadness is not welcome anywhere here, so immediate reunions when you arrive are very important. Please . . . join me."

"Of course!"

Kuynipper and Juan walked down the path.

"Let me first show you a place that you may have heard of before," Kuynipper said. "To your right is the home-base of The Dozen angel group. You're familiar with Mick, are you not?"

"Oh yes!" Juan exclaimed. "We've worked together in the past."

"The building to your right is now called the 'locker room.' This is where his group, The Dozen, is stationed."

"That's wonderful. Is Mick in Heaven right now?"

"He's not currently in the locker room. But come; we must go. You are the guest of honor at a great celebration."

They continued down the path.

"I always heard there are no temples or churches in Heaven," Juan said. "Is that true?"

"It is indeed," Kuynipper said. "Everything in Heaven shouts with the glory of God, and every thing that has breath praises the LORD. There is no need for a temple or church here."

"I see."

After a short walk, they arrived at a huge clearing. This marked the entrance to their destination—the forest lodge—which was set in a peacefully shaded, tree-lined area, not far from the Flaming Sword terminus. This particular venue was often-used by Mick and other angels for heavenly celebrations.

The forest lodge was unique due to its distinctive four chimneys, which topped the mighty celebration hall. A steady stream of smoke was slowly billowing out of all four stacks, covering the area with a pleasant blanket of rustic aroma. This always signaled that the celebration inside was ready to begin.

Kuynipper led Juan towards the lodge.

"Why are there four chimneys?" Juan asked.

"In part, it symbolizes that someone arriving in Heaven has been forever joined together with Father, Son, and Holy Spirit—one God joined together with His redeemed child arriving Home. The fires from the four chimneys blend together to form one aroma. As you have already learned, you are now joined with the LORD's very heart."

"That's awesome," Juan said.

Once they ascended the six steps up to the front porch, the angel said, "This is what your soul has longed for, Juan. But I must now leave you. Another angel has been assigned to be your orientation coordinator. She is inside the lodge, and will guide you after this gathering is finished. But please know this; you will never experience sadness ever again."

"Thank you, Kuynipper. I'm very grateful."

Kuynipper nodded. The angel then opened the huge, medieval wooden door for Juan, who joyfully stepped inside.

All of the excited conversations in the forest lodge came to an abrupt halt as Juan entered the main hall. Kuynipper gently shut the door behind him. The bright light inside the forest lodge stood in stark contrast to the peacefully muted light surrounding the area directly outside. Juan stood there with anticipation; his excitement was palpable.

Once again, and for a third time during his new journey, a presence on his right moved towards Juan, touching his arm. There was a great quiet in the lodge now, as everyone in the group of people in front of him remained completely still.

The next words that Juan heard were the most incredible words that anyone who loves the LORD can ever hear:

"Well done, good and faithful servant."

As Juan looked to his right, he was greeted with the most amazing sight he would ever see for all of eternity. This poignant event was the absolute moment of truth for what every true Christian longs for in their heart the most—physically meeting Jesus Christ for the very first time.

Juan's joy was beyond compare. Standing there before him—in his very presence—was the LORD Jesus Christ. Juan didn't know what to say.

"I love you, my son," Jesus said, breaking the silence. *"You have indeed fought the good fight for me. Because of this, I will never allow you to feel pain ever again."*

"I love you too, my LORD," Juan said humbly. "Everything here seems so different. But at the same time, very familiar."

"That is the desire I have for my children," Jesus said. *"In my home, you will see every thing as I have always intended it to be. During your brief time on Earth, you have only seen the corrupted version of my creation. Now that you are home with me forever, you will only see things as I desire."*

"Thank you, my LORD."

"Join me, Juan; I have some others who are excited that you're home." Jesus led Juan by the arm into the throng of visitors. As they proceeded into the lodge, a group of guests folded into a circle behind them. Juan then proceeded to gaze into the faces of the lodge's numerous guests.

He recognized them all.

A thought suddenly entered his head, but before he could say anything, Jesus spoke.

"Juan my son . . . your suffering on Earth was only temporary . . . it is now time to reunite with those who love you . . . it is now time to be with your permanent family in my eternal home. Welcome, my son . . . ."

Moving from behind several friends, Juan saw his wife Cecelia, his son Juan, and his two daughters Isabella and Lourdes. They all stepped forward, smiling brightly.

No words could adequately describe the magnitude of his emotions.

The first amazing event since dying a short time ago was Juan's physical transformation, which is described in *1 Corinthians 15:42-44 . . . So will it be with the resurrection of the dead. The body that is sown is perishable, it is raised imperishable; it is sown in dishonor, it is raised in glory; it is sown in weakness, it is raised in power; it is sown a natural body, it is raised a spiritual body. If there is a natural body, there is also a spiritual body.*

Then, after briefly glimpsing the most amazing kingdom in existence, Juan was able to gaze upon the face of his beloved Savior, Jesus Christ. Now, as he stood among many old friends from his time on Earth, Juan was finally reunited with his wife and children.

Other than physically meeting Jesus for the very first time, he knew in his heart this was the most amazing reward any Christian can ever have—a long-awaited, permanent reunion with loved ones who died before him in Christ.

Juan was overwhelmed.

This singular moment of once again seeing his wife and children was the event which Juan had longed for in his heart since his family had been inadvertently and callously gunned down several years before. At that time, his family's departure from Earth had ripped his life to shreds. Now, Juan felt a tremendous sense of completeness and peace once again. Every good thing that had been temporarily lost was now restored.

Mick stood in the back of the room, watching the scene unfold. Juan had been an excellent soldier for Mick on Earth, and his presence would be greatly missed. However, the angel always knew this particular joyous moment would occur one day.

It always did.

Mick's heart leapt when he witnessed events like this; moments when the LORD's tremendous healing and restoration overcame the devil's attacks from down on Earth.

Cecelia and the kids joyfully ran into Juan's arms as everyone in the forest lodge began to heartily cheer and clap with much enthusiasm. Juan and his family then smothered each other with hugs of relief and joy.

The long, arduous journey for this family had finally reached the finish line. And of course, this final victory belonged to Jesus Christ and his boundless Grace.

The corruption that once was . . . the pain that had endured . . . the tears that had fallen . . . all of these were now wiped away; neither to be seen nor experienced ever again.

Juan was finally home with Jesus Christ and his beloved family.

Forever.

It was indeed, another spectacular day in Heaven.

Methuen, MA
October 9th

**"As the mountains surround Jerusalem,
so the Lord surrounds his people both now and forevermore."
Psalm 125:2**

A thin layer of frost snuck its way into New England that morning, bringing forth a subtle omen that frigid weather was indeed on its way. With the remnants of summer safely tucked away in the rear-view mirror, vibrant orange pumpkins and jack-o-lanterns dotted the urban landscape, joyfully announcing the peak of the autumn season.

The previous afternoon was a triumphant one for Wyatt and Cam as the author was released from the hospital only a few days after his near fatal attack. Wyatt's doctors and nurses were absolutely amazed he had recovered to the extent that he could be released so quickly. Nurse Hendricks declared it to be an absolute miracle.

Wyatt and Cam heartily agreed.

Joining Cam in his return to their home in Methuen was Wyatt's cousin Frank, and oddly enough, Alistair McClellan. With spare bedrooms available in the upstairs of Wyatt and Cam's house, both visitors were able to relax the previous two nights in comfortable accommodations. After Cam assisted Wyatt in getting settled into his man-cave in the basement the previous evening, Cam, Al, and Frank watched the original <u>Raiders of the Lost Ark</u> together.

Assisting in the logistics the previous afternoon, Frank had generously chauffeured Al to the hotel to retrieve his personal belongings, then followed him to Logan Airport so he could turn in his rental car. The oddly-paired twosome then drove to Wyatt's house for what was quickly evolving into an adult version of a sleepover.

Cam stood in the kitchen in sweat pants and a Pittsburgh Steelers sweatshirt, busying himself with tending to his guests. The enticing aroma of freshly brewed coffee wafted into the living room from the kitchen, thereby announcing that the morning festivities had officially begun. Cam had already gathered together an assembly line of coffee accoutrements for his honored guests, which included a soon-to-be-arriving pony-tailed angel named Mick.

The centerpiece for that morning's "gourmet" breakfast were three boxes of freshly made donuts from a local shop, which Cam had fetched earlier that morning. To round out the definitively male-oriented repast was the scintillating smell of freshly sizzling, hickory-smoked bacon, which Cam was busily preparing.

The doorbell suddenly rang over the sound of the morning news blaring through the home theater system in the living room, where Frank and Al were relaxing.

"Do you want me to—?" Frank began.

"No, I'll get it Uncle Frank," Cam said. "You and Al take it easy."

"That'll work for me," Frank said.

"Indeed," Al added.

"By the way, the coffee's ready," Cam said. "Help yourselves."

Cam then proceeded to the front door and opened it.

To his utter amazement, his brother Danny and good ole Mick stood in the doorway, grinning widely.

"What's happening, bro???" Cam said.

Danny and Cam shook hands and man-hugged.

"Nothing much," Danny said. "Good to see you again!"

"Yo Mick," Cam said. "How come you didn't tell me Danny was flying in?"

"I'm afraid that's *angel business,* dude."

"I see," Cam said, wearing a smirk. "C'mon in, guys."

Everyone said their hellos and appropriate introductions went all around. After a couple of minutes of chatter, Mick dispatched Danny and Cam to retrieve Wyatt from his room in the basement so he could join their breakfast gathering.

After being so far away in Seattle when Wyatt was attacked a few days before, upon his arrival downstairs, Danny was absolutely elated to see his father.

Using Danny and Cam's minor assistance with climbing the stairs, Wyatt appeared at the top of the basement stairwell, onto the main level of the house. When the author saw Mick he began to speak, but Mick beat him to the punch.

"Hey there dude. Fancy seeing you again so soon."

Wyatt chuckled. "Back atcha, Mick."

Instinctively, Wyatt knew that his vision within the dream two days before was strictly between himself and Mick for the time being.

"Is that perchance the aroma of freshly brewed coffee?" Mick asked. "If so, I'd sure like to partake in some of it, please."

"Why are you sounding so officious?" Cam asked. "You don't have to ask permission to grab a cup of java around here. You know that!"

"How right you are," Mick said. "So what've you brewed up today?"

"One of your favorites—Seattle's Best number four."

"Excellen-tay!" Mick said.

"After that's done," Danny added, "I brought some fresh stuff directly from the coffee capital for our little pow-wow today."

"Cool, bro!" Cam said. "What did you bring?"

"A coffee staple—some Starbucks Espresso Roast—right from their store in Pike Place Market. You still have that fancy espresso machine, dontcha Cam?"

"We sure do. Pop and I have actually assembled together quite a collection: a Keurig for single cups, a regular Bunn coffee maker for large pots of coffee, and also a pretty cool espresso machine for lattes and whatnot. We're pretty much armed and ready."

"That sure sounds good," Danny said.

"But first," Cam continued, "let's all partake in some of this *gourmet grub*. The bacon is just about ready and the donuts are fresh."

"You can keep the bacon," Mick added, "but those donuts sure sound good."

After the five men and one slightly unorthodox angel enjoyed their dude-oriented feast, Cam and Danny brewed up lattes for the entire group. When everyone had what they wanted, they all settled-down in the living room for a little chat.

"So Al," Mick began. "How does it feel to have a cup of joe with a *real* angel?"

"Well I must admit," Al said. "Everything I've seen for the past few days has been quite an eye-opener. Although I must say; you're at least the fourth different angel who I've encountered."

"That's true," Mick said. "I'm quite sure these past few days have been somewhat of a whirlwind for you."

"Indeed they have."

"I'm guessing that you and Frank have gotten to know each other pretty well during this time, huh?"

"We certainly have. Frank tells me that our families once battled against evil forces together back in my hometown of Dundee, Scotland."

"He is correct," Mick said. "In fact, your folks—the McClellan clan, the Baugh family—Jacques and JJ's people, and the Hunter family once banded together against a huge force of evil across the pond."

"So when did this happen?" Al asked.

"It was a few hundred years ago," Mick said. "Listen; one day we'll get into the history of what happened back then. But not today. The good news for today is that the LORD has chosen to reveal Himself to you in a big, big way, huh?"

"He most certainly has," Al said. "And I honestly cannot wait to see what's next. Frank and I have spent a good deal of time during the past day or so talking about God. And I must admit, I'm learning quite a bit. To me, it's amazing how much having belief in Jesus Christ makes so much more sense; that is, once you've removed two essentially detrimental elements. I'm sad to say, I've mistakenly allowed these negative things to influence my spiritual life thus far."

"Oh—?" Mick asked. "What elements are they?"

"Firstly; once I witnessed the battle the other night between angels and demons, I obviously dropped the whole, *putting God on trial* thing."

"What do you mean by that?" Cam asked.

"I can now see that in the past, I was being purely and utterly arrogant," Al said. "And I'm afraid that many of my academic contemporaries follow that very same script when they either question whether God exists—just as I once did—or outright deny His existence. Once I saw the evidence of this *spiritual war,* as Frank so aptly puts it, I realized that I'm but a small pawn in the reality of life. At that point, I understood that attempting to make an all-powerful God prove Himself to me—a mere speck of dust on the horizon of humanity—well, let's just say that I'm embarrassed that I ever had the arrogance to put the LORD on trial . . . so to speak."

"That makes sense," Cam said. "The LORD has absolutely nothing He needs to prove to any of us."

Al nodded. "So basically, the first detrimental item which kept me from knowing Jesus Christ was my own, stubborn, self-centered pride."

"That's true for all of us," Wyatt added.

"Secondly," Al continued, "once our dear chap Frank explained his faith in Christ to me in such a *non-religious* way, it sure made a lot more sense."

"What exactly do you mean by that?" Danny asked.

"Faith in the LORD should not be based on religious traditions," Al said. "It should be based on a *relationship* with Jesus Christ. In the past, I've allowed too many religious people to influence my understanding of the LORD. However, once I was past that, I realized the LORD desires our *hearts* more than anything else. In my own heart, many things fell into place after that."

Mick nodded emphatically. "Religion is fake . . . Jesus is real."

"Anyway Al, welcome to our group," Wyatt said. "I'm confident you'll be a tremendous ally in our war against Satan's evil ways."

"Thank you, Wyatt."

"So Frank," Wyatt began. "I haven't actually seen you in a couple of years there, cousin. What—or should I ask *who*—asked you to show up on my near-death bed a couple of days ago? You sure are a long way from your home in Bloomington, Indiana."

"What can I say, cuz?" Frank said. "A certain angelic, mutual friend of ours told me that it's finally time that you and I discuss what I do for God's kingdom."

"Really?" Wyatt asked. "I wonder who told you that?!?!?"

"Alright guys," Mick nodded, chuckling, "let's stay on topic. But before we get started, I have a few things I need to say."

"Go for it," Frank said.

"First off," Mick continued, "our friend Juan's funeral is coming up soon, but it will be very low-key. We're having it in the next week or so out in California in order to lay him to rest with his family. You see; his wife and daughters were tragically killed a few years ago. So of course, Juan is now reunited with them in Heaven."

"That's awesome!" Wyatt said. "It seems that I was pretty close to joining him up there in Heaven, myself."

"Thank God you didn't," Danny said.

"Amen," Cam agreed.

"The next thing," Mick continued, "is a Scripture that I want all of you to concentrate on as some great mysteries get revealed here today. You'll need to remember this passage as all of you take the next step in our war against Satan and his demons. It's from *Galatians 5:22-23* . . . *But the fruit of the Spirit is love, joy, peace, forbearance, kindness, goodness, faithfulness, gentleness and self control. Against such things there is no law.*"

"I see," Cam said. "We should take the Gospel out to the world in the spirit of love and joy, etc.—right?"

"*Ding-ding-ding!*" Mick said. "Way to go, dude. That's absolutely correct. If we're going to wage war *God's way*, these fruits of the Holy Spirit are how you need to continue to conduct yourself as witnesses to the world. Remember—to some people, you may be the first or *only* true witness to them of our LORD, Jesus Christ. So please; don't take this responsibility lightly."

"I think we all agree with that concept," Cam said. "No offense, but why do you keep bringing it up?"

"I have to keep reminding you guys of this because all of you are men. Let's face it; men can sometimes be macho knuckleheads. Puffing your chests out and banging on them is obviously *not* the LORD's way."

"Acknowledged," Cam said.

"Anyways," Mick continued, "I also need to advise everyone that Wyatt, here, is going to be moving back to the Seattle area very soon. He's dong this so he can concentrate on his novels."

"Really?" Cam asked. "Why does Pop have to move away? I mean; we've had such an awesome time during the past few months. Why does it have to end so soon?"

"I think you know the answer to that question," Mick said. "It's time to fess-up and tell everyone how you really feel about Maria."

Cam remained quiet.

"Listen son," Wyatt added. "I never thought I'd be living with you forever. After all, you're a young man, and I always knew you'd be starting a family one day. So don't worry about me; I'll be living near your brother in Seattle, and I'll still be involved with our group. But as for me going out and doing any demon-bashing . . . well . . . I probably won't be doing a lot of that. But of course, you never know."

"I hear you Pop," Cam said softly. "I just didn't want you to think I didn't love you because I'm considering asking Maria to marry me one day. If things proceed and we do get married, the prospect of you living with us would never have posed a problem."

Wyatt smiled. "Don't go thinking it's okay to mess around with my man-cave downstairs, son. Planes fly from Seattle to Boston all the time, you know. Don't forget the fact that I'm not moving to another planet. It's just that I feel the LORD's call for me is to concentrate on the message in my novels. My work for Him is actually just beginning."

"Don't worry Cam—we'll be seeing dad quite a bit," Danny added. "Mick tells me he'll actually be living across Puget Sound on Bainbridge

Island, so he'll only be a short ferry ride away. I expect that we'll be seeing him a lot."

"That's cool," Cam said. "And I suppose you can always call Pop to cover a shift for you at the book store in Pike Place Market if you really need him to."

"Pike Place Market is absolutely my favorite place on Earth," Wyatt declared. "So that won't be a problem. Besides, I'm not sure I can live another day without seeing my dog Baby. I really miss her, you know."

"She also misses you," Danny said. "We'll have to work out a visitation schedule or something."

"That'll work," Wyatt said, winking.

"So Wyatt," Frank said. "Why do you like this Pike Place Market so much? What's the big deal about it?"

"It's kinda hard to explain that, Frank," Wyatt said. "To me, it's just a magical place. There's just a certain something about when I'm there that gives me a great sense of peace."

"You'll have to give me a tour of it some time soon."

"Good idea!" Wyatt said. "You know, it's weird, because when I think about going to Heaven, I often wonder what the markets up there will be like. I've been told they're absolutely magnificent."

Wyatt winked at Mick, who simply shrugged.

"Anyways," Mick said. "Before we get into Frank's personal ministry, I want to give you guys a warning, right up front. The passage I'm going to read to you is from *Luke 9:42-43 . . . Even while the boy was coming, the demon threw him to the ground in a convulsion. But Jesus rebuked the impure spirit, healed the boy and gave him back to his father. And they were all amazed at the greatness of God.*"

"So what's up with that passage?" Danny asked.

"Dealing with demons is *serious* business," Mick said soberly.

"Hmmm," Cam mumbled. "What is it that you do, Uncle Frank?"

Mick nodded at Frank to proceed.

"First off, let me give you guys a little history," Frank said. "My father, Billy Hunter, is the younger brother of Wyatt's daddy Earl. And believe me when I tell you this—dad and I were *sooo* happy when we heard that Uncle Earl surrendered his life to Christ before he died last February. His salvation was of great concern to us."

"Isn't that the truth," Wyatt murmured.

"Unfortunately Wyatt, dad and I were on a mission and couldn't attend his funeral."

"No problem Frank."

"Anyway, unbeknownst to you, Wyatt, my dad has been involved in some very unique ministry work for many years now. The truth is; no one else in the family except dad, myself, and my wife Nadine, know the details of what we do. Actually, the stuff dad was originally assigned to do has now been passed down to Nadine and me. Anyway, since we're unable to conceive any children, I'm not really sure who'll take over for us after we're gone . . . if anyone at all."

"C'mon Frank," Wyatt bemoaned. "You've really got my curiosity piqued. Please spit it out—whatever it is you have to say."

"Well . . . basically . . . Nadine, me, and your Uncle Billy are demon hunters."

"You're what???" Wyatt asked, incredulous.

"You heard me right. Demon hunters. You see; demons are deceivers, and they often manifest themselves as many things in our world . . . including vampires."

"Wait a minute! I thought vampires were only mythical. Am I missing something here?"

"No Wyatt, you're not missing anything," Frank said chuckling. "What I really mean is this: Throughout the world's history, demons have been sneaking around committing atrocities under the guise of many evil things—including the mythical vampires. So yes, there is at least a little bit of truth to them. You see; legends of monsters and vampires are steeped in virtually every culture the world has ever seen. And while it's true there's been a ton of fiction developed about demons over the years, make no mistake about it—demons are deceivers who'll carry out their evil agenda under the deceptive guise of many evil and scary things . . . like vampires . . . and werewolves . . . you get the picture. Hunting down nests of these deceptive demons and driving them out of their hosts is what you might say is our part of the ancient *Hunter family mission* . . . so to speak."

"First off; I want you to know I have a bunch of questions," Wyatt said. "But please go on. This is really interesting."

"Dad is mostly retired now, so he usually stays in the background at home—much like Jacques does for JJ."

"You know Jacques and JJ?"

"Of course I do," Frank said. "I've been working with them for many years now."

"I see. So what else do you know?"

"Let's see; my dad knew that when your father Earl left your mother Abbie back in the sixties, that Caleb wasn't really dead. That's just the lie Uncle Earl told everyone. Your Uncle Billy had been brought into kingdom service by Mick well-before then, and dad knew what his brother was doing was hugely wrong."

"Then why didn't Uncle Billy intervene?" Wyatt asked.

"Our dads really didn't get along very well and rarely spoke," Frank said. "Also, my dad was instructed to stay out of it. You have to remember this—when you've been chosen to serve God, you also must obey His commands, even if they don't make any sense to you at the time. By being obedient, you avoid getting in the way of God's will for the events that are unfolding. I don't know about you, but I sure don't want to get in God's way."

"That makes sense," Cam said.

"So what else do you have to say, Frank?" Wyatt asked.

"I've actually kept up with things in your life pretty closely, Wyatt. When Vanessa died—which I believe was the last time I saw you before this week—I surmised that you'd soon be getting an official visit from our good ole friend Mick. You see; I know all about the Hunter family missions of engaging in spiritual warfare throughout history. I also know that most of the men of our family end up *in the game,* so to speak."

"So you knew that Mick was putting together our group, Flaming Sword Communications, huh?"

"I sure did. Believe me; it's been a little frustrating not telling you about this over the years. But it's all proceeding according to the LORD's plan. So I'm obviously good with that."

"This is really getting weird," Wyatt bemoaned. "So you're in some kind of *deliverance ministry,* huh?"

"Not exactly," Frank said. "There are indeed deliverance ministries throughout the world, but ours is a little different."

"How so?" Danny asked.

"First off, we don't use special methods and whatnot. Although driving out demons is extremely serious business—*and should absolutely not be dabbled in*—we use more of a providential method in what we do. Actually, the approach we utilize is vastly different than what many others use, which is an in-your-face warfare utilizing certain methods. The bottom line is that we use the power of the Holy Spirit to deal with demons, instead of some esoteric man-made methods."

"I've never heard of the providential approach before," Cam said. "That's very interesting."

"Truthfully, our methods aren't very fancy, but we understand *exactly* what we're engaging in. Trust me; it takes years of practice to effectively do what we do. Not only that, but we end up dealing with many of the same demons, over-and over."

"Hmmm," Wyatt mumbled. "So when did Uncle Billy bring you into this ministry?"

"As you might remember, when I was about fifteen, my mother Connie was murdered. However, it wasn't due to a bunch of robbers breaking into our house; like what was reported in the news."

"So what happened to Aunt Connie?" Wyatt asked. "I remember when it happened many years ago."

Frank sighed. "Dad actually made a minor error when he drove out the lead-demon from a nearby nest. So when dad and I were at a movie a few nights later, a group of five demon-led lunatics broke into our home and killed my mom. The cover story was that it was a robbery-gone-bad, but that wasn't true. Demons attacked and killed her. That was all they wanted."

"That's shocking. So what happened after that?"

WADE J. CAREY

"A friend of ours named Pete, who is with a special division of the FBI, helped dad keep the whole thing out of the media. But the end result was that mom was killed by demon-possessed lunatics."

"I see," Wyatt said. "Satan and his demons sure seem to enjoy attacking the women of our family."

"Unfortunately, they do," Frank said, then turned to Danny and Cam. "You guys need to be *extra* careful in protecting your wife and girlfriend. I suggest praying for their protection every single day, as well as being aware of what's going on around them at all times."

"We sure will," Danny said. Cam nodded.

"Anyway," Wyatt said. "So does this Pete-fellow help you guys in your specialized ministry? Does he drive out demons as well?"

"Not exactly," Frank said. "Although he is sometimes forced to get involved in things like that. Believe me; Pete knows he shouldn't casually mess around with evil spirits, because demons are quite dangerous. If you don't believe me, check out what happened to the Seven Sons of Sceva in *Acts 19:13-16*. Those guys really messed up by dabbling with demons without knowing what they were doing. They also apparently didn't have the proper faith in Christ. Trust me; our G-man Pete is smart enough to know the difference."

"Hey Mick," Cam began, "is this Pete fellow the same one who helped with the cleanup the other night when dad and I were attacked by that disgusting legion-demon?"

"That's correct," Mick said. "Pete deployed some of his associates to handle that situation. That's part of what he does for us."

"Anyway Frank," Wyatt said. "Do you get involved in any other paranormal activities? I mean; other than shutting down groups of demonic psychos?"

"Sometimes we do," Frank said. "We've actually done some work with driving away evil spirits in different situations."

"Such as . . . ?" Cam asked.

"Like demonic spirits infesting houses . . . the occasional alien-abduction deceit—which always includes demonic activity . . . Bigfoot sightings . . . and a few other oddball paranormal activities. Things like that. Please know that everything we do is to destroy Satan's lies and deception and to bring the glory to God. You have to remember this: by their very nature, demons are liars. My job is to cut through the deception and bring them into the light."

"Gosh Frank," Wyatt began, "are you, Uncle Billy, and Nadine some kind of *Christian Ghostbusters* or something???"

Frank chuckled. "I suppose you could say that's at least partially true."

"You mentioned earlier, Uncle Frank, that you and Aunt Nadine aren't able to have any children," Danny said. "So what will happen to your work when you're gone?"

Frank shrugged. "I'm not really sure Danny. All I know is that you and Cam are the youngest of the Hunter dynasty who loves the LORD, so the fate of our family will likely happen through both of your heirs— at least on the godly side. You see; this is the smallest group of men who are fighting for Jesus in the history of our family. So I expect that your son DJ, and any future sons that you and Cam may have, will be the ones involved in any future biblical end-times events."

"Really?" Wyatt asked. "I guess I hadn't thought about that."

"Listen fellas," Mick said. "Let's not get into all of that end-times stuff right now. We have more pressing things to be working on today."

"Like where Caleb is?" Wyatt asked.

"That's correct, dude."

"So what's the next step?" Cam asked.

"First things first," Mick said. "Al is fixing to head to the airport tomorrow so he can go home and see where his new life in Christ is leading him. Also, Frank has an assignment coming up back in the Midwest, so he'll be heading towards the house tomorrow."

"Other than coming to see me," Wyatt began, "is Danny in town for anything else?"

"He sure is," Mick said. "For today, we're supposed to just sit-tight and relax. Very soon, Danny and Cam will be joining Moo, Bobby, Ben, and JJ on the trail of Caleb. But for today's assignment, we need to just chill-out and spend some time together."

"That sounds good to me," Wyatt said. "Before we break out some movies to watch, do you have any other official business?"

"Actually, I do," Mick said. "I have one last thing . . . Al . . . do you have anything you want to say?"

"I certainly do."

"Don't be shy—go ahead."

"My dearest new friends," Al began, "Due to the many things which I've witnessed the past few days, coupled with Frank's gracious assistance, I'm now ready to ask the LORD Jesus Christ for forgiveness of my incredible arrogance, rebellion, and overall sinfulness against Him. Although the events upon which I came to know that Jesus is LORD of all were very unique; nevertheless, I'm ready to surrender the rest of my life to Him. I'd like to ask all of you to join me in this endeavor."

"Wyatt my friend," Mick said. "Would you mind leading Al in his prayer of repentance?"

"I certainly will," Wyatt said. "With pleasure."

Quechee, Vermont
October 9th

"For the LORD Almighty has purposed, and who can thwart him?
His hand is stretched out, and who can turn it back?"
Isaiah 14:27

The rustic diner on Route 4 in the quaint village of Quechee was sparsely patronized that afternoon, and due to what was about to go down, this was probably a good thing. With various members of the forces of God gathered together in this quiet town on the edge of a massive river gorge, one could almost feel the imminent confrontation between good and evil approaching. Very soon, a fateful tremor from the ongoing earthquake of battles between the forces of light and dark would be thrust upon the Flaming Sword crew as the IFI showdown drew near.

The restaurant's largely leaf-peeping lunch crowd had long since resumed their inspection of the colorful bounty from the area's maples and oaks, so the group was mostly alone. Overcast skies had now moved in, replacing the early morning's sunshine. As the diner's closing time of two-thirty beckoned like the two-minute warning in a football game, the troops relaxed in two adjacent booths; it was very much the calm before the storm. Included were Pete and Spiro, the angel Ben, and JJ, Moo, and Bobby.

The five humans and one angel had just finished a late lunch. Although they had intentionally avoided discussing the mission at hand by engaging in small talk about sports and current events, Ben had been somewhat quiet as the others chatted away. After the waitress cleared their tables and everyone had finished gulping down their coffee, Ben suggested they gather outside on the gravel driveway for even further privacy.

Pete's government sedan was parked next to JJ's Dodge Intrepid. The six of them now stood between the two vehicles. Moo and Bobby's rental SUV was parked on the other side of JJ's car.

"Okay gentlemen," Ben began, "it's time to get down to business. First off, I want to thank Pete and his newest associate, Spiro, for joining us here today. I also want to thank JJ, Moo, and Bobby for their brave work in storming the Synagogue of Satan's dungeon of death during our recent battle over on the coast. I must say; it was a very unpleasant and dangerous task indeed. For that, I thank you gentlemen."

They all nodded.

"I can also assure you that we will soon be back on the trail of Caleb Hunter," Ben continued. "But our orders for today are to first deal with this treacherous situation at IFI—"

"Listen Ben," Pete interrupted. "I know I'm speaking for all of us when I say we're sure glad the LORD sent you here to help us today. I've really enjoyed working with you in the past, and I know you'll be a real asset in helping us with what's about to go down. As you well-know, my usual angelic mentor, Carlton, isn't really suited for these types of front-line duties."

A sly grin slipped onto Ben's face as he nodded.

"And I'd like to also add," JJ began, "I think it goes without saying that we're all terribly sad about losing our friend and brother Juan in that battle over in Maine. But at the very least we know that Juan is home with the LORD now."

"He most certainly is," Ben agreed.

"So JJ," Pete began, "did my associates do a good job assisting you guys the other day? Their report back to me was that things went smoothly over at the Pritchard estate after Juan's murder."

"They sure did," JJ said. "I was amazed at how quickly they showed up after I contacted you. To tell you the truth, after your guys arrived, we really didn't have very much to do. They did a great job in arranging for several members of that satanic cult to be taken into custody. I understand they even arranged for Juan's body to be sent home to California."

"We're accustomed to coordinating those types of situations," Pete said. "My contractors handle the arrangements, and I use my government authority to get things done. The crew I sent in there is actually among the very best. Of course, my people had to cooperate with the local officials since there were deaths involved. But since Cape Elizabeth is a quiet area, I think the local cops were glad to have our federal assistance. At least, in this case they were."

"So how is all of this going to play out?" JJ asked. "You obviously can't let it get in the news that what went down was a battle between devil-worshippers and the forces of God, right?"

"No worries," Pete said. "In this case—as it typically is when we deal with The Servants—we really won't have to worry about keeping things quiet."

"Oh, why is that?" JJ asked.

"Because the man who killed Juan will gladly sign a confession and will be processed through normal due-process channels. The reason for this is that The Servants are content to do their time in prison in order to protect their group's anonymity. I suspect that the rest of those who we apprehended the other day—the ones that Moo clobbered—will be processed in much the same way. In reality, those members of the Synagogue of Satan are nothing more than glorified terrorists; they'll gladly die to protect their master, Satan, and his evil demons."

"I suppose that makes sense," Moo said. "It's twisted, but logical."

"Let's not forget," Pete continued, "that even though Juan's killer was possessed by a demon when he committed the murder, he was also an ardent member of that evil satanic group. So believe me; I'm sure he'll also gladly take the blame for Pritchard's killing, which was obviously done in self-defense. That'll help to keep things quiet."

"Really?" Moo asked. "That's odd; why would he confess to something he didn't do?"

"Like I said," Pete said. "All of the members of the Synagogue of Satan will do whatever they can to protect their anonymity. Their members will actually do everything within their power to ensure that the world doesn't discover who they really are. To tell you the truth, they're very much like a cult in that once you're a member, you're always a member."

"It sounds like you're loading up the prisons with a bunch of loyal Satanists," JJ said. "It almost sounds like The Servants are building an army within the prison system."

"That's one way of looking at it," Pete agreed.

"So what will happen with Pritchard's house?" JJ asked.

"We won't have to worry about any more satanic activities down in that cave," Pete said. "Pritchard's buddies will likely destroy all evidence of what they did down in that dungeon. Now that their group location has been exposed to us, The Servants will simply find somewhere else to set up shop. I hate to tell you this, but those guys are not only very slippery, but their organization is huge. They actually have home-bases set up all over the world. We're fortunate, however, in that their members appear to be concentrated right here in the United States and Mexico."

"So where do you think Caleb escaped to?" Bobby asked.

"It's difficult to say," Pete said. "But I recently arranged for Candace and Jacques from your group—along with one of my technicians in Washington—to work together on pinpointing them. Between the three, they're working together to see if we can figure out where Damon, Donovan, and Caleb fled to. We're all guessing that it can't be too far away; probably somewhere still in New England."

"I see," JJ said. "Not to change the subject, but how did Spiro here get hooked up with you Pete? I've been in contact with you over the years, but I've never heard you mention his name before."

Pete nodded at Spiro. "For many years," Spiro began, "I was Sampson's right-hand man at IFI. After I fled from them a few years ago, Ezekiel took over for me."

"Oh, I see," JJ said. "Not to pry or anything, but Ezekiel has done a number of executions for IFI. Is that something you did when you were with them?"

"Unfortunately yes," Spiro admitted.

"Actually, that's a fair question," Pete added. "But let me first say this: several members of the group Spiro just joined are ex-black ops agents. In order for them to become authorized contractors and cooperate with the U.S. government in this unique way, I've had to issue them blanket immunity for their past deeds of mercenary and vigilante activities. You see; I have the authority to issue this once-in-a-lifetime immunity in exchange for what is basically a lifetime commitment to serving the Two Seals Warriors and its godly initiatives. I'm happy to say that Spiro has now agreed to this deal."

"That's very interesting," JJ said. "Please go on."

"That's basically it. We would have never taken-in Spiro if we didn't believe him to have truly repented of his terrible sins of vengeance. Even though Spiro will never be legally prosecuted for his former vigilante activities, his real forgiveness can only come from our LORD, Jesus Christ."

"So let me get this straight Pete," Bobby said. "The Two Seals group you cooperate with is chock-full of ex-military and/or CIA types who help you fight against true evil? Some of these guys and gals have a checkered past, but they still have a bright future of fighting for the LORD?"

"Something like that, Bobby," Pete said. "My personal job is unique in that my expenses are privately funded, but I have full government authority through my position as Director of Paranormal Religious Activities. Essentially, I work in a completely autonomous fashion as a covert division within the FBI."

"For real?" Bobby asked.

"Absolutely," Pete said. "And oh-by-the-way Bobby, speaking of a checkered past, I was actually at the accident scene when Hank crashed into Wyatt's car in Athens a couple of years ago."

"You were?"

"I certainly was. That night, I was working with Mick, so he and I took care of things. I'm sure you probably don't remember very much about it Bobby, because you were passed out when we arranged for Hank—who was completely sober—to get you home safely."

"I suppose I need to thank you for that," Bobby said.

"There's no need," Pete said. "That was a fairly easy gig to handle; at least as it's compared to some of the other messes I've gotten involved in over the years."

Bobby nodded. "Well anyway, I do thank you."

"It's good to see you've dedicated your life to Christ," Pete said. "I love it when that happens. Since Mick was with me on the accident scene that fateful night when Wyatt's wife was killed, I figured you were somehow going to fit into God's plans down the road some day."

Moo patted Bobby on the back.

"So anyway guys," Pete continued. "Like Ben said, there'll be a resumption of the chase for Caleb and the Synagogue of Satan after we handle our business today. In the meantime; let me first give you all a little history: JJ and I spoke after Juan was killed the other day. Well, we ended up discussing the fact that Spiro had just joined my group. When I told JJ that Spiro had previously been involved with IFI, he advised me that he-himself had just met with them a couple of days before. Now this surprised me a great deal, because I know all-too-well how IFI operates. Sampson and I have been familiar with each other for a number of years now."

"So how does Sampson operate?" Moo asked. "What exactly do you mean by that?"

"It's my belief that Sampson likely has plans to execute JJ some time in the near future, after he finds him no longer useful. You see; right now, Sampson considers JJ to be an ally—that is, until Caleb Hunter is apprehended or killed. Once that's done, I'm afraid JJ would simply be a loose end. And I think we all know what IFI does with loose ends."

"There's no doubt that JJ would never have been allowed to live after Caleb was apprehended," Spiro added. "When JJ turned down Sampson's offer to go to work for them, his death sentence was thusly pronounced. Basically, Sampson and Ezekiel are trying to use JJ as a pawn to help them find Caleb. Once that's done, since JJ had already turned down the opportunity to go to work for IFI, his death sentence would have been carried out."

"Is that why we're fixing to go confront them?" Bobby asked.

Pete nodded at Ben.

"I'll now give you a little more history," the angel said. "Sampson's real name is Matthias Schmidt. He is from Germany. For some odd reason, those who are members of IFI are instructed to adopt Old Testament names when they are initiated into their order."

"Why is that?" JJ asked.

"I suppose it makes them feel more religious," Ben said. "Many people throughout history have claimed they believe in the LORD. Unfortunately, however, many of them project their faith with great arrogance instead of the requisite humility that a true experience with knowing Jesus Christ brings."

"I see," JJ said. "So what was your IFI name, Spiro?"

"I used the name Joshua," Spiro said. "Of course, I stopped using that name once I fled from them."

"For a number of years," Ben continued, "Pete and Sampson have been shadowy reflections of each other. The difference is that Pete has always served the LORD, while Sampson has only served his own, personal religious fervor. Sampson is very much convinced that he's serving the LORD by killing the wretched criminals of society. But by breaking the law, he only serves his own sanctimonious lust for revenge."

"I may be off-base here," Bobby said, "but I kinda understand why he'd want to take out murderers, rapists, and whatnot. Am I an idiot for feeling this way?"

"No Bobby," Ben said shaking his head. "Your disgust at evil is a part of being made in the image of the Most High God. But it's very important that you realize that *feeling* the need to exact revenge is natural; *acting* on that feeling is what is potentially dangerous."

"I suppose you're right," Bobby said. "Mick has stressed this with us many, many times."

"Listen Bobby," Pete added. "On a daily basis, I make sure to read *Hebrews 10:30*, which says . . . *For we know him who said, 'It is mine to avenge; I will repay,' and again, 'The Lord will judge his people* . . . The reason I do this is because I constantly need to remind myself that the war on evil belongs to the LORD. At the same time, I need to remember that seeking revenge on those who oppose God also belongs to the LORD—and Him alone."

"So getting back to Mick," Ben began, "many years ago, he appeared to Sampson . . . that is . . . Matthias Schmidt . . . while he was in seminary. You see; Matthias is a very-well educated man in matters of theology. I'm sad to say, however, while Matthias was working on his doctoral thesis, his only son was murdered in their home town outside of Munich, Germany. After that, Matthias chose to distort biblical teaching and seek out revenge as a twisted attempt at serving the LORD. So let me remind you all of something very important—you do *not* serve the LORD when you ignore His Holy Word. You only serve yourself when you do that."

"I'm confused," Moo said. "What actually prompted us coming together for our confrontation with IFI today? On the drive over here the other day, JJ told me he had made a commitment to Sampson about not disclosing the whereabouts of their home-base. Even though Sampson appears to be a very misguided man, I'm sure JJ would hate to go back on his word."

JJ nodded at Spiro.

"I can answer that," Spiro said. "Something apparently terrible was uncovered a few years ago that ultimately led to me leaving IFI. So it's *I* who am actually leading us to them—not JJ."

"What happened?" Moo asked. "What was this terrible thing?"

"I'm afraid I don't know. It's actually something my dearly departed wife Beatrice discovered about IFI. You see; something caused Sampson to have my wife Bea executed for treason against the group.

Unfortunately though, I have no idea what caused that to happen. But I believe it was something significant."

"It was very significant indeed," Ben said. "And very soon, we will be dragging that situation from the darkness into the light."

Pete's cell phone began ringing. "Hello?" Pete said, answering his phone. "I see," he continued, nodding. "We'll start heading that way."

Pete hung up.

"Who was that?" JJ asked.

"That was Saul," Pete said. "He works as a kind of personal assistant for Sampson and Ezekiel."

"Really? I met Saul the other day," JJ said. "Is he some kind of double-agent or something?"

"I guess you could describe him that way," Pete said. "He's actually a deep-cover angel."

"Saul is an *angel?*" JJ asked, surprised.

Pete nodded. "He sure is. I recently discovered that Mick has had Saul stationed at IFI for quite some time now."

"Listen JJ; I was shocked to discover this also," Spiro said. "I had no idea that for all those years of being around him, that Saul was actually an angel. I mean; I saw him most every day, but I had no idea."

"Wow," JJ said. "I guess God really does work in mysterious ways."

"He certainly does," Ben said. "Come; we must go now . . . ."

Heaven
October 9th

**"For he will command his angels concerning you
to guard you in all your ways"
Psalm 91:11**

The Agora central market in Heaven bustled with its usual activity once again as another day in Paradise lingered without hurry. In keeping with tradition, many of the participants from Juan's arrival celebration two days before also joined him for this gathering, which was among the first scheduled activities on Heaven's orientation agenda.

During that celebration at the forest lodge, Juan experienced the utter bliss of being reacquainted with many of his dearest friends from down on Earth. Among those blessed reunions, Juan especially enjoyed seeing the key people in his life who had helped him in his walk with Christ.

But what really surprised him that day were his numerous discussions with many citizens in attendance who had only played a minor role in his life. Some of those earthly intersections were only brief, passing moments. But upon entering Heaven, those moments ended up being retrospective surprises from the LORD. Juan had absolutely no idea that those seemingly insignificant people in his life were actually a part of God's plan of drawing him into eternal salvation.

Juan also met his orientation coordinator that day; a member of the heavenly hosts named Annabelle. She had been one of his guardian angels. Annabelle, who had beautiful red hair and soulful hazel eyes, had been overseeing Juan and his ancestors from Heaven for many generations now. Since a person's guardian angel or angels often lead new citizens during this phase of their acclimation into Heaven, the angel had been very busy lately with Juan and his family.

"So Annabelle," Juan said. "Please tell me more about Agora and why we're here today. This market is amazing! I mean; there are *sooo* many wonderful things here. The products are absolutely beautiful, and the diversity of the people who brought them here from the outer reaches of Heaven is beyond compare."

"I agree," Annabelle said. "But before we get started, let me first remind you of something very important."

"Oh, what's that?"

Annabelle grinned. "Please don't forget that you don't need any money here at Agora—it has absolutely no purpose. In fact, no currency of any kind exists in Heaven."

"Right you are!"

"So to answer your question, Juan, coming to Agora is an important part of your initial agenda, because the market atmosphere is something which is very familiar to citizens who are brand new to Heaven. The LORD plans it this way so He can demonstrate some of the similarities that Heaven has with what you experienced down on Earth—*like walking through a market.* So coming here is really just a part of your ongoing fellowship with the LORD."

"I see. So let me ask you another question. Why are so many of my friends from the forest lodge celebration joining us today? Please don't get me wrong—this is absolutely wonderful. It's just that I'm not accustomed to having celebrations which don't end abruptly with the sadness of saying goodbye. After a party or gathering down on Earth, I always seemed to have to get back to work or something. But up here, things seem to be totally different in that regard."

"They sure are," Annabelle agreed.

"Anyway, there must be fifty fellow-citizens with us; not to mention several angels. Including yourself."

"Due to your move from the fallen world and into your permanent fellowship with the LORD, the lack of running around in a frantic rush is one of the many positive changes you'll notice between Earth and Heaven. We don't have any pain or stress here, and there are generally no deadlines; at least, not in the earthly way. Anyway, you're observation is quite natural."

Juan lovingly squeezed his wife Cecelia's hand as they walked through the market with Annabelle. While they were married down on Earth, Juan often did this as a way of telling Cecelia how much he loved her. And of course, a pure love like that survives for eternity in the home of the LORD.

"You know something Annabelle?" Juan began slowly. "I've thoroughly enjoyed so many of the unexpected and amazing gifts from the LORD since I first arrived here."

"Oh, what gifts are you speaking of?" Annabelle asked, grinning.

"One of them was when I was greeted at the forest lodge by several acquaintances who I barely knew during my life on Earth. I even had a wonderful talk with one of my elementary school teachers who I really didn't care for when I was a kid. It was absolutely amazing to see her again; this time in her full glory in Heaven."

Annabelle nodded. "So who else did you meet?"

"I also ran into a fellow truck driver who I only briefly met at a truck stop in Wyoming many years ago. I remember that blustery winter night so very well. You see; I was parked next to this poor fellow named Jarvis who was flat broke—I mean, he had absolutely no cash to even buy a cup of coffee with. So because of his predicament, all I did was simply pay for his meal that night. It wasn't a really big deal you know; but I was amazed that such a small act of kindness on my part became such a wonderful rallying cry for celebrating the Lord's greatness in Heaven."

They continued perusing Agora's many items of food and hand-crafted artwork as they walked.

"That's how things work in the home of Jesus Christ," Annabelle said. "Since you already loved the Lord with all your heart, the many good deeds you did down on Earth were actually acts of worship to Him. In fact, all good deeds done by those who love Jesus mean *everything* to the heart of the Lord. Although Jesus doesn't want you to run around bragging about the things you do to help others, He always remembers—*and very much appreciates*—even the smallest acts of kindness from those who love Him. In other words, once you love Jesus Christ, no good thing ever goes unnoticed in the Kingdom of God."

"That's very cool," Juan said. "But I have another question for you."

"And that is . . . ?"

"I was a little surprised at the people who were not actually here in Heaven when I arrived. I knew many men and women on Earth who I believed loved the Lord, but they're not here. I suppose their faith must have been a façade or something. To tell you the truth; I was actually more than just a little surprised when I discovered that they're not here. Can you shed any light on this for me?"

"To answer that question, I must first quote an important Scripture to you Juan. *Romans 10:9* says . . . *If you declare with your mouth, 'Jesus is Lord,' and believe in your heart that God raised him from the dead, you will be saved* . . . The important thing to remember is this: Only the Lord knows someone's true feelings and whether they trust and obey Him. From the human perspective, the actual saving process is very simple in that the Holy Spirit provides the saving miracle—*not* any person. Your friends who are now battling evil down on Earth are simply called to proclaim the Gospel to the lost. God will handle the rest."

"I understand that part, Annabelle. But when the angel named Atoggishem escorted me into Heaven when I first died, he asked me a very curious question."

"Oh, what was that?"

"He asked me if I was surprised to be heading towards Heaven. I must admit; I thought it was a little odd. It was as if he wondered how strong my faith was."

"That's not why he asked you that question," Annabelle said. "Atoggishem was merely demonstrating to you the suddenness of that poignant moment when your eyes shut on Earth and open in Heaven for the very first time. For those who love Jesus, that is a wonderful moment when you leave sin behind forever. But for those who don't love Jesus, the darkness in their lives becomes much more pronounced when they die. In fact, it's absolutely terrifying."

"Hmmm," Juan mumbled. "So . . . does the LORD understand a person's fear of death?"

Annabelle shook her head. "Jesus never wants you to fear for anything. He wants you to have confident faith in Him and His promises."

"I see. But do you think the LORD understands a person not wanting to die down on Earth?"

"Of course He does," Annabelle said. "Since Jesus is the only One who can lift you from physical death into eternal life in Heaven, He knows *exactly* how you feel. Don't forget the fact that Jesus personally went through the same process of physically being born and dying. The LORD is the first fruits of life, death, *and* resurrection."

"He sure is."

By this time, the group arrived at a café within the market where they were planning to enjoy a feast together. Everyone began to assemble around several tables on the east end of the dining area.

As Juan sat there holding Cecelia's hand, he looked over at his children, Juan Jr., Isabella and Lourdes. A wave of joy exploded in his heart as he realized that he would never experience separation from them ever again. Because he had placed his faith in Jesus Christ and had lived his life as a living sacrifice for his Savior, Juan was now experiencing the eternal rewards of God's gift of Grace.

Juan smiled and nodded as many of his new extended family arrived and began to sit around the adjoining tables. Many of Wyatt's family members were there in attendance—Abbie, Earl, Patrick, and

Cammie. There were also Willie, Menelik, and Robert from Candace and Charlene's family. To Juan's right were several members of Mi-Cha and Moo's family, including the venerable Chung-Hee Kim. Many others followed.

As everyone continued to get settled at their tables, Juan pondered the startling difference between himself sitting there in total peace, and what his fellow warriors on Earth were currently doing to combat the evil forces of Satan. He prayed for his friends to persevere through their tribulations until they could one day sit in this very place, experiencing this unbounded joy.

And on that day, Juan would be the one joining his newly redeemed friends as they became the center of the celebration for leaving the fallen Earth behind forever . . . just as Juan was doing that very day.

It was indeed, another spectacular day in Heaven.

Woodstock, VT
October 9th

**"And no wonder, for Satan himself
masquerades as an angel of light."
2 Corinthians 11:14**

Leaving behind the rental SUV in Quechee, Moo, Bobby, and Ben piled into JJ's Dodge, joining him in following Pete and Spiro in their government sedan into nearby downtown Woodstock. As they turned north on Route 12, JJ found himself recognizing the trail which he had followed up to the IFI house just a few days before. This time, however, he felt much less intimidated due to the fact that he had such a powerful team behind him, including two angels—Ben and Saul.

Overcast skies continued to hover over the group as they made their way up the serpentine driveway and onto the gravel circular entry to the main house. Before turning counter-clockwise to move around towards the front door, JJ could see the black-suited Saul standing across the grass field at the bottom of the front porch. He marveled that only five days before when he had first met Saul, he had absolutely no idea that the man was actually a deep cover angel, assigned to infiltrate IFI.

Once both cars were parked in front of Sampson's black SUV, Pete jumped out and made a bee-line towards Saul, with Spiro joining him. Ben and the threesome in JJ's car followed closely behind.

"Greetings Spiro," Saul said. "It's good to see you again."

"Hello Saul. Fancy seeing you again under these circumstances." Saul nodded.

"Although this place creeps me out," Spiro continued, "I'm glad to be back here working for the good guys now."

"Indeed," Saul said.

"And I-myself didn't think I'd be back here so soon," JJ added.

"I can't say I'm surprised JJ," Saul said. "After your meeting with Sampson and Ezekiel last week, I felt like the LORD would soon be bringing His Light into this darkened place."

"What caused you to believe that?" JJ asked.

Saul grinned. "As you humans like to say, *this ain't my first rodeo.* After you turned Sampson down to join this wicked group, I combined the expectation that Ezekiel would have most certainly come to execute you very soon, with the understanding that your work for Flaming Sword is just beginning. The result seemed to indicate an apparent end to the lies and sanctimonious evil going on in this place."

"I see," JJ said. "I've been told over-and-over that you angels only know what God tells you, so you don't always know the entire plan. Right?"

"That's correct," Saul agreed. "Sometimes God tells us the whole plan, and sometimes He does not."

"So . . ." Pete began, "Ben and Saul . . . what's our plan here? Not to be rude, but time's-a-wasting."

"Saul and I will lead off the discussion when we get inside," Ben said. "We are here to confront this mysterious founder of IFI, who is currently meeting with Sampson and Ezekiel. After we begin the discussion, Saul and I will stand-by to ensure that our mission is successfully accomplished. At that point, Pete and Spiro will lead the proceedings. Are we clear?"

Everyone nodded.

"Please follow me," Saul said.

Saul showed the others the way inside. Once they were gathered in the entry way, the angel led the group—single file—to the right, towards Sampson's library.

Instead of knocking as he usually did, Saul opened the door and held it open for the others as they piled into the room. After the five humans and two angels were all inside, Saul closed the door behind them.

Sitting at the large round table were the recognizable faces of Sampson and Ezekiel, who both sported astonished expressions. The Founder of IFI sat in-between them, wearing a curious look of what was quickly evolving into an expression of mild horror.

"What in the world are you doing, Saul???" the Founder barked. "This intrusion is outrageous!"

Saul moved to the front of the group with Ben, but said nothing.

"Madam Founder," Ben said. "We are here today to discuss with you the subject of your group's involvement in countless criminal activities. I must say; you certainly do not serve God when you take the law into your own hands."

At this, Sampson and Ezekiel both bolted to their feet. The Founder remained seated.

"Oh . . . what criminal activities are those?" she asked brazenly.

"First off," Ben continued, "I am an angel of the Lord. Because of this, I *strongly* suggest you control your underlings." He nodded at Sampson and Ezekiel. "If you fail to do so, I will be forced to deal with them in a *most* unpleasant manner. Am I making myself abundantly clear?"

In response, The Founder waved Sampson and Ezekiel to sit down. They reluctantly complied.

"Now then," Ben continued, "I believe we were about to discuss your heinous vigilante activities—"

"May I at least have your name?" The Founder interrupted.

"Of course. My name is Ben. And your name is *Mildred Fountainhead*—founder of the IFI vigilante group. Please forgive my manners, but I'm *not* very pleased to make your acquaintance. You are indeed, an evil woman."

"What on Earth are you talking about?" Mildred leveled. "We're a charitable organization—"

"That is a lie!" Ben interrupted.

"Now you listen to me," Mildred said slowly, her face turning red. "IFI stands for 'Investment Finance Institute.' We're merely a charitable organization which helps small businesses get on their feet financially."

"You're still lying," Ben said. "You cannot fool me."

Sampson vaulted to his feet once again. Ezekiel joined him.

"Every single one of you is intruding on our property!" Sampson declared. "I am perfectly within my right to shoot all of you for barging in here and threatening us. And by the way Saul . . . *you're fired!*"

Saul remained quiet.

"Ahhh Sampson," Ben said. "I fully expected your substantial bravado to introduce itself to us early in these proceedings. It appears that I was correct."

Ezekiel slowly reached for the pistol inside his jacket. JJ had already brandished his own weapon before Ezekiel had a chance to retrieve his. He then pointed it directly at the IFI goon.

"Stand down Ezekiel—right now!" JJ shouted.

The bald, bushy-mustached Ezekiel slowly raised his hands above his head in submission.

"Put the piece on the table and slide it towards me," JJ demanded. "But do it *slowly.*"

Ezekiel complied.

"I'm sorry to say this JJ, but I'm afraid you're a dead man," Sampson said with deadly confidence. "We both know that I warned you about betraying our location to anyone."

"It wasn't JJ who betrayed you Sampson," Spiro added, stepping from behind Moo and Bobby. *"It was I."*

Another look of utter astonishment passed over both Sampson's and Ezekiel's faces.

"You see," Spiro continued, "We've come here today to take you all into custody. That includes you, Mildred."

Mildred also stood up. She was of a medium build and clearly in her sixties. Her gaunt face was framed by her gray hair, which was done-up neatly in a bun. She wore a Victorian-like ensemble, which gave her the appearance of a woman fully entrenched in high-society.

"*Wait a minute,*" JJ said suddenly. "Now that I'm thinking about it; I've heard that name before—Mildred Fountainhead. Yeah, I remember now. I saw a dossier on you among Earl Hunter's files. *You're* the one who raised Caleb Hunter to be a leader for the Synagogue of Satan. *You were Caleb's nanny!*"

"Preposterous!" Mildred said. "I will *not* tolerate any more of this insolence. Either you leave here immediately, or I'll—"

"*Or you'll what?*" Spiro said through clenched teeth. "All of you are now done with your crimes of vengeance. If I hadn't already left your cult, I'd surely be on my way to prison with you."

The room remained uncomfortably quiet for a few moments.

"Let's get back to this nanny-thing," JJ said. "Hey Saul, am I off base here, or what? If I remember right, this woman is still an integral part of the Synagogue of Satan. Not only that, but she's probably inhabited by a demon or demons right now. After storming the Pritchard house the other day, we figured out that many of The Servants are *proud* to have demons inhabit them. It's some kind of honor among some factions of their group."

"You are not off base," Saul said. "I suggest you continue on your pathway towards the truth."

"Why are you asking my chauffeur what he thinks about anything?" Sampson asked, pointing at JJ. "Saul drives me around and fetches me tea in the afternoon. I think you may be—"

"*Shut your face, Sampson!*" Spiro shouted. "You're so blinded with your lust for revenge; you didn't even know that Saul is an angel of the Most High God. And believe me; I know you've met Mick before, so you're well aware that holy angels are for real."

"Spiro my good man, don't be so foolish," Sampson said coolly. "Why would the Lord send an angel to merely be my butler?"

"Why?!?!?" Spiro asked. "I can't believe how blinded you are by your pride, Sampson. The LORD sent Saul here because you don't serve God like you think you do with all of these revenge killings. I'm afraid I know that all-too-well now. I know that all of that killing we did together was being led by Satan and one of his cohorts. *That's you,* in case you're wondering Mildred."

Mildred stared straight ahead, but said nothing.

"What Sampson—you don't believe me?" Spiro continued. "Well now; we do have a biblical way to test the spirits, so to speak. Since you have a doctorate in theology, why don't you merely ask Mildred a few questions about who she serves? Have you ever thought about doing that before???"

Sampson was dumbfounded. He remained quiet.

"If you're so sure she's not being led or inhabited by demons in this IFI-thing," Spiro continued, "then I suggest you prove it to yourself and us right now. Tell me something; do you have the *guts* to do that?"

Sampson gazed sheepishly at Mildred. "Madam Founder," he began. "Why don't we go ahead and put this whole thing to rest so we can resume our duties. As you well-know, we're doing the work of God through all of our initiatives. And since JJ currently has a gun pointed at us, I'm going to ask you a few questions to appease their curiosity."

Mildred's eyes were red with fear, but she said nothing.

"*1 John 4:1-3* exhorts us to test the spirits," Sampson continued, "so I'll ask you a few questions to put their minds at ease. Since we serve God in all we do, this shouldn't take but a few moments."

Mildred began to slowly hyper-ventilate, but tried to suppress it.

"So Madam Founder," Sampson said. "Please answer this question: Did Jesus Christ come in the flesh—both fully God and fully man—into our world to save it from its sin? Please answer this question so we may dispense of these hooligans who have so rudely interrupted our meeting."

Mildred's head began to slowly circle as if she was holding back an intense wave of uncontrollable anger. This was something out of the ordinary for her, and Sampson knew it.

"Mildred . . . *please* . . . answer the question. Jesus is the unique son of God who came to save the world. He is the one and only way to eternal life in Heaven. You do believe in this basic tenet, don't you?"

Very slowly, Mildred spoke. *"I . . . acknowledge . . . that Jesus Christ . . . is the son of God . . . ."*

At this, Sampson's street-wise instincts clicked on.

"Mildred . . . that isn't what I asked you. Please now; acknowledge that Jesus Christ was born both fully-man and fully-God . . . that He did indeed appear in the flesh . . . that He was physically resurrected from the dead . . . that He is the only way to eternal life with God our Father in Heaven."

By now, Mildred's face had turned fully red. Sampson and Ezekiel found themselves totally stupefied at her cryptic response to such a simple question for a Christian to answer.

The dam suddenly broke.

"You fools!!!" Mildred shrieked. *"You have NO idea who the real power in this universe belongs to, do you?!?!?!"*

Sampson and Ezekiel slowly backed away from Mildred, who stood there in total defiance, continuing to hyper-ventilate.

"If you'll allow me, Sampson," Spiro said. "I think I can help you with this."

Sampson nodded nervously.

"Tell them Mildred," Spiro continued. "Tell them that you worship Lucifer and are one of his disciples; tell them that you would *never* have allowed them to harm a single hair on Caleb's head; tell them you raised Caleb to be the progenitor of the growing army against Yeshua and his followers . . . *tell them now!"*

Mildred breathed in, slowly regaining her composure. When she spoke this time, it was of an unearthly timbre; her voice echoed with an other-worldliness that summoned with it an army of goose bumps among the others in the room.

"Those of you who worship Yeshua are the most absurd people who have ever lived on this planet. Why? It's because you worship a god who creates you to enjoy certain things; then he says you can't indulge in them.

Meanwhile, for some inexplicable reason, you all get down on your knees and say that you love him. Fools! Every single one of you are fools!"

"Tell me something madam," Pete said. "Are we speaking with Mildred, or are we speaking with the evil spirits inhabiting her? Tell us *right now* who you are! In the name of Jesus Christ, *we demand to know!"*

Mildred's head tilted slightly upward, looking into the space above their heads; almost like she was looking into a completely different realm. Her bright eyes reflected a ghastly expression as she calmly continued.

"All of you still have a chance to follow Satan, because he will defeat Jesus Christ in the end. You have NO idea how powerful he is. You also have NO idea how powerful the army we are building will become. This Earth belongs to us, and we will not relinquish our power on it."

"Who *are* you demon???" Pete demanded. "Tell us now!"

Mildred sneered.

"Oh, there are many of us in this woman," Mildred replied, eerily. Her voice was now deeper and echoed with a frightening intonation. *"We have been stationed here for many decades now."*

"Why did my wife have to die?" Spiro asked. "Why did you have her killed?"

Mildred responded by smiling with glee.

Sampson shook his head in disgust. "I had absolutely no idea Spiro; I didn't know we were being led by a demon. You *must* believe me!"

"Tell me what happened, Mildred," Spiro demanded, ignoring Sampson.

"Beatrice was merely weak," Mildred said. *"She didn't deserve to live another moment. She was an absolute coward."*

At this, Spiro brandished his own pistol, aiming it right at Mildred.

"You're going to tell me *exactly* what happened to Beatrice," he demanded. "And you're going to tell me *right now!"*

Mildred, along with her cast of internal demons, laughed heartily.

"Oh, let's just say that Beatrice figured out that IFI was being led by the real god of this universe – Lucifer. I suppose you could say that she tested me in a similar way you filthy flesh bags just did."

"So what happened after she was on to you?" Spiro asked.

"I merely gave Sampson and Ezekiel the order to execute her because she had gone over to the side of Satan. Pretty ironic, huh? These two idiots were so blinded by their blood-lust for killing; they simply complied without asking any questions."

Spiro cocked his weapon.

"Okay Spiro, let's take it easy," Pete warned. "I can't help you if you shoot Mildred for no reason. We're going to take her into custody now. Please my friend, lower your weapon."

Spiro trembled with anger. After a few moments, he complied.

"So Mildred," Pete said. "All this time, you've been protecting Caleb from the one organization—IFI—which has been obsessed with finding and killing him. I must say; it was rather ingenious of you."

Mildred grinned. *"Keep you friends close . . . keep your enemies closer."*

Sampson sat down at the round table and buried his face in his hands in disgrace. In the meantime, Ezekiel slowly edged towards the back of the room. With everyone concentrating their attention on Mildred, no one else seemed to notice.

"So what now?" JJ asked. "What're we going to do with these scumbags?"

"They'll immediately be taken to a special place we have set aside for these kinds of offenders," Pete said. "But first, we must—"

"Do you mean to tell me that Spiro isn't going to be joining us?" Mildred asked sarcastically. *"Surely you know of what he's done for us in the past, Pete."*

"I do indeed," Pete said. "But do you really think I was unprepared for you to accuse my newest associate? This isn't my first run-in with demons you know."

"Oh, I absolutely know that to be a fact," Mildred said. *"We actually consider you to be quite a formidable adversary. In fact, we've all had many discussions about where this demon prison of yours is. I must say; you're very clever."*

"C'mon Mildred," Pete said. "The flattery ploy? Really? Surely you know I'm not going to fall for *that* little trick of yours."

Mildred grinned. *"Well . . . it was worth a shot."*

"So what is this demon prison she's talking about?" JJ asked.

"That's on a need-to-know basis," Pete said quickly. "And I'm afraid you're not ready to know that yet."

"Wait a minute!" JJ said. "Where is Ezekiel?"

Everyone looked around the room, then towards the fireplace at the far end. The trap door in front of the fireplace had been open during the proceedings.

"He must've exited through the prison downstairs," Saul said. "Shall I pursue him?"

Pete shook his head.

"No, Saul" he said. "JJ—why don't you go see if you can track Ezekiel down. And Bobby; since you're also packing, you go with him. But please; be very careful! I don't recommend getting into a shoot-out with Ezekiel. He's a very good shot."

"Hey, I'm not so bad myself," JJ bragged.

Pete nodded. "I gotcha. Anyway; we'll stay here and see if we can extract the location of Caleb, Damon, and Donovan from our new friend Mildred. Go now!"

JJ and Bobby proceeded into the tunnel under the house.

"Oh Mildred dear," Pete continued. "Before we take you away from here to a very special place, I'm going to ask you to tell us where Caleb is located. Actually, I'm going to *insist* you tell us. But to be totally honest here, I'm afraid this isn't a *polite* request. In fact; you're going to tell us *exactly* where Caleb is, whether you like it or not."

"Never!!!"

Pete nodded.

"Have it your way demon," he said. "Saul and Ben . . . I'm going to need your assistance, along with Moo. Oh, and Sampson . . . would you like to show some repentance and help us out here?"

"I absolutely will," Sampson said solemnly. "But only if you call me by my proper name—Matthias. I shall never be called *Sampson* ever again."

"I can do that," Pete said.

A pleased expression slipped onto the agent's face.

Seattle, WA
October 11th

"Be very careful, then, how you live—not as unwise but as wise, making the most of every opportunity, because the days are evil."
Ephesians 5:15-16

"We live in treacherous times indeed," Miss Charlene said sadly. "If you don't think the spirit of the antichrist is alive and active in the world today, then all you have to do is flip on the news for about *five* minutes. Oh, you'll see people doing awful things to their fellow man that are so self-obsessed; I'm surprised these people even notice anything outside of their twisted little worlds."

"Amen to that Miss Charlene," Pete said.

Lowell's restaurant in Pike Place Market was unusually quiet that morning as Charlene Harris sat in a booth against the window with Pete, Spiro, and Pete's assignment angel named Carlton. The group had just ordered their breakfast during the restaurant's mid-morning lull. It was now time for them to settle in for a little chat before their repast.

Pete, Spiro, and Carlton had arrived in Seattle late the night before. Carlton was the angel within Mick's group assigned to lead Pete's efforts in his cooperation with the Two Seals Warriors. Before the group's next appointment to discuss some important issues with Candace and Mi-Cha, it had been decided they would have a general strategy meeting over breakfast that day.

"So Carlton my friend; how's your cup of tea?" Spiro chided. "Is it acceptable?"

"Oh, I suppose it'll do," Carlton said. "But what this restaurant may lack in offering a proper cup of British tea, it certainly makes up for with this fabulous view of the waterfront. I must say; it's spectacular."

Charlene shook her head, grinning.

"Trust me Carlton; you'll also enjoy our breakfast when it arrives," Spiro said. "The food here is fantastic. When it gets down to it, that's the most important thing, huh?"

"Oh, I suppose you're right," Carlton relented.

"Out of all the possible angels that could've been assigned to bring missions to me, I'm working with a proper British-type. I feel *sooo* lucky," Pete joked. "Tell me Miss Charlene; how did you and your group luck-out and end up with a coffee-lover like Mick; while myself and the Two Seals got assigned tea-aficionado like Carlton?!?!?"

"I beg your pardon," Carlton said. "And after all we've been through together, Pete. Really! Now you're intimating that I'm some kind of snob or something. Come now; I think you should reconsider your position."

Pete chuckled.

As was his duty, the angel Carlton recently appeared to Pete to guide his work. On this particular occasion, it was after the unpleasant proceedings with IFI in Vermont two days before. Of course, the angel wore his traditional attire when appearing on Earth—an understated jacket on top of a shirt and tie. His slightly British-style accent blended nicely with his tall, slender frame, old-style spectacles, and neatly trimmed hair, set within the framework of typical male-pattern baldness. Above it all, the angel's mannerisms were very proper.

"Carlton my friend," Pete said. "You *really* should've been there during the confrontation with IFI the other day. It actually got a little rough when we had to hold ole Mildred down to extract the information we wanted. The demons inhabiting her were not real happy with our presence, you know."

"I'm sure," Carlton said.

"Anyway, Mildred didn't exactly want to cooperate by telling us where Caleb was hiding. Fortunately, however, we ended up getting what we needed."

"Indeed."

"But tell me something Carlton; why did your fellow angels, Ben and Saul, have to do all the dirty work?"

"Ben and Saul are merely better suited for dealing with those kinds of situations," Carlton said curtly.

Pete shrugged. "It must be nice to simply show up after all of the rough work is done, huh?"

Carlton shook his head admonishingly. "By now Pete," the angel began, "you must know that I'm more of an advisor than a warrior. Although I've been known to wield a sword on occasion, it's really not my calling. As you well-know, there are others in Mick's group who are much better suited to deal with . . . How shall I say this? . . . Ruffians and whatnot. It's not that I *cannot* deal with them; it's merely a fact that the other angels are better suited for those types of duties. As a result, I tend to stay out of such confrontations. Moreover, Pete, I'm just like you in that I stick with the assignments the Lord gives to me. You're familiar with *Ephesians 2:10*, are you not?"

"What do you mean by that?" Pete asked.

Carlton bristled. "God designed various duties for angels in a similar way He did for humans. I merely carry out what the Lord wants me to."

Pete held up his hands in a stop motion, grinning. "No problem Carlton," he said. "I get it. I'm just busting your chops."

"I see," Carlton said. "Now then; if you don't mind, I'd like to get on with the business at hand."

"I don't mind at all," Pete said.

"Now don't you go listening to these boys, Carlton," Charlene said. "I equally enjoy working with Mick, yourself, and any of the other angels the LORD sends down here. As far as I'm concerned, every single one of you is a blessing to us in our ongoing battles against evil."

"Thank you Miss Charlene," Carlton said. "I can always count on you for a kind word."

Charlene nodded. "By the way, where's Mick?" she asked.

"Mick is actually with the others in New England, chasing down Caleb," Carlton said. "He was assigned to be there today when the final confrontation with Caleb goes down. But no worries—Ben is also with him."

"And where is Saul?" Charlene asked.

"I'm afraid Saul is dealing with a grieving Sampson today," Carlton said. "Actually, I meant to say *Matthias*. Anyway, we're not sure if Matthias is going to prison, or if he'll be joining the Two Seals in some capacity. Either way, since IFI has a substantial apparatus in place, it's going to take a lot of effort to dismantle all of it. And believe me; Matthias is all-too happy to accommodate this."

"And if Matthias does end up joining us," Spiro added, "I've already forgiven him—*to his face*—for ordering Ezekiel to execute my wife Beatrice. I know that Matthias was only trying to carry out his duty—which unfortunately was being dictated by demons. To tell you the truth; I feel sorry for him and the repentance he's facing. I felt much the same way when I left IFI a few years ago."

"And I commend you for your proper attitude on that issue," Carlton said. "Jesus tells you to love your neighbor as you love yourself. As far as I'm concerned, that's an unambiguous command."

"I agree," Charlene said. "But let me ask you something Carlton. Did Mick stay with Danny and Cam to look over Wyatt's recovery, or was it because he was assigned to help my boys apprehend Caleb? I ask you this because I know that Mick stayed with Wyatt and his sons when the rest of you boys were storming IFI the other day."

"There was a good reason for Mick staying with Wyatt," Carlton said. "The reason is that he's focused on the Hunter family and their current mission-at-hand, which is to ensure that Caleb is apprehended."

"Oh, I see," Charlene said.

"Actually Miss Charlene," Carlton continued, "Mick—along with Danny and Cam—have now joined up with Moo, Bobby, JJ, and Ben to apprehend Caleb. The three of us," Carlton nodded towards Pete and Spiro, "had a brief meeting with some of the others after the IFI situation was secured the other day. We did this before Ben led his men towards Wyatt's house to meet up with Mick and Wyatt's sons. From there, the entire group—minus the ailing Wyatt—is planning a raid on Caleb's latest hideout. Like I said, this confrontation should actually occur sometime today. Perhaps very soon."

"So why aren't Pete and Spiro joining Mick and the others in apprehending Caleb?" Charlene asked.

"The Caleb matter is a personal one for the Hunter family," Pete added. "Our instructions from Captain Tea here," he nodded at Carlton, "was to come out here to work with the rest of the group today. Although the IFI takedown was a personal one for those of us involved with the Two Seals Warriors, the situation with Caleb and what he's done to the Hunter family was another matter altogether. Truthfully, what Caleb has done is an utter disgrace, so it's better handled by those directly involved. But don't worry; I have our crew in the Boston area on-site—just in case things get ugly today."

"I see," Charlene said. "So tell me Carlton; you've told me all about the situation with Matthias and Saul tending to him. But what actually happened to Mildred and Ezekiel?"

Carlton nodded at Pete.

"Unfortunately, Ezekiel escaped," Pete said. "His whereabouts are currently unknown."

"Oh. That's obviously not good. So what about Mildred?"

"I'm afraid that Mildred did what some of the demon possessed people in high-ranking positions within The Servants do when they're *out-ed*; so to speak."

"And that is—?"

"She committed suicide."

"I see," Charlene said. "That's very sad. Although I can't say I'm surprised. I know that on some occasions, you gentlemen take these demon-possessed people directly into custody and they're prosecuted; while other times, you first take them to that mysterious *demon prison* of yours."

"We really don't like to talk about the place we refer to as the *demon prison,*" Pete said soberly. "It's a place better left unspoken of."

"Hmmm," Charlene mumbled. "Can you tell me anything about it? I've obviously been curious about it over the years."

Pete sighed. "I suppose I can at least give you an overview. Ultimately, those who we take into custody are processed through the normal, legal, federal prosecution channels. But on occasion, when we're forced to deal with an unusually heinous demonic crime or crimes, we have a short-term lock-down facility where we first interrogate demon-possessed people. Of course, after we're through with them, the individuals—*minus their evil spirits*—get processed through the normal due-process channels. But as you know, that sometimes takes a while."

"How do you keep all of this out of the news?" Charlene asked.

"Trust me Miss Charlene," Pete said. "Those who are genuinely engaged in demonic activity are always—*and I mean always*—ready to go to the grave instead of letting their true satanic work get out into the public domain."

"Why is that?"

"It's because true followers of Satan are led by his demons who have made their soldiers give a blood-oath to remain anonymous. You see; if the members of the Synagogue of Satan were to be discovered, Satan's deceptive ways would be brought out into the open and therefore into the light. And believe me; that's the last thing in the world they want to happen."

"Have you ever had someone attempt to leave their ranks and try to help you?" Charlene asked. "Has anyone ever left The Servants?"

"Not that I know of," Pete said. "But we're still hoping someone will ultimately come forward."

"Not to change the subject," Charlene said. "But I remember the day when Mick had his first real meeting with Wyatt about a year ago. That morning, I had Wyatt mail three letters for me when he was headed up to the market to unknowingly meet with Mick. Wyatt did indeed mail those letters for me, but I don't think he ever realized they were letters I had written to some of those poor souls who have left that demon prison of yours and are now in federal prison."

"That's interesting," Pete said. "Maybe one of those prisoners will end up leaving The Servants and assist us with tracking them down. Anyway, I'm sure that Wyatt also doesn't know that his cousin Frank has been working with me for many years on apprehending some of these demon-possessed serial killers who work like the mythical vampires and other monsters. If Wyatt only knew some of the atrocities his cousin and uncle have seen over the years, he'd be shocked beyond belief."

"Perhaps not as much as you may think," Carlton added. "These men of the Hunter family are actually some pretty tough hombres as it relates to spiritual warfare. They typically take to spiritual battles like a duck takes to water."

"Perhaps you're right," Pete conceded.

"Don't forget about the people of my family also," Charlene said. "My ancient ancestors first became acquainted with Wyatt's people during Christ's earthly ministry—right before He was crucified. Our family has also been at this for a long time."

"Indeed," Carlton said. "And for all of the proceeding years since then, there's certainly been a lot of tension between the people of African descent, and those with Anglo descent. But as you know, the LORD has continued to weave the brotherhood of your two families together underneath all of that nonsense. It just goes to show that it takes someone like the Savior Jesus Christ to lift people out of their sinful prejudices and into true brotherhood as His children."

"Amen Carlton," Charlene said.

The angel nodded. "Now then . . . getting down to our other business at hand . . . I have a couple of things to discuss with the three of you before they're revealed to the others. The first thing, Miss Charlene, is that as is our customary way of doing things, you'll continue to guide the Flaming Sword group from behind the scenes. Candace will continue to remain out in front, running the daily operations. But since you have the deepest spiritual maturity of the lot, we still need your guidance down here on Earth."

"Thank you Carlton," Charlene said. "And let me say once again that I'm delighted that Spiro has now joined the Two Seals Warriors. We can certainly use all the help we can get."

"Absolutely," the angel agreed. "And as you also know, Miss Charlene, Pete's group often gets pre-warned about volatile situations just before they occur. Of course, when that happens, I'm the one who delivers the message to Pete, who then dispatches the Two Seals Warriors to be in place."

"That's true," Pete said. "For example, that actually just happened the other night when Carlton appeared to me when Wyatt and Cam were being attacked in Boston by Damon and company. Around the same time, Saul was dispatched to protect them."

"That's correct," Carlton said. "As usual, we-heavenly types are often called-on to protect humanity. Of course, most of the time, you humans never even know about it."

"I suppose we're just blessed to be among the few who get to know some angels before we arrive in Heaven," Charlene said, smiling.

Pete and Spiro nodded in agreement.

The waitress arrived at the table and gave everyone their meal. After some minor chit-chat, they resumed their discussion while they ate.

"So Miss Charlene," Carlton began, "what do you think about Wyatt returning to Seattle?"

"I'm absolutely *delighted* to have him returning home. As you know, he's very much like a son to me. I've really missed him during the past few months. And like a mother, I'm always worried about him. Of course, I'm very grateful he survived that awful attack by Caleb and Damon."

"As we've already discussed," Carlton continued, "please ensure that Wyatt's sons go to see him often. Those boys are going to be quite busy as the Flaming Sword group moves forward. With Wyatt moving to Bainbridge Island to live all by himself, he's going to need some companionship to accompany the solitude he'll be experiencing in writing his novels. I sincerely doubt that Wyatt will ever begin dating again, so please make sure to look after him."

"Oh, you know I'll continue to mother him as if he was my own son," Charlene said. "But tell me something Carlton—you haven't met Wyatt yet, have you?"

"No, actually I haven't. At least, not directly. But the LORD has a plan for all of us to meet and work together at some point. Although you humans don't always see what's going on, Jesus is always at work in His kingdom."

"He sure is. So after we're through here, did you gentlemen say we're going to stop by our bookstore before the meeting with Candace and Mi-Cha?"

"We certainly are," Carlton said. "I want Pete and Spiro to meet the store's newest employee named Cheryl. She's the mother of one of the children in Mi-Cha's baby group."

"Oh," Charlene said. "Do you mean the other two babies—Cookie and Roberto—who Mi-Cha often baby-sits?"

"Yes, the very ones. Cookie's mother is your employee, Cheryl. Unfortunately, Cheryl has had a lot of difficulty in raising her daughter, due to an abusive ex-husband. But the LORD has brought them all into your lives for a reason. In fact; there's a very important reason why Mi-Cha's son DJ, Cookie, and little Roberto have been brought together. However, we need to save this part of our conversation for when we're with Candace and Mi-Cha."

"I understand," Charlene said. "When we're finished up here, we'll stop by the bookstore. Then we'll head down the hill to attend our meeting with my sister and Mi-Cha."

"Very well then," Carlton said.

"Do we need to cover anything else before we head out in a little while?" Charlene asked.

"I hate to ask," Carlton began, "but do you mind if we stop at the Market Spice store downstairs? I'd like to see if they have a supply of my favorite tea."

"That'll be no problem whatsoever Carlton," Charlene said.

Pete shook his head as he finished up his breakfast.

Salem, MA
October 11th

**"The eyes of the arrogant will be humbled
and human pride brought low;
the Lord alone will be exalted in that day."
Isaiah 2:11**

Members of various local pagan groups were sprawled across the grassy Salem Common, basking in the beautiful autumn sunlight. The relatively small annual pagan festival being celebrated that day was a peaceful gathering of several different groups, all of which would be relocating to a nearby state park to continue with their festivities later that afternoon. Although these pagans were generally non-intrusive, they provided a good cover for the real evil that was infesting the area—Caleb's satanic hideout, which was only a few blocks away.

Caleb always relished the fact that he had chosen Salem as his primary residence. Ironically, the "Witch City" had turned out to be the ideal locale for his home base. This was due to the prevailing—though largely false paradigm—that witches were direct worshippers of the devil. Using this deception as a clever ruse, Caleb had capitalized on the foolishness public opinion. Being that he had also grown up in neighboring Peabody, Salem seemed to make perfect sense.

Caleb understood that the various pagan groups, including those who identify themselves as witches, largely had nothing directly to do with the worship of Satan. Only members of his group, the *Synagogue of Satan,* were true worshippers of Lucifer. However, if people were going to be foolish and believe otherwise, so be it. This mind-set fit in nicely with Caleb's deceptive plans.

The one thing Caleb did know was that he had to remain anonymous if he was going to follow his master Satan's prime directive, which was to operate outside of the spotlight. So when the abandoned factory and warehouse property he ultimately purchased the previous February became available, it provided an unbelievably good opportunity. Being a disciple of Satan required tremendous guile, cleverness, and deceptive abilities, and Caleb had been a top-of-the-class student in these areas over the years. When the run-down warehouse he had been keeping track of arrived on the real estate market earlier that year, Caleb was ecstatic. He had long-since outgrown his house near the waterfront, and he very much needed some more space. After thoroughly investigating the warehouse property, Caleb made his triumphant purchase.

What had clinched his decision about purchasing his new base of operation was something very interesting he had uncovered during his diligence in researching the old blueprints of the property. This unique quality was very likely an unknown aspect to the local realtor, but it was absolutely perfect for what Caleb needed.

Overall, the warehouse property actually fulfilled the one requirement that every member of The Servants required of their home; a quality which every member simply must pursue: their home must be able to hide in plain sight. In other words, no one should ever suspect that their neighbor was a dedicated member of Satan's burgeoning army.

Damon had drilled the importance of deception into Caleb's head for all of his life, and Caleb had ardently listened to his master; he followed Damon's advice in everything he did. After all, Damon was his angelic mentor, and he certainly knew how to wage war against God and his minions.

The two demons, Damon and Donovan, stood with Caleb in the run-down warehouse. Although the building's doors were partially open on the side, the threesome was not visible from the street. Numerous holes in the roof of the decrepit facility provided gateways for opportunistic beams of sunshine to drill-down into the debris-filled, metal-walled structure. A fire blazed in a rusty, fifty-five gallon drum, which sat squarely in the center of the group as they planned their next move.

"So Damon; what's our next step?" Caleb asked. "This waiting around stuff isn't really gettin' it for me."

Damon remained quiet for a few moments. The demon had remained relatively un-talkative since he, Caleb, and Donovan fled the Pritchard estate a few days earlier.

Damon sighed wearily. "Let's just say that I'm racking my brain on how we're going to track down—*and then eliminate*—whoever it was that betrayed our location up in Maine to those maggots in Flaming Sword. So let me be abundantly clear—*somebody is going to pay for our loss!* Nelson Pritchard was a tremendous ally for our group, and his loss will be strongly felt throughout our entire network . . . especially this area."

"Don't worry Damon, we'll get our revenge," Caleb said. "I can assure you that those Jesus-loving scumbags won't get away with their crimes against us. Somebody's going to *die* for this. Perhaps many will."

"I agree," Donovan added. "They won't get away with this. I can assure you of that."

Damon tossed a couple of dried branches into the fire. "Caleb my friend," he said. "I mean no disrespect by this; but I don't think you fully understand the big picture of what Pritchard's loss actually means to us."

"What do you mean?" Caleb asked. "Pritchard was a great sponsor and all, but I think we'll be okay without him. We still have our overall mission to accomplish—which is the building of Satan's army of the millennium . . . don't we?"

"Of course we do, my fine young student," Damon said. "But since Pritchard was a single man, he has no heirs to succeed him. Trust me on this—we've experienced a tragic loss for our brotherhood in the war against Jesus Christ."

"Okay . . . ?" Caleb said slowly. "Can you please explain why?"

"Very well then," Damon said. "I suppose I've never told you very much about Pritchard's history, so now is as good a time as any to explain it to you."

"Please do," Caleb said.

"Let me first tell you about Pritchard's father, Nelson Pritchard II. When he was only a teenager, Pritchard II emigrated to Germany from Britain after World War I. Later on, as he stealthily made his way into the inner circle of rising stars on the German political scene in the 1920's, Pritchard was able to convince the Nazis that his lineage was purely Aryan. Due to the fact that he was actually an ardent member of our Synagogue of Satan, Pritchard hated the Jews—as do we, of course. As a result, he was a natural fit with the Nazis and their evolving, ambitious goals of genocide. So ultimately, Pritchard II was in place within the growing Nazi organization when Hitler formed his *SS* during their rise to power."

"I see," Caleb said. "Under your direction, I've studied a lot about World War II. So let's see if I can figure some of this out."

"Be my guest," Damon said.

Caleb nodded. "Even though the term *SS* is understood by history to stand for *schutzstaffel,* which is German for *protection squadron,* our people were involved with guiding their evolution. Ironically, the Nazis were never aware of the double meaning of SS. But of course, we utilized them because they represented so many of our blessed ideals. And in keeping with our modus operandi, The Servants had no problem staying in the background, helping the Nazis rise to power. Of course, they were completely unaware that we were guiding them all along."

"That is correct," Damon said. "After Hitler came sweeping into power, he was well on his way to taking over the entire world—as was our plan. However, he ultimately blew our chance to control the Earth when he became too aggressive and lost World War II. At that point, we in the Synagogue of Satan—*the real SS*—had to work on a new plan to raise an army against Jesus Christ."

"Yeah, it seems to me that Hitler wasn't patient enough to execute the game plan. If *only* he had just listened—"

"Absolutely," Damon interrupted. "In retrospect, I can see that we simply didn't have enough control over the Nazis. We certainly had the right amount of *influence,* but not the right amount of *control.* Anyway, when you and Wyatt were born in the mid-1960's as twins of the Hunter family—*my wretched enemies for over two thousand years now*—Satan hatched this wonderful plan to make you the father of our new army. Of course, our plan will take several decades to accomplish. We simply must be patient this time."

"The effort will be worth it in the end," Caleb encouraged.

Damon nodded. "I can assure you that we'll not be making the same mistakes the Nazis did. In fact, we're going to be *very* patient this time. In the end, the time we invest in growing an organic army of true disciples of Satan will be well-worth it when we defeat Jesus Christ at Armageddon."

"I see. So Pritchard III's recent death is really a blow to the legacy of what his family has accomplished over the years in serving our master, Satan?"

"Right you are," Damon said. "The Pritchards have served us very, very well over the years."

"Hmmm . . . that's very interesting," Caleb said. "And speaking of your plan to create a new army where the Nazis failed, I'd like to thank you once again for your forward-thinking strategy in setting up Mildred to be my nanny. Since I'm the honored one who's been chosen to sire our growing army, I must say, it's due in large part to Mildred always teaching me the truth about how our god Satan is the one who cares about human beings—not Jesus Christ. To tell you the truth; in my heart, Mildred is my true mother. She always has been."

"I understand," Damon said. "And I thank you for your kind words. I chose Mildred specifically because I knew she would do an effective job in raising you in *our* ways. I suspect her involvement in your life is the reason why you're not only our Grand Master, but also the father of the future leaders around the world who'll continue to multiply in the name of Satan. Indeed, your descendants—under our leadership—will one day lead our victory over Jesus Christ and his pathetic Christian followers."

"You got that right," Caleb said. "By the way, have you heard from Mildred recently?"

"No, actually I haven't. Why do you ask?"

"I haven't heard from her in a few days. This is highly unusual. I mean; aside from her reports to me about what those fools at IFI are doing in their silly attempts to locate me, I usually talk to her at least every other day or so. Like I said, she's pretty much my adopted mother. I suppose I'm just a little worried because I haven't heard from her."

"I see," Damon said. "Then why don't you call Chas or Blake across the street to see if they can use our various resources to contact her?"

"Good idea."

"But I wouldn't worry," Damon said. "Since Mildred is basically undercover, I'm sure she simply hasn't had the time to check-in with us."

"You're probably right."

Caleb called over to the main building across the street. However, Chas and Blake—who had now entered brand new hosts—failed to answer their phones.

"No answer," Caleb said. "Hey, you know what? I think our little ruse of this fire showing some activity here in the warehouse is good enough for now. Why don't we head back over to the main house?"

"Good idea," Donovan said. "Is that okay with you Damon?"

"Certainly. Caleb my friend, please lead the way."

Caleb led Damon and Donovan towards the back of the warehouse.

Since the time he had purchased the property, Caleb actually ventured over here every few days to burn a fire for a short time. He did this to make the area appear as if it was being utilized by a witch group to do whatever it is they do. Showing this activity was a wonderful trick to help conceal where Caleb was actually located.

Once they arrived at the back of the warehouse, the threesome descended the metal and concrete stairwell into the underground storage basement. After zigzagging through the carefully placed shelving and debris in the basement, Caleb stepped behind the large enclosed metal book shelf at the back of the room. After Damon and Donovan followed him into the landing area behind the bookshelf, Caleb flipped on a large flashlight and handed it to Donovan to lead the way.

Caleb then pulled the back of the book shelf by the handles he had installed on its rear side. The hidden wheels under the shelf slid back over the opening they had just entered into. Caleb then secured the top and bottom of the shelf into their metal locks. A distinct metal *clink* told him the shelf was now locked into place over the hidden entrance.

Donovan led Damon and Caleb down through a musty, dank old tunnel which had been built during the Prohibition era. Dangling wires and old cobwebs surrounded the tunnel, which was seven feet high by twelve feet wide. Caleb surmised that the builders of the tunnel had designed it that way to facilitate the storing and rolling of barrels of liquor; hence the need for a gateway that was wider than it was tall.

Once they had walked about a hundred yards or so, the two demons led the father of their evil army up some rickety wooden steps and into the basement of the old brick building across the street from the warehouse.

Caleb grinned as he thought about the times when he had witnessed the Flaming Sword and IFI idiots snooping around the warehouse, which was merely a clever subterfuge for Caleb's true location, right across the street, in this apparently abandoned brick building.

Caleb relished the fact that he had openly purchased the warehouse in his own name, knowing that both the IFI and Flaming Sword people would have found a record of his purchase. What they didn't know was that he had also utilized one of his shell corporations to purchase the building across the street. So right under their eyes, Caleb had remodeled the brick building as his home base. This little trick allowed him to hide in plain sight.

Bingo! Hiding in plain sight. Mission accomplished.

Once they had entered the basement of Caleb's building, they made their way up to the main parlor, which was on street level. The design of the four-storied building left no trace of habitability when being viewed from the street. However, the interior of the building was another story altogether.

Caleb had spared no expense in decorating the interior of his home, which served not only as a magnanimous place to live, but was also a satanic worship chamber, a fitness center, and a "love shack" for the impregnation of an almost countless number of women.

In Caleb's mind, he had it all: A supernaturally empowered angelic mentor in Damon, a pile of money, the ultimate home replete with an obscene number of creature comforts, and hundreds of women to impregnate; all of whom were brought to him by various members of his group.

Caleb felt like a true god.

As they entered the sprawling living room area, Damon asked, "Caleb my friend; do you mind if we crank up that fancy little espresso machine of yours? I'm feeling the need for a good latte."

"That sounds good to me," Caleb said.

A booming voice from the area of the front door jarred Caleb and the demons back to the reality of the war they were waging. Although this voice was unexpected, it was shockingly familiar.

"Normally I'd like to join you for a latte," Mick said, "but I'm actually here for another reason today. Hmmm . . . let's see if you can guess what that reason is . . . ?"

Caleb was stunned.

The maelstrom had begun.

"How *dare* you invade my home!!!" Caleb shrieked.

Danny, Cam, JJ, Moo, Bobby, and Ben stepped from behind the hallway to Mick's right, joining him.

"It's all over, Caleb," Ben said. "Your days of murdering, lying, and deceiving people in the name of Satan will be no more. To be fair, we're here to present the Gospel of Christ to you. After that, I'm afraid we have some FBI contractors waiting outside to take you into custody. In other words, your criminal activities will be ceasing as of this very moment."

"I'll never turn to Christ!!!" Caleb boomed.

Ben shook his head. "I didn't really expect you to. But you can never say you weren't told the Truth during your life on Earth. Let me say once again—Jesus Christ is the *only way.*"

Suddenly, a loud rumbling of stampeding feet sounded-off as two men hustled down the stairway from behind Caleb, near the kitchen. Chas and Blake then entered the room.

"What's going on here???" Chas shouted.

"Listen Chas; you just keep your mouth shut," Ben said calmly. "This is none of your business."

"Oh yes it is!" the demon snorted. "You can count on that!"

"Tell me Chas," Mick began, "how many times do I need to pound your head into the ground before you'll learn that God is in charge? I guess you're really not the sharpest tool in Satan's shed, are you?"

Chas began to charge towards Mick, but Damon held up his hand in an authoritarian stop-motion, halting his progress.

The room remained uncomfortably quiet for a few moments.

"So Mick . . ." Damon said calmly. "Tell me something, my dear old friend. How did you find us this time? I must admit; I never thought you'd be able to pull this one off. We've been very careful."

"You'll have to ask Ben that question," Mick said. "He's the one who had the pleasure of driving your fellow evil spirits out of ole Mildred Fountainhead."

"Wait a minute!" Caleb demanded. "Did one of you scumbags put your disgusting hands on my mother? *I'll kill every one of you for that!*"

"Shut your filthy mouth!" Cam shouted, unable to hold back his anger any longer. "You almost killed my father, not to mention the fact that you *did* kill my mother! *You're a piece of garbage!*"

"Ahh, my impulsive nephew," Caleb said sarcastically. "My only regret from last week is that I didn't get a chance to use my dagger on *you,* just like I did on your mother!"

This quickly ceased all dialogue.

In an impulsive rage, and to Mick and Ben's substantial dismay, Cam darted forward and dove into Caleb with a flying kick. Moo instinctively followed behind. When Chas and Blake converged on Cam in an effort to assist Caleb, a melee ensured.

However, it didn't last long.

Moo executed side-kicks on Chas and Blake, landing both of them on the floor. Interestingly, he had done the exact same thing to both demons earlier that year; albeit while they were inhabiting different hosts at the time.

As the chaotic scene charged out of the starting gate, JJ suddenly bee-lined towards Donovan, who was the demon in-charge of tormenting his family for many years now. But instead of engaging Donovan in hand-to-hand combat, JJ aimed his pistol right at Donovan's forehead. JJ's hand shook with anger, so the demon quickly held up his hands in submission.

He was rightly afraid.

JJ then glanced over at Chas and Blake, who were now being man-handled, along with Caleb. The three of them were in the process of getting the unholy daylights beat of them by Cam and Moo. Gooey redness covered both demons as their noses and mouths dripped a steady flow of blood. Since Moo and Cam were both skilled combat warriors, subduing the demons and Caleb didn't take very long. Bobby and Danny calmly pulled Moo and Cam off of their conquests, while Mick and Ben remained in the background.

Chas and Blake were both somewhat conscious, but lay still on the floor. Danny stepped towards Caleb, who was also down on the floor, but was sitting up. Blood continued to drip from Caleb's nose and mouth. Moo was now very calmly standing on Caleb's right, in a fight-ready stance. He was keenly prepared for any further offensive from the Satan-worshipping thug.

Cam, however, was another story. He had made the huge mistake of letting his emotions get the best of him, and as such, he hyperventilated with anger; he was just barely able to hold himself back from killing Caleb with his bare hands.

"Okay boys, I think that's enough," Mick said calmly.

The room fell into silence.

"Now then," Mick continued, looking at the men on the floor. "Like we were saying, Danny is prepared to present the Gospel of Christ to Caleb. After that, Pete's FBI contractors are standing-by to take all of you Satan-loving dirtbags into custody. Danny my friend, would you kindly do the honors for us pal?"

"I certainly will," Danny said.

"Wait a minute," JJ barked. "Where's Damon?"

Everyone looked around.

"He's trying to slip out the door like the coward he is," an ominous voice from behind them said.

Every one in the room wheeled around towards the back door. Greeting them was the imposing specter of Ezekiel holding Damon from behind. His left arm firmly held Damon in a headlock, while his right hand held a silencer-equipped pistol against Damon's head.

The demon looked frightened.

"Now then," Ezekiel continued, "everyone here is going to chill, until I sort this mess out. Understood?"

The room remained quiet.

"Good."

Ezekiel pushed Damon into the room.

Damon went over and stood by Caleb, who was now off the floor. Simultaneously, Ezekiel trained his pistol back on Caleb. At seeing this, JJ slowly raised his own pistol and pointed it at Ezekiel. As he did so, JJ pondered the irony at having to raise his weapon at Ezekiel in an almost identical fashion as he had just done two days previous.

Undaunted, Ezekiel sighed. "It seems that we're long overdue to get together to hash out all our differences—wouldn't you say?"

No one answered.

"I'm afraid I have some very bad news for you Caleb," Ezekiel continued. "You see; I wasn't very happy to discover that for all these years of trying to hunt you down, our pathetic leader, Mildred, was actually a demon-possessed lunatic leading us astray. In fact, Mildred was just like the rest of you lying, demonic weasels."

He nodded at Damon, Donovan, Chas, and Blake.

"Just for the record, Ezekiel," Caleb began, "I've never been inhabited by a so-called demon. Only a select few of us are strong enough handle this honor. I've chosen to serve Satan of my own accord."

"*Shut your disgusting mouth!*" Ezekiel shouted.

"Now let's just take it easy Ezekiel," Mick said. "No one needs to die here today. That won't serve the LORD in any way."

Ezekiel pointed his gun quickly at Mick, then back at Caleb. He suddenly and curiously appeared as if he was unsure what to do next.

As JJ looked on, he found himself surprised that Mick and Ben were largely staying in the background for this confrontation. Somehow, he sensed that God's instructions were for the angels to allow the human drama to play out as important decisions were being made. In this case, the angels were largely there for protection, not battling.

"I think you know those bullets won't hurt Ben or me," Mick said. "Please Ezekiel . . . haven't you done enough killing over the years?"

"Those demons lied to me!" Ezekiel shouted, shaking with furious anger. "They're going to *pay* for their deceit. I've been waiting for this day for a *looong* time!"

Mick shook his head. "If you had read your Bible without adding your own agenda," the angel said, "you would've known that revenge doesn't belong to any human being. In fact, it actually doesn't belong to anyone except the LORD Himself."

Ezekiel ignored Mick

"Mildred is dead," Ezekiel said coldly, looking directly at Caleb and Damon. "She killed herself a couple of days ago. That's right—she decided to take the old *dirt nap,* right after she told these Flaming Sword losers where you were located. I must say; tracking you down was pretty easy at that point. All I had to do was tail these idiots here."

Tears appeared in Caleb's eyes. "Mildred . . . would . . . *never . . .* betray me. I don't believe you for one second . . . *you're lying!"*

The room remained quiet for a few agonizing moments.

For the first time since his unexpected arrival, Ezekiel appeared calm and relaxed. Conviction gripped his face as he muttered his next words through clenched teeth . . . .

"Time for you to go to Hell, Caleb!"

Ezekiel then quickly aimed his pistol and fired three successive shots into Caleb's head.

Seattle, WA
October 11th

"Woe to you, teachers of the law and Pharisees, you hypocrites! You clean the outside of the cup and dish, but inside they are full of greed and self-indulgence. Blind Pharisee! First clean the inside of the cup and dish, and then the outside also will be clean."
Matthew 23:25-26

"Caleb has *how* many children?" Candace asked. "Did I just hear you right—did you just say Caleb has *hundreds*—or perhaps even *thousands* of children throughout the world?"

"I'm afraid that's correct," Carlton said. "The good news is that the other members of your group are now in the process of apprehending Caleb at his hideout back east. We actually should be hearing from JJ or one of Pete's associates very soon with the news of his capture."

"So tell me; what's the meaning behind all of this?" Candace asked. "Why on Earth do you think God has allowed an abomination like Caleb's satanic army to grow? I mean, *really???*"

Carlton shook his head. "You know, of course, the answer to that question falls under DP—Divine Privilege," he said. "We must all stand confident that in the end, God's will reigns supreme. It appears to me that all of these events simply must play out—even if they don't seem to make any sense to us at the time."

After finishing their late breakfast, Pete, Spiro, Miss Charlene, and Carlton ultimately joined Mi-Cha and Candace down in Mi-Cha's condo on the waterfront. Fortunately, Mi-Cha had just put her young son DJ down for his nap. Joining DJ in his sleeping soiree were two fellow babies of about the same age, Cookie and Roberto.

Pete and the others had stopped at the Flaming Sword bookstore as planned. While they were there, they enjoyed a nice visit with Cookie's mom Cheryl for a short while. Cheryl was a single mom who was very strong in her faith in the LORD. Coincidentally—or perhaps not— Roberto's father Carlos, who was also a single parent, had stopped by the book store while they were all gathered together. Carlos had come to the market to have an early lunch that day, and decided to visit.

"I suppose you're right about things having to play out, Carlton," Candace said. "So tell me; where do we go from here? I mean; we've already lost Juan. And I'm sure hoping no one else gets hurt as our guys take down Caleb and those demons. It's probably a good thing that Mick and Ben are with them today."

"I'm sure all of our men will be fine," Carlton said. "Believe it or not, after a while, you'll get used to the dangers which are always lurking around the corner due to what you do in Flaming Sword. You see; when you put your hands to the plow to serve the LORD, Satan will most certainly counter-attack you in retaliation. Although all of you must be cautious, you shouldn't be apprehensive at all. In fact, you absolutely *must* remember that Jesus Christ is always in charge."

"Of course," Candace said. "To be honest though, I suppose what's been bothering me lately is that I'm still confused by one of my recent dreams. I mean; most of the time, my dreams are readily understandable.

But other times—like this latest series—I'm not really sure what they're all about."

"Can you tell me more about them?" Carlton asked.

Candace sighed. "In my dreams, there are two opposing hills with a valley in-between. On the one hill is a normal looking castle. Now this castle isn't fancy by any means, but it's very solid. The king of that castle is warm, loving, and cares for his people. Moreover, this king doesn't try to impress his subjects with fancy exterior accouterments. Interestingly, however, the inside of this castle is replete with tremendous warmth and peace . . . ."

She stopped for a moment.

"Please, go on dear," Miss Charlene said.

"On the other hill is a fancy-schmancy castle with an ostentatious king. Now this king is all about impressing his subjects with his royalty. But inside this king's castle is utter coldness. I mean; his people are completely miserable. Essentially, all they do is serve their king's ego."

"So what's eating at you?" Pete asked. "It seems that your dream might be about a good king, Jesus, and an evil king, Satan."

"Not exactly," Candace said. "I already considered that, but I don't think that's right. You see; this dream would seem to indicate that these two kings are both human, and therefore equal. As you well know, Jesus and Satan—while being adversaries—are far from being equal. Sometimes, people forget that Jesus is vastly more powerful than Satan."

"Then what do you think the dreams are about?" Spiro asked.

"That's the part I'm unsure of. It's not a big deal or anything, but I'm just not sure why I keep coming back to this same dream."

Carlton nodded. "I think your dreams may be representing two important things for the Flaming Sword group," he said. "And that's why you keep having them. This is certainly not a coincidence."

"Oh . . . ?"

"The first thing," the angel continued, "is the tremendous difference between *religion,* which is all about outward appearances, and *relationship,* which is all about your inward feelings towards Jesus Christ."

"That makes sense," Candace said. "Please don't get me wrong—these dreams aren't creeping me out or anything. It's just that I've been unsure why I keep having them."

"I understand," Carlton said. "The second thing your dreams likely represent is the nature of your battlefield. Since Wyatt is moving back to this area soon, his writing will follow along with the many travails the rest of you in Flaming Sword will continue to encounter as you serve the LORD. The major theme for his books will continue to center on spiritual warfare and the trickery of the devil; with an emphasis on the perils of human pride. I'm sure that's of no surprise to you."

"No, it isn't," Candace said. "I'm with you."

"The other theme Wyatt will continue to point out is the true dichotomy between the choices for eternal life. And to that end, your collective battles—both yours and Wyatt's—will not only happen with the adamant unbelievers in this world. In fact, I'm afraid you can most assuredly expect an onslaught of hatred from the modern-day Pharisees who are so prevalent today."

"What do you mean by that?"

"In *Matthew 23:27*, Jesus warns about outward appearances, which often have an inward ugliness. Jesus is not impressed with outward appearances. He's only interested in what lies within each person's heart. Due to this fact, your entire ministry must center on encouraging others towards an *authentic* relationship with Jesus Christ—not merely a show of religious dedication. As you'll see when you read the passage I just cited, our LORD is not impressed with form. He is only concerned with *function;* that is, the function of your heart."

The living room remained quiet for a few moments.

"Tell me something Pete," Mi-Cha said. "What exactly does the *Two Seals Warriors* mean? I understand that you're not technically a part of them, but working with them seems to be your primary FBI responsibility."

Pete looked at Carlton and Spiro, then back at Mi-Cha.

"Their name is based on two of the seals mentioned in *Revelation 6*," he said. "But before you ask any more questions, let me say that they really don't like to discuss the details regarding their name."

"I see," Mi-Cha said. "I'm sorry if I offended—"

"Oh no—you didn't offend me in the least bit young lady," Pete said. "Let me tell you something; I believe both of these groups—the Two Seals Warriors and Flaming Sword Communications—will be working together *very* closely as we all move forward."

"Why is that?" Candace asked. "This is certainly good news, but why do you see us working together more closely now?"

"It just seems to be a natural fit between what each of you does," Pete said. "You guys in Flaming Sword are going to expand your ministry into all areas of the media, while my friends in the Two Seals will remain in the background. They'll continue to execute their duties—with my substantial cooperation—outside of the public eye . . . *or* the media."

"That makes sense," Mi-Cha added. "We'll be in front of the curtain, doing our work, and you and the Two Seals group will be behind the curtain; ensuring that we're protected."

"That's basically it," Pete agreed. "The focus of the Two Seals' original charter was to ensure that the spiritual battles between angels, demons, and the people involved stay out of the public domain. It's kind of ironic, huh?"

"Perhaps so," Candace said. "It'll be nice knowing you guys are getting our backs. We can use all the help we can get—"

"I also need to add something here," Carlton said. "Mi-Cha dear; your son DJ is a very important child in the kingdom of God. As an angel, I can only inform you of what the LORD permits me to share. You, of course, understand that, correct?"

"Absolutely," Mi-Cha said. "So is this bad news?"

"Definitely not," Carlton said. "What I need to tell you today is that you should embrace the fact that you're actually providing substantial support and assistance for your friends Cheryl and Carlos in caring for both Cookie and Roberto. They have all been assigned to you as a holy ministry."

"Really???" said Mi-Cha. "That's a little surprising. Gosh, I sure wasn't expecting something like that. I just thought I was helping out a couple of friends from church who are having a hard time being single parents."

"Yes. You see; these three children—DJ, Cookie, and Roberto—will always be friends. And one day, they will all be engaged in ministry together for the LORD. In fact, their work will be absolutely critical in many future kingdom affairs. So please keep this heavenly assignment in mind as you help care-for and assist these children *and* their parents."

Pete's phone rang. He held up the *hold on a moment* signal to the others.

"Speak" Pete said, answering his phone. After a minute or so of saying "yes," "uh-huh," and "okay," Pete hung up.

"Was that word from our guys?" Candace asked.

"Yes it was. Actually it was my Two Seals agent-in-charge over at Caleb's house in Salem; the one who is coordinating this mission."

"So what's up?" Candace asked. "What happened?"

"Let me first give you guys the good news," Pete said. "All of the Flaming Sword guys are safe and sound. They're all unharmed and uninjured."

"Whew," Mi-Cha said. "Thanks for sharing that before anything else. That's always my first question."

"Understandably so," Pete said. "But the bad news is that Damon somehow got away again. But you know; it really doesn't matter. The truth is; if Damon's current host had been gunned down or captured, Damon would have simply found himself another host with whom he could inhabit; he would still be able to perpetrate his evil plans."

"I suppose that's true," Miss Charlene said.

"Anyway," Pete continued, "Damon fled the scene, but the hosts who Chas and Blake were inhabiting are now in custody. If you think about it; Chas has been forced to enter an array of new hosts during these most recent battles. This is a little strange; even for a demon."

"So what else happened?"

"Oh, I almost forget the big news," Pete said. "Caleb was shot and killed by Ezekiel from the former IFI group. Caleb is now dead."

"Wow!" Candace exclaimed. "That's shocking."

"How did Ezekiel end up in the mix?" Mi-Cha asked. "I thought that IFI was being dismantled as we speak."

"Ezekiel was blinded by his thirst for revenge," Spiro said. "I used to be the same way myself, so I understand his way of thinking. Anyway, I'm sure he probably used his resources to follow the Flaming Sword guys to Caleb's house. I'm very sad to hear that he's continued with his violent rampage."

"He surely was blinded," Pete added, "After he shot Caleb, Ezekiel turned his weapon on the other demons and began firing. Fortunately though, JJ was prepared and halted Ezekiel's rampage before it went any further."

"JJ shot Ezekiel?" Mi-Cha asked.

"He did," Pete said. "He had to. If JJ had failed to do so, then several of your guys might now be dead. I'm afraid that Ezekiel was an expert assassin. But he's now gone. He was destroyed by his own anger and pride."

Carlton nodded. "Jesus said in *Matthew 26:52* . . . *'Put your sword back in its place,' Jesus said to him, 'for all who draw the sword will die by the sword* . . . Unsurprisingly, our LORD was correct."

Everyone remained quiet for a few reflective moments.

"So Caleb is really dead, huh?" Candace asked.

"Yes ladies," Pete said. "The man who killed Miss Charlene's husband Robert, Candace's husband Willie, and Cam's mother Cammie is now dead."

"But why don't I feel happy about that?" Candace asked.

"Because you shouldn't," Carlton said. "Believe me; Caleb is now going through quite a horrible experience. While Robert, Willie, and Cammie are now experiencing the unbounded joy of Heaven every day for eternity, I'm afraid that for Caleb . . . well . . . let's just say he's in store for a horrible shock."

Hell
October 11th

"They say there's a Heaven for those who will wait,
Some say it's better but I say it ain't,
I'd rather laugh with the sinners than cry with the saints,
The sinners are much more fun . . ."
Billy Joel,
the song, "Only The Good Die Young"

Darkness. Pure and utter darkness. Although Caleb was completely lucid and aware of his surroundings, his vision behind the curtain of death was instantly shrouded by a foreboding, black nothingness which engulfed everything in sight. It was at once shocking and uncomfortable.

Deep inside, he felt panicked.

There was no peace.

There was no joy.

There was no victory parade to greet him.

There was only an intense sense of desperation, which was slowly spreading throughout every fiber of his spirit and soul.

Nothing in existence could adequately explain the overwhelming and complete sense of remorse Caleb felt the very instant Ezekiel's three bullets suddenly took his life. After his eyes closed on Earth for the final time only moments ago, Caleb discerned that in that split second, the door of opportunity for his redemption had been simultaneously slammed shut behind him. He knew there would be no further dialogue or arguments about God.

His emotions were unbalanced, distraught, and frenetic with a jagged sense of fear.

As Caleb found himself suddenly thrust into a horrible, infernal darkness—which absolutely screamed of total abandonment—he knew there would never again be any joy in his existence. Every fiber of his being absolutely reeked with a sobering awareness that the judgment upon him was both immediate and final.

Caleb's overall sense was that of being thrown out of a snuggly, wintertime bed and into an erupting volcano. The shocking depth of this terrifying event was both agonizing and penetrating. Panic infused all of his senses.

However, the shock of this ontological seismic wave was still reverberating. All of it had not sunk in yet. So for the moment, Caleb's pride of denial was still struggling with this new reality within his soul.

During Caleb's life of living like the god of his own world, he ruled every day on Earth as if he was a king. He truly believed that nothing could knock him off his throne. But now, since his life had come to such an abrupt and unexpected ending, Caleb knew that for the rest of eternity, he would neither see any sunshine . . . .

Nor anything good . . .

Nor any thing beautiful . . .

Nor any thing peaceful . . .

And worse yet; he felt the unfathomable loss of all hope.

And the loss of all dreams . . .

And the loss of all true love . . . .

Every ounce of his self-awareness was now overshadowed by a rueful emptiness which defied description.

There was nothing cool about it . . .

There was nothing hip about it . . .

It was nothing to be proud of . . .

He could not brag . . . .

Deep down, Caleb felt utterly ashamed at his foolishness.

Due to the absolute finality of physical death, every single human being who rejects a relationship with the LORD Jesus Christ—no matter how subtle or overt it's accomplished—ends up facing the reality that their life on Earth is the ultimate litmus test of their pride. And without exception, there is no second chance. Unfortunately for Caleb, he now understood this essential truth.

Caleb knew he had failed.

His pride had won.

His soul had lost.

But pride is *hungry*. Pride is *unyielding*. Pride *destroys* . . . .

****

What on Earth is going on here?!?!? I'm Caleb Hunter – father of the future army of Satan's warriors in our holy war against Jesus Christ! I mean; what is this?!?!? I feel like I've been dropped into a bucket of burning acid. This is awful!

Damon always told me there'd be a parade of celebration when I left the Earth to triumphantly enter Satan's spiritual kingdom. Well . . . since I don't see anything yet . . . this has *got* to be some kind of horrendous mistake. I'm supposed to feel *happy*—not miserable.

Unless . . . .

Of course—that's it! This must be some kind of weird initiation rite or something. That's the only explanation I can think of. Anyway, since I can now see some firelight ahead, I think I'll just head towards it. What else am I gonna do?!?!?

Still though; this has *got* to be some kind of mistake. I feel so unbelievably *lousy*, not to mention scared. I mean, *really* scared. I don't understand why I feel this way. It feels like I've been banished or something. To be honest, I'm really not accustomed to fear—at least not experiencing it. Admittedly, I'm pretty good at dishing it out.

But somehow, I am now afraid.

Definitely afraid.

You know something? Damon and his fellow angels have always instilled in me the confidence that I'd live to be an old man. They also told me I'd have a chance to witness the blessed events unfold when my children and grandchildren take over the world's political and religious systems as the leaders of Satan's future army. I've always loved the fact that my heirs would be the honored ones to prepare every nation for Satan's ascension to the throne of this world.

But based on what's going on now, *did Damon lie to me???*

No. *Of course not.* Damon loves me like a son. He would *never* lie to me about anything. Still though; there must be some kind of explanation as to why I feel so completely panic-stricken right now. This isn't how the end of my life on Earth was scripted.

Oh, you can bet I'll get to the bottom of this all right! Oh yeah, someone down here is going to explain to me *exactly* why they totally blew my triumphant entry into Satan's kingdom.

Don't they know who I am???

Anyway, as I walk towards the firelight ahead, it appears to be growing larger and larger. This is good! It actually reminds me of our many human and animal sacrifices under Pritchard's house over the years. I'll just head towards the end of this black hallway and see who's there. Maybe someone can tell me what's going on!

You know; I can't *wait* until I get my hands on the one who is responsible for this terrible mistake. Someone is going to pay for fouling up my glorious arrival into the real paradise of this world. *Somebody is going to pay for this with their life – that's for sure!*

****

Caleb walked out of the dark hallway and into a wide open area. There in front of him, shrouded by an intermittent red fog, was the unexpected sight of three malefic figures sitting around a craggy, rock table. The three figures were all facing the black hallway from where Caleb had just come from. Curiously, they were all at full attention, eerily gazing at him with a penetrating intensity.

Although the darkest, most terrifying horror movie on Earth could not do justice to the ominous scene staring at him, Caleb instinctively walked towards the figures.

The arid landscape surrounding Caleb was parched and appeared to have no end. The darkened fog faded in-and-out as he moved forward. Caleb gazed at the sky above, which contained a mixture of varying shades of black, red, and dark orange. But there were no stars—only a seemingly endless void of nothingness, which hung as an austere canopy, draped over this land of immense sadness.

Deep down, Caleb knew something was wrong.

Horribly wrong.

But the denial of where he now was, kept him going.

Surrounding the plateau from behind him were darkened, jagged mountains, which stood as looming sentinels over this shadowy theater. A huge, seemingly shapeless rock wall stood directly behind Caleb, framing the black hallway from which he had just emerged. In the far distance on his front, left, and right sides, were indistinct smooth hills, giving the immediate area the appearance of a gargantuan arena floor.

And then there was the gloomy red fog; dark, penetrating, and seemingly alive. It moved about with a precise purpose; snaking its way around Caleb, as if it was a roaring dragon, preparing to blast him with a geyser of blazing fire.

The barren ground on which Caleb walked was a combination of various dry, geometric shapes, placed within a never-ending jigsaw puzzle. It actually appeared as if it was the dried-out floor of a long-defunct, ancient sea. There was a mild *crackle* under each step as he walked forward.

While he was absorbing his ominous new surroundings, Caleb's spirit felt completely lacking; like it was yearning for something lost; something which he dearly missed, but could not yet identify. It was this mysterious, missing element which had previously held everything together in his life. But for the moment, he had no idea what it was. Due to this mystery, his overall psyche felt an increasing sense of intense desperation.

This was at once, both frightening and puzzling to him.

Caleb continued towards the odd-looking figures. As he arrived at their stone table, a powerful wave of putrid sulfur assaulted his sense of smell. Making things worse, the atmosphere was extremely dry and he felt thirsty.

"Greetings Caleb," the figure in the middle said. "My name is Guyrichrorch. To my right is Sensindahl. To my left is Schlomazelgeg. We welcome you to your eternal destination."

"Wait just one minute," Caleb said. *"Is this Hell?* If so, I'm supposed to have—"

"Oh, I suppose this place gets called *Hell* more often than it should," Guyrichrorch interrupted. "But that is not accurate. This place is actually *Hades*—it's the place where banished humans temporarily reside until the Great White Throne Judgment of God at the end of this age. After that, I'm afraid all of us so-called demons, along with all of you condemned humans, will be thrown into the actual fires of Hell. But if you wish to call this place *Hell,* then we have no objection to that."

"Listen Guyrichrorch . . . or whatever your *weird* name is . . . I only want to know one thing pal—where's my parade? Where's my celebration? *Don't you know who I am???"*

The three demons all looked at each other and began laughing heartily. Because of their rudeness, Caleb mentally stepped back to examine the three demons more closely.

What he saw made his skin crawl.

The leader, Guyrichrorch, had an elongated, triangular face and greenish, lizard-like skin. He was only of a medium build, but his almond-shaped eyes were huge; they glowed like dark amber beacons. His laughter boomed with a deep, unearthly timbre, reminiscent of Jabba the Hutt from the Star Wars movies. The worst part, Caleb thought, was that Guyrichrorch appeared to be some kind of space alien.

To Caleb's left was Sensindahl. Even though this demon was sitting down, he appeared to be tall and lanky. Topping his narrow head was a crop of greasy, spiked hair. His yellowish skin had an almost alligator-like texture, and his laugh sounded like an old man gasping for breath.

But it was the demon on Caleb's right which had really caught his attention. This one really creeped him out.

Big time.

Schlomazelgeg had a large, bald head and facial features which favored the old Creature from the Black Lagoon from the fifties. He appeared as if he was a half-fish, half-human hybrid. Even worse, the demon's snicker was far beyond obnoxious. His laughter actually sounded like a rapid-fire machine gun: *ha ha ha ha ha ha ha ha!!!*

Caleb was disgusted.

"Now you three clowns need to listen up!" he demanded. *"I'm the father of Satan's army against Jesus Christ.* If you don't start showing me some proper respect, *I'll have all your heads on a platter!* Do you idiots hear what I'm saying???"

Uncontrollable laughter from the motley crew of demons now hit a fever pitch. When they calmed down, Guyrichrorch continued.

"Caleb Hunter . . . you have now been banished to this empty place referred to as Hell. Regardless of what you think you knew—or what status you believe you had on Earth—you have now been granted your every wish. However, I'm afraid the outcome of your desire is not going to be any where near as pleasant as what you might have expected."

"What do you mean by that?"

"It's clear that you have been *deceived.*"

"Now wait just one min—"

"Caleb . . . I'm afraid you chose Satan's way of the world over the genuine love of Jesus Christ. In a word, you chose *poorly.*"

"What is this nonsense? Listen Bubba—who do you report to??? If you think I'm gonna just stand here and listen—"

Guyrichrorch held up his hands in a stop motion.

"Please save your bravado Caleb," the demon demanded. "It is now time for you to realize just *exactly* what your poor choice on Earth now means."

"What are you talking about? Where is the demon in charge down here? I need to speak with him *immediately!*"

Snickering ensued among the demons once again.

"There are no demons in Hades," Sensindahl said. "Save for the three of us, as well as a host of other greeters."

"What do you mean by that?" Caleb asked. "This place is Satan's spiritual domain . . . right . . . ?"

"No," Schlomazelgeg added. "It most certainly is *not.* Irrespective of what the poet Dante said about Hell's inferno many years ago, there are no levels in this place—and there are no torture chambers. In addition, there are no demons who torment the souls of those who didn't make it to Heaven. That is *not* what this place is all about. Guyrichrorch, Sensindahl, and I are *only* here as an omen of your poor choice. Well, we're also here as a punishment for our own mistake. Anyway, our job is to explain to certain people who enter Hell what they can expect for eternity."

"I don't get it," Caleb said. "Hell is supposed to be the place where I'm given a huge crown of honor for being a loyal soldier in Satan's earthly army. What do you mean there are no demons here?"

"Let me put it to you another way," Guyrichrorch said. "Hell isn't evil; Hell is the place where evil gets punished."

"What are you talking about?"

The demons were quiet for a few moments.

"I can see that we're not getting through to you," said Guyrichrorch. "So let me describe this place to you another way. Hell is the place for God to punish His children who reject Jesus Christ. Hell is *neither* the place where the other inmates torture you, *nor* the place where demons punish the souls who arrive here. It's like we just told you— Hell is the place where God sends you when you reject His son, Jesus Christ. Essentially, whether you worship Satan; or whether you deny the existence of God; or whether you say you believe in God, but really don't. In all of these cases and more, a person ends up right here if they choose their own way over Yeshua's. In essence, this is *exactly* where you asked to be. I'm afraid you actually sent yourself here, so you're now the god of your own universe—completely devoid of Jesus Christ—just like you asked for. However, there *are* some drawbacks to this scenario."

"Such as???"

"You'll discover these things soon enough. However, you will not hear them from us."

"What do you mean?"

"You'll soon see that your egregious error was of spitting in God's face and telling Him that you'd rather be the god of your own world, instead of loving Him. During your lifetime on Earth, you lived by your own rules. By doing this, you made the greatest mistake any human being can ever make."

Caleb pondered this for a few moments. "If you guys really are true demons—or *angels* as I still like to call you—then you wouldn't just sit there and smugly admire Jesus Christ. News flash guys – *Jesus Christ is the enemy!!!*"

"Watch your filthy mouth!" Schlomazelgeg shouted in anger. He calmed down before continuing. "You must remember that as banished angels, all of us were once glorious hosts of the Most High God. But we—*as did you*—made a terribly bad choice when we rejected the love of the LORD and were sent away. Now we *all* must pay for our sins against God. We *all* have received exactly what we asked for."

Caleb shook his head. "This is going nowhere guys, so let's try something else. What is this place that we're in right now? I mean; this general area."

"Essentially, this is the atrium to what people call Hell," Guyrichrorch said. "But I'm afraid we're now finished speaking with you, Caleb. You must now continue towards the hills behind us, in the distance. It is there you will find your destiny."

"C'mon guys! What's all of this supposed to mean?"

Guyrichrorch looked at Sensindahl, then Schlomazelgeg, before he spoke again.

"Go," the lead-demon said. "We've done our job. It's now time for you to leave us."

"Where am I supposed to go? What am I supposed to do???"

The three demons all pointed towards the hills behind them.

****

I can't wait to find someone down here who can tell me the truth about what's going on. *Did those guys not hear me that I'm Caleb Hunter?* Yeah, the Three Stooges back there weren't real helpful in telling me why I'm here. But I'm sure going to find out, sooner or later. You can count on that!

In the meantime, I guess I don't have much choice but to move forward, towards those hills. To be honest, this whole thing is absolutely horrific. *This isn't what was supposed to happen!*

Anyway, you can bet your bottom dollar on this—I'm gonna find out who's lying about all of this. That's for sure!

****

The barren landscape spread out in all directions as Caleb continued his trek towards the indistinct hills in the distance. The fiery red fog continued to swirl about in a deliberate manner, summoning in him a severe sense of dread.

As Caleb trudged forward, the ominous, nagging feeling of this missing element in his spirit continued to vex his soul. But it wasn't merely because he felt thirsty and his soul burned with a rueful lament. It was because he was not yet able to identify the reason for his sorrow. This was a new experience for him.

Caleb moved ahead.

As the crackling under his feet on the barren floor of this indescribably vast plateau continued to mark the cadence of Caleb's ghastly walk of discovery, through the haze of the dark red fog, he noticed some other people to his right and left. Oddly enough, they were taking a similar pathway towards the hills, just like he was. Although these people weren't yet within shouting distance, he could nonetheless see them walking in a parallel fashion. And because they appeared to be human, he initially felt a sense of relief that he wasn't alone; that he wasn't the only person remaining in this never-ending, parched desert.

However, his sense of relief would not last long.

Caleb noticed that interestingly, the hills which he was moving towards didn't appear to be getting any closer as he moved ahead. But what his journey lacked in progress from a geographical sense, it had gained in the number of others around him. Although they appeared mostly as indistinct shadows, there were now many people within view.

This is weird, he thought. *This plateau seems endless.*

Caleb was now desperate to find something familiar in Hell—any thing at all. Just when he was about to explode with frustration, through the fog's haze, he saw a familiar person in his direct line of sight. Although this person was standing completely still, she appeared to be nothing short of an oasis in this desert; a desperate drink of water in this never-ending land of withered, unfertile territory.

Mildred.

The appearance of his spiritual mother made Caleb's heart leap. This was *exactly* the lucky break he was looking for. He quickened his pace in an effort to arrive at this much-needed, triumphant reunion with the woman who had raised him; the woman who he had always looked up to.

When Caleb arrived to within a few feet of Mildred, he noticed something very odd; something very distressing.

She was weeping.

Mildred's face was reddened with what appeared to have been a river of tears gushing down her cheeks.

This isn't good, Caleb thought.

When he arrived at Mildred's side, Caleb embraced her as tightly as he could. Although she returned his hug, something was definitely missing.

There was no passion.

There was no true love.

A realization then hit Caleb like a giant meteorite slamming into the Earth's surface: true love no longer existed in Mildred's heart.

Nonplussed, Caleb pulled back from their embrace and looked squarely at her. He held her firmly by the shoulders as he looked straight into her eyes.

"Well aren't you a sight for sore eyes!" he said.

She sniffled; then buried her face in her hands.

"What's wrong?" Caleb asked.

After a few moments, she looked up. "Caleb my son . . . ."

She began weeping again. This time, her crying was on the verge of uncontrollable.

"Has somebody done something wrong to you?" Caleb shouted. "If so, you need to *tell me,* so I can go beat the living daylights out of him!!!"

Mildred was quiet for a few moments. "Yes Caleb," she began, "someone did indeed do something wrong to me—and to you also. But I'm afraid it's too late to do anything about it."

"Who are you talking about? What did he do?"

She sighed, trying to regain her composure. "I'm afraid that Damon and those other demons lied to us about everything."

"Wait a minute! We're supposed to be crowned as heroes for what we've done for Satan. Why are you so upset?"

"It was all a lie."

"No it wasn't! Have you been brainwashed or something?"

"Listen to me son. I want to make this as easy on you as I can. Will you please indulge me? I'm actually doing this for your own good. But if you do agree to listen to me, you need to hear me out *completely.* Do you understand?"

Caleb was quiet for a moment. "Yes, I understand," he said. "I'll hear you out."

Mildred sighed once again as an expression of complete despondency gripped her face. "The first thing you need to know is that this sense of outrage your feel right now will very soon fade away. As you begin to absorb what I'm about to tell you, you'll come to understand that I'm speaking the absolute truth—you'll feel it in your soul. You see; I'm not angry that I've been sent to this place called Hell, and I have no sense of outrage. The truth is; God was righteous for sending me here. I don't complain about the pain I feel here; I feel *remorse* over my dreadfully bad decision; a decision that dates back to the time when I was a teenager and fell under Damon's evil influence."

"Wait a minute—*why are you talking about our master that way?"*

"Please don't forget what you just agreed to," Mildred admonished. "You need to listen to me. Please, let me finish . . . ."

Caleb nodded.

"Do you recall," she continued, "when I read you Scriptures from the Christian's Bible when you were growing up? Do you remember how all of the lessons I taught you centered on how those of us in Satan's army needed to study the Christian Scriptures in order to completely understand our enemies before conquering them?"

"I do."

"Now that I'm no longer on Earth, I've come to realize all too clearly that the Christian Bible was absolutely right all along—*we* were the ones who got it wrong."

Caleb wanted to object, but held back. "Go on," he said, wearily.

"Do you remember when I read to you the parable of the rich man and Lazarus in *Luke 16:19-31?* You remember it, don't you? It was the story of the rich man who was here in Hades."

Reluctantly, Caleb nodded.

"You see; the rich man didn't have any outrage that he was sent here. No, the rich man knew he had lived his life strictly for himself. Although he felt pain and remorse, he was no longer able to feel any *anger* towards God; he was no longer able to reject God, because God had judged Him. In other words, the error of the rich man's choice was completely obvious to him."

"But Damon always said the Bible was a book of lies."

"It's *not* a book of lies. Just look all around you. That passage tells the absolute truth. The liars were both Damon *and* our own pride."

This powerful truth continued to drill-down into Caleb's psyche. "So what other bad news do you have for me?" he asked facetiously.

"Actually, I have several passages which I need to recite to you. They'll explain things much better than I can."

"Okay . . . ?"

"Hebrews 9:27 says . . . *Just as people are destined to die once, and after that to face judgment.* Caleb dear; God's judgment has been pronounced upon us. There is nothing more we can do."

Caleb sighed heavily. "What else?"

"*Proverbs 11:7 says . . . Hopes placed in mortals die with them; all the promise of their power comes to nothing.*"

"But Damon promised me honor and riches if I followed Satan's way and served him. That passage can't be right . . . can it?"

"I'm afraid it is," Mildred said. "*Matthew 8:12 says . . . But the subjects of the kingdom will be thrown outside, into the darkness, where there will be weeping and gnashing of teeth.* Caleb dear; that's exactly where we now are. We've been removed from the complete goodness and true love of God. Haven't you noticed how empty and miserable you feel?"

"Uhmmm . . . actually, I have . . . ."

"I'm sorry dear. But there's more. *John 3:36 says . . . Whoever believes in the Son has eternal life, but whoever rejects the Son will not see life, for God's wrath remains on them.*"

"I see. So we're now experiencing God's wrath? Is that what you're telling me? Are we now being punished for doing things our own way? Are we now going to experience God's eternal punishment because we sided with those so-called demons? If so, that hardly seems fair."

"You're not *listening* to me," Mildred insisted. "Let me finish what I need to say."

"Fine . . . !" Caleb puffed.

"If you'll also remember, *Matthew 10:28 says . . . Do not be afraid of those who kill the body but cannot kill the soul. Rather, be afraid of the One who can destroy both soul and body in hell.*"

Caleb shook his head. "This news just keeps getting worse," he moaned.

"I'm afraid I've left the worst part for last," Mildred said. "This last thing I must share with you is by far the most painful part of being in Hell. You see, we won't rule in Hell. We also won't have any fun with all the sinners in Hell. Hell is not the place where all of the cool people who decided to reject God's allegedly bogus rules hang out. No; the worst part about being in Hell is that it's the place which is absolutely, positively devoid of God's loving presence. Unfortunately for us, this includes *all* of His wonderful attributes."

"That doesn't sound so bad," Caleb said. "I never wanted to be around God for eternity anyway."

"No Caleb. It's bad. In fact, *it's absolutely horrible.*"

"In what way? Isn't Hell the place where we can forever be separated from God's stupid rules?"

"No. I just told you it wasn't. Being able to do things our way in Hell *is a lie.* But that's not the worst part of it. By far, the worst part of being forever separated from God is that we'll never experience three wonderful godly attributes ever again. Unfortunately for us, these three things are all indelibly intertwined with the LORD, so they're not available to us in Hell. In *John 8:44* we were told that Satan is *a liar and the father of lies.* I'm afraid this is very true. Unfortunately, we believed Satan's lies. Satan is a deceiver, not a god."

"That's debatable," Caleb mused. "Anyway, what are these three things you speak of?"

"Scripture says in *1 Corinthians 13:13 . . . And now these three remain: faith, hope and love. But the greatest of these is love.*"

"And . . . ?"

"Caleb dear; without God, there is no love—at least, not in the truest sense. So even though you'll be seeing many others down here who you knew and loved on Earth—*including me*—you'll be woefully unable to have any kind of real relationship with anyone."

"Why??? That sounds ridiculous."

"Because without love—*God's true love*—love is not possible. At least; not in any real sense."

"But that wasn't how it was for us on Earth!"

"No, it certainly wasn't. But Earth was different."

"How so?"

"You see; on Earth, we essentially lived in a middle ground. Earth is a world that contains both good and evil. While it contained the good things of God, it was also Satan's playground. So when we woke up each day, we saw both the things of God, *and* the things of Satan. But down here in Hell, since God is essentially not here, His love is *also* not here. Do you hear what I'm saying? Am I getting through to you at all???"

As the penetrating truth of Mildred's words continued to impale his bravado, the bubble of Caleb's pride suddenly burst. A horrific, marauding wave of terror then began rampaging throughout his emotions, pillaging every ounce of denial that had remained in him.

It was absolutely unbearable.

Caleb's heart burned with remorse and utter anguish. Still though, he tried to hang on to any kind of hope as the realization of his terrible choice settled in.

"On Earth," he began, "I always lived with the hope that I'd be rewarded by Satan for my loyalty. So I suppose you're saying that's now gone???"

"Yes Caleb. All hope is now gone. And that's my whole point in a nutshell. Hell is completely devoid of God's gift of Hope. While a person is still on Earth—*which is only a temporary place for all people*—he or she always has those beautiful attributes of God to cling to—His gifts of Faith, Hope, and Love. But down here in this awful place, Hope *in particular* doesn't exist. This lack of Hope is what actually hurts my heart the most. In fact, Hope is nowhere to be found in Hell. *Ever.* The end result is that we have nothing whatsoever we can ever look forward to. My son, I'm afraid there's no bright future for us. There's nothing but the solitude of our own mis-guided, self-centered wishes. For us, Hope is dead, along with our bodies and our souls."

Almost like the snap of a guillotine suddenly dropping down on his neck, the last thread of Caleb's pride suddenly vanished. An enormous tsunami of shear and utter panic quickly followed, crashing into the seashore of his soul. An irreversible sense of consuming devastation then settled into its newest victim.

Caleb now felt the crushing weight of his own horrendous sins sitting squarely on his shoulders. There would be absolutely no forgiveness for his unrepentant soul. This caused him to begin weeping.

Caleb's agony was not only due to the fact he had been banished to Hell. He was overwrought because he knew he had forever lost his chance to be with God. There would never again be another chance at redemption for Caleb.

Ever.

Caleb had never wanted God to be in his life before. But now, he would do absolutely anything to be with Him.

Anything!

This loss of Faith, Hope, and Love—*God's true love*—left a consuming emptiness in his heart which burned in every fiber of his soul.

In fact, the burning was unbearable.

"I'm afraid it's our own fault Caleb," Mildred continued. "Our own pride destroyed us. Listen to me! If there's one thing I've learned, it's this: *Pride is hungry. Pride is unyielding. Pride destroys.* We rejected Jesus Christ when we were on Earth due to our own pride. That's *precisely* the reason why we're in Hell."

"But Damon and the other demons lied to us," Caleb said, still weeping. "How can we be held responsible for their lies???"

"It was our own choice, Caleb. Those demons merely fanned the flames of our own pride. *We* were the foolish ones who listened to them, completely of our own accord—it was our own fault. God loved us enough to allow us to make our own choices. But like I said earlier, we both chose poorly. I'm afraid there's nothing else we can do . . . ."

****

I just bid my spiritual mother, Mildred Fountainhead, a sad good-bye. She said that she'd see me around some time, but I really don't know what good that'll do. Without love, all of us down here have nothing to bind us together. All that's left for us is the numbing reality of where we are and what we've done. I wish so much that I could go back and do things differently, but I can't. I want so much to warn others about this place.

But once again, I can't.

Before Mildred and I parted, she told me that I must continue towards the hills in the distance. She said that I'd likely find some old friends along the way; and perhaps even a few others who weren't my friends.

But who cares? I can't go back and fix what I've done. I've already run into a few old buddies from back in the day. But unfortunately, they have the same expression on their face that I do. And it's not a happy one.

I am a fool!

You know; I always heard that *God is love,* but I guess I never really understood that expression. But now, I surely do. Without God's true love, nothing in the universe is binding. Nothing can function as it was made to function. Nothing works. Without God's true love, every single thing is broken. I suppose it's fair to say that since that's true, without Jesus Christ, everything is broken.

And then there's that not-so-small issue about losing all Hope. Actually, it's an unbelievably *big* issue. In fact, it's absolutely terrifying to look ahead and not see any opportunity for happiness whatsoever.

The loss of all Hope and Love is the worst thing I can possibly imagine!

Although my self-centered pride is now dead, I'm still very much alive—I did indeed survive my physical death. But ultimately, God gave me what I asked for.

And it ain't good.

Anyway, as I walk around this barren place, I'm seeing more and more people along the way now. But like I said earlier, it doesn't really matter. Love is gone. Hope is gone. And I only have myself to have faith in. Not God's blessed gift of Faith, but my own, miserable faith. I asked to be the god of my own world so I could make my own rules, and by golly, that's exactly what I got. Trust me when I tell you this—it ain't what it's cracked-up to be. Not by a long stretch.

You know something? The odd thing about this plateau of arid nothingness I'm forced to wander on is that it continues to grow. Unfortunately, this foreboding red fog continues to prowl around; almost like it's following me. I have no idea what this fog is all about. Maybe it's the manifestation of the consuming misery in this awful place.

Anyway, I've discovered something else here in Hell; something that hurts me beyond belief.

Actually, it's two things.

The first thing is that one bright light in the sky above. I can now see it in the distance. It shines as a brightened orb over this desolate plateau. It's beautiful beyond belief, but it's so far away . . . .

It's Heaven.

Sadly, those of us in Hell can see that Heaven is up there above us—at least for the time being. But we also know this chasm between Heaven and Hell will always keep us away from being in the presence of the LORD and His redeemed children; it will always keep us separated from God's Hope and His Love.

The second thing I can now see is on the horizon below us, but it's not beautiful. In fact, it's the most horrific thing I've ever seen.

It's Hell. I mean, the *real* Hell.

You see; the *real* Hell is a lake of fire, and it's been reserved for the devil and his angels—along with those of us who aligned with Satan— either aware or unaware—forever. The dry, cracked plateau upon which we wander actually ends at a precipice over this horrible lake of fire. In fact, it goes right up to its edge.

However, the lake of fire is reserved for us in the future. Of course, that ain't so good. So not only are we forced to look at what we missed out on in Heaven above, we also see our miserable future in the fires of Hell, below us. And you wanna know something?

I am completely miserable down here!

Anyway, I suppose I'll just have to live with my regrets forever. God was in no way evil for giving me my wish. *I* was the one who was evil for turning my back on Him. You heard me right—*it was my own fault.*

Oh, I almost forgot to tell you something interesting. In fact, it's *very* interesting. Of all the people I've encountered, I just saw Ezekiel down here. Well, at least, that's the name he went by when he was aligned with IFI on Earth. His real name is James something-or-other.

Anyway, Ezekiel was apparently killed right after he shot me in the head three times, ending my life on Earth. The interesting part was that when we spoke, we weren't angry with each other. In fact; we both only felt huge regret at our diametrically opposed—but nonetheless effective—pathways to Hell.

You see; as it relates to Ezekiel, you don't have to worship Satan to find your way into Hell, like I did. Those who claim to love Jesus, but who are actually hypocritical, religious Pharisees in disguise, can also end up in Hell. You have to remember something—Hell is the place for those who reject Jesus Christ and His teachings. In the end, you can't claim to love Jesus and not follow His commands. In Ezekiel's case, you can't do the work of Satan in the name of Jesus and think you're pleasing the Savior of the world. Why? It's because you can't please Jesus if you don't love Him *and* obey Him. In fact, if you truly love Jesus, you *will* obey Him. If you end up rejecting Jesus . . . well . . . trust me . . . you don't want to end up in this place.

That's all I have to say on this matter.

In closing, let me say that while I'll give you the fact that Damon and his army of demonic cohorts played a role in my destruction, ultimately it was my own choice. It was *me* who didn't want God in my life. And it's *me* who now knows there's no goodness without God . . . and there's no true love without God . . . and there's nothing worth living for, without God.

I know that now.

You wanna know something else? There's one word which best describes exactly how I feel about all of this; one word which I suspect will be the theme of my life for the rest of eternity.

Remorse.

I feel pure and utter remorse. My soul burns with it. My body burns with the physical pain of this place, but my soul yearns for something lost; something I was made for, but rejected.

How could I have been such a fool?!?!?

Trust me people; you don't ever want to feel like this.

I have one last thing for you. I often muse over this. It's what I think to myself when I consider those demons who influenced me with their constant fanning of my own flames of self-centered pride. In one way or another, the evil spirits on Earth will do whatever they can to keep you away from Jesus Christ—the only way to Heaven with God.

Actually, I often repeat this over-and-over to myself as I walk along this great plateau of desolation. In fact, you could call it my own, personal, unpleasant, eternal mantra:

They lied to me!

Seattle, WA
October 14th

"Half a truth is often a great lie."
Benjamin Franklin

The Seattle's Best Coffee café on Post Alley in Pike Place Market bustled with activity once again, as the old coffee house served up its delightful libations with a deliberate efficiency. The squealing sounds of milk being scalded in stainless steel pitchers provided the music behind the powerful aroma of coffee and espresso, which summoned with it the very perfume of Seattle.

After the chaos at Caleb's house in New England had subsided a few days before, Mick returned to Wyatt's house to tend to his recovering friend. To Mick's amazement, the author's miraculous recovery had continued to the point where Wyatt was able to travel.

God is truly amazing, the angel thought.

The entire group who had descended on Caleb's house—minus Pete's associates who still had much work to do—had a wrap-up dinner meeting at Wyatt's house later that night. Afterwards, since Mick had some kingdom business to tend to for a couple of days, it was agreed that he and Wyatt would reconvene here in Seattle today; only a few days later, on this unusually cool, bright sunshiny day.

As usual, Mick hung out in his favorite spot at the counter, which bumped up against the wall of the red-tiled bar. As the angel sat there, he patiently awaited the arrival of his good friend Wyatt, who was currently enjoying a little walk through the market. It had been several months since Wyatt was able to visit Pike Place Market, which coincidentally was the author's favorite place on Earth. Because of this, Mick waited for Wyatt to finish his mid-morning tour of this ancient bazaar; a locale that had seen an almost countless number of visitors in the past century or so.

Mick slowly sipped away on a quad-venti mocha as he reflected on the past year. This entire saga with Wyatt actually began in this very spot just twelve short months ago. Much had happened during this time, from Wyatt's shock of officially meeting an angel for the very first time; to the initial gathering of the Flaming Sword members at the Mall of America a few months later; to now, the aftermath of the final conflict and demise of Wyatt's evil brother Caleb. Indeed, so many life-changing events had taken place during this time. But there was still so much more to do.

"What's up, Captain Coffee?" Wyatt asked, interrupting Mick's daze. The author walked down into the café.

"Hey dudester," Mick said. "I was just thinking about how much has gone down since you and I first met here last year. Do you remember that morning?"

"How can I ever forget it?"

"Yeah, I guess you're right. I'm pretty unforgettable, huh?"

"Whatever, Mick," Wyatt said, grinning.

"Anyways, I suppose you could say that everything has changed in your life since our little *walk through the market,* huh?"

"Boy, is *that* an understatement."

Wyatt sat down next to Mick; to his right.

"So tell me," Mick began. "Do you have any further thoughts about your brother Caleb? You know; I hated to be the one to call you the other day with the news he was dead."

Wyatt sighed. "To be honest, I guess I still have mixed feelings about the whole thing. I mean; I thought I really didn't care about him—after all, he did try to kill me. But I'd be a liar if I didn't admit there wasn't some kind of bond between him and I. You know what I mean; something about being twins and all."

"I understand Wyatt. But isn't it also true that your real family in this world isn't necessarily who you're related to. Isn't your *spiritual family* in Christ the one which really matters?"

"Yeah, I suppose you're right."

Mick took a sip of his mocha.

"So I've been thinking about a possible name for your next book," the angel continued. "And I think I have a catchy title for it."

"Oh . . . ?"

"Yep. I think you should call it *The Cult of Me.*"

"Oh really? How in the world did you come up with that title?"

"Well, since you're books are about the biblical condemnation of human pride, I thought it might be an appropriate title. So tell me honestly—what do you think?"

"Actually, it's not too bad. But you need to remember that I'm also writing about a really odd 'fictional' angel who talks about Heaven and guzzles coffee. I'm not sure how all of that's going to fit together."

"Perhaps you're right," Mick said. "And speaking of Heaven, does it bother you at all that Caleb isn't there, waiting to see you again one day? Have you given that any thought?"

"Actually, I have," Wyatt said. "Although I know the punishment of Hell is something I wouldn't want for even my worst enemy, I still think about an old expression as it relates to Caleb."

"Oh . . . ?"

"You know the one, Mick—*If you're only born once, you'll die twice; but if you're born twice, you'll only die once.*"

"Amen, dude. I'm afraid those are the only two combinations available. But the truth is; you don't have to go as far as being a Satanist to go to Hell. Hell is actually the place for those who choose their own way instead of the LORD's way."

"How true," Wyatt agreed.

"Listen; I'd like for you to continue to remind your readers—both in your novels and your future blogs—that you can't *good your way* into Heaven. You need to keep telling folks that loving Jesus Christ is the only way to live with God forever. If people try to attain entry into Heaven strictly by their good deeds or their perceived holiness, I'm afraid they'll be in for a really lousy surprise."

Wyatt nodded. "So tell me something, Mick. How could Caleb be so arrogant that he'd choose Hell over Heaven?"

"That's easy, dude. Although Caleb had some evil people who fanned the flames of his self-centered ambitions, in the end, Caleb really only accomplished the damnation of his soul. Of course; he also betrayed his own heritage in the process, as well."

"What do you mean by that last part?"

"Think about it. Caleb is a *Hunter,* and you Hunter men have Jewish heritage, right?"

"Right. At least, that's what you told me last February. Actually, you informed me of that little tidbit right here; in this exact spot."

"I sure did," Mick said. "But that was no accident, my friend. I've become pretty attached to our little tradition of meeting here in Pike Place Market. It's actually something we should keep doing for a while. We'll just call it our little meeting spot."

"That's fine with me. It doesn't matter where we meet here at the market. I love this entire place."

"Yep."

"Anyway, what did you mean that Caleb betrayed his own heritage?"

"Oh yeah, I almost forgot. Think about it. Satan has been attacking the Jews throughout history with an eye towards killing them all. Of course, he's always lost his bid—and he always will. Anyways, if you think about things from Satan's perspective, there's probably no better way for him to execute his future plans to take over the world and to demolish the Jews than with a home-grown army of Jewish descendants who fight for *him,* instead of God. Am I making any sense?"

"Yeah, but don't forget that I'm also descended from Jews . . . as are my sons. You can bet your bottom dollar that we'll be doing everything we can to fight against this shadowy army of Satan. Even though Caleb is dead, didn't you say that since adulthood, he's been utilized to spawn hundreds—*or perhaps even thousands*—of heirs?"

"That's correct," Mick said. "And I'm afraid they're literally spread all over the world. Listen; we'll get into the details of that situation during our next mission. For now, let's just enjoy this awesome day God has given to us."

Wyatt sighed. "That's fine. Hey; do you think Caleb knew he was a Jew?"

Mick shrugged. "I'm actually not sure if Damon hid that from Caleb or not. In either case, it really doesn't matter."

"Why is that?"

"Because Damon is executing Satan's 'big picture' plan to take over the world. In times past—like with Hitler and Haman—Satan was unable to exterminate the Jews because God wouldn't allow it. But now, Satan is trying a different tact: to covertly use descendants of Jews to take over the world by building an army of Jew-haters."

"That's interesting," Wyatt said. "It's perverse and sickening, but interesting."

"The one thing you need to remember, Wyatt, is that in the case of your family fighting against Satan, the torch is now being passed down to your sons. *They* are the ones who'll largely be fighting these battles. One day down the road, this war will also include your grandsons."

"I see."

"*Your* job will be to guide, support, and assist Flaming Sword's initiatives, but only from the background. Trust me on this; you're going to be quite busy with your writing. I think the LORD has a *lot* of things He wants to tell others through your efforts."

"Wouldn't that be arrogant of me to acknowledge?"

"Nope. Not at all. God has a plan for every single person. His call to service is always there for everyone. The choice is up to each person whether or not they'll heed God's calling."

"I see," Wyatt said nodding. "You know; sometimes I believe people mistakenly think they need to do humongous things to please the LORD. As I grow older, however, I believe that's simply not true . . . ."

"Go on," Mick encouraged.

"Well . . . for what it's worth . . . the more I study about Jesus Christ and the Bible, the more I feel that He only wants us to do what He *calls* us to do—and nothing more. Sometimes, those things can seem really big—like leading evangelism crusades, missions, or pastoring a group of Christians. But far more often, I think the LORD merely wants us to fulfill whatever role He has specifically chosen for us."

"How true. Not only that, but someone who loves the LORD doesn't need to win a gazillion dollars and give it to their church to please God. If you really think about it—that's like trying to play Superman or Wonder Woman. Listen to me now; God doesn't expect things like that from you unless He specifically calls you for it. And callings like that are indeed, very rare. What He *really* wants you to do is to carry-out the seemingly little things that actually matter a great deal to Him."

"Like what?" Wyatt asked.

"Like random acts of kindness, encouraging someone who is down, and boldly proclaiming the Gospel to others . . . things like that."

"Oh," Wyatt said. "That's what I've been getting at. In other words, you agree that God works small miracles in the lives of His children more often than big miracles, right?"

"Basically, yes," Mick said. "Of course, Jesus often does do huge things in His kingdom. But far more often, it's the seemingly small things that really matter to Him. You see; when you love the LORD, those small things always warm your Savior's heart in a big, big way."

"I'm with you there, Mick. Anyway, I forgot to ask you a question the other night over dinner; after you guys raided Caleb's house and my brother was killed."

"And that is . . . ?"

"Wasn't it unusual for a bunch of civilians like our Flaming Sword team to lead the way in a criminal matter? In other words, shouldn't Pete or one of his FBI contractors have been the ones to confront Caleb and take him into custody?"

"Wyatt my man, that's an excellent question," Mick said. "However, you need to remember something very important: Pete and the Two Seals Warriors are specially commissioned so that the battles between angels and demons can take place without it becoming what we would nowadays call a You Tube or media sensation. Because of this, Pete's group allows the human drama to play out—under the guidance of the Holy Spirit."

"I'm not sure I'm following you."

"Think about it; God's invisible qualities are apparent so that no one has an excuse—"

"Romans 1:20, right?"

Mick grinned and nodded. "I suppose no discussion between you and I would be complete without us discussing that verse."

"How true. God's invisible qualities are apparent, so that no one has an excuse to not believe in Him."

"That's right. Although Pete's group has a dedicated angel to advise them—by the way, his name is Carlton—their ultimate mission is to ensure that these battles are dealt with through proper criminal channels. At the same time, these matters *must* be able to play out; but must also be kept out of the sensational media spotlight. This is a very tricky balance. So in the case of Caleb's takedown the other day, the mission was for all of the involved players, so to speak, to decide how they were going to handle the confrontation. Some of what happened was good; some of it was not so good."

"I see," Wyatt said.

"Anyways, Pete and his associates have been hugely helpful to God's kingdom in matters like these, long before Flaming Sword was formed earlier this year."

"For example, are you talking about how much Pete has helped my cousin Frank in his unorthodox work?"

"Exactly!"

"You know; that whole thing with Frank being some kind of demon hunter was kinda freaky," Wyatt said. "I'm still taking it all in."

"It's like I told you in your dream," Mick said. "I've actually been working around you for your entire life. It's just that I wasn't commissioned to officially introduce myself to you until a year ago . . . right here in Pike Place Market."

Wyatt nodded. "And speaking of the subject of you being around me my whole life, didn't you tell me you were at the accident scene when Vanessa was killed?"

"I sure was," Mick said. "And so was Pete. You see; later on, after the accident, the IFI bozos ended-up abducting Hank. You remember him, don't you? He was Bobby's friend who Damon possessed when he ran into your car that night."

"Yes, I remember you speaking of him."

"Anyway, Ezekiel at IFI executed Hank after they abducted him. But that wasn't the saddest part."

"What could be sadder than that?"

"Sampson and Ezekiel tried to force a salvation out of Hank before they executed him. I guess that made them feel good about themselves. Although they were still going to kill Hank no matter what, they thought they were actually saving his soul by forcing some kind of twisted altar call before they killed him. It's as if someone other than the Holy Spirit can convict a person to turn to Christ."

"That *is* twisted," Wyatt agreed.

"I can't believe those fools actually thought they were doing Hank a favor," Mick continued. "Of course, a forced salvation—taken out as some kind of mis-guided eternal insurance policy—isn't real. As a result, I'm afraid that Hank is not in Heaven. In fact, I know he's in Hell."

"How sad," Wyatt said. "So IFI really abducted Hank and killed him, huh?"

"Yep. Seeking vengeance is something that feels good to the sinful human spirit, but it's actually wrong. Very wrong. God understands that you feel a righteous desire for vengeance against evil and injustice, but that vengeance doesn't belong to anyone other than the LORD Himself."

"Do you want me to write about this or something?"

"Wow dude, you're awfully quick on the uptake," Mick said, wearing a smirk.

"And with that, I think it's time to get some coffee," Wyatt said, getting up from his chair.

"Make sure you get it to-go. We have some stuff we need to do."

"10-4."

Since there was no line at the register, Wyatt quickly got his latte. After he was armed with his paper cup of caffeinated nectar, Mick and Wyatt proceeded into the market to continue their chat.

They moved south on Post Alley towards Pike Place without delay, quickly landing on the Market's brick-laden main thoroughfare. Mick seemed to have a distinct destination in mind, so Wyatt simply followed along.

"Where are we going now?" Wyatt finally asked.

"Actually, I'd like to grab one of those big ole donuts from Pike Place Bakery."

"Seriously? Do you actually think you're man enough to eat the whole thing?"

Mick shook his head. "Have you forgotten that I'm an angel of the Most High God? I could probably wolf-down two or three, but I really don't want to show off today. We're pretty tough hombres, you know."

"Oh, so it now takes a *tough hombre* to eat a gigantic donut, huh?"

"Whatever dude. Let's go."

They made their way into the market's main entrance. After a quick right, Mick and Wyatt bellied up to the bakery's counter.

"Yes, I'll have one of those Texas Glaze donuts," Mick said to the lady in charge. She nodded and went over to get him one.

"I thought you said the other night you liked cinnamon rolls better than donuts," Wyatt said. "Did I misunderstand?"

"Nope. You heard me right. But my favorite cinnamon roll is a home-made version by a nice lady down in Georgia. Her rolls are actually much better than those you'll find in those mall stores. As a result, I'll have to hold out until I'm back in your home state before I can partake in cinnamon rolls. The others just don't measure up."

Wyatt shook his head in response.

"What do you expect, Wyatt?" Mick continued. "If I'm going to come down to Earth to work with you folks, I might as well partake in the best of what you have to offer, right?"

The bakery lady handed Mick his donut. Wyatt paid her.

"I suppose that makes sense," Wyatt said. "So where to next? You seem to be on some kind of mission or something."

"Let's go down to the Flaming Sword bookstore and visit with Danny for a few minutes. How does that sound?"

"That'll work."

Mick and Wyatt meandered downstairs into the nearby Down Under section of the Main Arcade. After descending a ramp and some steps, they walked into the Flaming Sword book store. The door's bell jingled as they entered the new shop. Standing behind the counter, Danny smiled as Mick and Wyatt headed towards him.

"Hey there son," Wyatt said. "Have you been busy today?"

"Actually, yes," Danny said, beaming. "We've had more than a few customers. And I have some good news! I just sold two signed copies of your book to some nice tourists—an older couple from Missouri. After they read the synopsis of your book, they wanted it for their collection of Christian novels."

"Good deal," Wyatt said. "Listen; I want to thank you again for helping me prepare for this trip out here. Sitting next to you on the plane the other day for such a long flight really helped me with the discomfort I'm still having. The pain isn't too bad, but being with you made it much more tolerable."

"No problem dad," Danny said. "Oh, and before I forget to tell you this, Candace and Miss Charlene are over on Bainbridge Island at the realtor's office, signing the papers. Candace just texted me a little while ago with the good news that your house is now officially owned by Flaming Sword Communications."

"Cool!"

"Congrats dad, you have a new home to live in for as long as you wish."

"Thanks, Danny. I'm really looking forward to going back to Massachusetts in a few days to make sure all of my stuff gets packed. Actually, your brother Cam is taking care of most of that for me. I'm very grateful to you both."

"We both love you dad," Danny said. "And we're more than happy to help you in any way we can. We almost lost you last week, you know. It was kinda scary."

"Your dad's job on Earth isn't finished, Danny," Mick added. "If you faithfully keep your eyes on the prize—which is ultimately being in Heaven with Jesus Christ—then you'll be able to deal with life's ups-and-downs much better than if you keep your focus on earthly things, which will surely pass away."

"Amen Mick," Danny said. "Being with Jesus is the only way I can imagine living for eternity. It's like you keep telling us when you're speaking about our group's message: if we don't also include the alternative to Heaven in our message—*in other words Hell*—then we're not really telling the whole truth. In fact, we'd be lying."

"Indeed Danny," Mick said. "You can't just tell others about the glory of Heaven without also including the punishment of Hell for those who reject Jesus Christ. Essentially, if you only tell half the story—about either Heaven *or* Hell—then I agree; you're basically telling a lie."

"A lie? Really?" Wyatt asked. "Why do you say that?"

"Because the Truth of the Gospel includes both Heaven *and* Hell."

"Oh, of course," Wyatt agreed. "I'm with you now."

"Anyway dad," Danny said. "Since Miss Charlene and Candace took their car on the ferry over to Bainbridge Island, you'll need to also take the ferry, then walk to the realtor's office. But don't worry; the office isn't very far from the ferry's landing."

"I gotcha," Wyatt said. "No problem."

"Oh, I almost forgot to tell you that your new house is not far from a street named *Wyatt Way* over on Bainbridge."

"For real?" Wyatt asked. "Hey Mick; why didn't you just tell Miss Charlene and Candace to buy a house on Wyatt Way?"

Mick chuckled. "That would've created *way* too many bad jokes."

"Anyway," Wyatt continued, grinning. "The walking will probably do me some good. I'll drive back via the ferry with the ladies. That is; once we go check out my new place. Candace said it's really comfortable."

"It sure is," Danny said. "But make sure y'all are back at our place for dinner at six. Mi-Cha's cooking a huge Korean feast for us. As you know, her folks are in town for a few days, so her mom is helping out."

"Cool! I can't wait, son. See you tonight."

Mick and Wyatt bid Danny goodbye.

Angel and human then made their way out of the Down Under area and onto Pike Place Hill Climb. They chatted intermittently as they slowly made their way down the hill. Due to Wyatt's recovering condition, they opted to take an elevator in lieu of walking for part of their descent to the Seattle Waterfront.

Once they arrived at the bottom of the hill climb, they made their way across the street to the western side of Alaskan Way. There, they turned left and began a slow, southerly stroll towards the ferry terminal. As they walked, Wyatt fell into an introspective trance. Mick sensed this, so they walked mostly in silence.

Wyatt knew that although his brother Caleb was now dead, the fact that Damon had used him to sire an innumerable army of current and future soldiers was quite disturbing. As he thought about it, there were literally no bounds to the evil that Satan and his demons could wreak upon the world with their own battalion of staunchly dedicated human disciples—all of whom were unfortunately descendants of Wyatt's family.

In truth, part of Wyatt was happy that the Caleb saga was finally over. But the other part would remain apprehensive due to the countless ways that Damon could now use Caleb's descendants for evil purposes. Part of the battle was now over; the other part had only just begun.

When Mick and Wyatt arrived at the ferry terminal, they walked up the steps and walkway, into the terminal building. Wyatt proceeded to purchase his passenger ticket over to Bainbridge from the ticket office, then sat down with Mick to wait for the announcement that the ferry was ready to board.

During this time, Wyatt's introspection turned into a mild sadness.

Although the author knew he would continue to see Mick and the other angels as the Flaming Sword crusaders moved forward, he still felt a slight emptiness due to the fact that this chapter in their history had abruptly ended. Even though the Flaming Sword folks were just getting started with their important ministries and initiatives, his bonding with the group was already strong. In fact, it was very strong.

"Before you depart dude," Mick began, "I have just one last thing to tell you. But take heart—it's all good."

"So what've you got for me?"

"The battles you'll continue to write about will actually center on one basic issue. Sadly, this one issue sums up the current state of affairs for humanity. It's the one thing which shows a total divergence of thought and philosophies of life. This one, simple issue is the current centerpiece of your entire work and ministry."

"Is it the difference between Heaven and Hell?"

"Actually, no," Mick said. "But that's a good guess. Heaven and Hell are merely the destinations based on what people think about this issue."

"So what's this issue you speak of?"

"In the cases of both believers and unbelievers, it's all about a *tree.*"

"A tree?" Wyatt asked.

"Yep—*a tree.* You see; those who reject the LORD essentially opt for a science-only approach to life. In that case, they end up believing in the modern-day version of Darwin's tree of life. You know the one; it's the idea that all species on Earth evolved from a single organism over billions of years."

"Yeah. The latest versions of Darwin's tree of life follow the same flawed basic premise: a molecules-to-man explanation for the origin of life."

"That's correct. Of course, you know that the Bible's Tree of Life is tied into the correct answer on the origin of life question, which centers on God and His creation. I know you understand that mankind once had access to that life-sustaining tree; that is, until Adam sinned and the LORD subsequently blocked him and his descendants from eating from it. Of course, Jesus and his work on the Cross once again gave mankind access to eternal life, but only through Him."

"How true."

"And one more thing Wyatt. Those who reject the fact that God is the power behind all that we see today are treating Evolution and Darwin's tree of life as nothing but false idols. In a way, with the massive advances in science today, Darwin's tree of life has very much become a modern-day version of pagan idol worship."

"Why do you say that?"

"It's because throughout history, those who don't love God inevitably turn to idols."

"Why do you think that is?"

"It's because idols require nothing in return for worship. On the contrary, Jesus requires *everything;* that is, if you truly wish to follow Him. That's where the divergence of thought happens. False idols require very little, and basically, they provide a mirror for the worshipper to admire them self. On the other hand, Jesus requires your *entire* heart. That, my friend, is why the road to Heaven is so narrow."

"Amen Mick," Wyatt said nodding. "I'll be sure to tell the truth about those two diametrically opposed trees as I continue to write my novels to God's glory—"

"Now boarding for Bainbridge Island," an announcement said, suddenly interrupting their chat.

Mick sighed. "I'm afraid it's finally time, dude. Here; let me walk you over to the gate."

They headed that way.

The few passengers who were waiting in line had already boarded by the time Mick and Wyatt had meandered over to the gate. It was now time to say goodbye.

"Are you sure you can't join me?" Wyatt asked.

"I wish I could, but I can't. I actually have some tasks I need to accomplish in preparation for our next adventure together."

"Oh . . . ."

"Cheer up, Wyatt. I'll be dropping-in on you at your new house before you know it. In preparation for that, I need you to do me this one, tiny little favor."

"What's that?"

"Don't forget to stock-up on good coffee for when I show up!"

Wyatt grinned and nodded. He then looked at the pony-tailed angel in his leather jacket. Although Mick was far from what he would have expected from an angel, there was nothing he would change about this unbelievably lovable messenger from the LORD.

They embraced.

As they both pulled back, Wyatt said nothing. But the mist in his eyes told the story.

Mick held Wyatt's shoulders and said his goodbye for now. "May the love of Christ always be with you my friend. Be well . . . stay safe . . . and for Pete's sake, never—*and I mean never*—drink lousy coffee. Your life on Earth is *way* too short for that."

Wyatt nodded. "Another coffee joke, huh?"

Mick shrugged. "That's kind of my thing, you know."

"Please come back soon, Mick. I've grown fond of our little chats."

"I promise I will. Don't forget—we still have lots of work to do."

With that, Wyatt nodded and walked through the gate. In a matter of moments, he was safely onboard the ferry. Before proceeding inside, Wyatt turned and waved at Mick. The angel returned the gesture.

After the indication that no further boarding would be allowed, Mick stepped outside, but remained in the terminal area. The unorthodox member of the heavenly hosts watched as his friend Wyatt entered what was likely the final era of his earthly life.

Of all the men that Mick had known in the Hunter family over the centuries, for some reason, Wyatt was his favorite of the bunch. Of that, there was no doubt. He enjoyed the fact that his and Wyatt's bond was at once powerful, but also had an everlasting feel to it. Their appreciation for each other was only outdone by their mutual love of Jesus Christ.

As a loyal and holy angel of God, Mick always carries out the LORD's commands. But once in a while, when an angel like him finds a special son of God who loves Jesus as much as he does, it's indeed something special.

Mick watched as the ferry pulled away from the dock. The greenish waters of Elliott Bay churned under the powerful engine of the behemoth boat. A booming horn sounded as the ferry carried Wyatt into a brand new destiny.

The angel continued to watch for a while until the ferry was but a small speck on the watery horizon. The cold bay waters behind the craft slowly returned to normal as the ferry's once pronounced presence slowly faded away, disappearing into Puget Sound.

Of course, this fading away was also true of most things on Earth. The physical things that humans leave behind when they die inevitably subside, like smoke on the wind. But something important does indeed survive when a person leaves this Earth. In fact, it's the one thing which never fades away: *the loving imprints we leave on someone's heart.* They, of course, last forever.

And for those who love Jesus Christ, God's love lasts forever.

Mick pondered *Psalm 103:17 . . . But from everlasting to everlasting the* LORD'*s love is with those who fear him, and his righteousness with their children's children—*

Mick thought about this reality as he slipped into a quiet, deserted area in the ferry terminal and suddenly left Earth, heading back to Heaven. In an instant, the angel had disappeared from the fallen land. Although Mick was gone for the time being, he was most certainly not forgotten by those who he had touched with his messages from God.

One day soon, Mick would indeed return to see his friend Wyatt on another mission. And on that day, Wyatt's sons would be leading the charge against a seemingly invincible satanic army of incredible evil. But most importantly, the bond which Mick enjoyed with Wyatt would continue to bless both of them, and to all whom they encountered.

The fact that Mick would return one day soon to see Wyatt with a new mission was something the angel was absolutely certain about:

> *Because there was more work to be done;*
> *and more battles against evil to fight;*
> *until that glorious day,*
> *when the Lord returns . . . .*

EPILOGUE

Traverse City, MI
October 14th

"This is the verdict: Light has come into the world, but people loved darkness instead of light because their deeds were evil."
John 3:19

"So tell me something Alejandro," Damon said into the speaker phone. "How does it feel to be the new Deputy Grand Master of the Synagogue of Satan? Can you feel the power? Do you realize just how important you are to the great things we're destined to accomplish together?"

There was silence on the other end for a few moments.

"Of all the sons of Caleb, I'm very pleased that you've chosen me to compete for succeeding my father in serving our master," Alejandro said. "And I'm instructing my assistants to prepare for your arrival down here next week. While you're here, I'm confident you'll be very pleased with the work we're doing to serve the initiatives of The Servants."

"Very good, Alejandro. I always look forward to my visits to those beautiful mountains in the heart of Mexico. Your estate is as beautiful as it is serene. Since I've not seen you in nearly a year now, I'm sure our time together will be one of great fellowship."

"It will indeed, Master Damon."

"Let me also say once again that I'm sorry about what happened to your dear father Caleb. But I can assure you of one thing—those maggots at Flaming Sword will *pay* for what they've done to Caleb. Of that, there is no doubt!"

"Thank you, my master."

"I'll also remind you of one more thing, my fine young disciple," Damon continued. "Since you're the right-hand man to your boss Luis, the most powerful leader of the so-called Mexican drug cartels, you must remember that one day, he'll be gone. And on that day, *you* will be the most powerful man in Mexico. We strategically placed you in Luis's organization when you were young in order to infiltrate his ranks with one of our own. Of course, our ultimate goal is to not serve Luis, but to take his organization away from him, so we may accomplish our own, loftier goals."

"I certainly understand our mission," Alejandro said. "The war we are waging will one day help us take down the United States. The Americans clearly stand in Satan's way of one day ruling the entire world, so they must be weakened. I will allow *no one* to stand in our way of world-wide domination."

"Very good!" Damon said. "While you tend to your very important mission to ultimately take over as the chief lord in our southern war, I'll continue to mentor your fellow siblings of Caleb. As you well-know, many of your father's descendants are moving into place to inherit powerful positions throughout the world. Yours is but the first of many, my friend. Indeed; although we've suffered a great loss with your father's death, his legacy for Satan will most certainly continue. Truthfully, I'm sure that Caleb would be most pleased with what you're about to accomplish. In fact, I can picture him right now celebrating in Hell as an absolute hero."

"Thank you Lord Damon. I look forward to seeing you next week."

Damon heard a knock at Alejandro's door over the speaker phone. *"Who would dare to interrupt our call???"* Damon demanded.

"Oh, it's nothing," Alejandro said. "I have an appointment to meet with our new assistant."

Damon sighed. "I see."

"No worries, Master," Alejandro said. "It's just that in this case, I've allowed my chief-lieutenant to hire someone to replace my former chauffeur; you remember the one who I had to execute for thievery, right?"

"Yes, I remember him," Damon said, calming down. "So . . . can I expect to hear from this new assistant of yours with my travel arrangements in the near future?"

"That is correct. I will instruct him to advise you as to when my private plane will pick you up next week."

"I suppose that's acceptable."

"Please Lord Damon; don't worry yourself with such trivial matters. I will ensure that it's taken care of promptly. If not, someone's head will most certainly roll."

Although Alejandro could not see it, Damon smiled widely.

"Very well then, Alejandro," the demon said. "I look forward to seeing you next week. In the meantime, you be safe."

"And you as well, Master Damon."

****

Damon hit the speaker button, ending the call.

"The human propensity towards intense greed and overall avarice never ceases to amaze me," Lord Jiyott said. "You've got that kid practically eating out of the palm of your hand."

Damon looked at Satan's personal messenger with a begrudging respect. Since Damon had failed to protect Caleb from being killed, Satan had dispatched Lord Jiyott to oversee the Synagogue of Satan's move from New England to this beautiful upper Great Lakes city.

"I have this situation under control," Damon said. "I see no reason why you've been dispatched to baby sit me, Lord Jiyott. No offense."

"None taken. Once again Damon, let me say that you're still a valuable asset to our master Satan. In this case, he felt that you needed some assistance. Since many of the first wave of Caleb's children are old enough to begin our massive assault on the body of Christ, your workload has increased dramatically. Of course, very soon now, every knee in this world will bow to our master, Satan. If not, that person will lose their head. This is *our* world, and we will not relinquish it to Jesus Christ."

Damon gazed at Lord Jiyott, trying to mask his contempt.

"I accept your assistance with open arms," Damon said. "But you must know that Alejandro is just like all of the other children of Caleb—they believe our lies as being the absolute truth. With deception as our weapon of choice against all humans, I can assure you that I am in complete control."

"I see," Lord Jiyott said. "Let me also say that you've chosen an ideal location for our new headquarters after we lost both the Pritchard house and Caleb's building over in New England. This former winery located on the eastern arm in Grand Traverse Bay is an absolutely perfect locale from which we can continue our work."

Reluctantly, Damon said, "Thank you Jiyott. I appreciate your help."

"You're certainly welcome Damon. But I do have another question for you. When do you plan to go after Cameron's girlfriend Maria? Since she's the estranged niece of Alejandro's boss Luis, shouldn't you be trying to execute her?"

Damon shook his head in anger. "No, Lord Jiyott," he said. "The time is not right. Like I've told you before, we *must* wait until Alejandro has taken over Luis's operation before we can begin to backtrack and take care of matters like that. Let me assure you of one thing—any pain we can bring to Cameron, or *any* of those losers in Flaming Sword Communications, we will most certainly accomplish. Of that, you can be absolutely certain . . . ."

****

Alejandro's chief-lieutenant brought their new assistant into the large, circular-shaped office of the rising star within Luis's organization. The new assistant stood there at attention, directly in front of Alejandro's desk. The lieutenant then left them alone, closing the door behind himself.

"Please sit down," Alejandro said. He was pleased that their new employee had shown the proper respect by waiting until being invited to sit down before doing so.

"Thank you sir," the man said.

He sat down.

Alejandro looked the assistant over. "No offense my friend, but you look just like a gringo. I mean; with your shaved head and all."

"I understand sir," the man said. "But I can assure you, I'm not from the United States."

The new assistant's Spanish dialect was spot-on for the region where Alejandro's estate was located. This disarmed Alejandro's suspicions to a large degree.

"My lieutenant tells me your background checks out completely," Alejandro said. "And believe me; we're extremely thorough in our investigations into matters such as these. I'm sure you know that what we do here isn't exactly *legal*. As a result, the impotent government is always trying to infiltrate us with spies. We can't be too careful about who we bring into our organization, you know."

"I can assure you, I don't work for the government," the man said. "And I can absolutely understand your need to be cautious. But please let me make this clear, right up front: I'm here because you pay your employees well, and I'm very good at what I do. As far as I'm concerned, your business enterprises are your own, personal business. I'm just happy to now have a good job with a solid organization."

"I see," Alejandro said. "Well I suppose I should welcome you aboard. But please forgive me for asking—what was your name again?"

"My name is Saul. I thank you for this opportunity, sir."

"Welcome aboard Saul. I'm sure you'll be a real asset for us."

"I certainly will," Saul said. "Of that, you can be sure."

THE MYTHOLOGY FOUND IN A WALK THROUGH HEAVEN & HELL:

I'd like to start off this section with several excerpts taken from the mythology segments from the first two books in the Flaming Sword Series, "A Walk Through The Market," and "A Walk Through The Mall." In addition to these subjects, I have provided some additional information on various items relevant to "A Walk Through Heaven & Hell."

Previous excerpts from "Market" and "Mall": <u>Separating Fact & Fiction</u>

Although the Bible provides everything we need to live our lives giving glory to God, it does not tell us everything there is to know. Therefore, when one deems to write about Heaven, angels, and how angels interact with humans, there is much we likely won't know until this life is over. In other words, we will likely only understand how this works when our eternal lives begin with the LORD in Heaven.

However, in writing these novels, even though they are fictional, it is my steadfast desire to always write story lines which are consistent with the Bible. Novels are not, by their very nature, biblical exposition. In this section, I wish to clarify right up front where literary license has been taken so you will be able to separate the two things—biblical fact and reasonable biblical speculation (fiction).

It is important to note that I will never intentionally write anything that directly contradicts Scripture. These story lines are only designed as a means to present the Word of God in a way which I believe is easy for the reader to understand. However, we must be cautious as we explore the possibilities regarding some of God's wonderful mysteries in the story lines as being just that—possibilities.

Studying and discussing the Holy Word of God is something we all should engage in every day. I truly hope this story has drawn the reader towards the Bible, and has helped to further open your eyes to spiritual warfare. In the end, whether you agree or disagree with my use of fictional mythology, if you are drawn towards studying the Bible because of it, I am delighted!

The Flaming Sword

After Adam and Eve sinned, God placed a flaming sword at the entrance to the Garden of Eden to keep mankind out *(Genesis 3:24)*. Beginning with the first book, *A Walk Through The Market*, I have used the flaming sword as a fictional portal for the angel Mick (and other angels) to travel between Heaven and Earth. Essentially, I treat the flaming sword as a barrier between Heaven and the sinful world mankind currently dwells on—Earth.

Demonic Activity

The only demon structure presented in the Bible is "legion," which is found in the Gospels (for instance *Luke 8:26–38*). The activities of demons written into this book may or may not be presented in the Bible in the strictest literal sense. However, these actions are quite consistent with what the Bible presents as the activities of the evil ones and their violent, rebellious, and deceitful ways.

Invisible Dimension

I have coined the phrase "invisible dimension" for the general abode of demons (see *Ephesians 6:12*). Some of the characters, including the angel Mick, often use this term to describe the place where demons roam; one which is not visible to the human eye. The full answer for where demons dwell is under Divine Privilege (more on this later).

Dreams and Interpretations of Dreams

In the Bible, God often uses dreams for instruction, encouragement, or as a way to impart a message (for instance, see *Matthew 1:20–21*). However, this appears to be a rare activity. The dream sequences in this story are fictional, and possibly have no relationship to God's biblical use of dreams. They merely enhance the story and are a speculation about how God could *possibly* use dreams.

Angels

There are many passages in the Bible where an angel delivers a divine message to someone living on Earth. In fact, the word angel itself means "messenger." However, for a human, meeting an angel is clearly a rare thing, and likely only happens when a divine message is absolutely necessary.

The casual communication between angels and humans presented in this book is fiction, since it is beyond what is found in the Bible. However, as *Hebrews 13:2* explains, there is surely much more interaction with angels than we are aware of.

The angels who travel from Heaven to Earth in the story are shown to have "human-like" bodies when they are visiting people. Unlike the mis-perceptions of some, this is not without biblical likelihood. For example, in *Genesis 18*, the pre-incarnate Jesus appeared with two angels and had a meal with Abraham. In that same passage, the two angels then traveled to Sodom. When they arrived, their appearance was so human-like, the men of Sodom assumed the angels were men.

A couple of the characters in this book who are angels are given female names; this of course is also fiction. Any time angels appear as humans in the Bible they are presented as male. However, that does *not* necessarily mean we will only meet angels in Heaven with masculine attributes. It merely means that God has chosen to present His holy angels to us as men.

Heaven

Several scenes in this book take place in Heaven. They are strictly fictional accounts of what I anticipate Heaven might be like. We do know that Heaven is the dwelling place which God has created for us to live in, and the Bible tells us that God chooses to dwell in Heaven.

I take the position that Heaven is a very familiar place—a real, physical place—rather than an ethereal, non-physical place, as some claim. This is a reasonable conclusion, since we were created with physical attributes. This is also substantiated by the fact that the Bible speaks of Heaven in physical terms (for instance, the great multitude of *Revelation 7* are wearing white robes and carrying palm branches in their hands).

Discovering how the LORD brings His children to Heaven, what our bodies will be like, and what we'll do in Heaven, are exciting subjects to speculate on. Even if you don't agree with my speculations, we should all keep our eyes focused on God's eternal kingdom, knowing that it will be a vast improvement over our lives on the current sinful, fallen Earth.

Theology

To be honest, navigating the world of theology for a "regular dude" like me can be quite daunting. My personal writing is an attempt to decipher the complex world of theology, and what the experts have to say on spiritual matters and issues (this can often be a minefield, indeed!). I then attempt to present these positions in a way that is easy for a non-theologian to understand. Essentially, that's the reason why I write novels such as these—to draw the reader towards God's Holy Word in the Bible, which is much more valuable than a pot of gold. The Bible is where all the answers are. In fact, the Bible *is* a pot of gold!

Coffee

While I cannot unequivocally prove that coffee exists in Heaven, I sure am hoping it'll be there! Having a *cup of joe* with some friends is an often used scenario in this story, but there's a good reason for that. It's not only because of my love of the wonderful beverage; but also, having coffee with friends is a very common and comfortable socializing event for many people around the world. For my non-coffee-loving readers, I beg your forgiveness.

Items specific to "A Walk Through Heaven & Hell": Divine Privilege

Beginning with my first book, "A Walk Through The Market," I have utilized the term "Divine Privilege" or "DP" with the characters whenever possible. I believe this allows for a smoother flow in the story without too many digressions.

Although the Bible is silent on some issues (like whether our pets are in Heaven), that does *not* necessarily mean the answer is bad news. This is a seemingly default conclusion for some people. I believe that the Bible being silent on an issue simply means that God's focus in His Holy Word is to give us a necessary revelation of His holiness during our brief lifetime on Earth. In other words, the Bible tells us what we need to know to live godly lives, and ultimately, how to get to Heaven. I'm sure the LORD will give us more specifics later on. It's all in His mighty hands.

Essentially, instead of speculating on every single issue on which the Bible is silent, "DP" allows me to tell the story without digressing.

In other words, it's God's "Divine Privilege" to not tell us everything we may want to know.

More about Heaven . . .

The many scenes in Heaven in this book reflect my guess as to what *some* of our activities in our eternal home with Christ *may* be like. While they cannot be taken as literal biblical fact, they should be understood as *possibilities*.

Without question, my personal speculations about our possible activities in Heaven reflect a true dichotomy: I believe that Heaven will be at once, very familiar; yet also beyond anything we can currently imagine. From the bottom of my heart, I believe that Heaven must be an absolutely *fascinating* place, so full of wonder and awe that it will always bring tremendous excitement. Worshipping Jesus Christ will definitely be our primary focus in Heaven. Along with that, I see no reason why we won't explore, build, celebrate, feast, play sports (possibly baseball???), and . . . well, you get the idea. It's certainly not going to be anything boring—that's one of Satan's most egregious lies. However, there will certainly be uncountable joys, far beyond what we can now imagine.

At this point, I would be remiss if I neglected to recommend one of the "Heaven" books by Randy Alcorn as a wonderful resource for studying the subject of where Christians go when we die. The book "Heaven" absolutely changed my life and helped to draw me closer to Jesus Christ. It just may do the same thing for you.

About Hell . . .

Although Jesus warns us of Hell throughout the Gospels, not a lot of specific information is given to us. The term, *"there will be weeping, and gnashing of teeth"* is often used to describe Hell, but we really don't know where Hell currently is. We do know that at the final judgment, those who reject Jesus Christ will end up in the "lake of fire" with Satan and his fallen angels.

In conducting my research for this book, the biggest disagreements about Hell seem to reside with the subject of fire: *are the fires of Hell literal, figurative, or both?* I think it's both. Truthfully, the specific attributes of Hell can only be known after death for those who go there. But for those who trust in Jesus Christ for salvation, you are bound for Heaven and will never see what Hell is like.

My personal take on Hell is obviously written into the story. Once again, I don't claim it as absolute truth. It's merely a possibility based on my studies of Scripture.

Demons & Possessions

Demon possessions are presented in the Bible in many places. There is also a wealth of testimony about the result of demonic possessions today, and can be found online. However, the process of how demons are able to possess humans is strictly under "DP." As a result, the way demon possessions are described in this book must be listed as fiction.

Synagogue of Satan

The "Synagogue of Satan" as mentioned in *Revelation 2:9* and *Revelation 3:9* has a lot of mystery surrounding its exact meaning. One of the schools of thought is that it will be a false religion of the antichrist in the end-times. In this story, I have gone beyond what the Scriptures say about this subject, but have kept the story consistent with my interpretation of these passages. If you investigate this subject for yourself, you'll see there are widely differing opinions on what this evil "synagogue" is, may be, or one day will be.

Essentially, the presentation of the Synagogue of Satan in this book (and any future books) **is strictly fiction**. I do not claim it as any kind of essential biblical truth. It is presented as a *possible* way that Satan could raise a future group of false believers in Jesus Christ. Being aware of Satan's past, present, and future deceit is the important issue here. To that end, this mysterious synagogue and its direction in the plot lines is something that I expect will continue to be a central theme in future books.

Heaven, Hell, & Luke 16:19-31

The pivotal chapters in the first three books of the Flaming Sword Series culminate in Chapter 23 (Heaven) and Chapter 31 (Hell) in this book. In contemplating how to go about writing these chapters on Heaven and Hell, I felt that the parable of the rich man and Lazarus in *Luke 16:19-31* was not only the best—but also the theologically *safest* place to base them. Of course, there is some substantial storytelling in these chapters, as well. But their basis is steeped in this incredible story from the words of Jesus-Himself in this passage. I strongly suggest the reader slowly read this Scripture to absorb what God is telling us.

One more thing regarding this subject. The three demons in Hell are strictly fictional. I don't believe that demons or evil spirits are currently in Hell/Hades, but it may be possible as it is presented in the story.

Miscellaneous Subjects

Pete Canon's FBI job and The **Two Seals Warriors** are strictly fiction. This seemed to add an interesting layer of mystery for the reader, so I created the back story to enhance your enjoyment.

The **vision within a dream** with Wyatt, Mick, and Bob at the edge of Heaven is fictional. Bob's office is also fictional. It merely fits the story line for this book.

Everything having to do with **IFI** is fictional. I wrote that group into this series as a way to explore the difference between our natural lust for revenge, and what Jesus teaches us via Scripture.

FOR MORE INFORMATION. . . .

For more information and current news on all things related to the books of author Wade J. Carey, please visit:

http://flamingsword.us

or

http://rybdude.com

There, you'll find information on current events, future books, videos, music, articles, book history, daily scripture emails, and many other encouraging resources.

Oh, and one more thing . . .

RYB, Dude!!!

PRAYER OF SALVATION

I am excited that even seekers of biblical truth who are not yet committed to Christ would be drawn to this novel, and I pray that your heart would be open to salvation. The amount of information now available for those seeking to find answers to their questions is nothing short of amazing. Finding faith in Christ is not about acting religious or having to dress a certain way. It's about surrender to the Creator of all that we see; the One who loves us more than we can imagine; the One who died for our sins; and the One who loves you, no matter what you have done.

It's important for you to know that it's absolutely normal to have questions and objections regarding matters pertaining to life in Christ. However, failing to truly seek the answers to your questions is extremely inadvisable. I ask you to consider going into an investigative mode, and to not let previous potentially false paradigms about matters of faith corrupt your investigation. In other words, please go into your investigation with an open mind. I believe it will not be hard for you to find the answers to what you seek. However, you must remember that only the Word of God is inspired by the Holy Spirit. Therefore, even though there are tremendous ministry tools available to aid you in your quest, they must always be synchronized with the Bible. If they fail to do that, they're absolutely false.

If you find yourself ready to find true joy for the first time in your life; if you're ready to change your days from hopelessness to hope; and if you're ready to secure your future for eternity; then please consider praying this simple prayer. If you pray this prayer in earnest sincerity, please understand that it's just the *beginning* of a long and incredibly enjoyable walk with the LORD. You'll need help along the way, so finding a local, Bible-based church with strong Christian leadership to disciple you in your walk is the next step.

Jesus,
I confess that I have sinned and fallen short of your glory.
I believe that you suffered and died on the cross for me,
And when you did that,
You paid the full price for the punishment due me, for my sins.
Please forgive me for my sins,
And accept me into your kingdom.
Until right now,
I have only lived for myself.
From now on,
I will only live for you.

Thank you for your incredible sacrifice,
And please also show me
How to help others.
When it is my time,
I look forward to being received
Into your glorious presence.

Please come into my life
Now,
And forever . . .

Welcome to the family!
Don't stop now, there's work to be done.

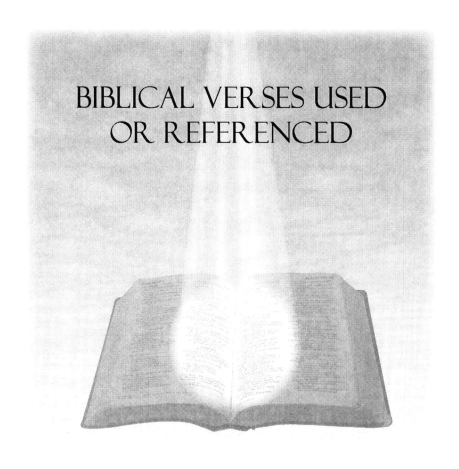

BIBLICAL VERSES USED OR REFERENCED

CPSIA information can be obtained at www.ICGtesting.com
Printed in the USA
LVOW11s0818180114

369915LV00002B/111/P